"Wicked writing gets noticed, and first-time novelist Kelley Armstrong has written a deliciously wicked book. . . . This is no ordinary werewolf tale, but a werewolf mystery with a huge dollop of romance thrown in."—*Toronto Star*

"The plot of *Bitten* has echoes of the best crime thrillers . . . the story is fast and entertaining. But what makes the novel so gripping is Armstrong's talent for vivid description and her interest in both the sensuality and psychology of werewolfhood, a fascination that greatly enhances the world she creates while never slowing down the breakneck plot. At every turn, her depiction of physical sensation is precise and compelling. . . . Surely one of the sexiest, most energetic novels published in a long time." —*Gazette*

"Armstrong has a definite talent for sensual descriptions. The wolf creatures are vividly created in gestures and behaviour, and most of the sexual encounters would knock one's socks off (not to mention other things)."—*National Post*

"*Bitten* is hip and postmodern. . . . Those who enjoy the vampire books of Anne Rice, or Canadian vampire writer Nancy Kilpatrick, will love it."—*Globe and Mail*

"A very contemporary, funky supernatural thriller with a particularly provocative heroine."—*Hello!*

"A hair-raising story for the she-wolf in us all."—Shannon Olson, author of *Welcome to My Planet*

"Entertaining new take on an old thriller story form. Makes Buffy look fluffy."—*Daily Express*

"A tasty confection of werewolves, sex and vendettas . . . after the first nibble it's quite hard to stop. . . . Elena and her acid repartee successfully steal the show throughout; she has bags of charm. Gory, sexy fun."—*SFX*

"A thrilling adventure . . . who'd want to be human? Great fun."—*Big Issue*

"Good slick fun; expect the television series soon." —*Guardian*

STOLEN

"[A] fast-paced story."—*Orlando Sentinel*

"Demonstrates a sharpening of Armstrong's narrative skills."—*Rocky Mountain News*

"A sure-footed follow-up to *Bitten*."—*Publishers Weekly*

"Richly done."—*Kirkus Reviews*

"In *Stolen*, Kelley Armstrong delivers a taut, sensual thriller that grips from the first page. Elena Michaels is at once sublime and sympathetic, a modern heroine who shows that real women bite back."—Karin Slaughter, *New York Times* bestselling author of *Faithless*

"Armstrong has created a persuasive, finely detailed other-worldly cosmology—featuring sorcery, astral projection, spells, telepathy and teleportation—that meshes perfectly with the more humdrum world of interstate highways and cable news bulletins. . . . More than just a thriller with extra teeth, *Stolen* is for anyone who has ever longed to leap over an SUV in a single bound, or to rip an evil security force to shreds, or even just to growl convincingly."—*Quill & Quire*

DIME STORE MAGIC

"[A] sexy supernatural romance [whose] special strength lies in its seamless incorporation of the supernatural into the real world. A convincing small-town setting, clever contemporary dialogue, compelling characterizations and a touch of cool humor make the tale's occasional vivid violence palatable and its fantasy elements both gripping and believable."—*Publishers Weekly*

"Kelley Armstrong is one of my favorite writers."—Karin Slaughter, author of *Faithless*

"From the first page, *Dime Store Magic* captures the attention and never lets go. Magic, mayhem and romance all combine to create a novel that pleases on every level. The pace is fast, the dialogue witty, and the characters totally unique and enjoyable. . . . First-rate suspense, action packed, and an all round terrific read, I highly recommend *Dime Store Magic* and proudly award it *RRT*'s Perfect 10!" —*Romance Reviews Today*

"There are so few authors out there who can write this well and it makes the perfect read for a few hours of escapism. If you enjoyed the first two books, *Dime Store Magic* is a refreshing change of direction that looks set to keep the series going for a good few books yet."—*SF Crow's Nest*

"After only three books, Kelley Armstrong has proven her talent in creating a truly imaginative and trendy realm. If you're into supernatural stories with a fresh twist, *Dime Store Magic* is just what you're looking for." —BookLoons.com

"Kelley Armstrong continues to dazzle . . . With such crisp, stylish writing and a tautly suspenseful, well-crafted plot, this new installment in the 'Otherworld' series showcases Kelley Armstrong at her best."—CurledUp.com

"*Dime Store Magic* is the best book in this series that has been excellent since Book I."—*Huntress Reviews*

"A terrific contemporary fantasy that makes sorcery and witchcraft seem genuine . . . The action-packed story line is fast-paced and provides strong characterization."—*Midwest Book Reviews*

INDUSTRIAL MAGIC

"Set in a supernatural but credible underworld of industrial baron sorcerers and psychologically crippled witches . . . breakneck action is tempered by deep psychological insights, intense sensuality and considerable humor."—*Publishers Weekly*

"Dark, snappy and consistently entertaining . . . Armstrong never loses the balance between Paige's sardonic narration, the wonderfully absurd supporting characters and the nicely girlie touches that add a little lightness to the murder and mayhem. . . . There's never anything that could be described as a dull moment or filler and for nearly 600 pages, that's quite an achievement. The series, in general, is developing into something more interesting and less predictable with every installment."—*SF Crow's Nest*

"Armstrong's world is dangerous and fun, her voice crisp and funny . . . a solidly engaging novel."—*Contra Costa Times*

"Not to be missed. The action is fantastic and the drama is very intense."—*Huntress Reviews*

"I found a lot to like in the humor and diversity of Armstrong's world."—*Denver Post*

"*Industrial Magic* is a book not to be missed. The action is fantastic and the drama is very intense. Kelley Armstrong creates such fun characters that really jump off the pages. The book is fast paced with lots of unexpected turns. Like the other books in the series, I wanted more after finishing *Industrial Magic*."—SFSite.com

"One of Armstrong's strengths is the creation of plausible characters, which is a real bonus in a series based on the premise that there are supernatural creatures walking and working beside us in our contemporary world. . . . *Industrial Magic* is a page-turner and is very hard to put down." —Booksluts.com

HAUNTED

"Another fantastic adventure in the *Women of the Otherworld* series . . . Kelley Armstrong is an author to be lauded. Instead of cranking out another adventure using werewolves, witches, or sorcerers, she has created an entire mythological inspired afterlife that exists as another layer to the series. . . . *Haunted* is well worth reading. Kelley Armstrong has created an entertaining novel and stretched her wings. Many writers in her position simply rest on their laurels, but Armstrong has instead decided to create something entirely different. And it works as an entertaining piece of fiction."—SFSite.com

Also by Kelley Armstrong

BITTEN

STOLEN

DIME STORE MAGIC

INDUSTRIAL MAGIC

HAUNTED

BROKEN

KELLEY ARMSTRONG

BANTAM BOOKS

BROKEN

A Bantam Spectra Book / May 2006

Published by Bantam Dell
A Division of Random House, Inc.
New York, New York

Bantam Books, the rooster colophon, Spectra, and the portrayal
of a boxed "s" are trademarks of Random House, Inc.

ISBN-10: 0-553-58818-4
ISBN-13: 978-0-553-58818-7

Printed in the United States of America
Published simultaneously in Canada

www.bantamdell.com

OPM   10 9 8 7 6

To Jeff

Acknowledgments

A huge debt of thanks is owed to my agent, Helen Heller, and my editors—Anne Groell at Bantam US, Anne Collins at Random House Canada, and Antonia Hodgson at Time Warner UK—for putting up with my endless fretting and fussing on this one. They were as patient and supportive as any writer could want . . . though I wouldn't blame them if, at times, they wanted to throw *me* in a dimensional portal.

Thanks to my readers, Laura, Raina, and Xaviere for catching my gaffes, and saving me the embarrassment of answering "how come?" questions from confused readers.

Finally, this time around I want to give a shout-out to Xaviere Daumarie, the cover artist for all my online novellas and stories. In 2005, I did a short story a month, and she somehow managed to do a wonderful piece of original cover art for each . . . even when all she had to work with some months was "I haven't written the story yet, but I think it'll be something about . . ."

BROKEN

Changes

CLAYTON DOESN'T DO "UNOBTRUSIVE" WELL. NOT EVEN when he tries, and that afternoon, he was trying his damnedest. He was downwind of me, at least two hundred feet away, so I couldn't smell him, see him or hear him. But I knew he was there.

As I stood under the oaks, I couldn't suppress a twinge of resentment at the pressure his presence added to an already gut-twisting situation. Yes, I'd been the one to suggest the run, leaping up from the lunch table and declaring I was ready. He'd asked if he should stay inside—possibly the first time in our fifteen-year relationship that Clay had been willing to give me space. But I'd grabbed his hand and dragged him out with me. Now I was blaming him for being here. Not fair. But better than to admit that what I felt was not resentment but fear—fear that I would fail, and in failing I would disappoint him.

I took a deep breath and filled my lungs with the loamy richness of a forest emerging from winter, the first buds appearing tentatively, as if still uncertain. Uncertain . . . good word. That was what I felt: uncertainty.

Uncertainty? Try abject, pant-pissing, stomach-heaving terror—

I took another deep breath. The scent of the forest filled me, called to me, like Clay's presence out there, beckoning—

Don't think of him. Just relax.

I followed the sound of a rabbit thumping nearby, upwind and oblivious of me. As I moved, I saw my shadow and realized I was still standing. Well, there was the first problem. I'd undressed, but how would I Change if I was still on two legs?

As I started to crouch, a pang ran through the left side of my abdomen and I froze, heart pounding. It was probably a random muscle spasm or a digestive complaint. And yet . . .

My fingers rubbed the hard swell of my belly. There was definitely a swell there, however staunchly Jeremy swore otherwise. I could feel it with my hand, feel it in the tightening waistband of my jeans. Clay tried to avoid the question—smart man—but when pressed he would admit I did seem to be showing already. Showing, when I was no more than five weeks pregnant. That shouldn't be. Yet one more thing to add to my growing list of worries.

At the top of the list was this: the regular transformation from human to wolf that my body required. I had to Change, but what would it do to my baby?

My fear over losing my child came as a revelation to me. In the nearly three years I'd wrestled with the thought of having a baby, I'd considered the possibility that the choice wouldn't be mine to make, that being a werewolf might mean I wouldn't be able to conceive or carry a child to term. I'd accepted that. If my pregnancy ended, I'd know that I couldn't have a child. That would be that.

Now that I was actually pregnant I couldn't believe I'd been so cavalier. This was more than a collection of cells growing in me, it was the actualization of a dream I'd thought I'd lost when I became a werewolf. A dream I was certain I'd given up when I decided to stay with Clay.

But I had to Change. Already I'd waited too long, and I could feel the need in every muscle spasm and restless twitch, hear it in my growls and snaps whenever someone spoke to me. Twice I'd come out here with Clay, and twice I'd been unable—or refused—to Change. Make it a third, and Clay and Jeremy would be flipping coins to see who locked me in the cage. That was a safety precaution—being Change-deprived makes us violent and unpredictable—but given my surly behavior this past week, I wouldn't blame them if they fought over the privilege.

Just Change, goddamn it! Get down on your knees . . . See? That feels fine, right? Now put your hands on the ground . . . There. Now concentrate—

My body rebelled, convulsing so hard I doubled over, gasping. Change into a wolf? With a baby inside me? Was I crazy? I'd rip, tear, suffocate—

No!

I pushed up onto all fours and cleared my head, then opened the gate only to thoughts bearing the pass-code of logic. Was this my first Change since I'd become pregnant? No. It was the first since I'd *learned* I was pregnant, two weeks ago. I must have Changed a half-dozen times between conception and testing.

Had anything happened during those Changes? Bleeding? Cramping? No.

So stop worrying. Take a deep breath, smell the forest, dig your fingers into the damp soil, hear the whistle of the April wind, feel the ache in your muscles. Run to Clay, who'll be so happy, so relieved . . .

My skin prickled, stretching, itching as fur sprouted—

My brain threw up the brakes again and my body tensed. Sweat trickled down my cheeks. I growled and dug my fingers and toes into the soft earth, refusing to reverse the process.

Relax, relax, relax. Just stop worrying and let your body do the work. Like constipation. Relax and nature takes over.

Constipation? Oh, there was a romantic analogy. I laughed, and my changing vocal cords squeezed the sound into a hideous screech, more worthy of a hyena than a wolf, which only made me laugh all the harder. I toppled sideways and, as I lay there, laughing, I finally relaxed.

The Change took over, spontaneous. My convulsions of laughter turned to spasms of pain, and I twisted and writhed on the ground. The pain of a Change. Yet some still-panicked part of my brain convinced me this wasn't the normal kind of pain—I was killing my child, suffocating it as my body contorted.

I must— Must stop— Oh, God, I couldn't!

I tried to stop—fighting, snarling, concentrating on reversing to human. But it was too late. I'd waited too long, and now my body was determined to see it through.

Finally, the pain ended, gone without so much as a lingering ache, and I lay on my side, panting, then leapt to my feet.

Damn it, not so fast! Be careful.

I stood there, motionless except for my tail, which

wouldn't stop whipping from side to side, as if to say "Well, we're Changed. What are you waiting for? Let's run!" The rest of my body didn't disagree with the sentiment, though it let the tail do the shouting, settling for subtler displays of restlessness: heart tripping, ears swiveling, muscles tensing. I refused to move, though; not until I'd taken inventory, made sure everything was as it should be.

First, my belly. No obvious signs of distress. I panted, letting my chest rise and fall, testing whether the movement seemed to hurt anything. It didn't, though my stomach did let out a growl as that nearby rabbit's scent wafted past. You wouldn't know I'd just devoured a three-course lunch. Ungrateful stomach. But the other part of my belly, newly filling with life, felt fine.

I lifted my paws one at a time, stretching and rotating my joints. Good. My nose and ears had done fine picking up that rabbit. And the still-wagging tail was obviously working. Okay, enough of this.

I stepped forward. One paw, two, three, four . . . No sudden scream of complaint from my belly. I broke into a lope, then a run, then a headlong dash across the clearing. Still no signs of distress.

Next, the tougher moves—the wolf maneuvers. I crouched, wiggled my hindquarters, then leapt at an imaginary mouse. As I hit the ground, I wheeled around, teeth bared as I snapped at an unseen foe. I bounded across the clearing. I jumped and twisted in midair. I pranced. I lunged. I charged. I chased my tail—

A wheezing sound erupted behind me and I froze, the tip hairs of my tail still caught between my teeth. There, across the clearing, was a huge, golden-haired wolf, his head between his forepaws, eyes closed, hindquarters in the air, body quivering with that strange wheezing noise. His eyes opened, bright blue eyes dancing with relief and amusement, and I realized what that noise was. He was laughing at me.

Laughing? I'd just gone through a horrible trauma, and the guy had the nerve to laugh? I knew half of that laughter was relief at seeing me Changed, and I admit I probably looked a little silly gallivanting alone in the clearing. But still, such indignities should not be tolerated.

With as much grace as I could muster with tail fur hanging out of my mouth, I swept around and stalked in the other direction. Halfway across the clearing, I wheeled and charged, teeth bared. His eyes widened in "oh, shit" comprehension and he backpedaled just in time to get out of my way, then bolted into the forest.

I tore after him. I loped along the path, muzzle skimming the ground. The earth was thick with the scent of my prey—a deliberate move, as he weaved and circled, permeating this patch of forest with his smell, hoping to throw me off the trail.

I untangled the web of trails and latched onto the most recent. As I picked up speed, the ground whooshed past beneath me. Ahead, the path opened into a clearing. I pitched forward, straining for the open run, but before I hit the edge of the clearing, I dug in my claws and skidded to a graceless stop.

I stood there, adrenaline roaring, urging me to find him, take him down. I closed my eyes and shuddered. Too eager. Keep that up and I'd run straight into a trap. After a moment, the adrenaline rush ebbed and I started forward again, cautious now, ears straining, muzzle up, sniffing as I walked.

My eyes saved me this time. That and the sun, peeking

from fast-moving clouds. One break in the cloud cover and I caught the glint of gold through the trees. He was downwind, crouched to the left of the path's end, waiting for me to come barreling out.

I retraced my last few steps, walking backward. An awkward maneuver—some things easily accomplished on two legs are much more difficult to coordinate with four. Once I'd gone as far as I could, I craned to look over my shoulder. The trees closed in on me from either side. Not enough room to guarantee a silent about-face.

I took a careful step off the path. The undergrowth was soft and moist with spring rain. I prodded at it, but it stayed silent. Hunkering down to stay below branch level, I started forward, looping to slink up behind him. Once close enough to see through the trees, I peered out. He was crouched beside the path, as still as a statue, only the twitch of his tail betraying his impatience.

I found the clearest line of fire, hunched down, then sprang. I hit him square on the back and sank my teeth into the ruff around his neck. He yelped and started to rear up, then stopped. I let out a growling chuckle, knowing he didn't dare throw me off in my "condition." All I had to do was hang on—

He dropped, letting his legs fold, his body cushioning my drop, but the suddenness of it was enough of a surprise that I let go of his ruff. As he slid from under me, he twisted and pinned me, his teeth clamping around the bottom of my muzzle. I kicked at his underbelly. He snorted as my claws made contact, but made no move to fight back.

He looked down at me, indecision flickering in his eyes. Then he released my muzzle and his head shot down to my throat. I wriggled, trying to pull out of the way, but he only buried his nose in the ruff around my neck and inhaled deeply. He shuddered, legs vibrating against my sides. A moment's hesitation. Then a soft growl, and he twisted off me and dove into the woods again.

I scrambled to my feet and set off in pursuit. This time he had too much of a head start, and I could only get close enough to see his hindquarters bounding ahead. He flicked his tail up. Mocking me, damn him. I surged forward, getting close enough to hear the pounding of his heartbeat. He veered and crashed into the forest, off the trail, and I chortled to myself. Now I had him. Cutting a fresh path would slow him down just enough to let me—

A brace of ptarmigan flew up, almost under my feet, and I slid to a halt, nearly flipping over backward in my surprise. As the panicked birds took to the sky, I got my bearings again, looked around . . . and found myself alone. Tricked. Damn him. And damn me for falling for it.

I found his trail, but before I'd gone a hundred feet, a gurgling moan rippled through the silence. I stopped, ears going up. A grunt, then panting. He was Changing.

I dove into the nearest thicket and began my own Change. It came fast, spurred by a healthy double shot of adrenaline and frustration. When I finished, he was still in his thicket.

I crept around to the other side, pulled back a handful of leaves and peered through. He was done, but recovering, crouched on all fours, panting as he caught his breath. By the rules of fair play, I should have given him time to recuperate. But I wasn't in the mood for rules.

I sprang onto his back. Before he could react, my arm

went around his neck, forearm jammed against his wind-pipe.

I leaned over his shoulder. "Did you think you could escape that easily?"

His lips formed an oath, but no sound came out. His shoulders slumped, as if defeated. Like I was stupid enough to buy that. I pretended to relax my grip. Sure enough, the second I did, he twisted, trying to grab me.

I slid off his back and pulled him down sideways. Before he could recover, I was on top of him, my forearm again at his throat. His hands slid up my sides, snuck around and cupped my breasts.

"Uh-uh," I growled, pressing against his windpipe. "No distractions."

He sighed and let his hands slide away. I eased back. As soon as I did, he flipped me over, still far more gently than usual, and pinned me as securely as he had in wolf-form. He eased down, belly and groin against mine. He slid his hands back to my breasts and grinned at me, daring me to do something about it now.

I glared up at him. Then I shot forward and sank my teeth into his shoulder. He jerked away. I scrambled up, then pinned him, hands on his shoulders, knees on his thighs. He struggled, but couldn't get me off without throwing me.

"Caught?" I said.

He gave one last squirm, then nodded. "Caught."

"Good."

I slid my knees from his thighs and slipped over him. He tried to thrust up to meet me, but I pushed down with my hips, keeping him still. I moved into position. When I felt the tip of him brush me, I stopped and wrig-gled against him, teasing myself. He groaned and tried to grab my hips, but I pinned his shoulders harder. Then I closed my eyes and plunged down onto him.

He struggled under me, trying to thrust, to grab, to control, but I kept him pinned. After a moment, he gave up and arched against the ground, fingers clenching handfuls of grass, jaw tensing, eyes closing to slits, but staying open, always open, always watching. When the first wave of climax hit, I let him go, but he stayed where he was, leaving me in charge. Dimly, I heard him growl as he came, and by the time I finished and leaned over him, his eyes were half lidded, a lazy grin tweaking the corners of his mouth.

"Feeling better?" he said.

I stretched out on top of him, head resting in the hollow below his shoulder. "Much."

Prisoner

WE LAY THERE FOR A FEW MINUTES, THEN I CAUGHT A whiff of blood and lifted my head. Blood trickled from Clay's shoulder.

"Whoops," I said, licking my fingers to wipe it off. "Got a bit carried away. Sorry about that."

"Didn't hear me complaining." He brushed his fingertips across a fang-size hole under my jaw. "Seems I gave as good as I got anyway." He yawned and stretched, hands going around me to rest on my rear. "Just add them to the collection."

I ran my fingers over his chest, tracing the half-healed scabs and long-healed scars. Most of them were the residue of friendly fire—dots of too-hard bites or the paper-thin scratches of misaimed claws. I had them too—tiny marks, nothing to draw stares when I wore halter tops and shorts. Even after fifteen years as a werewolf, I had few true battle scars. Clay had more, and as my hands moved over them, my brain ticked off the stories behind each. There wasn't one I didn't know, not a scar I couldn't find with my eyes closed, not a mark I couldn't explain.

He closed his eyes as my fingers moved down his chest. I stared up at his face, a rare chance to look at him without him knowing I was looking. I don't know why that still matters. It shouldn't. He knows how I feel about him. I'm having a child with him—it doesn't get any clearer than that, not for me. But after ten years of pushing him away, trying to pretend I didn't love him—wasn't still crazy-in-love with him—I'm still cautious in some small ways. Maybe I always will be.

Gold eyelashes rested against his cheeks. His skin already showed the glow of a tan. Now and then, when he was poring over a book, I caught the ghost of a line forming over the bridge of his nose, the first sign of an impending wrinkle. Not surprising, considering he was forty-two. Werewolves age slowly, and Clay could pass for a decade younger. Yet the wrinkle reminded me that we were getting older. I'd turned thirty-five last year, right around the time I'd finally decided he was right, and I—we—were ready for a child. The two events were, I'm sure, not unconnected.

My stomach growled.

Clay's hand slid across it, smiling, eyes still closed. "Hungry already?"

"I'm eating for two."

He chuckled as my stomach rumbled again. "That's what happens when you chase me instead of something edible."

"I'll remember that next time."

He opened one eye. "On second thought, forget it. Chase me and I'll feed you afterward. Anything you want."

"Ice cream."

He laughed. "Do we have any?"

I slid off him. "The Creamery opened last week. Two-for-one banana splits all month."

"One for you and one for—"

I snorted.

He grinned. "Okay, two for you, two for me."

He pushed to his feet and looked around.

"Clothing southwest," I said. "Near the pond."

"Are you sure?"

"Let's hope so."

I stepped from the forest into the backyard. As clouds swept overhead, shafts of sunlight slid over the house. The freshly painted trim gleamed dark green, the color matching the tendrils of ivy that struggled to maintain a hold on the stone walls.

The gardens were slowly turning the same green, evergreens and bushes interspersed with the occasional clump of tulips from a fall-gardening spree a few years ago. The tulips ended at the patio wall, which was as far as I'd gotten before being distracted and leaving the bag of bulbs to rot in the rain. That was our typical approach to gardening: every now and then we'd buy a plant or two, maybe even get it in the ground, but most times we were content just to sit back and see what came up naturally.

The casual air suited the house and the slightly overgrown yard that blended into the fields and forests beyond. A wild sanctuary, the air smelling of last night's fire and new grass and distant manure, the silence broken only by the twitter of birds, the chirp of cicadas . . . and the crack of gunfire.

As the next shot rang out, I pressed my hands to my ears and made a face. Clay motioned for us to circle back along the woods and come up on the opposite side. When we drew alongside the shed, I could make out a figure on the patio. Tall, lean and dark, the hair that curled over his collar as sporadically clipped as the lawn. Standing with his back to us, he lifted the gun over the edge of the low stone wall and pointed it at the target. Clay grinned, handed me his shoes, then broke into a silent lope, heading around the other side of the patio.

I kept walking, but slower. By the time I neared the wall, he was already vaulting over it. He caught my gaze and lifted his finger to his lips. As if I needed the warning. He crept up behind the gunman, paused, making sure he hadn't been heard, then crouched and sprang.

Jeremy sidestepped without even turning around. Clay hit the wall and yelped.

Jeremy shook his head. "Serves you right. You're lucky I didn't shoot you."

Clay bounced back, grinning as he brushed himself off. "Live dangerously, that's my motto."

"It'll be your epitaph too."

Jeremy Danvers, our Pack Alpha and owner of Stonehaven, where he, Clay and I lived and would doubtless stay for the rest of our lives. Part of that was because Clay was Jeremy's bodyguard and had to keep close, but mostly it was because Clay would never consider leaving.

Clay had been no more than five or six when he'd been bitten. When other kids were heading off to kindergarten, he'd been living as a child werewolf in the Louisiana bayou. Jeremy had rescued him, brought him to Stonehaven and raised him, and this was where Clay would stay.

Now it was my home too, really had been since the day

Clay had bitten me. It's no sacrifice. I'm happy here, with my family. Besides, without Jeremy to mediate, Clay and I would have killed each other years ago.

Jeremy watched as Clay bounded back to me. As he glanced my way, relief sparked in his eyes. If Clay was in such a good mood, my Change must have gone well. I knew they'd both been worried, though they'd tried to hide it, knowing I'd been panicked enough and that the alternative—not Changing—would be even more dangerous.

I handed Clay his shoes. Jeremy's gaze slid down to Clay's bare feet. He sighed.

"I'll find the socks next time," Clay said. "And look, Elena found her top."

I held up a sweater I'd "misplaced" in the woods a few months ago. Jeremy's nose wrinkled as the smell wafted his way.

"Toss it out," he said.

"It's a little funky," I said. "But I'm sure a good washing, maybe some bleach . . ."

"In the garbage. The outside garbage. Please."

"We're going into town for ice cream," Clay said. "Wanna come?"

Jeremy shook his head. "You two go. You can pick up steaks at the butcher. I thought we'd have a barbecue, take advantage of the warm day. It may still be early in the season, but since you seem so energetic, perhaps I can persuade you to cart out the lawn furniture and we'll eat outside tonight."

"Let's do that now," I said, swinging toward the shed. "Build up an appetite for those banana splits."

Clay caught my arm. "No lifting, remember?"

I was reasonably sure you couldn't damage a fetus the

size of a pea by lifting a patio chair, especially not when werewolf strength made it the equivalent of picking up a plate. Yet when I looked over at Jeremy, he busied himself unloading his revolvers.

Since I'd first decided to try for a baby, Jeremy had read just about every book ever written on pregnancy. The problem was that no matter how many books Jeremy read, he couldn't be sure they applied to me. Female werewolves were very rare. For one to bear a child, even to a human father, was a thing of legend. Two werewolves reproducing? Never happened. Or, if it had, there was no record of it, and certainly no maternity guides.

So we were being careful. Some of us more than others. Not that I disagreed. Not .... really. After all, it was only nine months. I could handle not picking up lawn chairs for a while. It was the "not doing anything at all" part that was driving me nuts.

I could argue that I'd just Changed into a wolf—surely lifting chairs wasn't any more strenuous than that. But I knew what they'd say—that Changing was a necessary stress, and all the more reason for me to reduce all other physical activity to compensate. Remind them what I'd just done, and Jeremy would probably cancel our trip to town and replace it with an afternoon of bed rest.

"You can grab the lanterns," Clay said finally. "But I'll get them down."

"Are you sure?" I said. "They are oil lamps, you know. I could set myself on fire."

Clay hesitated.

I bit back a growl, but not before the first note escaped.

"I'm thinking of the oil," he said. "Is it okay for you to breathe that stuff in?"

"Hmmm, you have a point. And what about the air? I caught a whiff of manure out there today. God knows what kind of drugs they're feeding cows these days."

"I'm just saying—"

"Clay, get the chairs. And the lanterns. Elena, I need to speak to you."

As Clay walked away, I braced myself for "the lecture." Not that Jeremy ever really lectures—you need to say more than a few sentences for that. In this case, I already knew those few sentences by heart. He'd agree that Clay was being overprotective, and so was he, but they knew how important this pregnancy was to me, and they just wanted to make sure it went smoothly. Just eight months to go. Thirty-four weeks. Two hundred and thirty-eight days . . .

"Have you been taking the new vitamins?"

I gave him a look. He lifted a finger, then darted his gaze in Clay's direction, telling me to play along.

"Yes, I've been taking the new vitamins and, no, they don't seem to be upsetting my stomach like the last concoction. Next time, though, as long as you're mixing up a batch, could you add some cherry flavor? Maybe mold them into little animals? Bunnies would be good. I like bunnies."

Clay's chuckle floated back to us, and he quickened his pace. Jeremy glanced over his shoulder, estimating werewolf hearing distance, then lowered his voice.

"You got a call while you were out," he said.

Clay stopped.

"It was Paige."

Clay's shoulders tightened. He hesitated, then shook it off and resumed walking.

"Now this is the part of being coddled I *do* like," I

murmured. "He doesn't even complain about Paige phoning. Does she want me to call her back?"

Jeremy said nothing, just kept watching Clay's back, letting him get farther this time before continuing.

"She was relaying a message. Someone's been trying to reach you. Xavier Reese."

At that, Clay wheeled. Jeremy grimaced.

"You tried," I said.

"Reese?" Clay strode over. "The guy from the compound?"

"That's the only Xavier I know."

"What the hell does he want?"

I had my suspicions. "Did Paige leave his number?"

"You're not going to call him, are you?" Clay said. "After what he—"

"He saved my life."

"Yeah? Well, if it hadn't been for him, your life wouldn't have needed saving. And I'm sure you'd have been fine without his help. The only reason he jumped in to 'save' you was so he could hold a marker over you—" He stopped, jaw setting. "That better not be why he's calling."

I took the message from Jeremy. "I'll know in a few minutes."

"Hey, Elena!" the voice crackled across a weak cellular connection. "Remember me?"

"Uh-huh."

I settled onto the sofa and pulled my legs up under me. Clay sat on the other end, making no effort to look like he wasn't eavesdropping—enhanced hearing meant he could hear both ends of the conversation. I didn't care. If I had, I wouldn't have let him in the room.

"Uh-huh?" Xavier said. "That's all I get after three years? We spent a harrowing week together, locked in an underground prison, fighting for survival—"

"I was fighting for survival. You were drawing a paycheck."

"Hey now, in my own way, I was just as much of a prisoner as you."

I snorted. "A prisoner of your greed."

"Trapped by my shortcomings. It's tragic really."

"Know what'd be even more tragic? If you teleported into the middle of a wall and got trapped by your shortcomings there. Does that ever happen?"

"My momma taught me to always look where I'm going."

"Damn."

"What did I ever do to you—er, better not answer that."

I glanced over at Clay, who motioned for me to hang up.

"What do you want, Xavier? I was just about to head out for ice cream."

"And that's more important than talking to me? No, wait, don't answer that either. Since you're obviously not going to play nice, I'll cut to the chase. You owe me a favor."

"No, *you* said I owed you one. I never agreed. As I recall, you offered the trade in return for giving me two pieces of advice about the compound, but you hightailed it out of there yourself after only telling me one."

"The second was about the dogs. They had trained bloodhounds and attack dogs."

"Right, *that's* what nearly ripped my throat out. Left a nice scar on my shoulder too. Thanks for the warning."

"Okay, so you only owe me half a favor, and I'm really only using that as an opener for a fresh deal. I'm a useful guy, Elena. I could really help you out."

"Uh-huh. So who's chasing you?"

"No one. Let me finish. I started thinking about this last year, that I should get in touch with you and renew our acquaintance."

"Uh-huh. Who was chasing you *then*?"

"A Cabal, but that's not the point."

"I'm not a bodyguard, Xavier."

"That isn't what I have in mind. This particular proposal has zero violence potential. It involves another of your . . . specific skills. In return, I can tell you where you'll find that rogue wolf you've been hunting."

I glanced over at Clay. "What rogue—?"

"David Hargrave. Killed three women in Tennessee. Your Pack has been looking for him for almost five months."

"Who told you—"

"Contacts, Elena. I'm a regular Rolodex of supernatural contacts. Point is, I know where Hargrave is hiding. That got me thinking. If I gave you that information, you might be willing to do a little something for me in return."

"So I do this 'little something' for you, and you give me an address, and I show up to find Hargrave cleared out a week ago . . ."

"No. If you agree to the deal, I'll tell you where to find Hargrave right away. Not only that, but I'll wait until you have him, and *then* you'll do the favor for me. I don't con anyone who can rip out my liver with her bare hands."

"What's your end, then? What do you want?"

"It . . . takes some explaining. Come to Buffalo tomorrow and I'll tell you."

"Buffalo? Too far. Meet me halfway, in Rochester."

"Buffalo *is* halfway. I'm in Toronto. Your hometown, if I remember the compound records. Hey, maybe you can recommend a good sushi—"

"What are you doing in Toronto?"

"That's where the, uh, service would take place. Should make it easier for you, right? Operating on familiar ground? Anyway, I'm here setting it up, so I'll meet you halfway, in Buffalo, tomorrow. Got a place all picked out. Nice and public. A daytime meeting. Absolutely nothing for you to worry about . . . so there's no need to bring the boyfriend."

"Uh-huh."

"I like all my limbs just where they are."

I rolled my eyes. Clay mouthed something, but I waved him off and took down the time and address from Xavier.

"It's Buffalo, not the Gaza Strip," I said as we returned to the study with Jeremy.

I plunked onto the sofa. Clay tried to sit beside me, but I swung my legs up to stretch out. He reached to yank them off his spot, then stopped, remembering my "condition," and stalked across the study to sit on the fireplace hearth.

"I need to get out of the house," I said.

"You got out yesterday," Clay said.

"To go to the grocery store. And last week, you let me go to Syracuse for a movie. The highlight of my month so far, dinner afterward and everything . . . oh, wait. I didn't get dinner, because you thought it was getting too late for me, so we ended up grabbing sandwiches to eat on the way back to jail . . . I mean home."

"Fine, you want to go out? We'll take a trip to New York next weekend, visit Nick. You're not traipsing off to Buffalo—"

"Traipsing?"

He fixed me with a look. I returned the glare, then glanced at Jeremy, who only leaned back in his chair. No sense appealing to him anyway. I knew which side he was on. Prison guard number two.

I took a deep breath. There was only one way to win Jeremy over. Steer clear of histrionics and mount a logical defense.

"You don't want mutts knowing I'm pregnant," I began. "And I agree. But Xavier is half-demon. He can't smell that I'm pregnant, and unless I wear a tight shirt, he won't be able to tell by looking. I'm certainly not going to volunteer the news. All I want from him is David Hargrave." I paused and met Jeremy's eyes. "We do want Hargrave, don't we? He's killed three women—"

"You don't need to remind me of Hargrave's crimes." *And you can't guilt-trip me with the reminder,* his eyes added. "I have every intention of making this meeting with Reese. Either I will or Clay will—"

"Absolutely. Despite Xavier's hopes, I'm not planning to show up alone. Call Nick, call Antonio, even call Karl if you can find him. I'll take whatever precautions you want."

"Clay can handle it by himself, with backup from Nick."

"Clay? Oh, you mean the guy Xavier expressly warned me not to bring?"

"What's wrong with me?" Clay said.

"You scare him."

"He's never met me."

"Sorry, let me rephrase. The *idea* of you scares him. But I'm sure, once he meets you, he'll see that all those nasty rumors are completely unfounded."

"I'll send Antonio," Jeremy cut in before Clay could respond.

"If you send anyone, even yourself, Xavier will be out of there in a flash. I'm the only Pack member he knows, so I'm the only one he'll talk to."

"Too dangerous," Clay said, crossing his arms and leaning back against the fireplace, as if that settled the matter.

"Dangerous? Do you remember what Xavier's power is? Teleportation. *Limited* teleportation. The guy can move about ten feet. Worst thing he can do to me? Poke me in the eyes, go 'nyuk nyuk nyuk' and zip away before I can smack him."

One look at Jeremy and I knew I was losing "calm and reasonable" points fast. When he opened his mouth, I cut him off.

"Yes, the first time I met Xavier, I ended up as a guinea pig for mad scientists and a play-toy for a sadistic industrialist. I could argue that it took him two tries and a good dose of my own stupidity to finally nab me, but it's still a valid point."

"You think?" Clay muttered.

I glared at him. "I admitted to the stupidity part. Don't push it. Yes, it's possible that Xavier has found someone willing to pay big bucks for a female werewolf, and he's said, 'Hey, I can get you one of those.' But I doubt it. He learned enough last time to know that if he tries it, he'd better spend that money fast, because he's going to end up in little bitty pieces when either I get free or Clay catches up with him. But it *is* a possibility. That's why I won't even suggest going alone. The meeting will be held in a public park, which we'll scout first. You can bring the whole Pack as backup if you like. I'm taking Clay too, whether Xavier likes it or not. But I want to catch David Hargrave, and if this is our shot, I say it's a chance worth taking."

Clay opened his mouth.

"Let me rephrase *that* too," I continued. "I want Hargrave caught. I do not intend to play any role in catching him. For the next eight months, I'm out of the mutt-chasing business. I not only accept that, I whole-heartedly agree with it. No matter how bored I get, I won't take chances. Talking to Xavier, though, is a rea-sonable balance of risk and reward."

Clay and Jeremy looked at one another, and I knew I'd won . . . this time.

Ripper

I SQUEEZED THROUGH A BARRICADE OF STROLLERS AND past a small army of parents circled shoulder to shoulder around the playground, like a herd of bison protecting their young. A toddler shrieked. Her father swooped in and rescued her before she was trampled by a swarm of school-age boys who'd claimed the lookout tower. The father glared at the boys, then took his daughter out of the line of fire and wiped away her tears as she sobbed that *she* wanted to climb the tower. I had a mental flash of my own child in her place, Clay as the father charging in to find that someone wanted to keep his child off a piece of equipment and—

Oh, God, what was I getting us into?

On the other side of the playground was a cluster of picnic tables. Only two tables were occupied. At one, a mother divvied up animal crackers to three howling preschoolers, all the while shooting furtive glances over her shoulder at the lone man sitting a few tables away. He was brown-haired and in his late thirties, with a thin scar running down his cheek and no attached kids in sight. When the man met her gaze with a level stare, she looked away and doled out the crackers faster.

I snuck up behind him, then leaned into his ear.

"She thinks you're a pervert," I whispered.

Xavier jumped, realized it was me and grinned.

"Is that it?" he said. "Whew. I thought she was trying to pick me up."

The woman at the other table breathed a nearly audible sigh of relief as I sat across from him.

"I was starting to think you weren't going to show," he said.

"Good thing I did," I said. "A few more minutes and she'd have been calling the cops."

He shot a look in the woman's direction. "You know, she doesn't seem completely convinced. Maybe if you gave me a big 'hello, honey' kiss . . . Did I mention you look good?" He grinned. "Damned good. I forgot how—"

"Hard I hit?"

"That too." His grin broadened. "Wanna refresh my memory? Really give momma hen a reason to gawk?"

"You've given everyone enough reason to gawk already. So much for keeping a low profile."

"Hey, I wanted you to feel safe. Nothing safer than a playground. Absolutely no reason to regret not bringing the boyfriend."

I glanced over the crowd by the play equipment. "How do you know I didn't? You've never met Clay."

"I've seen pictures, remember? Blond curls, big blue eyes, everything but the goddamn cleft chin." He shook his head. "Brains, looks and the lovely Elena on his arm. I'd feel really inadequate . . . if he wasn't a raging lunatic. Score one for the half-demon. I may be a little nuts, but no one's ever called me a psycho."

I shook my head and sighed.

"Hey, don't tell me I'm wrong. I've heard the stories. Saw a photo too. You ever seen those pictures?"

"No, but I've heard about them."

"So you think they're fakes?"

"I'm sure they're not."

"And . . . that's okay with you? Your boyfriend spent his teen years hacking up people and taking pictures? But hey, high school was rough on all of us. Everyone has his own way of coping."

I could have set Xavier straight, told him the pictures were of one trespassing mutt, and Clay had his reasons—as alien as his reasoning might be to the rest of us. But to clear the record would be to wipe away the reputation Clay had so painstakingly built for Jeremy's protection, so I kept my mouth shut and shrugged.

Xavier leaned forward. "Sarcasm aside, you don't need a guy like that, Elena. Maybe you think you do—only female werewolf and all that—but hell, I've seen what you can do—tied to a chair, up against a male werewolf. You can do that, you don't need some fucking psychopath like Clayton Danvers—"

He stopped, noticing my gaze.

"He's standing right behind me, isn't he?" Xavier murmured.

"Uh-huh."

Xavier tilted his head back, saw Clay and disappeared. He reappeared on the opposite bench, pressed up against me. I looked over at him, eyebrow raised. He swore under his breath and teleported to the far end of the other bench. Then he stood and turned to Clay.

"You must be—"

"The fucking psychopath," Clay said.

"Er, right, but I meant that in the most respectful way. Believe me, I have the utmost regard for, uh . . ."

"Raging lunatics," I said.

Xavier shot me a glare.

"Oh, sit down," I said. "He didn't bring his chain saw."

Clay circled the table and slid in next to me. Xavier waited until he'd sat, then took his original place across from me.

"Clay, this is Xavier, Evanidus half-demon. Specialty? You just got a little demonstration of that."

"A pretty damned indiscreet demonstration," Clay said, shooting a look over at the playground.

"No one saw," Xavier said. "And even if they did, they've already explained it away. Humans only see what they expect to see. I bet you guys could change into wolves right here and you'd have twenty parents grabbing their cell phones—not phoning CNN to report a were-wolf sighting, but calling the Humane Society to pick up a couple of really big dogs that are definitely violating the leash laws."

"Speaking of violating leash laws, you *do* know where David Hargrave is, right? And he'll still be there when we arrive?"

"He should be. If he bolts, it won't be because I tipped him off. And if he does bolt, I'll get you a new location or you don't owe me a thing. This guy killed three women. I say you're welcome to him. I may not be the most moral guy, but with something like that, I'll gladly turn him in to the proper authorities. Which, in this case, would be you guys."

Clay snorted. "How long have you known where he was before your sense of civic duty kicked in?"

"Let me guess," I said. "Just long enough to find something you could ask for in return. Don't give me the wounded look. We want Hargrave. What do you want?"

Xavier eased back in his seat. "You guys ever hear of the *From Hell* letter?"

"No, and from the sounds of it, I'm not sure I want to."

Clay said, "If this is some kind of demon thing, we're not interested. The werewolves don't get involved in—"

"It's nothing demonic. It's just a letter. Supposedly sent by Jack the Ripper to the police. At some point over the next hundred years, it went missing."

I frowned. "You want us to find—?"

"Oh, I know where it is. It was never really missing. Not to our side of the world, that is."

When Clay and I glanced at one another, Xavier rolled his eyes. "*Our* side. The supernatural side. You guys rejoined the council; that puts werewolves back in the middle of the whole supernatural community. Didn't you get your membership cards?"

"About this letter," I said.

"All the Jack the Ripper files were sealed up for a hundred years. When they were opened in the eighties, the *From Hell* letter was missing. Not surprising, considering it was stolen back in the twenties. The theft was commissioned by a sorcerer."

"Why? Is it magical?"

"Nah. The only way of getting it was with supernatural aid, so it stayed on our side of the line. But just think— that letter could tell us the true identity of Jack the Ripper, and some rich spellcasting son of a bitch is hoarding it for himself. Disgraceful. We are about to rectify that."

I glanced at Clay. "Not liking the sound of that 'we.'"

"Me neither," Clay said.

"I hope you aren't going to ask us to steal that letter—"

"You can't steal stolen goods. What I'm asking is for you to right a very old wrong."

"And return it to the London Police. Gee, that's mighty big of you, Xavier." I turned to Clay. "See, there is a sense of civic duty there after all."

"Ha-ha. I'm passing it on to a buyer, yes, but he wants to have it analyzed by a team of DNA experts so the world can know once and for all the identity of Jack the Ripper."

"Damn," I murmured. "That *is* a righteous cause. Now we can finally catch that murdering bastard and lock him up in prison where he belongs."

Before Xavier could open his mouth, I continued. "What's the guy looking for: a book deal or a movie deal?"

Xavier hesitated, then said, "Book . . . and probably movie eventually, but he's investing over a hundred thousand dollars in this crusade—"

"In return for a book deal that I'm sure will net him a pittance."

I glanced at Clay. He shrugged. He was right. As offensive as I found this guy's reason for wanting the letter, it wasn't doing anyone any good where it was now. And we needed to find David Hargrave before he went on another killing spree.

"Why us?" Clay said. "You can teleport through walls." He met Xavier's gaze. "Unless there's a reason you want someone else to do it."

"There is, but not the one you're thinking. There's zero danger involved. No electric fences or armed guards. Just a spell. A very special spell. That's how it was protected the first time too, probably by a sorcerer judge or prosecutor who wanted to keep all the Ripper letters safe, so he cast a spell that would detect any living being who came near them. To get the letter, then, the guy who wanted it stolen found himself a very special thief, one without that telltale beating heart."

"A vampire," Clay said.

"Whoa. You're good. When he got the letter, he cast another protection spell around it—one that will detect anything in human form. He figured that was safe. Sure, someone could send in a specially trained bird or whatever, but no bird could open the sealed glass box."

"Ah," I said. "So, to retrieve it, you need someone not in human form. A wolf, perhaps."

"You got it."

I leaned forward. "Problem number one: as you doubtless noticed back at the compound, we change into full wolves. Wolves with paws. Operating a glass cutter? One of those things that requires opposable thumbs."

"True, but as I also recall from the compound, you can change just your hand."

"From human to wolf, yes. Vice versa? Not so simple." I glanced at Clay, who gave a half-shrug. "Not *impossible*, but not easy either. How many locks are we talking? Is the box locked or just sealed? And I assume the room is locked too?"

"The box is just sealed—a solid glass box bolted to the table. As for the door to the room, it's locked, but more to keep out the housekeeper than serious thieves. The spell covers that. Once you get the door open, you just need to change forms before you get too close to the glass box. As for changing just your hand back, that's pretty much essential. Change any more and you'll set off the alarms, so if you can't—"

Clay cut in. "We'll deal with it. Bigger problem for me?

What's to say this sorcerer hasn't used both the spells: the one to detect a pulse and the one to detect human form?"

"Can't. If you double up high-powered spells like that, you're almost guaranteed nasty side effects. Don't take my word for it, though. Check it out with your spellcasting buddies. Either this sorcerer didn't think about werewolves, like the last one didn't think about vampires, or he figured there was no real risk. Vamps are known for stealth, weres for killing."

"So this letter is in Toronto?" I said.

Xavier nodded. "Owned by the grandson of Theodore Shanahan, the sorcerer who had it stolen from the police archives. Guy's name is Patrick Shanahan. Lives alone. Typical investment banker—keeps his life very ordered and dull, with a strict routine. You won't show up and find he's moved the letter or skipped a client dinner to stay home unexpectedly. If he does? Abort, and we'll try again. No rush. No pressure. This letter isn't going anywhere."

I glanced at Clay. Another shrug, but this one merging into a nod.

"Let me think about it," I said.

"Really?" Xavier cleared his throat. "I mean, sure. Right. Think about it, do your research, make sure everything's on the up and up. I'll give you everything you need. I've bought a contact with access to the house, so I'm working on that now. All you'll need to do is go in and get the letter."

It would be Jeremy who made the final decision, but I wanted to do my homework before I decided how strongly I'd support Xavier's offer. I'd start with the letter. I hadn't wanted to admit the depths of my ignorance in front of Xavier, but say "From Hell" and "Jack the Ripper" to me, and the only association sparked was the Johnny Depp movie, which I'd wanted to see and Clay hadn't. Nick and I had ended up ditching him at the multiplex, sending Clay in to see *Training Day* and telling him we'd catch up after we got the popcorn.

Took thirty minutes for Clay to realize we weren't coming back, and another ten to get past the ushers and track us down in *From Hell*, whereupon he declared that if we'd really wanted to see it, we could have just said so. Then he plunked himself into the seat beside mine and spent a half hour grousing about how much he hated serial killer flicks before I shoved my Milk Duds box in his mouth, and Nick and I moved to a spot with no empty adjoining seats.

A typical night at the movies. The upshot being that my memories of the movie had big Clay-induced plot holes, and if there had been a mention of the letter that had inspired the title, I didn't remember it.

As we walked into the house, I said, "I'll go online and see what I can find out about this letter."

"Let's ask Jeremy first."

"Jeremy?"

Clay shrugged. "He likes solving mysteries. He might know something."

"About a case like Lizzie Borden maybe. Jack the Ripper is definitely not Jeremy's style."

"Maybe."

The study door opened down the hall and Jeremy walked into the foyer.

"That was quick," Jeremy said. "Was there a problem?"

"Questions needing answers," I said. "He's serious about giving up Hargrave—says if his tip doesn't pan out, we don't owe him anything. Hard to argue with that. But the favor he wants in return is . . . a little strange."

"Jack the Ripper," Clay said. "What do you know about him?"

Jeremy frowned. "Jack the Ripper?"

"Victorian serial killer," I said. "Killed some prostitutes—"

"Five women in Whitechapel in the fall of 1888," Jeremy said. "I know who he is, Elena."

"Obviously," I said. I tried to keep the surprise from my voice, but the corners of Jeremy's mouth twitched.

"Come into the study," he said. "I'm hardly an expert on the subject, but I'll see if I can start you in the right direction . . . after you tell me what this has to do with Xavier's request."

Jeremy didn't "start us in the right direction." He got us all the way to the last stop, and then some. I guess I should have known. As Clay said, Jeremy did love a mystery, and there were few crimes with more questions and theories than those of Jack the Ripper.

First, Jeremy skimmed the particulars. "Then there are the letters," he said, propping his feet on the ottoman. "Hundreds of letters sent to various members of the police and local press."

"I thought only modern killers did that," I said. "Establishing a correspondence with a reporter in hopes of getting more inches on the front page, keeping their crimes in the spotlight."

"That may very well be what he was doing," Jeremy

said. "One of the first media-savvy criminals. But it's more likely that the majority of those letters didn't come from him. Had he really written them all . . . well, let's just say his wrist would have been too tired to wield a knife."

"Fakes," I said. "Written by people in serious need of a life."

"Presumably that's where most came from, though some are believed to have been written by reporters themselves, frustrated by the lack of news between killings."

"Next they'll be saying the Ripper himself was a journalist, killing people to boost paper sales," I muttered.

"You know, newspaper sales did skyrocket during that period . . ."

I shook my head. "So this letter Xavier wants is a fake?"

"Perhaps. And yet . . . Imagine you're the killer. Someone else is writing to the press and the police, claiming to be you. Dozens of people, signing your name to letters, putting their words in articles that are supposed to be about you."

"Identity theft, Victorian style. You'd want to set them straight. So you send real letters proving you're the killer."

Jeremy nodded. "There are three letters many believed to be genuine. The first, sent to the Central News Agency, appears to hint at a double murder committed a few days later. The second, sent to the same place, refers to the original letter, and includes details of the crimes that hadn't yet reached the papers. Still, there were doubters, those who believed the references in the first were too vague and the details in the second could have been leaked. Two weeks later, a third letter came in, this one sent instead to the chairman of the Whitechapel Vigilance Committee."

"The *From Hell* letter," I murmured.

"Called so because that was the return address on the envelope: *From Hell*. Enclosed with the letter was half a human kidney, and one of the victims was indeed missing her kidney. Tests indicated it came from a woman approximately the victim's age but that was the best they could do at the time, so whether it was a hoax or not was never determined. Obviously the man who wants to buy it believes it's the real thing. Yet all that matters, for our purposes, is that the letter does indeed exist and is indeed missing, as Xavier claims."

"What happened to it?"

"It was boxed up with the other evidence and packed away for a hundred years. When they opened the files in 1988, the *From Hell* letter wasn't there. It may have simply been misplaced. Conspiracy theories speculate that it was 'removed,' either by the police to cover a misstep, or by 'interested parties,' who feared it contained an important clue. Most likely, the truth is exactly what Xavier believes, that it was stolen for its value on the collectors' black market."

He paused, tilting his head slightly, eyes unfocusing as he retrieved something from his memory. "There *was* a story that it was bought by a Canadian collector. Interesting, given where Xavier claims it is now. I don't think there was ever much credence given to the rumor. It wasn't very interesting, given the other possibilities."

"That's the problem with the truth," I said. "Making things up is so much more fun. So what do you want us to do?"

Again, Jeremy paused, this time for a few minutes.

Then he pulled his feet off the ottoman and straightened. "Look into it more before you get back to him. Be thorough, but be quick. If we can get to Hargrave, I want to make this deal before he decides to move on. Start by confirming what I've just told you. It's been years since I took an interest, so make sure the letter hasn't turned up in the meantime."

"I'll search the wire services—" I began.

"No, give Clay your access." He turned to Clay. "You can do that, right?"

"Simple enough."

"Then, Elena, you get back to Xavier. He said he'll make this easy, but I want specifics. Make sure he can give us blueprints, security codes, keys, anything we might need. This isn't our area of expertise, so I want all the professional work done for us and provided in advance so we can get a second opinion."

"Karl?"

Jeremy nodded.

"I'll get on it," I said.

"That leaves the spell," he said. "I'll verify that."

"Spell?"

"Xavier claims this letter is protected by a spell that will stop anything in human form. I want to be sure such a spell exists—or that it could exist. Paige or Lucas should be able to tell us that, or find someone who can."

Diversion

WHEN WE FINISHED OUR RESEARCH, JEREMY HAD ME CALL Xavier to accept his offer and get David Hargrave's new address. Clay and Antonio took care of Hargrave right away. And no, that didn't mean they took him aside and gave him a stern talking to. Sometimes that's all that's required, but if a mutt catches the Pack's attention, it usually means he's gone beyond the "occasional slip-up" stage, and needs more than a warning.

They found Hargrave right where Xavier had told us he'd be. So we were ready to uphold our end of the deal. Yet it seemed that wouldn't happen anytime soon. When I called Xavier, things weren't going well on his end. Although he assured me he was just working out some kinks, I got the impression the buyer was waffling. When a month passed, with no word from Xavier, we figured the deal had fallen through.

Two more months passed. Spring became summer, then headed toward autumn. I was racing through the forest, hot breath billowing smoke signals into the cool night air.

Adrenaline rippled through me with each stride. A glorious late summer night, capped off by a perfect run.

I lunged through a stand of trees and launched myself. In midflight, pain ripped through my abdomen, and I crashed sideways to the forest floor. When I tried to get up, machine-gun bursts of cramps doubled me over and pushed me back down.

I lay on my side, moaning, claws scrabbling against air. A burst of wetness under my tail. The smell of blood filled the air. Still racked by cramps, I managed to twist around. Blood pooled in the leaves under my backside. Fur clotted the blood; fur too dark to be my own.

Oh, God, no. Please—

A tremendous wave of pain ran through me, so intense I thought I was spontaneously changing back to human form. Then a horrible wet plop, as something fell onto the leaves.

At first I saw only a dark lump, black against the blood. Then in a flash, I saw everything—the tiny limbs contorted by their own Change, the head nearly perpendicular to the body, neck snapped, broken by me, by my Change, my selfishness, my thoughtlessness.

I screamed.

"Shhhh." The wind whistled through the trees overhead. "Shhhh."

I tried to move, but something held me fast, something warm and solid. My eyes flew open and I saw the full moon overhead, bright blue against the night. A full moon? Hadn't it been a quarter moon earlier? I blinked, and saw two moons hanging over me.

"Elena?"

Another hard blink, and the blanket of sleep fell away. Clay's face, twisted with worry, hovered over mine.

"What did you dream?" he whispered.

I opened my mouth, but only a whimper came out. His arms tightened around me. I started to relax, then the images from the dream flew back and I jerked away. I ran my hands over my rounded belly. Still there. So big. Too big. I was barely past the halfway point, and already people were stopping me in the supermarket to ask how many weeks—or days—I had left.

Jeremy insisted it was the wolf blood accelerating my pregnancy, but he was only guessing. No one knew. I ran my fingers over my stomach again, trying to feel a heartbeat or a kick, but knowing I wouldn't. For as far along as I seemed to be, my baby was strangely quiet. Jeremy assured me he heard a heartbeat, though, and I kept growing, so I had to tell myself that was good enough.

Clay laid his hands over mine.

"I can't Change anymore," I whispered. "It isn't safe for the baby. It can't be."

"If it wasn't, then you wouldn't need to Change while you were pregnant. You can't have a species physically incapable of reproducing—"

"We are not a species!" I said, pushing myself up. "*They* are a species, not us. They inherited it. We were bitten. Don't you get that? You're infected, I'm infected, and no sane person with something like that intentionally tries to reproduce!"

I took a few deep breaths and concentrated on hearing that voice of reason in my head, telling me I was overreacting again, that everything would seem better in the morning. But my pounding heart drowned it out.

Goddamn it! Why couldn't I get past this? After I'd Changed that first time, everything had seemed fine. But every Change since had been just as nerve-wracking.

Logically, as my pregnancy progressed without complications, my fears should have eased. Instead, they grew worse, like a shipwreck survivor swimming to an island, with each stroke thinking, "Oh, God, I've made it this far, please, please, please don't let me fail now."

As hard as I tried not to, every day I made new plans for our child—"I can't wait to show him this" or "I have to remember to teach her that." If something went wrong, I'd lose hopes and dreams and plans, and a baby that was already as real to me as if he or she were lying in a bassinet beside my bed.

"You'll be okay," Clay murmured. "You're doing great so far, right?"

I took a deep breath. "I know. I'm sorry. I'm so—"

He put his hand over my mouth. "You're worried. Nothing wrong with that." He lowered me down to the bed. "What did you dream?"

An image flashed. The blood, the clotted fur, the—

Heart hammering, I crushed my face against his bare chest and took a deep breath, grounding myself with his scent.

I pulled back, not looking up at him. "I just want—I need to sleep."

A slight tensing of his shoulder muscles, as if fighting the urge to prod. After a moment, he relaxed, pulled me against him and, eventually, I fell back to sleep.

I woke up the next morning to the sound of Clay's snoring. I eased out of bed so I wouldn't disturb him, then leaned over to brush my lips across the top of his curls, too light a touch to wake him.

As I headed downstairs, I heard Jeremy in the kitchen.

When I smelled what he was cooking, I knew he'd heard me wake up screaming last night. I leaned against the wall and cursed my performance, knowing even as I did that it wouldn't be the last. No matter how embarrassed and guilty I felt the next morning, in the darkness of night all my fears and insecurities came out to play.

I took a deep breath, pushed open the kitchen door and looked at the tottering stacks of pancakes and sliced ham on the counter.

"You don't need to do this," I said.

Jeremy fished the bottle of maple syrup from the back of the fridge. "The plates are already in the sunroom. Can you carry the pancake platter for me?"

"Really, you don't need to do this. I'm being silly, and what I need is a swift kick in the rear, not comfort food."

"What you need is baby furniture," he said, handing me the platter. "Plus a nursery to put it in, but I thought we'd start with the furniture and choose the decor from there. I'm sure Syracuse has fine stores, but I propose a trip to New York. We'll spend a couple of days, stay with Antonio and Nick, make a trip out of it. We'll leave today."

I shook my head. "I'm not ready, Jer."

"We'll go whenever you are. We have to wait for Clay anyway, although if we're lucky, we'll be able to leave him with Nick while we go into the city and shop."

"I don't mean— I'm not ready for a nursery. If something went wrong— I'm not ready."

Jeremy laid down the ham and looked at me. "That's why this is exactly what you need. Everything is going fine, and the best way for you to recognize and accept that is to keep moving forward, making plans and preparing." A quarter-smile. "At the rate you're progressing, we'd better get cracking, or we may end up with a baby and no place to put him. We'll be fashioning diapers out of dishcloths."

I tried to return the smile, but my lips wouldn't budge. I looked away. "I can't. Soon, I promise. Just . . . not yet."

The kitchen door opened before I got to it. Clay popped his head in.

"Look who smelled breakfast," I said.

As I brushed past him, I dipped my hand to his and squeezed it. An awkward apology for last night.

"I'll take that ham," he said to Jeremy.

I didn't turn, but I knew more than the platter passed between them. After I'd fallen asleep again last night, they'd probably snuck downstairs to devise "distract Elena" plans. Option one: baby shopping in New York. Jeremy would have signaled Clay that the idea had been torpedoed, so they'd have to find a way to segue to option two over breakfast.

I turned into the sunroom and put the pancake platter down, then reached for the coffee urn and started filling mugs.

"We should invite Paige up," Clay said as he rounded the doorway. "For a visit."

"No segue required," I murmured. "Silly me."

I exchanged his ham platter for a steaming mug of coffee, and sat down to fix my own. Decaf of course. Every bit of coffee in the house was decaf. I tried telling the guys, really, you can drink regular coffee in front of me, but they were having none of it. If I sacrificed, they sacrificed. A communal pregnancy. It was starting to drive me a little bonkers.

"Invite Paige here? Your desperation is showing."

He shrugged and slid into his seat. "We've had her up before."

"At *my* invitation. With you gritting your teeth the whole time."

"I was never gritting my teeth. I'm fine with Paige. And if Lucas can make it . . . All the better. Maybe they'll be working on a case, something to get your mind— Something to talk about."

I'd rather take a trip to Portland to visit *them*, but I knew that was out of the question. Having Paige here would be nice, and if Lucas came along, Clay would enjoy the distraction just as much as I did.

Lucas had filled a space in Clay's life that I'd never realized had been empty. Logan used to tell me how, when he'd first joined the Pack, Clay would drive him nuts with "lessons," always showing him how to fight better, train better, Change better. He'd figured it was just Clay's way of reminding Logan that he was the newest and youngest member, keeping him in his place.

When I saw Clay with Lucas, I realized there had been more to it than that. Clay had genuinely wanted to teach Logan, to assume the role of mentor to a younger werewolf. Maybe that was the wolf in him, instinctively wanting to pass on his life experience to the next generation. In the Pack, though, there was no next generation . . . not yet. With Lucas, Clay had found a substitute after Logan's death—if not a werewolf, at least an intelligent, thoughtful young man who not only accepted Clay's counsel, but sought it out.

Most of Clay's ideas for dealing with problem mutts weren't the kind of thing Lucas would ever use on rogue sorcerers. He didn't have the personality—or the stomach—for that. Yet he was astute enough to take

Clay's teachings and pick out the principles that worked for him. In seeing them together, I'd realized that Clay's desire for a child had to do with more than pleasing me. For the first time, I'd seen him in the role of father . . . and not been scared shitless by the image.

After breakfast, I waited until it was a reasonable time to call Oregon. Then I phoned Paige. As I listened to her answering machine, my hopes plummeted. I didn't bother leaving a message. The one on her machine told me Paige was off on an investigation with Lucas. Of course, the message didn't say that, but it was one she used to let her fellow council members and supernatural friends know she was out of town, and they should call her cell phone instead.

"We'll try again next week," Clay said. "She's never away long. Not with Savannah in school . . . or, I guess, Savannah isn't in school right now, is she?"

"Summer break," I mumbled.

That reminded me that this was the first summer in four years that Savannah wouldn't be spending a week with us. We'd planned on it, but then my nightmares started, and I'd been afraid of spooking her. The last thing any teenage girl needs is to see something like that—might scare her off having kids herself someday. Savannah had been understanding, and we'd promised to make it up to her at Christmas, but I knew she'd been disappointed, which only made me feel guiltier, as I screwed up another person's summer . . .

"Jaime," Clay said.

"Invite Jaime? I'm sure she's too busy—"

"What about that documentary work you two were talking about? Not really your type of writing, but you seemed interested when she brought it up."

I hesitated, then nodded. "Sure. Work. That'd be good. Something new might be just what I need."

I grabbed the phone book from the drawer, opened it and dialed. Again I got an answering machine. This time I left a message, just a vague "give me a shout when you get a chance." I suspected it would be days before I heard back—Jaime spent most of her year touring, a few days here, a week there. God only knew when she'd get the message.

"She might have just stepped out," Clay said.

"Sure. Maybe."

"You want to give Nick a try?"

I shook my head, murmured a "maybe later" and slid from the room.

Strategy

THE PHONE RANG EARLY THE NEXT MORNING.

"I'll get it!" I said.

I rocketed from the table so fast that I temporarily forgot my new center of gravity and nearly landed face-first on the floor.

"You expecting someone?" Clay called after me, as I righted myself and hurried to the study.

"Work," I said. "A . . . job assignment."

Like I ever moved so fast to get work. The sad truth was that I wasn't expecting a call—I just wanted contact with the outside world. Any contact. At this point, a vacuum cleaner salesperson would do.

Just last week, when our tenacious local Avon lady had dropped a catalogue in our mailbox, as she'd done for the last four years without ever getting an order from me, there had been a moment when I'd thought, "Huh, maybe I should give her a call, get a makeup consultation." It didn't matter that I hadn't bought new makeup since the nineties. Even when I recalled Jeremy's story about the last Avon lady that showed up at Stonehaven, I wasn't deterred. After all, Clay had been only seven or eight years old, and even if he did terrorize the Avon lady again, as bad as I would feel about that, it certainly would liven up an afternoon.

The phone hit its fourth ring. I dove for the answering machine, and hit the off button, then glanced at the caller ID as I reached for the receiver. A pay phone tag flashed past. A pay phone? Maybe Jaime calling back or Paige checking in.

"Hello?"

"Elena!" a voice boomed.

"Xavier!"

Silence. A bit too enthusiastic on my part, I guess. He was probably trying to figure out whether that was a happy shout of greeting or a warning snarl.

"Good to hear from you," I added.

Silence. Then, "What'd I do?"

"Nothing. It's just . . . good to hear from you."

Clay appeared in the doorway. I mouthed "Xavier." He scowled. I turned to face the wall.

"So what's up?" I said. "Have you heard anything about that letter? Or do you have something else you need us to do? We still owe you for the Hargrave tip, don't forget."

He paused, certain a trap lurked behind my enthusiasm. "Uh, no, I haven't. It's the letter. Things have fallen back into place—"

"So we're on? Great! When do you want it?"

"The, uh, buyer would like it within the next couple of weeks, but if that's not enough notice, I can probably swing something—"

"A couple of weeks? Perfect. Just send us the updated plans and we'll be on it. Do you still have my fax number?"

He did. We discussed a few final details, then I hung up and turned, beaming, to Clay.

"Absolutely not," he said. "So don't even ask."

"Ask? Since when do I need your permission?"

I bounced past him out the door.

"He's going to say the same thing," Clay called.

We'd see about that.

Wrangling a day pass from Jeremy . . . take two.

Since I'd started showing, Jeremy and Clay hadn't wanted me leaving Pack territory or meeting with any supernatural who wasn't a good friend. As overprotective as that sounded, there was logic behind it. They wanted to keep my pregnancy a secret from the werewolf world for as long as possible.

Being the only female werewolf always made me a target. Becoming Clay's mate had upped the ante. There were plenty of mutts who wanted to get to him, and wouldn't mind doing it through me. But we'd learned to deal with that . . . or I'd learned to deal with it, and Jeremy and Clay had learned to trust that I could deal with it.

But now I was carrying Clay's child, and my growing belly already hampered my ability to fight, or to run from a fight. So they'd laid down the law. I was to stick to New York state—Pack territory. As much as I wanted to argue with that, I knew what mutts were capable of. Maybe I was willing to take the risk, but I had no right to subject my unborn child to it.

But Xavier wouldn't have to see me. I could conduct all arrangements by phone and courier. Plus, it was mere larceny, with no violence or personal threat involved.

"The plan will stand as we decided two months ago," I said. "I'm not arguing with that. Jeremy takes the letter and Clay stands guard. My job will be to escort Jeremy into the house, so he doesn't have to worry about opening doors in wolf form."

"And what if—" Clay began.

"The doors are rigged with deadly gamma ray trip wires?" I bit back the sarcasm. "Sorry, I mean, what if it's not safe for me to go inside the house? Then I don't. Jeremy, you wanted Karl to go over the plans. I agree. If he has any safety concerns, then I won't go in."

"That's *any* concern," Clay said. "Not a high risk or a moderate risk. Karl even brings up a potential risk, you don't go, right?"

"Right."

"And anything goes wrong, we get out of there."

"Absolutely."

"And it's there and back, just an overnight trip."

"Fine by me."

"And you stay in my sight or Jeremy's sight at all times, the entire trip."

"Except for bathroom breaks."

He hesitated. I glared.

"Fine," he said. "Except for bathroom breaks."

We looked at Jeremy.

"All right," he said. "Let's get this over with, then. Elena? Call Karl, and see how soon he can look at those plans."

Karl Marsten arrived two days later. Prompt for Marsten, who had spent the last three years dragging his heels on another matter: joining the Pack. Five years ago Jeremy had granted him territory for helping us when a group of mutts tried to overthrow the Pack. Since he'd been part of that group, though, his last-minute change of heart had only won him territory in Wyoming, which I'm sure is a lovely state . . . if you aren't a cosmopolitan jewel thief.

While Marsten did a good trade robbing celebrities in Jackson Hole, after a year he'd decided maybe he'd join the Pack after all, see whether he could get territory farther east. Jeremy hadn't fallen for that. He'd laid out the responsibilities Marsten would be expected to follow as a Pack member. That made Marsten back off, but not give up. For three years he'd been fence-sitting, attending our meetings, and helping us when we asked for it.

His help, though, usually came slow . . . like a week after we needed it. Then last spring he'd come to *me*. He'd met a half-demon tabloid reporter who wanted to help the council and asked me to "mentor" her. An odd request from a guy who never lifted a finger to help anyone unless it would benefit him. Since then, Marsten had been quick to come when I called.

When he declared the job looked sound, we left for Toronto.

Larceny

A DROPLET OF SWEAT PLUNKED INTO MY EYE. I GAVE A SOFT snarl at the salt-laced sting, then swiped my hand across my forehead and looked up at the sky, half obliterated by leaves. The sun was long gone, but the humidity held on, determined to see the season to the very end.

Though I was sure my huge belly had something to do with the rivulets of sweat streaming down my face, the heat wasn't unexpected. After all, this was August, and it was Toronto. Unlike visitors who crossed the Canadian border with skis strapped to their roof rack—in July—I knew what to expect. The city as urban furnace— six hundred square kilometers of baking pavement, sky- scrapers ringing the core like sentinels, on guard against any cool breeze.

It had been a cool summer, here and at home in Bear Valley, but as Labor Day approached, August had thrown off her lethargy for a farewell heat wave. What had been a pleasant summer week in Bear Valley was downright uncomfortable in Toronto. The smog didn't help. I vis- ited Toronto a few times a year, and the smog always seemed worse than I remembered. This time, pregnancy had ratcheted up my sense of smell, so even here, amid the designer trees and golf-course lawns, the air quality seemed to have plunged to New York City levels.

Patrick Shanahan's house, half hidden by evergreens, wasn't what I'd expected. Sure, I'd seen the blueprint. I even knew the neighborhood—modest homes where you pay more for the address than for the square footage. And yet . . . well, I couldn't help it. Tell me that a place contains a priceless historical document, and I expect a labyrinthine mansion on a hill, surrounded by an electrified fence and patrolled by armed guards. The letter would be in the center of that mansion, in a fortified, hidden room, rigged with infrared heat detectors, and I'd have to lower myself from the ceiling, *Mission Impossible* style, to retrieve it.

I looked at the ranch-style house and sighed. There was a camera at the front door, more to ward off salespeople than to foil thieves. The only security system was a key-coded entry point alarm—the kind that, if triggered, would call forth an unarmed twenty-year-old security guard, accustomed to showing up and finding sheepish homeowners who'd forgotten their codes. It was all very Canadian.

From behind me came the soft padding of paws on grass.

"Doesn't look like you can hope for much mayhem in this adventure," I said.

A grunt and I turned to see, not the golden-haired wolf I expected, but a jet black one.

"Er, and that's good," I said quickly.

Jeremy's dark eyes rolled. As he passed me, his tail whacked the back of my knees.

"I was talking about Clay, not me," I said. "I'm not looking for any mayhem. I already promised. I won't do anything to make this adventure more fun—I mean, dangerous."

He tilted his head, eyes meeting mine, then gave a soft chuff, knowing I was only teasing, and padded to the line of trees to peer out at the house.

Was I kidding about wanting something more exciting? On a conscious level, yes. My nightmares were all the warning I needed. This had to be as uneventful a pregnancy as I could make it. Yet there was that gnawing restlessness, not to do anything dangerous, but to get my adrenaline pumping, to burn off all this excess energy. With any luck, this excursion would be just what I needed—a safe adventure to tide me over for the next few months.

Another sound came behind me, this one the sharp scuffle of dead leaves. Then the ground vibrated as Clay pounced and landed at my side.

"You don't dare tackle me now, do you?" I said. "I should have known Jeremy wasn't you—you're never that quiet."

Clay slipped his head under my dangling arm, letting my hand slide over the top of his head and down to the ruff behind his neck. I ran my fingers through the thick fur, over the coarse top hairs and burrowed down to the soft fluff underneath.

Five years ago, I'd have pulled away the minute he brushed against me. Having him in wolf form while I was human had made me uncomfortable. I'd accepted what I was, but it had taken longer to hit the next step, to embrace it, and see the two forms not as separate identities, but dual aspects of one.

These days, I could talk to Clay as a wolf, touch him as a wolf, and know him as my lover. Know him in a nonbiblical sense, I mean. Any other way . . . well, that was a wall neither of us was interested in breaching.

I crouched beside him. He leaned against me and I let my hand rest on his shoulder. We sat there for a minute, looking over at the house. Finally, he let out a sigh.

"Pretty disappointing, huh?" I whispered, too low for Jeremy to hear.

Clay leaned into me hard enough that I had to put out my free hand to keep from toppling over. As I recovered my balance, he rumbled deep in his chest—a wolfish laugh. Then he craned his head back over his shoulder and licked my other hand.

"Apology not accepted," I growled.

I caught his muzzle. He wriggled free, grabbed my hand between his teeth and gave it a fierce shake. And that was as rough as our play got these days. As I stifled the urge to say "to hell with it," knock him flying and have a real tussle, I reminded myself that things would be back to normal soon enough.

I smiled, gave Clay one last brisk rub, then pushed to my feet.

"Okay, who's up for a little grand larceny?"

Turned out the experience wasn't as dull as I'd expected. My adrenaline started pounding when I touched the security keypad. As my latex-clad finger punched the buttons, my mind raced through every conceivable risk. What if I mis-hit a key? Could that seven on the paper really be a one? What if the homeowner had changed the code?

I punched in the last digit and held my breath as I braced for the alarms. Even when they didn't go off, I paused, half expecting a wailing car to rip into the driveway.

When the key caught in the lock, my gut did a back-flip. Had the lock been changed?

One last desperate jangle and the lock popped open. I turned the handle and pushed, still ready for the alarm. None came. I listened for footsteps, then looked around for any sign that Shanahan was there. According to Xavier, Shanahan gave a monthly investment seminar to prospective clients tonight, something he never missed. But there was always a first time . . .

Finally, with Jeremy right behind me, I zipped to the keypad. A green light flashed. Good. Or was it? Why was it flashing? Maybe flashing green meant security had been breached. If so, why was there a dimmed red light? It could be reverse psychology—green meant danger, red meant okay, letting unwary thieves think they were safe.

Something hissed and I jumped.

A cat stood in the doorway, some long-haired pampered thing that wouldn't last five minutes in an alley. One halfhearted growl from Jeremy and the cat tore off.

Jeremy's nails clicked against the parquet flooring as we set off. He slowed, put more weight on his pads and all went silent. My heart was pounding, every muscle tensed and ready for trouble.

We found the locked room easily enough. It was just a spare bedroom with the window bricked over and the door locked. The locking mechanism was so simple Xavier hadn't bothered providing a key—a sharp door-knob wrench of werewolf strength snapped it open.

We entered a library. Bookcases lined the walls, containing lots of knickknacks and a smattering of actual books. There were a couple of uncomfortable-looking leather chairs and a full bar. As I spied it, I tried to remember the last time I'd had a drink. I'd never been much for alcohol, but it's funny how much more you miss things when you can't have them.

Jeremy grunted.

Ah, right, the letter.

A table near the center held numerous glass boxes, containing artifacts, small statues and bric-a-brac. Among them was the box that held the letter.

All this I saw from outside the door. I couldn't go any farther, as we didn't know how much of the room the spell covered.

Jeremy took one careful step inside and paused. Both of us strained to hear some indication of a tripped alarm, yet we didn't know what would happen if the alarm *was* tripped. Lucas had said that depended on the spell-caster, and could be anything from flickering lights to wailing sirens to the room being sucked into a hell portal. I think he was kidding about the last part, but we'd seen enough in the past few years that a room-sucking hell portal really wouldn't come as a surprise.

When nothing happened—nothing obvious, at least—Jeremy padded over to the table. Now came the tricky part.

Jeremy had to start the Change, with particular attention to his hand, then stop at the point where he could fish the glass cutter from the bag around his neck, cut open the box and put the letter in the bag. I was glad Jeremy was the one doing it. While I wouldn't mind the challenge, Jeremy had the most control over his Changes and was most likely to be able to manipulate the glass cutter and letter while still in largely wolf form. ·

I didn't watch. My comfort level with the dual form may never extend to that in-between Change state. Having accidentally seen werewolves in it, I had no desire to watch it intentionally. I don't consider myself vain, but *I* don't want to be seen like that, and I assume others feel the same. Well, except maybe Clay, but Clayton's way can never be confused with the norm.

So when Jeremy stopped at the foot of the table, I turned away and stayed turned away until a cold nose pushed against my hand.

"You got it?" I whispered, then saw the rolled paper in the bag around his neck. I grinned, and patted his head. "Good boy."

He nudged me with a "get moving" growl.

Clay met us at the edge of the evergreen patch. After a quick "everyone okay?" snuffle, he dove into the trees to Change back. I untied the bag from around Jeremy's neck, and he loped off to his own spot.

I turned over the bag containing the rolled-up letter and squinted to see words. From my research, I knew what it was supposed to say, but Ripper enthusiast or not, when you get hold of something like this, you want to see it for yourself. But if the bag was opened, it needed to be done carefully. Last thing I needed was to leave my own DNA on it.

I was still trying to read the letter when Clay grabbed me from behind, swung me up and around to face him. A resounding smack of a kiss, and he put me back on the ground.

I looked him up and down. "Don't tell me you misplaced your clothes *here*."

"Nah, just thought I'd come see you first. Everything went okay then? No complications?" He took the bag and started opening it. "So this is the letter?"

I snatched it back. "Yes, and it's a valuable historical document, so don't touch."

He snorted. "A letter from a fucked-up killer or a fucked-up wannabe. Historically valuable only in that it proves humans were no less screwed up a hundred years ago than they are now."

He plucked the bag from my hand and tossed it to the ground, then put his arms around my waist—or as close as he could get to it. I knew I really should protest the illtreatment of the valuable historical document but, well, he *was* naked, and my heart was still tripping from the excitement of the heist.

"So," he said, lips against my ear. "How'd it go?"

"Complication free . . ."

"Disappointed?"

"I'll live." I put my arms around his neck and leaned in as close as my belly would allow. "I probably had as much excitement as the doctor would allow. How about you?"

"Could have used a couple of good guard dogs. Got all ready for trouble, thinking Xavier would have lied to us about something and then . . . nothing. Damned disappointing."

"Definitely. All revved up . . ."

"No place to go." He nipped my ear. "Can't be healthy." His hands slid under the back of my shirt. "Should do something about it."

I twisted my hands in his curls and tilted my face up, lips a hairsbreadth away from his. "Got a cure in mind?"

"Got two. First, the obvious—get the hell out of here, back to our hotel room and lock the door until noon."

"And number two?"

He pulled back. "What? You don't like that one?"

"Didn't say that. But you said you had two ideas, so I'm checking out all the options first."

"I'm not sure you'd like the second one . . . it's not really your kind of thing. Nah, maybe I shouldn't mention it . . ."

I tweaked a lock of his hair. "Talk."

"Well, number two ends the same as number one—"

"Shocking."

"—but it starts with a run. In the city."

I shivered and pressed against him. "Mmm, yes."

"You'd like that?"

There was genuine surprise in his voice. Normally, I *did* love city runs. They were forbidden fruit, not being the kind of "safe werewolf activity" Jeremy endorsed. Lately, though, my attitude toward running in general had been far from my usual. Yet now . . . Well, I'd had a taste of excitement and wasn't quite willing to hurry home.

I slid my hands down his back, my lips going to his ear. "I'd love it."

From behind us came a sigh, then a mutter that sounded like "Figures," followed by "Elena, get off Clay. Clay, get dressed. Now."

"We were just—"

"Oh, I know what you were doing, but you can wait ten minutes, until we get to the hotel."

I pulled away from Clay. "Please, do you really think we'd interrupt our getaway for sex?"

Jeremy just gave me a look.

"Okay, maybe we would, but not tonight."

Jeremy scooped up the letter. "Clay? Get your clothes on. Meet us at the car."

"You go on," I said. "I'll wait—"

Jeremy grabbed my arm and led me away.

Victoriana

JEREMY HAD WANTED TO HEAD STRAIGHT TO THE HOTEL, but I convinced him I wasn't ready to turn in yet. Wrangling permission for a city run wasn't something I could do on the fly.

So I claimed restlessness and dehydration, circumstances that would prevent me from getting the good night's rest I needed. The cure? A warm milky drink and a long walk. Since we hoped to turn that walk into a city run, I asked if we could grab that drink at a popular late-night coffee bar close to downtown. Then we headed into the quiet residential Cabbagetown area for our walk.

I strolled down the narrow street, listening to Clay talk about some article on bear cults he'd read last week. Jeremy and I nodded at appropriate junctures and sipped our coffees. Mine was a latte, of course—for the milk. Whole milk. Seems odd, specifically requesting whole milk, but Jeremy insisted. He also insisted on plenty of ice cream and cheese and other whole-fat dairy products. He said it was for the milk content, but I suspected he was trying to fatten me up for motherhood.

Besides my stomach, the only thing that *had* plumped

up were my breasts. Yes, for the first time in my life, I actually had breasts—the kind that could be seen even under a baggy shirt. Not that it mattered. My belly stuck out farther.

As the midnight hour passed, the heat lifted and a cool night breeze found its way through the armor of skyscrapers into the narrow residential streets. I liked Cabbagetown. I'm not much of a city dweller anymore, but this is the kind of place I'd choose, a quiet old neighborhood just a few minutes' walk from the bustle of downtown.

The narrow street was lined with small, two-story, multihued houses, the tiny front yards jealously guarded by fences of every description, from stone to wrought-iron to white-picket. The era was Victorian, and every architectural detail I associated with the period was evident in a single sweep—gingerbread, gables, wrap-around porches, balconies, cupolas, spires, stained glass.

Though we could hear the roar of Yonge Street a few blocks over, there was a hush here, as if the trees arching over the road were an insulating blanket, letting the residents sleep amid the chaos of the city core. We walked down the middle of the road, our footsteps echoing softly, our voices barely above a whisper.

To our right was a line of parked cars. The houses predated driveways and didn't have enough room between to add them. Most of the cars were midpriced imports, with few minivans or SUVs. This was a neighborhood for seniors and couples, not families.

Jeremy drained the last of his coffee and looked around, but of course there was no place to toss the cup.

"Here," I said, and opened my bag.

I'm not a fan of purses, and certainly not big ones, but

tonight I was carrying a small knapsack-style bag for the *From Hell* letter. Jeremy had decided this was the safest way to transport it. We hadn't wanted to leave it in the hotel or the Explorer, so I'd brought it along.

Jeremy took a tissue from his pocket and wiped out the inside of the cup before crushing it and tucking it into my knapsack. The letter was still in its plastic bag, but I guess he wasn't taking any chances with stray coffee droplets. I started to zip up the knapsack, then stopped and took out the letter.

"Are we going to . . . ? I mean, can I take a look? Before we drop it off?"

Jeremy hesitated.

"I'll be careful," I said. "I've got these." I tugged the latex gloves from my pocket.

He still hesitated, but I could tell he was as curious as I was, so after a moment he nodded.

We moved to the side of the road, under a streetlamp. I set down my latte on the curb, then put on the gloves, opened the bag, reached in and took out the letter. I expected it to be brittle, but it was oddly supple, almost clothlike, as if it had softened with time.

I unrolled it. The paper was brownish, the color uneven. I doubted a drop or two of Jeremy's coffee would have made much difference. It was already spotted with ink and other substances. I remembered reading that the letter had come packed in a cardboard box that included part of a kidney preserved in wine. I really hoped the reddish splotches were wine.

The writing was a near-indecipherable scrawl, with a quarter of the words mangled. If I hadn't known what it was supposed to say, I wouldn't have made out half of it.

"Looks deliberately misspelled," I said.

"That's the general consensus with the other Ripper letters as well," Jeremy said. "The spelling is erratic, with some words spelled correctly once, then misspelled—"

Clay slapped my upper arm. I spun so fast I almost tripped.

"Mosquito," he said.

I glared at him.

"They have West Nile here, don't they?" he said.

"Just like at home," I said through my teeth.

"But at home you've been wearing that special stuff Jeremy got for you. You didn't bring it, did you?"

"Clayton's right," Jeremy said softly. "I know the risk is minimal, but if you've forgotten the repellent, you really should be wearing long sleeves after dark. If you contract the virus, it can be passed on—"

"To my baby, I know. But considering what else I'm already passing on to my baby, West Nile virus seems the least of my concerns." I shook my head, then leaned toward Clay. "Smack me again, and I smack you back. Maybe you can smack harder, but I *dare* to smack harder."

A small smile. "You sure about that?"

"You wanna test me?"

"Uh-uh," Jeremy said. "No smacking challenges. At least, not while you're holding that letter. Here, better put it away. Looks like it's already creased."

I looked down. When Clay swatted the mosquito on my arm, my hand had automatically clenched on the letter.

"Shit!" I quickly straightened it. "There. No harm—"

The mosquito was still on the paper, now a squashed dark splotch. It must have bounced onto the paper before I'd clenched it.

Jeremy shook his head. "No matter. It's dirty enough. I'll take a closer look before we drop it off. Now roll it up. Quickly."

"Before I drop it in the gutter and trample it," I muttered. "I can't believe I did that."

"Wasn't your fault," Clay said.

"That's right. It wasn't." I turned a mock scowl on him. "Bug killer."

"Yeah, but I *only* killed it. You squashed it."

"You didn't squash it *when* you killed it?"

Jeremy sighed.

I looked at him. "And you thought we were ready for kids?"

"No, I just thought one more wouldn't make much difference. Now, if I could have the bag please?"

I put it into my knapsack and handed it to him. He looked down at the knapsack—lime green with a daisy on the front.

"Hey, I didn't pick it out," I said. "You bought it; you can carry it."

He took the knapsack with a slow shake of his head. "Let's get this back to a hotel, examine it for damage and send it off to Xavier."

Clay and I looked at each other, seeing our opportunity for a city run vanishing.

"Uh, Jer," Clay said. "Elena and I were wondering . . ."

He stopped, eyes narrowing as he stared at something over my shoulder. I followed his gaze to a curtain of smoke rising from the road. It looked like sewer steam . . . only there wasn't a sewer grate or manhole cover in sight. I walked over and looked down to see a hairline crack in the asphalt. Clay grabbed my arm and yanked me away.

"Don't give me that look," he said as I caught my balance. "You don't know what that is."

"An underground volcano ready to bury us all under a mountain of spewing lava?"

The smoke wafted up, a thin, slow moving line that dispersed before it hit waist level. Jeremy crouched for a closer look.

"Probably some kind of trapped steam," he said.

Clay rocked on the balls of his feet, fighting to keep from yanking Jeremy out of the way too.

"I don't think it's West-Nile-carrying steam," I said.

When Clay didn't move, I laid my fingers on his arm. He nodded, but I could feel the tension strumming from him as he watched Jeremy.

"Jer?" I said. "We should probably get going."

"Mm-hmm."

He waved his fingertips through the smoke. Clay let out a strangled sound.

I tapped Jeremy's shoulder. "We really should go. Before one of the residents notices the smoke. And us."

"Yes, right."

He pushed to his feet. Yet he didn't move, just stared at the smoke, a frown-crease between his brows. Then his head jerked up, body going rigid. I followed his gaze and saw nothing, just the trees, leaves rustling—

"Clay!" Jeremy shouted.

Hands grabbed my arms and I flew backward, stumbling, then lifted, feet flying off the pavement, fingers tight around my upper arms, half shoving me out of the way, half carrying me. My back hit the low wall of a fence. A flash illuminated the night sky as a transformer overhead exploded in a shower of sparks. All went dark as my rescuer's body shielded me from the falling cascade.

"Clay!" The voice came from above me, and as my brain cleared, I realized it was Jeremy, not Clay, who'd been shielding me, that he'd thrown me clear of a transformer . . . before it blew.

"Clay!"

"Over here," came a voice beside us. "Where's Elena?"

"She's here." Jeremy looked at me. "Are you all right?"

"Still seeing sparks," I said.

I blinked and realized I was still seeing sparks because there *were* still sparks, on the ground, coming from a power line that had fallen from the exploding transformer . . . and landed right about where we'd been standing.

The line sputtered, then went dark . . . as did everything around it. I waited for my night vision to kick in, but the moon had disappeared behind cloud cover and I could only make out shapes.

"Whatever that was, I didn't do it," Clay said as he got to his feet.

Jeremy shushed him and motioned for him to stay still. Again, I followed Jeremy's gaze. Again, I saw nothing. Then, twenty or so feet away, a shadow moved. I squinted, and could make out a dim figure crouched in the middle of the street.

I tried to move forward, but Jeremy's hand clamped around my arm. I caught a whiff of something—the smell was downwind, but strong enough to carry. It was the stench of an unwashed body, mingled with the faint "off" smell of sickness. My brain jumped to the closest approximation it knew—a homeless person.

When I looked back at Jeremy, his eyes were trained on the shape, squinting, that same furrow between his brows. Something in his expression sent a chill through me. Without even looking my way, he patted my hand. Then he motioned for me to stay put, shifted into a stooped hunch and started forward.

I glanced at Clay. He was already moving toward Jeremy, but Jeremy shook his head. When Clay hesitated, Jeremy lifted his hand and firmly waved him down. A soft growl rippled through the air, cut short as Clay swallowed his protest.

Jeremy didn't head straight for the figure, but circled to the left, trying to get downwind. I watched him, my gaze flicking between his dark shape and the other. It looked like a man, with an oddly shaped head, crouched on the road. His head moved, and I realized he was wearing a hat—a black bowler.

The man grunted. Then he pushed to his feet. A sharp grating sound, then the flare of a lit match. The light illuminated the bottom half of a man's swarthy face. Thick lips, dark whiskers, a missing front tooth. The match sputtered out. Another strike of a match, then a snap as it broke and a tap-tap as the broken end hit and rebounded off the asphalt. Another grunt. Then the sound of hands rustling over fabric. Searching his pockets for more matches.

"Bloody 'ell," he muttered in a thick English accent.

I could make out the pale moon of his face as he looked around.

"Huh," he grunted.

A screen door slapped shut and a beam of light ping-ponged around us. I ducked. Out of the corner of my eye, I saw the man in the street freeze.

"You there!" someone shouted.

The man wheeled and ran.

"Jeremy?" Clay hissed.

"Go," Jeremy said.

I pushed to my feet and dashed after Clay. Jeremy called after me, as loudly as he dared. I knew I hadn't been included in his command, but if I didn't hear him expressly tell me to stop, then I didn't have to obey. That was the rule. Or my interpretation of it.

When I caught up, Clay just glanced over at me and nodded, then turned his attention back to his prey. The man was heading north, moving at a slow jog. He veered out to cross the road . . . and ran smack into the side of a parked minivan.

The man stumbled and swore, the oath ringing down the empty street. A quick look around, to see whether he'd been heard. Clay and I stopped, frozen in place. We were both dressed in jeans and dark shirts, and the man's gaze passed right over us.

He turned back to the minivan and put both hands out, palms first. He touched the side of the van and jerked back with a grunt, as if expecting to touch a wall of brick or wood, not steel. He looked up and down the street, his body tense, eager to be off, and yet . . .

He reached out and pressed his fingertips to the minivan door. His hands moved across the panel, hit the handle and stopped. His fingers traced the outline of the door handle, and he bent for a closer look but only grunted, making no move to open it. Then he straightened. His hands resumed their exploration of the door. When they reached the window, he looked closer, peering through it. Then he backpedaled, sending up another too-loud oath.

Breath tickled the top of my head and I wheeled to see Jeremy behind me.

"What should we do?" I whispered.

He hesitated, eyes on the figure, about twenty feet from us.

"Clay? Take him. Carefully, and before he reaches the main road. Elena?" He paused, then said, "Help Clay. Make sure you stay back—"

The screech of tires cut him short as a car ripped around the corner. Headlights flooded the darkened street. The man let out a wail of absolute terror and threw himself to the ground—in the middle of the road. At the last moment, the car veered around him. Someone shouted from the open passenger window.

"Go," Jeremy hissed. "Now. Quickly."

Clay bolted for the man, with me jogging behind. The man was still on the road, his face pressed against the asphalt. We made it halfway to him, then a second carful of teens careened around the corner. This time, the man didn't cower in the street and wait to be mowed down. He leapt to his feet and raced for the side of the road.

From there he had two directions to choose from. One would've brought him straight into our arms.

He hit the sidewalk and ran in the other direction, heading north again.

Still jogging, I glanced over my shoulder at Jeremy. He hesitated, gaze meeting mine, and I was sure he was going to call me back. After a moment, he motioned for us to keep going, in silent pursuit, and head the man off someplace safe.

Parked

WE REACHED THE AUTO REPAIR SHOP ON THE CORNER JUST as the man crossed the road. He paused and stared up at the replica gaslight streetlamps, then squinted down the street. Clay glanced at me, but I shook my head. Too public.

Seconds later, the man took off again, darting down a narrow road between two yellow brick houses. Before we could sprint across, a short line of cars, released from the stoplight, reached the corner. I bounced on the balls of my feet, leaning and ducking, trying to track the man's figure as he disappeared down the dark road. The moment the last car passed, we dashed off the curb and to the other side.

He was gone. As Clay raced down the narrow road, I slowed and took a deep breath, getting the scent. Then I followed. When I hit an alley between two tall buildings, the trail ended. I whistled, and veered without waiting to make sure Clay understood. He would.

The alley was clogged with garbage bags, stinking in the summer heat. I skirted around them, and the rows of gray and blue recycling bins, and came out on the east side of Sherbourne. As I paused to find the man's scent under the stench of the busy street and the garbage, Clay tapped my back, grunted "there," pointed across the road and strode past me. At this hour, the four-lane road was quiet, and we crossed easily, earning only one polite warning honk from an oncoming driver.

On the other side was a block-sized park surrounding the square-domed Allan Gardens Conservatory. That's where our target was heading, straight down the rose-lined walkway to the glass building.

Clay glanced at me for instructions. That was how we worked, and it had nothing to do with dominance or power. Put Clay with a werewolf of roughly the same hi-erarchical position, whose judgment he trusted, and he preferred to follow orders . . . which was fine because I preferred to give them.

The choice now was: split up or stay together. Still moving, I scoped out the park and our target's path, and made my decision. I signaled the plan. There was no rea-son why I couldn't talk—we were far enough away that the man wouldn't overhear—but when I switched to hunt mode, my brain switched to nonverbal.

Clay nodded, and we broke into a slow jog. In the dark, our outfits looked sufficiently joggerlike to get away with that. The biggest danger we faced was alerting our target, but if he hadn't looked over his shoulder yet, he probably wasn't going to. He had other things on his mind. As for *what* . . . well, I had my suspicions, but this wasn't the time to consider them.

We ran along the gauntlet of trees, old-fashioned benches and lampposts that lined the main path. As we neared the conservatory, we slowed, and I motioned Clay into the shadows with me. The man had stopped in front of the historic site marker. His lips moved as he read it, brows furrowing in confusion.

I glanced at Clay. He stood motionless, tensed and waiting, blue eyes glittering as he watched his prey. Without looking away from the man, he leaned sideways toward me, his hand brushing my hip, lips curving. Our eyes met. He grinned, and I could read that grin as clearly as if he'd spoken. *Even better than a city run, huh?* I grinned back.

The man finished reading the plaque and walked to the window. As he stared at the huge tropical trees inside, I nodded and Clay slipped away, looping around to the other side. I crept to the stairs. I made it halfway up before the man turned. He saw me. I kept climbing, gaze fixed on a spot to his side, just another nighttime visitor, a pregnant woman, nonthreatening and—

He bolted.

He ran for the north staircase. I raced up mine as Clay flew from the south. A look my way. I waved him back and he nodded, wheeling to head around the building and cut the man off. While I scrambled down the north steps, the man raced between the garden beds and toward the greenhouse. I ran after him. I rounded the corner and nearly bowled over two police officers.

A mental "Oh, shit!" Then I checked my pace to a jog, flashed a tight smile and prayed they wouldn't try to stop me. I made it three strides.

"Miss!"

Play dumb. No, deaf. Just keep—

"Miss!"

A hand touched my arm as one of the officers ran up behind me. Couldn't ignore that.

I forced myself to stop, turn and smile, trying hard not

to bare my teeth. My heart pounded, adrenaline racing, reminding me that my prey was getting away.

"Are you all right?" the first officer, a beefy graying man, asked.

"Sure, I was just—" I stopped before I said "jogging." My outfit might pass from a distance, but not this close. I caught sight of a terrier across the park, and remembered this was an off-leash area.

"Walking my dog," I said. "Chasing him, actually. He took off on me and—"

"It looked like someone was chasing *you*."

"Me?"

"There was a man running behind you. We noticed from the other side of—"

"There you are," said a voice to my right.

Jeremy walked out from the shadows. "I caught the dog. He's back at the car now. Sorry for the inconvenience, officers." A small smile. "It seems he's not ready for off-leash walks quite yet."

"There was a man following your—"

"Wife," Jeremy said, his arm going around my waist. His face gathered with concern. "A man was following her?"

"A blond man."

Jeremy looked at me. "Did you notice . . . ?"

"No, but I was looking for the dog."

Oh, come on! Problem solved, officers. Dog's found, helpless pregnant lady safe with her husband. Now move on.

Clay was out there, chasing someone, thinking I was there to back him up. It took everything I had to keep from blurting "Thanks, officers," and running after him.

Jeremy did the right thing, trying quickly but patiently

to bring the encounter to a close. He confessed to the officer that maybe these nighttime dog walks weren't such a wise idea, but I'd been having trouble sleeping lately, with the baby kicking and all . . .

As he handled it, I struggled to hold myself still. Had Clay caught the man? Was he holding him, waiting for us? Had something gone wrong? Was he hurt, while we were stalled, parked out of sight behind this greenhouse—

"Ready to go, hon?"

I started out of my thoughts. Jeremy smiled down at me.

"Getting tired finally, I see."

He turned back to the officers, thanked them again, then led me away. I counted ten steps, then started to look over my shoulder.

"Not yet," Jeremy whispered.

"But Clay—"

"I know."

"But—"

"I know."

I bit back a growl and counted off ten more steps.

"No," Jeremy said, before I even started to turn.

"But—"

"He lost him."

"How—?"

"Look right. Along the sidewalk."

There was Clay, walking along the north sidewalk on Gerrard, his path set to intersect with ours. Jeremy gestured—the slightest flutter of his right hand—and Clay paused, then turned and walked across the road. We crossed at the lights, and found Clay around the corner, hands jammed in his pockets, eyes seething.

"Lost him," he said.

"I got waylaid by—"

"The cops. I saw."

He pulled his hands from his pockets and stepped toward me, hand brushing mine, reassuring me that he didn't blame me, wasn't angry about that. The reassurance was nice, but I knew what he was upset about. The same thing I was: a failed hunt.

"By the time I got around the building, he was gone," Clay said. "I think he went north, but I couldn't pick up the trail. We should circle back and maybe Elena—"

Jeremy shook his head. "The police saw you following Elena. I don't want either of you back in that park."

"What if we weren't recognizable?" I asked. "If one of us Changed, we could find the trail for sure. And it is a popular park with dogs."

Jeremy wouldn't even dignify that with an answer.

"Okay," I said. "Then we'll wait. Those officers will move on, then I'll go back—"

"No."

"But—"

"One, he'll be long gone. Two, it's not worth our time simply to satisfy our curiosity."

I opened my mouth to argue, but Jeremy had already moved away. I looked at Clay. His jaw worked, and he glanced back toward the park.

"We could find him," I whispered.

"Yeah."

"We *should* find him."

"Yeah."

Jeremy didn't turn, but his voice floated back to us. "Just in case I wasn't clear? That was an order."

We glared at his back, then jogged to catch up.

* * *

Jeremy had picked a hotel from a cluster near the QEW, the highway that would take us back toward Buffalo. The hotel was nothing fancy—this was just a sleep-and-go stopover. Or it was for Jeremy. Having been deprived of our quarry and our city run, neither Clay nor I was in any mood for sleep. A hasty good night at the door to Jeremy, then a fumbled throwing of the deadbolt and we fell on each other, nips masquerading as kisses, clawing as fevered gropes.

"Bed?" Clay gasped as he came up for air.

I looked over at it, looming five feet away. "Too far."

He chuckled and his mouth went back to mine, kissing me deeply enough to stop the air in my lungs. My hands went under his shirt and I stripped it off, with only a split-second break in the kiss. His leg hooked the back of my knees, ready to drop me to the floor, then he checked himself just in time and carefully lowered me.

My shirt and bra went next, yanked off as one. His fingers went to my breast, kneading and pulling, fingers tugging the nipple hard and insistent. An ache rippled through me. As I gasped, something warm and sticky trickled out.

"What the—?" I began.

Clay laughed. "That's new."

He cupped my breast in his palms and squeezed, his fingers digging in, pulling me to him in another kiss. My hands slid down his belly to his fly. I snapped the button open, tugged his jeans down over his hips, then reached inside his boxers.

My fingers wrapped around him, my grip tight. He reared up to give me better access as he growled and nipped my lower lip hard enough to draw blood. A few tight, urgent tugs and he growled again, this time warning me to stop before it was too late.

"So soon?" I said, pulling back and arching an eyebrow.

Another growl, sharper, and his hands dove to my waist, yanking down my elasticized jeans and panties so fast I heard a seam give way. His fingers plunged into me without so much as an exploratory touch and I jumped, then arched back, snarling and pushing into his hand. A few thrusts and I dug my fingers into the carpet, back arching higher.

"Stop," I hissed between clenched teeth.

He arched a brow. "So soon?"

I reared up, growling, and grabbed him around the neck in a bruising kiss, fingers digging into his shoulders so hard I knew he'd bear the marks in the morning. He only laughed and kissed me back.

We rolled to the floor, kissing and nipping and tussling, both instinctively avoiding my stomach. Once I got the upper hand, but quickly relinquished it. I wasn't in the mood for that, not tonight. So when he grabbed my wrists, grip tight as he pulled them up over my head, I made only a token struggle, then arched my hips to meet him, my legs parting, heart racing, straining, ready—

He'd stopped. Crouched there, above me, poised to take the plunge, but not moving, a clear "Oh, shit" on his face. For a second, I thought we'd pushed the foreplay too far. It happens, particularly when we're revving on high before we begin. I was fighting to keep the disappointment from my voice as I opened my mouth for the obligatory "that's okay." Then I looked past my belly and saw that he certainly did not appear to be done. My gaze went back to my stomach and I realized why he'd stopped.

"Oh, shit!" I said, pushing up on my elbows. "I completely forgot."

"And I almost did." He rolled his shoulders, shuddering, as if trying to suppress the wish that he hadn't remembered in time.

Two weeks ago, after a relatively unathletic round of lovemaking, I'd started spotting. Jeremy was pretty sure it had been nothing serious, but it scared the crap out of Clay and me, so we'd made a decision: no intercourse until the baby came.

Sounds easy enough. There were plenty of other things we could do. The problem was that for Clay and me, foreplay was just that—a precursor to the main event. Anything more than a few minutes' worth was teasing, deliciously postponing what we both really wanted. I could say that's the wolf in us, but I suspect it's just our natures.

Still, four months without intercourse shouldn't be so hard. Or so it had seemed, in that still-panicked moment of reflection after the spotting scare. But lying here, beneath him, looking up at him, his blue eyes lust-glazed, lips parted as he panted, sculpted chest and arms shimmering with sweat, the thin line of golden hair stretching between his nipples and his stomach equally sweat sodden, a dark path leading down to—

My gaze dropped.

"Oh, goddamn it!" I snarled, fists pounding the carpet.

Clay caught me up with a growling laugh. "My sentiments exactly, darling."

His lips went to mine, our kiss even rougher now,

edged with frustration. He broke away first, his lips going to my ear.

"Tell me what you want me to do," he whispered. "Anything."

"What I *wished* you could do? Or what you can do, under the circumstance?"

His face moved in front of mine, the tip of his tongue slipping out, his eyes rolling back as my hand wrapped around him.

"What you want me to do," he said, finger sliding into me. "What you wish I could do."

So I told him, in every way and turn of phrase I could think of, half of which would make me blush under any other circumstances. I hadn't even exhausted my repertoire when the words caught in my throat as I threw my head back, growling, thrusting against his hand, and pretending with every bit of creative visualization I could muster that it wasn't his *fingers* inside me.

Clay's mouth went to mine, and I felt the answering snarl of release vibrate up through his chest into his throat. A moment later, he shuddered, and started to lie down atop me, remembered it wasn't possible these days, and lowered himself to my side.

He bit back a yawn. "After the baby comes, you'll get that."

"Repeatedly, I hope."

He grinned. "As 'repeatedly' as I can manage, which, after four months, I figure I should be able to manage pretty often." He paused. "Well, with short breaks."

"Which we'll probably need . . . for feeding and diaper changing."

"Hmm, hadn't thought of that. Not going to be pulling those half-day sessions for a while, are we?"

I sputtered a laugh. "Half-day? More like half-hour."

He growled and pulled me onto him. "You've gotten half-day . . . with short breaks." He looked at me. "Lots of short breaks."

"Don't ever hear me complaining, do you? Slow is good for teasing, but for satisfaction?" I grinned down at him. "Give me fast and hard any day. Pretty soon, speed will be a good thing, or this baby's going to be hampering our sex life for more than these few months."

"Can't have that."

I curled up beside him. "Definitely not."

"Kidding ourselves, aren't we?"

I chuckled against his chest. "Oh, yeah."

Homeward

BY THE TIME WE WOKE UP THE NEXT MORNING, JEREMY had already scoured the papers for any mention of last night's events. He'd found nothing. On the radio, a local station reported that hydro crews were still working to recover power lost last night in a Cabbagetown neighborhood, but before the newscast even ended, they announced that the problem had been fixed. That was it—one blown transformer, already repaired. Not a single mention of a whiskered man in a bowler hat.

"So we're leaving?" I said as Jeremy folded a shirt and put it into his bag. "We may have unleashed Jack the Ripper, and we're just going home?"

He didn't answer, so I moved to the foot of the bed where I could see his face. "You do think that's what we did, don't you? Unleashed Jack the Ripper?"

"Because we dropped a dead mosquito onto a letter possibly written by the man over a hundred years ago?"

I thumped onto the bed. "My hormones are acting up again, aren't they?"

I could imagine what Clay would have said about my

wild logical leap, but luckily he was still in our room, showering and shaving.

Jeremy only gave me his crooked smile as he took his pants from the chair, then said, "Considering some of the things we've seen, it's not as crazy as it sounds. Something did happen last night, something . . . unusual."

I remembered his reaction, the odd look on his face when he'd seen the smoke, how he'd glanced up at the transformer and pushed Clay and me out of the way before it blew. I longed to ask him about it, but as with everything else in Jeremy's life, if he didn't volunteer, I rarely dared to ask.

"That guy didn't come from a community theater production," I said.

"I know."

"So what do you think happened?"

"I don't know."

He moved to the bathroom to clear his toiletries.

"You want me to shut up and go away?" I said.

"Of course not."

"Then you just want me to stop talking about it."

"No."

I gave a low growl of frustration.

"Can I see the letter?"

"It's packed."

He said this without hesitation, inflection, facial expression or anything else to suggest he didn't want me seeing that letter. But when you live with someone for as long as I've lived with Jeremy, you just know.

I moved to the bathroom door. "What's wrong with the letter?"

"Nothing. I just need to repair the damage before we

hand it over. And I'm not eager to hand it over until I've done what I should have done before—researched it."

"We did research it. I pulled up everything I could find on the history of—" I looked at him. "You mean supernatural history, don't you? Whether the letter has any kind of supernatural background. It *was* owned by a sorcerer. Maybe there's an invisible spell written on it. Or the paper could be magical. Maybe it's—"

"Made from the skin of a thousand killers?" drawled a voice behind me. "Pasted together with the tears of their victims? Dried in the fires of hell? It *does* say it's 'from hell.' Could be a clue."

I glared, and Clay grinned, grabbed me, pulled me against him and kissed the side of my neck.

"I was just—" I began.

"Theorizing. And I was helping."

"All 'theorizing' aside," Jeremy said. "While I'm not convinced that whatever happened last night has anything to do with that letter—"

"Sacrifice!" Clay plunked me onto the bathroom counter. "We sacrificed a mosquito. I bet that's what did it. It was probably a virgin too."

"I've contacted Robert Vasic to investigate," Jeremy continued.

"The mosquito?" Clay said. "It's kind of squashed, but sure."

Jeremy crossed his arms and waited.

Clay sighed, then picked up the toiletry bag. "I'll toss this in the car."

As Jeremy watched Clay go, his expression softened. I knew what he was thinking—the same thing I was—that it was good to see Clay happy. There had been months, even years after Clay had bitten me when neither of us had seen that side of him. But now he had everything that was important to him—his home, his Pack, his Alpha and his mate. And, soon, a child. Every reason to be happy. For now . . .

I put my hands against my belly and willed myself to feel a kick, a jab, some sign of life . . .

Nothing.

"You can listen with the stethoscope when we get home," Jeremy said softly. "The heartbeat is somewhat erratic, but the books say that's not unusual—"

"You called Robert already? What did he say?"

A soft sigh at the change of subject. Jeremy took his used towels from the rack and tossed them into the tub before answering. "He wasn't home, but Talia said she'd have him call later this afternoon."

We had a late breakfast before leaving. There was a restaurant in our hotel, but it didn't open until noon, so we popped over to a place a few doors down and ate there.

We were walking back—driving the short distance had been more trouble than it was worth—when I caught a whiff of something that stopped me midstride. Jeremy and Clay took another few steps before realizing I was no longer between them. Jeremy stayed where he was, as Clay circled back.

"What's up?"

I tilted my head and inhaled, then rubbed my nose and made a face. "I hate that. You catch the faintest smell, your brain says 'hey, that's someone I know,' then it's gone."

Clay looked around. We were in the middle of a strip of grass between the road and the hotel parking lot. Cars zoomed past, but there was no one around. A busy road and no sidewalks didn't invite pedestrian traffic.

"Maybe someone you knew drove by with the window down." He glanced at the strip mall to our right. "Or stopped here."

I nodded. "Probably, whatever—whoever—it was, it's gone now."

We caught up with Jeremy and headed for the SUV.

I flipped between Toronto radio stations all the way to Buffalo, listening to the private stations for news at the top and bottom of the hour, then tuning to CBC as the other stations switched to music. By the time we moved out of Buffalo and the Canadian stations faded to static, I was convinced that Jeremy was right. Whatever had happened last night, it was safe enough to leave.

We pulled off at the Darien Lake exit to fuel up with gas and food. We would stop for lunch in a favorite restaurant outside Rochester, but it had been two hours since breakfast, and our stomachs were complaining. Well, Clay's and mine were complaining; one could never tell with Jeremy.

Jeremy shooed us off to the store, getting me away from the fuel fumes. Inside, I scooped up a doughnut and chocolate milk. Convenience food—they didn't offer much else.

The store was busy, there were only two cashiers, and one was fiddling with her register, so the lineup stretched back to the refrigerators. People kept brushing past me to get to the pop fridge. I've never been one to enjoy personal space invasions but, lately, close contact with strangers set my fight-or-flight instincts on high alert.

Stuck there in line, in an enclosed place, with too many people, my gaze kept drifting to the exit, to freedom and fresh air. Especially fresh air. The mix of BO and cheap cologne and fried food from the restaurant made my stomach churn . . . and made me wonder whether I'd be able to eat my snacks at all.

A passing trucker jostled my shoulder so hard I wobbled back into the shelf. He reached to catch me, blasting coffee breath and halitosis in my face. Another hand caught me from behind. Clay glared at the trucker, who mumbled something vaguely apologetic and shambled past.

Clay took my milk carton and doughnut, and piled them onto his and Jeremy's snacks.

"Hey," grumbled a man behind us. "There's a line here, you know. You can't just—"

Clay turned and looked at him, and the man's mouth snapped shut. I leaned out to see why the line wasn't moving.

"You okay?" Clay whispered.

I swept a glance around. "Just . . . claustrophobic."

He nodded, but didn't comment. He didn't need to. Clay hated crowds, always had, and I'd always faulted him for it, chalking it up to his dislike of humans. But now, looking into his eyes and seeing my own response reflected back—discomfort not distaste—I knew I'd never again snipe at him about avoiding a crowded mall or packed movie theater.

He shifted over, his hip brushing mine. "Go on outside. Get some air."

"I'm—"

He bumped me with his hip, causing his stack of junk

food to sway. "Go. Stretch your legs. There's a field out back, isn't there? Behind the building?"

"I think so."

"Find a picnic spot then. Grab Jeremy and I'll meet you there."

"Thanks."

Jeremy was just outside the doors, eying one of those new SUV hybrids.

"Looking for a trade-up on the Explorer?" I asked.

"I was thinking of you."

"I have a car."

"Which is half dead, has no air bags, no child restraints, and is definitely not baby-friendly." He waved at the SUV wannabe. "This is cute."

"Cute? It looks like a minihearse. Yes, I know I'll need something new. But not that. And if you mention minivan—"

"I wouldn't dare."

I told him Clay's picnic plan.

"That's fine," Jeremy said. "I need to use the restroom. You can wait for me or, if Clay comes out first, I'll meet you both out back."

He started to walk past me, then stopped to watch a vehicle pull in a few spots down. A Mercedes SUV.

"Perhaps something like that," he said. "It's a luxury vehicle, sure to have all the top safety features, plus be quite reliable in bad weather, but not as big and unwieldy as the Explorer. I'm sure you'd find it quite peppy."

"Peppy? That's almost as bad as 'cute.'"

"It would be the perfect vehicle for a—"

"Suburban soccer mom."

A slight furrow of the brows.

"Never mind. Just . . ." I waved at the car. "Not me. Not now. Not ever. I'll find something. But not—" I looked at the Mercedes and shivered. "That."

He shook his head and walked toward the building.

I followed the walkway along the north side of the service center. Behind the building, the path cut on a diagonal to the southwest truckers' lot.

The whir of the huge air-conditioning unit and the distant rumble of idling trucks blocked out the roar of the highway to the north. To my right was a white storage silo. Beyond that was a swamp.

I thought the swamp was what I'd smelled when I first picked up the scent of something heavy and overripe. But the smell came on the south wind, blowing toward the swamp, not from it. The scent carried other notes too, all human—the smell of an unwashed body and unwashed clothes, male, seemingly healthy, but underlain with that faint scent of overripeness. Of . . . rot.

It was the same scent I'd smelled on the man in the bowler yesterday. Not sickness but rot, so faint I had to get a noseful before I was sure. I realized it was the same thing I'd smelled walking back from the restaurant after breakfast.

I dismissed it. No one—and nothing—could track us like that. We were 185 miles from Cabbagetown. Even I would've lost the trail the moment we'd driven away last night. If this guy came from where I thought he did—nineteenth-century London—well, let's just say he couldn't hop into a car and give chase.

So it was impossible. Even when I glimpsed a figure

darting between the rigs in the southwest lot, and caught another whiff of that distinctive scent, I knew it couldn't—shouldn't—be him. But follow logic too far and it can lead right into the jaws of folly.

Jeremy had asked me to wait for him or Clay, and I hadn't meant to ignore him. But after fifteen years of being able to walk through deserted parking lots without a spark of fear, I was ill-accustomed to needing an escort.

Someone was following me, possibly hoping to cut me off when I was far enough from the service center, and from my male companions. At the very least, I should stop and wait for Jeremy and Clay.

Yet, the moment they showed up, my pursuer would run. So I kept going slowly and concentrated on picking up some sense of Clay. No luck. I stopped to tie my shoes and scope out the playing field.

Swamp to the right. A good place to throw my pursuer off-kilter, but the stink and the water would make tracking difficult. The field in front of me was too open. Behind it was a forest, which screamed "pick me, pick me." My ideal environment. But it was too far away, and I risked losing him on the trek across the open field. The parking lot had lots of places to hide, and that's where he was now. But the noise, the stink of diesel fuel and the possibility of bystanders would complicate matters. The best choice was also the closest—that thirty-foot-wide storage silo to my right.

Rotten

I WALKED SLOWLY PAST THE SILO, STILL STRAINING FOR A sense of Clay. When I reached the other side I felt that little twinge of relief and anticipation that told me he was nearby. As for where exactly he was, I had no idea. But he'd be looking for me.

With a half-dozen strides, I was close enough to touch the silo, and I started circling toward the back. Quick steps pattered over the pavement—someone running across the parking lot, footfalls too heavy to be Clay or Jeremy, the slightly awkward clomp of one unaccustomed to silent hunting.

I caught a whiff on the breeze, heavy with rot. On that same breeze came a more familiar—and certainly more pleasant—smell. Clay was getting closer. I smiled and picked up my pace to lure my pursuer farther behind the silo.

The clomping footsteps sped up, closing the gap. Closing in fast. Waiting for Clay wasn't going to be an option.

I spun around and found myself a hairsbreadth from being skewered by a butcher's knife. It was probably more like two feet away, but any time a knife that big is pointed at you it seems a whole lot closer.

I roundhouse kicked . . . and flew off my feet as my new center of gravity took over. My foot barely brushed my attacker. The ground sailed up to meet my stomach. My hands shot out to break my fall, but I managed to twist around and find my balance.

As I veered up, the man rushed me. I kicked again, this time low, snagging his calf and yanking. As he fell, the blade veered my way, but I skated out of the way—not nimbly or gracefully but unscathed. I pounced onto his back and he crumpled, arms flying out, knife pinging off the side of the silo and tumbling to the grass.

A shadow crossed over my head, but I stayed where I was, on all fours on the man's back.

"You want me to take that for you, darling?"

"Please."

Clay put his foot onto the man's neck and pressed down until he let out a strangled grunt. I recovered the knife—the sort that graces gourmet home kitchens everywhere, and rarely carve anything more than take-out rotisserie chicken.

"Impressive." I gave it a trial swing and made a face. "Unwieldy, though."

I knelt beside the man. It was definitely him—though he'd gotten rid of the bowler hat. He'd shaved his whiskers and changed into modern dress—ill-fitting slacks and a golf shirt that looked expensive enough to have come from the same house as the knife.

He tried to stay facedown, but Clay booted the other side of the man's head and kicked his face toward me. Then he pressed harder on the man's neck so he couldn't turn away again.

Sweat beaded on the man's forehead, but he only curled his lip. I adjusted my grip, lifted the knife, then plunged it down a handbreadth from the man's face. After a second, he opened his eyes. He stared at the knife, buried to the hilt in the ground.

"Who are you?" I asked.

He didn't answer.

"Where'd you come from?"

His lips pulled back, showing blackened teeth and the missing incisor I'd noticed the night before. "From hell."

"Good," Clay said. "Then we'll know where to send you."

Jeremy rounded the silo, walking fast, then saw us and slowed.

We spent the next few minutes interrogating the man. Who was he? Where did he come from? How did he find us? Why did he come after us? He wasn't talking. A more thorough "interrogation" was out of the question here, in midday. Finally, Jeremy eased back onto his haunches.

"Let's see if we can get him someplace better." He looked around, then nodded at the swamp. "Down there."

As Clay yanked the man to his feet, I stood, brushed myself off and turned to walk around the silo. A shadow leapt behind me, splayed on the sunlit side of the tank. I wheeled to see the man in Clay's grip, caught in midlunge, his gaze on Jeremy. I leapt forward to knock Jeremy out of the way, but Clay already had his forearm around the man's neck.

"Try that again," Clay hissed against his ear, "and I—"

The man wrenched forward, as if still trying to attack Jeremy, but so far away that Jeremy didn't even move. Clay jerked the man back, more warning than genuine effort. A sensible man would have felt that iron grip, seen how far he was from his target and noticed he'd lost his chance at a surprise attack. But he kept struggling, kicking and swinging. When his fist swung a little too close to me, Clay jerked him back, hard. A dull snap, like the crunch of celery. The man went limp in Clay's grip.

"Goddamn it!" Clay muttered, teeth clenched to keep his voice down. "I'm sorry, Jer. I didn't mean—"

Jeremy waved off the apology and took the knife as Clay lowered the body to the ground.

"Standard self-defense advice," I said. "Never let yourself be taken to the second location. He knew we weren't taking him there for a pleasant chat."

Jeremy nodded, then knelt and put his fingers to his neck.

"Dead?" I said.

"Presuming he had a pulse before." As he backed up onto his haunches, his nose wrinkled.

"Smells pretty ripe, huh? Maybe it's just me, but I swear it's getting stronger."

"It's certainly not getting better." Jeremy looked around. "We'll need to dispose of the body . . ."

"Swamp's best," Clay said. "Unless you want him to take a little trip in the back of a transport."

The man moved. I jumped forward instinctively, getting between Jeremy and danger. Clay stomped on the man's neck. His foot passed clean through to the ground.

"What the—?"

The body jerked again and this time, we saw that the movement was the man's body collapsing into itself like a rotting melon. There was a whispering crackle as the body stiffened and went hard. Then it just . . . disintegrated.

"Huh, guess that solves the disposal problem." Clay watched the sprinkling of dust settle into the grass. "Wish all my corpses would do that."

"Now is anyone still going to tell me he was just a normal guy?" I said.

"Doesn't matter." Clay waved at the grass. "Threat eliminated . . . or disintegrated."

"That's it? We just blow away the dust and go home?"

"Far as I'm concerned."

I looked at Jeremy. He finished wiping off the knife, then whipped it. The knife flew about a hundred feet before landing in the swamp with a splash. Perfect aim, as always.

"Elena? I'd like you to follow his trail. Perhaps we can figure out how he got here . . . and make sure he came alone."

That was easy. Not only did the taint of rot give it away, but his path went straight around the south side of the service center and into the front lot. He'd known exactly where I was.

The trail led to the nearly empty northeast corner. Only one car was there—a burgundy midsize with Ontario plates. As we drew closer, I could see red streaks on the driver-side window.

"Don't slow down," Jeremy murmured as the three of us continued our "stroll." "When we walk alongside it, glance inside, but we'll keep heading for the road."

We knew what we'd see when we passed the car, and we weren't wrong. A man's body lay stretched over the front seats, pushed down out of sight, his wide eyes staring at the roof, throat gaping open.

"Keep going," Jeremy murmured.

We walked to the road, then headed along the front of the service center.

"Chauffeured at knifepoint," I said.

"So it would appear," Jeremy said. "I was keeping a watch behind us, but I don't recall seeing that vehicle— or seeing it for long enough to appear suspicious."

"Meaning he followed at a distance."

"Doesn't matter," Clay said. "He's gone. Ashes to ashes, dust to dust, time to go home."

I turned back to Jeremy. "It must be the letter, right? We did something with that letter last night, and opened a time hole into the nineteenth century—"

Clay snorted.

I turned on him. "Oh, sorry, is my explanation a little too far-fetched for *you*? The guy who turns into a wolf a couple times a week?"

"I'm just saying—"

"That there's a logical explanation. Sure. How's this? He's a mugger with retro fashion sense, and he was hiding under a sewer grate in Cabbagetown, waiting for a mark to wander past. That transformer fell, scared the shit out of him and he jumped from his hole and ran for his life. Then he saw us chasing him, realized we could identify him—by his serious BO if nothing else. He decided he had to take us out before we reported him to the police for sewage-hole trespassing with intent to commit robbery."

"Yeah? Well, it's no less likely than 'he jumped through a time hole,' is it?"

Jeremy motioned for us to resume walking. "I'll have to agree with Elena. A supernatural explanation is most probable, something connected to the letter. Presumably, he came through that time hole or portal or whatever it might be, and wanted the letter back."

"And was somehow able to track it after he got away last night," I said.

"None of which matters," Clay said. "Because only one guy came through that portal, and now he's dust."

"True," Jeremy said. "With any luck, that's the end of it. But we'll need to make sure."

Clay opened his mouth to protest, but Jeremy continued. "It will be a quick trip. We go back, we scout the area, make sure nothing else has happened and there are no traces of anyone else passing through. If all goes well, which I expect it will, we'll be sleeping in our own beds tonight."

Soundbite

WE MADE IT BACK TO TORONTO BY EARLY AFTERNOON AND headed for Cabbagetown.

When I walked toward the crime scene, it was Jeremy at my side. Clay would keep watch.

At the end of the street there were no obvious signs of trouble—no police cars, no ambulances, no fire trucks. Yet something was wrong. Residents were out in their yards and on the sidewalks, talking in pairs and trios. Gazes skittered up and down the road, and the clusters disintegrated at the first sign of an unfamiliar face, people making beelines for their front doors, as if suddenly remembering they'd left the kettle on.

The cause of their unease? Probably something to do with the small swarm of journalists buzzing along the street. Across the road, a camera operator was getting setting shots, filming the other side of the street, the peaceful side, preparing for the "Today, in this quiet Toronto neighborhood . . ." intro. As for "what" had happened in this particular quiet Toronto neighborhood, I wasn't so sure I wanted to find out.

I steered Jeremy toward a scattering of print reporters,

all scouting for contacts and sound bites. We stopped on the sidewalk.

"It looks like something happened," I said in a stage whisper. "Do you think it has anything to do with our power going out last night?"

It took less than five seconds for a reporter to bite.

"Excuse me. You folks live around here?"

We turned to see a potbellied man in serious need of a hairbrush, razor, clothes iron and eye drops. I'm sure he cultivated that look—the rumpled newshound, always on the hunt, low on sleep, coasting on caffeine—but it was about fifty years out of date. Almost certainly not a representative of Toronto's journalistic constellations, the *Star*, the *Globe* or even the *Sun*.

"We're a few blocks over," I said with a vague wave.

"Did you know Mrs. Ashworth?" he asked, pen poised above his paper. "She lived right down there, in the green house. Old—older woman. Lived by herself."

"I believe we met her at the barbecue last month," Jeremy said. "You talked to her for a while, hon, remember? About her roses?" He frowned at the reporter. "She isn't hurt, is she?"

"No one knows. Disappeared this morning. And I do mean disappeared. Neighbor claims he saw her crossing the road and then . . . poof."

"Poof?" Jeremy's frown deepened.

"Gone. Just like that."

We stared at him. He leaned back on his heels, relishing the moment.

"She probably wandered off," I said, then lowered my voice. "We have a lot of . . . older residents here."

The reporter scowled, as if he'd already come to this

conclusion, but would really rather be writing the "poof" story than another sad tale of Alzheimer's.

"Still," I said. "It is strange, coming right after those fireworks with the transformer last night." I glanced at the reporter and tried to look nervous. "There's no connection, is there?"

A smug smile. "You never know."

Jeremy rolled his eyes. "No, hon, there's no connection. A blown transformer and a missing elderly woman, just two random events, not uncommon—"

"Plus, the woman in petticoats," the reporter said. "You did hear about that, didn't you?"

"Petticoats?" I said slowly.

"The cops got two calls last night, right after that transformer blew, people seeing a woman in petticoats running down the middle of the road. This very road."

"Probably a lady in her nightgown, running out to see what the fireworks were," Jeremy said. "I hear it was quite a show."

The reporter muttered something about a deadline, and stomped off to find a more receptive audience.

We'd returned to Toronto to reassure ourselves of two things: that the bowler-hatted man had been the only "portal escapee," and that nothing else had happened as a result of last night's events. The possible disappearance of the elderly woman thwarted our hopes of a hasty resolution on the second count. And now a sighting of a woman in petticoats suggested we weren't going to have any more luck with the first. Something told me we wouldn't be sleeping in our own beds tonight.

Jeremy and I spent the next hour discreetly scouting

the area for a second trail with that distinctive rotting
smell. Bad enough I couldn't change to wolf form, but
having the area under media and police scrutiny made
the search twice as hard or, more aptly, twice as large. Instead of scouring the road where the bowler-hatted man
had appeared, I had to search all the perimeter streets,
while trying to look like a restless pregnant woman and
her doting husband out for a prolonged neighborhood
stroll.

We'd made it almost all the way around when I found a
second trail. A woman's scent, mingled with rot.

I bent and retied my shoes—a simple act that was getting increasingly difficult.

"Definitely a woman," I said as I took a deep breath.

"We'll pick up the trail after dark and find her, see what
she can tell us."

In the supernatural world, it's sometimes tricky to know
who to call when things go awry. Take a portal. It could
be magical, in which case we'd want to contact a witch or
a sorcerer. Or it could be connected to the nether realms,
and then it would fall under the jurisdiction of a necromancer. The last time we'd been peripherally involved in
a case with a portal connection, Paige and Lucas had
been in charge, and they'd turned to a necromancer. So
we did the same, and called Jaime Vegas.

We phoned from the hands-free setup in the Explorer so
Jeremy and I could both hear Jaime. Clay waited outside,
standing watch.

"Hey," she said when she answered. "Let me guess.

You've got that other matter settled, and you're ready to work on my film." Last time we'd spoken, she'd been returning my message, ready to meet to discuss her documentary, only to hear that I'd made other plans in the meantime.

"Mmm, not quite yet. Seems we ran into complications. Something you might be able to help with."

When I described what had happened last night, she barely let me finish.

"Dimensional portal," she said.

"That common, huh?"

A small laugh. "No, definitely not, thank God. But given the choice between that or a time tear, odds are way better on the dimensional. Time travel makes great fiction, but in real life, that's where it stays."

"Pure fiction."

The connection crackled, as if she was getting comfortable. "I wouldn't go that far. Never say never in this world. My Nan used to tell me stories about time tears, but even she said they were just that: stories. Anyway, you have the classic signs of a dimensional portal. I wouldn't go looking for horse-drawn carriages to start galloping through downtown Toronto anytime soon."

"And what are the classic signs?" Jeremy asked.

Silence.

"Jaime?" he said.

"Uh, Jeremy. Hi. I . . . didn't know you were right there. You're so . . ."

"Quiet?"

She gave a nervous laugh. "Umm, right. So, what did you ask? Oh, the classic signs. Well, zombies would be the big one."

"Zombies?"

"That guy you dusted." She laughed, more relaxed now. "I've always wanted to say that. You see it happen in movies all the time, but real life? Vamps don't explode in a shower of dust."

"But zombies do?"

"Er, no. Well, not usually. But any zombie I've ever met was raised by a necro. When a spirit materializes through a portal, you've got something a bit different. Probably shouldn't even call them zombies but . . . well, we have enough beasties out there without inventing new names. When a formerly-human entity manifests in the living world, we call it a zombie. You get that rotting meat stink, which is a dead giveaway . . . pardon the pun."

"But this thing didn't act like a zombie," I said.

"Because it didn't shamble around, moaning and trying to eat your brain?"

"Let me guess: more movie fiction?"

"Yep. Not that you guys would know that. Zombies are the dirty little secret of the supernatural world. We know they exist, but we try not to think about them. Most necros go their whole lives without ever raising one. They're just . . . nasty. And I don't just mean the smell. A zombie is a ghost returned to a corpse. Not nice for anyone, especially the spook. Last one I saw was a dog raised by a kid necro. Like in *Pet Sematary* . . . only the dog had been hit by a car, and the kid thought the raising would fix him, and of course it didn't, so his uncle calls me in and . . ." She paused. "And that story, while instructive to any teen necromancer, isn't going to help you. Where was I?"

"Zombies. Which don't normally disintegrate into dust."

"Right. If yours turned to dust, dimensional zombies must be different. I'll have to look that one up."

"You said this was a dimensional portal," Jeremy said. "And that we're dealing with corporeal ghosts. So is this another door into the afterlife?"

"Probably not. You're dealing with things that just don't happen often enough to be properly documented. It sounds like you have a spell-triggered dimensional portal. Spellcasters probably have a fancier term, but that's the gist of it. A spellcaster, usually a sorcerer, creates a . . . balloon or a pocket, something that exists between dimensions where he can shove inconvenient things— usually people—for safekeeping. They stay there, frozen in time, until someone releases them. You'll have to check with Lucas, but I'm pretty sure the spellcaster creates a 'trigger'—some item that will let him open and close the portal."

"The letter," Jeremy said.

"Probably."

"So how did we activate it?" I asked.

"A trigger is like a combination lock, and only the sorcerer knows the code. It's usually some special sequence or event that will set off the portal, but there can be alternate ways of triggering it. Backups, in case the first one fails."

"Would blood do it?" Jeremy asked.

"Blood?" I glanced at him. "How—?"

I stopped as I remembered the mosquito, and the dark blotch on the letter. That's why he hadn't wanted me seeing it in the hotel room. Because, in the light, I'd have realized that the dark patch wasn't only mosquito guts.

"The mosquito," I murmured. "It had my blood in it."

"That's a new one," Jaime said. "But sure. That could

have been the backup trigger. It's not something that's likely to happen accidentally in storage. If the primary failed, the sorcerer could break in and activate the backup."

"So some sorcerer created the letter, stuffed two people into it, and then, before he could release them, it was stolen."

"If he ever planned to release them. That can be tricky, especially if you wait too long. When you seal up people like that, it's like a mini time capsule. Release them and . . . weird things can happen." She paused. "You haven't had anything weird happen, have you?"

"Besides possibly releasing and killing a zombie Jack the Ripper?"

"What else could happen?" Jeremy said.

"Hard to say. Creating portals isn't something you find in every spellbook, and not many sorcerers could make one if they had the recipe right in front of them. Oh, for example, there's a documented case of a sorcerer in the Wild West who caught some outlaw, tossed him into a portal and hauled his ass back to the East for trial. Caused a minor smallpox epidemic."

"Because the outlaw had smallpox," I said. "And he was brought into an area that didn't."

"Nope. The outlaw was smallpox free . . . but when he was tossed into the portal, it was in a region known for periodic outbreaks. It's like he took some of his environment with him."

That was all Jaime knew, but she promised to canvas her contacts.

When we'd signed off, I started lifting a hand to wave Clay back to the car, but Jeremy laid his fingers on my arm.

"When you tell him what Jaime said, leave out the part about the smallpox," he said.

"You think that's a concern? I've been immunized, and it sounds like something specific to the period, not to portals in general."

"I agree. However . . ."

His gaze slid to Clay, who was leaning against a tree, a pedestrian taking a shade break from the late-day heat, but his eyes were continually scanning the street, body tense, as if a horde of zombies might descend at any moment.

"No sense giving him one more thing to worry about," I said.

"Exactly."

When I went to put my cell phone away, I noticed I had a message. It was Robert, returning our earlier call. Robert Vasic was a former council delegate who now served as the go-to guy for esoteric research. Jeremy called him back, told him what had happened and he promised to start hunting through his library.

"We can't track this woman until after dark," I said when we were all back in the SUV. "The best source of information on the letter itself would be the original source . . . or as close to it as we can get. Patrick Shanahan's grandfather commissioned the theft of that letter, and I'm sure Shanahan knows why. We should pay him a visit." I glanced at Clay. "A friendly visit."

"Sure," Clay said. "We'll show up on his doorstep and

say, 'Excuse me, we're the ones who stole your letter last night, and it's giving us some trouble. Can we ask you a few questions about it?' "

"Let me think about it," Jeremy murmured. "Just start driving over there."

Routine

LESS THAN AN HOUR LATER, WE WERE BACK WHERE IT ALL started, at Patrick Shanahan's house. His street looked different in daylight. You could see the houses through the trees, and they looked dead. Empty driveways, drawn blinds, blackened windows, a lawn-care crew the only sign of life. If you lived in an upscale neighborhood like this, you worked—both spouses, all day, every day.

A "wrong number" call to Shanahan's house on the way had confirmed that the sorcerer was home, either working from there or taking the day off to inventory his collection, making sure nothing besides the letter had been stolen.

At just past 4 P.M., Jeremy and Clay were striding up Shanahan's driveway. I got to eavesdrop at a window. As Clay said, I did have another option. I could wait in the car and let them fill me in later. So, eavesdropping it was.

As I waited around the corner, I heard Jeremy ring the bell. A moment later, the door opened.

"Are you Patrick Shanahan?" Jeremy asked.

"Yes . . ."

"Owner of a historical document once residing in the London Metropolitan Police files?"

"Do you have it?"

"You don't?" Jeremy glanced over his shoulder at Clay and they exchanged a tight-lipped look, then Jeremy turned back to Shanahan. "Mr. Shanahan, are you aware of certain occurrences in Toronto in the last twenty-four hours? Occurrences our employer believes are related to the document *previously* in your possession?"

In the silence that followed, I knew Shanahan was taking a second, longer look at the two men on his doorsteps, seeing them not as associates of whomever stole his letter, hoping to "sell" it back, but as supernatural agents, most likely dispatched from a sorcerer Cabal. While one could argue that the Cabals needed policing more than anyone *outside* their infrastructure, they often played the role of law enforcement in the supernatural world, if only to protect their own interests.

Shanahan let them inside.

As they moved through the house, I could catch only Shanahan's boom of a voice as he complained about the heat, the humidity, the smog—the kind of chatter that fills space and says nothing.

He didn't ask how Jeremy knew he'd owned the *From Hell* letter. As Xavier had said, it was common knowledge among a certain subset of supernatural society, and Cabals had plenty of access to that subset. Nor did he ask which Cabal his visitors were with, or even confirm that they were from one. When dealing with Cabals, curiosity could sound dangerously close to challenge.

They stopped in the living room. As they sat, I moved around to that window. It was closed, of course, as they all were to keep the air-conditioning inside, but with werewolf hearing I could make out enough to follow the conversation.

Jeremy explained the events taking place in downtown Toronto. Shanahan expressed surprise, which seemed genuine enough—blown transformers and missing senior citizens weren't the sort of news tidbits a man like Shanahan would follow, not while the stock exchange was still open.

"I'm not sure I understand what that has to do with my letter."

"It was the combination with a third event that caught my employer's interest. There were reports of a man and a woman, both dressed in Victorian garb, seen in the area of the power outage and the disappearance. Our experts detected signs of a dimensional disturbance—a recently opened portal."

"P-portal?" A too-hearty laugh. "I'd never own a letter that contained a portal. Dangerous things, you know. Very dangerous. And damned near impossible to make. Way outside my very limited magical abilities." A self-deprecating chuckle. "I can pick a stock a lot better than I can cast a spell, let me tell you. Ask anyone."

"Presumably the portal was already within the letter before it came into your possession. Otherwise, it wouldn't contain people from the nineteenth century."

"Oh, er, of course." Shanahan paused. "Listen, I'm a man of great practicality—particularly when it comes to money. If I'd inherited a letter containing an active portal, I would have put it on the market immediately. I know how much a Cabal would pay for such a thing. If that letter held a portal, which—no offense to your employers, but I doubt—I knew nothing about it."

I could smell the bullshit in every word, yet Jeremy

was stuck. As much as Shanahan claimed to be a weak spellcaster, our experience with sorcerers had left us wary enough to know they could be formidable opponents. And Shanahan, already nervous, would be expecting attack.

Jeremy let Shanahan think he believed him, and promised that, if the letter was recovered, his employers would indeed want it and would pay a fair price to Shanahan, the rightful owner. As he and Clay left, Shanahan was handing out business cards, scribbling his home number on the back, and asking to be kept in the loop.

I met them by the road.

"He's lying," Clay said.

"I know," Jeremy replied, and kept walking.

Clay looked from me to the house, and I knew it killed him to leave it at that.

"We're going back, aren't we?" I asked. "When we can catch him off guard."

Jeremy nodded. "Tonight."

Robert had left a message. He'd found a mention of one case similar to ours, where a sorcerer had sacrificed a man in a portal creation spell. The soul of the sacrifice had been bound to the imbued object—in this case, a scroll—and when the portal was activated, the dead man had come through as a zombie.

That explained why we had rotting zombies. They weren't people who'd been stashed in the portal for safekeeping—as Jaime postulated—but those who'd been sacrificed to create it. As for the other case, according to the brief mention Robert had found, the zombie had been laid to rest and the portal closed. It just didn't say how the latter had been accomplished.

He'd e-mailed me some other stories. Since we still had a bit of time to kill before dinner, I found a cybercafe and read them, with Clay leaning over my shoulder, his chair pulled so close I might as well have sat on his lap.

Most of the "evidence" on portals was anecdotal. That's typical with anything supernatural, like the Pack's Legacy. Even those who seek to compile research, like Robert, are left with what really amounts to stories, and the closest thing to proof is multiple eyewitness accounts. Nice when you can get it, but how often does someone conducting a black magic ritual invite a dozen acquaintances over to watch? Even if he does, how many of them will take him up on the invitation . . . and how many will think "participate in a human sacrifice and risk being sucked into a faulty dimensional portal?" and decide they'd really rather stay home for the evening.

Although portal spells were available to any sorcerer willing to search enough and pay enough, there were few recorded instances of them being used. They were notoriously tough to cast, and the chances of them failing were rivaled only by the chances of them malfunctioning. Like the Austrian sorcerer who decided to use his portal to lie low until his legal troubles passed. A friend was supposed to free him after two years, and I'm sure he would have . . . if the paper that contained the portal trigger hadn't accidentally been sucked into the portal itself, leaving the sorcerer stuck in his dimensional bubble for eternity.

Then there was the genius in medieval Japan who'd tapped into the wrong dimension. His portal belched out a very pissed-off demi-demon, who'd proceeded to flay and disembowel the sorcerer, his family, and half the village before it figured out how to click its ruby slippers and return home. Start circulating a few stories like that, and your average sorcerer will decide dimensional portals aren't something he needs to add to his repertoire.

We headed out for dinner. We tried to find a quiet corner, and seemed to succeed, getting a table with a cushion of empty ones around us but it was not to be. Two tables over, a pair of emergency room nurses were complaining about an influx of stomach flu that had them working late that day and missing the commuter GO train home.

As sympathetic as I am to the plight of overworked hospital staff, I don't think a restaurant is the appropriate forum for airing complaints, especially when those complaints are sprinkled with graphic descriptions of the byproducts of gastronomic upset. When I started showing signs of losing my appetite, Jeremy asked the server to relocate us. We decided on the patio, which was hot enough to bake potatoes on, but quiet enough to discuss our next criminal enterprise.

The upside to our forthcoming home invasion? Having just invaded the same home the night before, we already knew the floor plans, security features and codes. The downside? Having been invaded the night before, Shanahan might have changed those codes.

"Nah," Clay said. "You get robbed, what's your first priority? Assessing damage and figuring out how it hap-

pened. Making sure it doesn't happen again comes later,
after you remember where you filed the instruction book
for your security system."

"What if he's a little more organized?" I said. "Or a little
more paranoid?"

Clay shrugged. "We'll deal with it. This is an interrogation. Subterfuge is secondary."

At eleven-thirty at night, Patrick Shanahan's house was
still ablaze with light. He hadn't gone to bed yet. Nor had
he activated the outside lights, which made sneaking up
to the side door very easy.

The side door was locked. Instead of trying Xavier's
key, Jeremy and Clay made the rounds to check the other
doors while I was consigned to the bushes again.

They got lucky with the oft-forgotten sliding patio
door, and slipped inside. I bounced on my tiptoes, straining to hear voices, wondering whether I could interpret
"stay there" as "stay outside," rather than "stay behind
that particular bush." Just as I decided Jeremy's command was indeed open to wider interpretation, the patio
door moved again.

Clay walked onto the deck and motioned me in. I
jumped forward so fast I nearly impaled myself on a marble obelisk. Then I raced to the deck and leapt onto it, ignoring the set of stairs on the far side.

"Don't laugh," I muttered as I swept a sweat-soaked
strand of hair from my face. "I'll make you hide in the
bushes next time and see how fast you come running." I
moved up beside him. "So what's up?"

"Not home."

"Shanahan? But the lights—and the doors—oh, shit."
I met Clay's gaze. "He bolted, didn't he?"

"Looks that way."

There were no signs of foul play, as the cliché goes, nothing to indicate a real Cabal security agent had swooped
down and snatched up Patrick Shanahan. We found
clothing laid on the bed and a couple of drawers open, as
if someone had packed in a hurry. A handwritten note on
the kitchen counter told his housekeeper he'd be gone
for a few days, and asked her to leave the mail in his
home office.

Shanahan must have opted for an impromptu vacation
until the mess was sorted out. Either that or he didn't
want to be in the city while a dimensional portal was active.

Clay and I had experience conducting residential
searches without the owner's knowledge, enough to earn
a rookie's spot on a crime scene team. Trouble was, we
were used to looking for evidence of a crime, usually
homicide. Suspecting a mutt of man-killing wasn't
enough. We needed evidence. Not an unreasonable requirement, considering the death penalty was at stake.

We also had experience searching for clues to help us
find a mutt-on-the-run, but we weren't trying to find
Shanahan. What we wanted from him we hoped to get
right here: clues on how to close the portal.

Jeremy directed us to search books and files, the first
on supernatural artifacts, portals or Jack the Ripper in
general, and the second on Shanahan's collection—as-
suming, as a careful investment banker, he'd keep detailed records.

Jeremy went in search of hidden books or ones hiding in plain view. Most reference texts on the supernatural don't need to be hidden—anyone who stumbled on them would just think you had unusual reading tastes.

The file duties were split between old-fashioned and new—paper files and computer ones. I got the computer. While I knew how to recover files from the recycle bin or the "deleted" folder on my e-mail, when it comes to things like cracking encrypted data or finding files that have been wiped clean, I was lost. I read through Shanahan's e-mail and hard drive files, finding nothing useful. Clay saved me from further digging by announcing that he'd found paper-based files on Shanahan's collection.

"Where?" I asked, swinging around in the computer chair.

"Right here." He pointed at the file cabinet. "Bottom drawer."

"Out in the open? Are they written in code?"

"Don't need to be. He found an easier way. They're all listed as fakes—curiosities, not artifacts." He lifted a folder and flipped it open. "One Baphomet idol, reportedly taken from an unnamed Templar castle in Britain. Later discovered to be a late eighteenth-century forgery." He thumbed through a few pages. "It goes on to describe the significance of Baphomet in the persecution of the Knights Templar." He handed me the file. "The usual stuff. How they were accused of worshipping Baphomet, presumably a Pagan deity of some kind. Problem was that no one's ever *found* a Pagan deity called Baphomet."

"So an idol of it would be significant."

"And valuable, if only from a scholarly point of view."

He frowned and glanced at the doorway. "Where did you say he kept his collection?"

"Uh-uh. No side trips. We have work to do. You can't get into that room in human form, so you'd have a heck of a time getting a good look at it." I paused. "Though I could see a few things from the doorway. Remind me to show you when we're done."

He nodded his thanks.

I waved the file folder. "So they're all written up like that? Purported fakes?"

"All the ones I've skimmed. Good idea. Most of them, like the Baphomet idol, are historically significant and widely believed to either not exist or not to have the supernatural powers attributed to them. They're written up as such—a collection of supernaturally-themed curiosities."

"And the letter?"

He bent to the drawer again. "Still looking. Tried P for portal, L for letter, J for Jack. Nothing yet."

"Here, hand me a bunch."

He did. Jeremy joined us about twenty minutes later and took a share. His book search hadn't revealed anything. Seems Shanahan wasn't much of a reader. The only hidden stash Jeremy found was a half-empty bottle of rye whiskey, presumably belonging to the housekeeper.

An hour later, we'd gone through every page in every file, and found no mention of the *From Hell* letter or anything related to Jack the Ripper.

"He's detailed everything," Jeremy said. "It's unlikely that the letter is the only undocumented artifact."

"Don't forget," I said. "It *was* stolen."

"So was his copy of John Dee's *Necronomicon*," Clay

said. "According to the pages copied into the file, it went missing in 1934, from Oxford. Shanahan just says he inherited it from his grandfather's collection."

"So, chances are, there is a file for the letter. Either he took it or he destroyed it." I looked around the office. "Does anyone see a shred—"

"Here," Clay said, heaving to his feet and walking over to it. He took off the top. "Recently emptied."

"Damn. What about the recycling box? He could have put the pieces in there."

"Or burned them in the fireplace," Jeremy said.

Clay nodded. "Or stuffed them in the garbage."

"Everyone can check out the place they suggested," I said.

"Excellent idea," Jeremy said, and headed off to the fireplace as I grabbed the recycling box.

Clay looked over at me and at Jeremy's quickly retreating back, then stalked out, grumbling.

Marked

IF SHANAHAN HAD SHREDDED THE FILE, HE'D TAKEN THE pieces with him. By the time we'd confirmed that, it was late enough to hunt down the second portal escapee.

When we left Shanahan's house, I checked my voice mail and learned that Robert had called while we'd been inside. We called him back from the hands-free setup in the Explorer.

"I believe I have some good news for you," Robert said.

"You know how to close the portal," I said.

"You were already on the right track and halfway there. To close a dimensional portal involving human sacrifice, all you need to do is return the sacrificed souls to the other side."

"In other words, kill the zombies."

"Precisely. Better yet, you aren't even doing them a disservice. Instead of returning to that dimensional portal, they'll go to their normal afterlife."

"That one we dispatched earlier today might not be so happy about that, considering he seemed pretty handy with that knife of his. He probably didn't much like where he ended up."

A light laugh. "True enough. But I'm sure this other poor woman will go someplace better."

"So that's what happened last time—someone killed the zombie and the portal closed?"

"Well . . . not exactly. In that case, the portal was opened shortly after it was created. That meant that the sorcerer who created it was still alive and had control of the zombie. To kill the zombie, they needed to kill the controller."

"Like with one raised by a necromancer?"

"Somewhat. Both types, if under someone's control, cannot be killed. Had yours been raised by a necromancer, a lethal blow simply wouldn't have been lethal."

"Like in the movies. You keep hacking, they keep walking."

"Precisely. But dimensional zombies with a controller—" He stopped and gave a small laugh. "Sorry. Talia's making faces, telling me that I'm veering far from the topic and probably confusing you. You don't need to know about controlled zombies, because that clearly isn't what you have. To contain zombies from the nineteenth century, your portal had to have been made around the time the letter was written. Only a sorcerer can create a portal, and they have normal life spans, meaning whoever made this one is long dead."

"Hence any connection is already severed," Jeremy said.

Clay nodded. "So all we need to do is kill the second zombie."

"Thereby returning the portal to a balanced state," Robert said. "Opening the portal allowed those souls to cross dimensions. That causes imbalance. Return them to the other side, and anyone who wandered into the portal will be released. Balance is restored. The portal closes."

We were counting on the woman being easy to find and at the end of an unbroken scent trail. Even after twenty-four hours, that wasn't as improbable as it might seem. She was from another century, and unlikely to have hopped on a GO train and headed for the suburbs.

The bowler-hatted man had adjusted to modern transportation quickly enough, but carjacking was probably little different from commandeering a horse or buggy, and I suspected he'd had some experience at that. He'd figured out that cars were the modern equivalent of a coach-and-four, grabbed one and let the driver do the tricky part.

As for how he'd tracked us, we assumed it had something to do with the letter. As for why he'd wanted it— that puzzled even Robert. He could only guess that he'd tracked us like a domestic dog following a rabbit's scent—only because instinct told him to. To avoid the problem this time we'd left the letter in the car, hidden in a place that would require werewolf strength—or a hydraulic jack—to access.

We began the hunt in human form, starting a block from the portal site where I'd picked up the woman's scent earlier that day. I tracked it for five blocks.

When the trail hit an industrial area riddled with abandoned or semiabandoned buildings, it meandered, as if she'd lingered there. Eventually it led into one of these buildings—where she must have rested—then snaked out of the neighborhood and over to a busier street, still rife with industrial buildings and warehouses, but many converted to lofts and nightclubs. It continued down the street of nightclubs, past lines of people waiting to get inside.

"She crossed the road here," I said.

We only got a few steps when I picked up the smell of rot again, stronger and fresher.

"I'm getting it too," Clay said. "She's close."

Halfway across, I stopped as a fresh wave of the scent came over on the breeze. I looked up to see a short, sturdy figure under a dim streetlight. She wore a hooded cloak of some kind, high heels and a short skirt. Her back was to us.

A car honked. Clay grabbed my elbow and hurried me across into the alley. I peered out, then ducked back around the corner.

"So how do we handle this?" I whispered.

"Mercifully," Jeremy said.

"No questioning then?"

"Don't need to," Clay said.

Jeremy hesitated, and I knew he was thinking it would be nice to question her. Personal curiosity, of course, but it could be concealed under the guise of education, wanting to add to the supernatural world's knowledge of portals.

After a moment, he shook his head. "Quickly and mercifully is best. Clay? Go out and ask her into the alley."

Clay looked at Jeremy as if he'd just been told to dance the rumba on a public thoroughfare.

I bit back a laugh. "Just walk over to her and point at the alley. Maybe say . . . I don't know . . . something like 'fifty bucks.' " I looked at Jeremy. "Does that sound right? Fifty?"

His brows shot up. "Why are you asking me?"

"I wasn't— I just meant, as a general . . ." I threw up my hands. "How am I supposed to know how much a hooker costs?"

"Your guess is as good as mine."

I sighed. "Fine, fifty bucks sounds good. It's not like *she* knows what the going rate is anyway. Just say that and nod at the alley. She'll follow."

Clay continued to stare at us in silent horror.

"Oh, for God's sake, you're ready to break her neck but you can't—"

"I'll do it," Jeremy said, then shot a look my way. "Not that I have any more experience soliciting prostitutes than Clay does."

"Never crossed my mind."

A mock glare, then he headed out.

I'm sure "fifty bucks" and a nod to the alley would have been enough, but Jeremy chatted to her for a couple of minutes first. Then he led her into the alley.

When she saw us blocking the other end, she stopped. Jeremy, at her heels, moved fast, intending to snap her neck before she knew what was happening. Quick and merciful. But we'd tipped her off too quickly and she ran—right for me. I feinted left and pulled back my fist, ready to swing . . . only to see her wide-eyed and cowering.

One look at her expression, and I knew she'd run to me for protection. I reminded myself that killing her was a mercy—it would send her to a decent afterlife. But I couldn't do it.

I looked over at Jeremy and Clay, but they were both caught off guard. So much for quick and merciful.

When no one moved, she bowed her head and started to sob. What I'd originally thought was a cloak was a shawl, pulled up around her face, so she could stay hidden in its shadow. That was probably the only way she could ply her trade in Toronto. From the glance I'd had at her face, she could have passed for sixty—and a hard-drinking, hard-living sixty at that.

"Who are you?" I asked.

Clay shot me a glare. I returned it. As long as we were standing here, working on plan B, I might as well ask some questions. Not like anyone else was doing anything.

She gave a snuffle and wiped her nose on her gloves.

"I—I don't know," she said. "I don't remember. I was . . . someplace awful. For so long." Her shoulders bent with a stifled sob. "Purgatory, it were. That's where 'e sent me. I might not 'ave led a Christian life, but I didn't deserve that."

"It was a mistake that will be corrected," Jeremy said, and looked at us as if to say, "Well, go ahead. Correct it."

Clay stepped forward, but I shook my head. His idea of mercy would be a quick death, but he'd let her see it coming, reasoning it would be over before she had time to think about it. I could do better. I motioned for Jeremy to ask her another question, so I could get behind her without her noticing.

"You said 'he,'" Jeremy began. "You were murdered?"

As he spoke, I slid to the side, but her head whipped around, eyes following me.

"Almost due, ain't you, luv?" she said with a gap-toothed smile. "Such a pretty girl. You'll have a beautiful baby. Handsome and 'ealthy. You want me to tell you wot it'll be?" She stepped toward me, her hands out. "It's an old midwife's trick, but it always works."

"Um, thanks," I said, "but I'd rather be surprised."

"Humor me, child," she said, still coming toward me. "It'll only take a moment. I just lay me 'ands—"

Clay leapt between us. The woman stumbled back. Jeremy jumped to catch her. The shawl fell away. Clay yanked me away so hard I saw only a split-second flash of the woman's face, covered with a red rash and dotted with lesions.

I moved to help her up.

"No," Jeremy said sharply. "Don't touch her."

I frowned at him. "It's not contagious. She must be decaying—"

"No, that's not the problem. And this *is* contagious—maybe not by touch, but we aren't taking the chance."

"All 'ad a good eyeful, 'ave you?" the woman snarled, still on the ground. "Getting a good look at poor Rose?"

She turned to look at me.

"Do you think you're safe now, girl? A big man to protect you?" She spat. " 'E'll use you up, and toss you aside. Weren't me work that gave me this—" She lifted her spotted hand. "It was me own 'usband. Gave me the pox, then left me to die." She smiled, showing teeth as rotten as her face. "But I got me revenge, yes I did. Sent many a man to 'ell looking just like me, and already got a couple more 'eaded there. Then or now, it's all the same. Long as your cunny works, they don't ask to see your face."

Syphilis. I took a slow step back toward Clay.

"Your 'andsome man can't protect you, girl. Not with that mark you're bearin'."

"Mark?" I said.

" 'Twas your blood that opened the portal." She smiled. "Long as you're alive, we can find you. Just follow the mark."

"Yeah?" Clay said. "Works both ways, though, doesn't it? You can only find her as long as *you're* alive, which—" He wrapped his hands in her hair. "—isn't going to be long."

A quick wrench, and her neck snapped, then he leapt out of the way before her falling body touched him. She'd barely hit the gravel before she started to disintegrate.

"We done here?" Clay said.

Jeremy nodded. "We're done."

We'd left the car back near Cabbagetown. A bit of a hike, so we stopped partway for cold drinks, taking seats on the outside patio just as an employee had been about to close it down for the night.

"So she had syphilis," I said. "And she's been spreading it."

"If she has, it was the guy's fault for not wearing protection," Clay said. "Anyone stupid enough to do that deserves syphilis or whatever else he gets."

I gave him a look, but didn't argue. It wasn't worth it.

"But if someone does get syphilis—"

"Then it's his own fault." Clay's gaze met mine. "Not yours, because your blood opened some portal and let her out. Wasn't even your fault the portal opened. I hit the mosquito. You want to blame someone, blame me."

"Even if someone does contract it, it's treatable today with penicillin," Jeremy said.

"She's dead," Clay said. "Threat eliminated. Now what about this mark business? That must be why that guy came after Elena yesterday. Not following the letter, but the mark."

I nodded. "If they—whoever—want the letter back, the fastest way to find it is to find the person whose blood opened the portal. But that doesn't matter now. Like you said, the zombies are dead and gone to dust. So what are we going to do with the letter?"

"You want to head back tonight?" Clay asked as we walked back to the car, lagging behind Jeremy. "Or find a hotel and take off after we've slept?"

"If you feel up to driving, tonight's fine with me. I know you want to get home."

He shook his head. "Doesn't matter. You don't sleep well in hotels, but you probably won't sleep any better sitting up in the car. Your choice."

I squeezed his hand. "Thanks. I *am* ready to go home, but maybe . . ." I shrugged. "I don't know. I'd rather wait until morning, make sure everything's back to normal."

Jeremy slowed to let us catch up. "We should sleep first. We've had two late nights. Rest up, and then we'll head home."

Back at the hotel, Clay and I did what we did most nights before bed—when we weren't going for a late-night run. We shared a drink and conversation, winding down for sleep. These days, the drink was more likely to be hot chocolate or herbal tea than brandy. Tonight it was tea, from the bags the hotel provided. Another deviation from the norm was that we were alone; Jeremy had retired as soon as we returned to the hotel.

So we were stretched out in bed, drinking our tea and eating cookies, trying not to scatter crumbs on the bedding.

"Well, I hate to admit it," I said, "but I think I've had enough excitement to last me through the rest of this pregnancy."

"Tired, huh?"

"Not really—" I bit back a yawn and laughed. "Okay, I guess I am. I've had my little burst of activity and now I'm ready to go home and hole up for the duration." I smiled over at him. "Bet you're glad to hear that."

He handed me another cookie. "I am . . . but if you start going stir-crazy again? You let me know and we'll do something. Get your mind off stuff with the baby."

"Fretting about the baby, you mean. It drives *me* crazy. We spent three years of hashing it out. What if I have a girl? How would she feel, growing up with werewolves and not being one? Is that fair? Or what if it's a boy and the genes don't pass on? What if he does carry the genes—is *that* fair, putting that burden on our child? What if I can't carry to term? What if—?" I growled and shook my head. "Every conceivable question debated and debated until we had all the answers."

"Or thought we did."

I gave myself a shake, turned around and slid under his arm, resting my head on his shoulder. "Time to stop talking and get some sleep. A few months from now, I'll be dying for a quiet night like this."

"*We* will. It's a joint venture, remember? I just wish I could do my share now, take half the burden of this part, half the worrying."

I snuggled into him and was asleep before he turned out the light.

Decision

WHEN WE WOKE UP THE NEXT MORNING, IT WASN'T MORN-
ing at all, but early afternoon. That's what happens after
two nights of staying up until nearly dawn. While I was
stretching and yawning, struggling to wake up, Clay
pulled on clothes, went downstairs and got breakfast.
Jeremy wasn't in his room, but had left a note, so Clay
wouldn't worry. Yes, fifty-seven years old and he still
couldn't walk out the door without letting someone know
where he was. Such is the life of a Pack Alpha.

We ate and talked while we got ready to leave. Showers
and shaves could wait until Stonehaven.

"It'll be nice to get back to my own bed," I said, stretching out the kinks in my back. "Speaking of which, I want
to start on the nursery. Should we use my bedroom? I
hardly ever sleep in it."

Clay shook his head and crammed half a croissant in
his mouth, talking as he chewed. "Keep it. That's your
space. You need it."

Five years ago, those words would have never left his
mouth. Hell, he would have suggested turning my room
into a nursery the moment we decided to try for a baby.

I tore off part of my blueberry muffin and handed it to him as I started dressing. "We'll use the guest room then. It's at the other end of the hall, but—"

"Jeremy suggested Malcolm's room. It makes sense—right next to mine, closer to yours than the guest room . . ."

I sniff-tested yesterday's shirt, then pulled it on. "Is Jeremy okay with that? Using his father's room?"

"I think he wants us to." He finger-combed his curls and gave the job a cursory mirror check. "Room's been closed for twenty years. Time to make use of it. Open it up, clear out Malcolm's shit, air out the . . ." He shrugged.

"Air out the ghosts?"

A light rap at the door. Clay opened it.

"Good morning, I see you're—" Jeremy snatched the coffee from my hand. "That water hasn't been boiled, has it?"

"Boiled?"

"There's a problem with the drinking water. Likely the municipal supply." He held out a newspaper. "Remember those nurses last night? Talking about an influx of stomach complaints?"

I glanced down at the headline. My gut went cold. "Contaminated city water? That can't be. After Walkerton, Toronto's water supply is locked down tight."

I'd done a series of articles on Walkerton, an Ontario town with a mismanaged water supply a few years ago. Seven people had died, and there'd been ongoing health problems. Since then, water safety had been a hot-button issue in the province.

"When they investigate, they'll find it's bottled water," I said. "Lot more Torontonians drink that anyway."

"Perhaps," Jeremy said. "But in the meantime—"

"We avoid all drinking water, tap or bottled. Got it. No big deal. We're leaving this morning anyway."

"Soon, but not just yet," Jeremy said. "That woman who disappeared in Cabbagetown is still missing."

"So?" Clay said. "Maybe she was disoriented after she came back, and wandered off. Or maybe she never went through the portal at all."

"True, but a second resident has gone missing, in the same area. A man in his thirties, apparently out for a jog, which rules out dementia-induced wandering."

"He disappeared this morning? After we supposedly closed the portal?"

"Still, it—" Clay began.

"Doesn't mean he fell into the portal," Jeremy cut in. "Or that it isn't closed. True. But unless we coincidentally have a serial killer preying on residents in the same area where we opened that portal, I'd say it's safer to assume we missed one."

"A zombie, you mean," I said.

He nodded. "I know you both want to go home, and now that we know Elena is a target, that might be wise. I can stay behind and scout today, and have Antonio here by nightfall to help me with the hunt."

Clay flung his half-eaten apple onto the tray. It bounced off. We watched it roll across the floor.

"You stay," I said to Clay. "If we call Nick now, he can probably make it to Stonehaven before I do."

Clay scooped up the apple and put it back on the tray, his jaw set.

"Or I can stay," I began.

"No."

"I don't see why not. Maybe I have some mark because my blood opened the portal, but does that really make me a target? What would they want with me? Probably just to tell them where to find the letter, right?"

Jeremy nodded. "That's Robert's theory. I called him this morning. He believes the zombies need the letter back—or think they do—and because your blood opened the portal, presumably you'd have the letter. As for this 'mark,' he's surprised they were able to track you all the way to New York State with it, but obviously they did."

"What about ditching the letter?" Clay said. "Send it back to Xavier. Make it his problem."

"Make the portal Xavier's problem?" I said. "I'm sure he'll rush right over to fix it."

Jeremy shook his head. "We caused the problem, we'll fix it. Even if the letter's gone, Elena would know where to find it, so they'd still come after her. And we don't want to get rid of something we may need to close this thing."

"Back to the question," I said. "Do I stay or do I go?"

Jeremy looked from Clay to me, then murmured, "I'll step outside."

"I don't want to fight about this," I said when Jeremy was gone. "All I care about is getting the damage undone, which means closing that portal. I don't care who does it."

"If you're in danger, I'm staying with you, here or at Stonehaven. My gut reaction? Stonehaven—even if we did miss a zombie and it can follow you that far, which I doubt." He took a deep breath and shook his head. "But that means leaving Jeremy behind, with some zombie who may have been following us and knows he's connected to the letter."

He went quiet for a moment, then said, voice soft, "I'm

trying not to freak out, Elena. When that guy came after you in the truck stop, you know what I wanted to do?"

"Drag me back to Stonehaven?"

"Yeah." A small, humorless laugh. "Big surprise, huh?"

His eyes turned to mine. Behind the anger, I saw frustration, fear and even an inkling of panic.

"Jeremy was right," he said. "We needed to come back and make sure this was over. Only, it's not over, is it? Now we've got these . . . zombies—" He yanked his hands from his pockets. "What the hell do I know about zombies? How can I—?" He bit off the sentence in a snarl.

"Protect me?"

"Yeah, I know, you can protect yourself. Any other time, I'd agree."

"But right now I'm pregnant. Very pregnant. Big, awkward, slow . . ."

He met my gaze, his eyes wary but determined, as if he knew he was sliding onto dangerous ground, but refused to backpedal.

"And you're right," I said. "I'm off my game. I know it. I also know that any risk I take, I'm not just taking for myself, but for our child. *Our* child. If you think I'm safer hiding out with Antonio and Nick, then I'll go."

"But that's not what you want, is it?"

"You know it isn't. I want to stay with you, and watch your back. Yours and Jeremy's, because, no matter which of us bears this 'mark,' I think we're all targets. I want to finish this, and I want to go home knowing everything's okay—that we're all safe and okay." I touched my fingertips to my belly. "All of us."

He nodded and looked away, eyes unfocused. After a moment, his gaze swung back to mine. "I want you here, with me, more than I want you gone. But there's one thing I'll need you to do."

"What's that?"

"Stay with me. Right with me. At my side. At all times. No arguing about space and privacy. I need to be beside you, to be sure you're safe."

"That's fine." I managed a smile. "But I still get those bathroom privacy privileges, right?"

"Depends on whether there's a window someone can crawl in through."

"Fair enough."

"And private bathrooms only."

I laughed. "You're going to follow me into public restrooms? That I have to see."

"You just might. Now let's go tell Jeremy. Then we'll finish this and get home."

Back to Cabbagetown. Four times around the perimeter, and twice down the portal street itself, and all I could find with that rotting scent were the two trails: the bowler-hatted man and Rose.

We knew there was a possibility that we hadn't found a trail because there wasn't one—that there was no missing zombie. We were basing our "portal closing theory" on a single two-hundred-year-old case. But, for now, it was all we had.

If we were missing something, we couldn't rely on Robert to find it. Having lost Shanahan, our best source for information was the person who'd gotten us into this mess. So I made the call I'd been dreading.

I phoned from our hotel. Clay stood by.

"Elena!" Xavier said. "What the hell happened? Where's my package?"

I told him. Silenced buzzed along the line, then, "Huh, well, that's strange but, you know, these things happen. I'm sure it has nothing to do with the letter, so just go ahead and send— Or, better yet, since we are running behind schedule, send it—"

"Directly to the buyer?"

"Er, right. Just, you know, in case—"

"It *is* demonically possessed?"

"Hey, I'm being careful. Send the letter, go on home and relax."

"After unleashing hell on Toronto?"

"From what I saw, Toronto could use a hell portal or two. Besides, you don't live there anymore. What do you care?"

I told him why I cared.

"Er . . . that's not good. And the . . . boyfriend. How's he taking this?"

"The fact that his mate is marked and on a zombie hit list? Here, why don't you ask him?"

I pulled the phone from my mouth. As Clay reached for it, Xavier's voice rang down the line.

"No, that's okay! Tell him I have no idea what's going on, but anything I can do to help, just ask."

"How about coming here and dispatching the zombies yourself?"

"Except that. But anything else, I'm your man. Oh, and don't worry about the letter. You can keep it."

"You're too kind. Now start by telling us everything you know about it."

It wasn't much. The buyer was a human with no super-natural connections, and he'd wanted it for the very reason Xavier had given: DNA analysis and a book/movie deal. Plus, Xavier had been the one to approach him with the offer—through his black market contacts, Xavier had heard the man was in the market for Ripper letters, and paying well.

"I could set you up with the original thief, Zoe Takano," Xavier said. "Maybe she knows more."

"The thief who stole it eighty years ago? Where is she? Shady Acres Home for the Supernatural Aged? She must be at least a hundred—oh, wait. She's a vampire, isn't she? Any idea where we'd find her?"

"Right there. Toronto born and bred. That's how the letter got there. The Shanahans are clients of hers. Have been for decades."

The thief knew Patrick Shanahan? Then we definitely wanted to talk to her.

"Do you know her?"

"Zoe and I don't move in the same circles. But I can tell you where you might find her. She's been doing her business out of the same bar forever. Creature of habit. Vamps are like that."

He promised to call back with an address and whatever details he could scrounge up.

Two minutes after I hung up, the phone rang again.

"Fast work, demon," I said as I answered it. "Keep that up and you might find your way out of my bad books."

Silence.

I glanced at the call display. I'd seen a semifamiliar long-distance number before answering . . . but now realized it wasn't the one I thought it was.

"Uh, Robert," I said. "Sorry about that. I was expecting—"

A soft chuckle. "Another demon?"

"Right, and one with a contact name and address, so I got a little overeager."

"No doubt. Wrong demon, perhaps, but I'm calling for the same reason. With a contact name."

"Oh?"

"I was making some calls myself asking about Jack the Ripper legends and supernatural connections, and someone suggested Anita Barrington. She's a witch running a bookstore in Toronto, and quite an expert on such lore. I know her only by reputation, but I thought if this was a potential shortcut to bypass my rather slow research . . ."

"We'll take it."

Lore

HECATE'S HAVEN WAS A TINY BOOKSTORE ON YONGE Street, wedged between a candy shop and a Korean take-out. When we arrived, a plump woman with a long silver braid was flipping the OPEN sign to CLOSED.

She looked out at us, her faded blue eyes crossing our faces with a questioning look, as if we weren't her usual clientele. Then her gaze dropped to my stomach, and her lips parted in a silent "Ah." She hurried over and opened the door.

"Let me guess," she said. "You're looking for something to protect you against the water contamination."

Before I could answer, she leaned forward, hand on my arm, and continued. "In times of trial, many of us feel the need to turn to the mystical. To be blunt though, dear, there's no ward that can protect you as well as common sense. Follow the health bulletins and avoid tap water, and that will serve you far better than any charm or amulet."

"Anita Barrington?" Jeremy asked.

She looked up at him. "Yes?"

"You were recommended to us by Robert Vasic."

A frown line appeared between her eyes, then she let out a small laugh. "Ah. Well, that's different, isn't it? Come in, come in."

She ushered us into the shop and locked the door, then closed a beaded curtain over the front window.

"You must think me a dotty old lady, jumping to conclusions, but you would not believe the day I've had."

She waved me to a stool pulled up to a counter stacked with used books.

"Is that too high?"

I hopped onto it.

"Excellent," she said. "Now, there's another one there if you gentlemen care to fight over it."

She headed behind the counter. "Such a day. Mind you, when one runs a bookstore with 'Hecate' in the name, one comes to expect shoppers looking for charms and wards and other New Age nonsense."

Still talking, she climbed onto a stool behind the counter. "Today, though, the phone hasn't stopped ringing, nor the chimes over the door. We consider ourselves such an enlightened society and yet, when our most basic fears are aroused, where do we turn? Magic and superstition."

She pulled the plastic wrap off a plate of bakery cookies and pushed them toward me.

"Eat up," she said, eyes twinkling. "While you still have the excuse."

I took two.

She continued. "Now, if Robert Vasic referred you, then I know you aren't here for charms against the water contamination. While humans are scrambling for supernatural cures, we supernaturals are renting cottages and stocking up on bottled water. So, how can I help you?"

I started by asking her about supernatural stories related to Jack the Ripper.

"Ah, our folklore," she said, eyes lighting up. "My specialty. I adore stories—they tell us so much about ourselves and our world, and our particular world has some of the most fascinating ones. However, in this case, I suspect you'll be disappointed. What fires the imaginations of humans does not necessarily fire our own."

"Because we've seen far worse than Jack the Ripper?"

"Exactly. If you look for human fiction and folklore speculating that Jack the Ripper was a supernatural, you'll be absolutely swamped by it. There's a wonderful story by Robert Bloch—" She laughed. "But that's not what you're here for, is it? Let's stick to our folklore. Now—"

"Nana?"

We turned to see a girl with a light brown ponytail peeking from behind a beaded curtain leading into the back rooms. She looked about twelve.

"Erin," Anita said. "My granddaughter." She smiled at the girl. "Done with your homework and thinking this sounds more interesting? Come get a cookie, then."

The girl took one, then Anita whispered to her, telling her she could listen from the back room, but not to disturb us.

Of the four stories Anita told us, two postulated that Jack the Ripper had been a sorcerer and the dead women were ritual sacrifices. In other words, the obvious angle, but very unlikely, she said. Brutality wasn't necessary for sacrifice, and even if a sorcerer preferred doing it that way, he'd never take the risk of performing the murder and the ritual in a public place.

The third story said the killings were done by a

werewolf and were part of a territorial dispute. One werewolf had been trying to scare another out of London, and hoped the killings would do the trick. Nice theory . . . if you didn't think about it too much. If you're a werewolf who wants to spook a fellow wolf with the threat of exposure, why make the murders only vaguely werewolf-*like*? Why not just change to wolf form and make them the real deal? Whoever started this rumor knew nothing about werewolves except for their reputation as the thugs of the supernatural world—very violent and none too bright. Typical.

The last tale was apparently the most popular, with multiple variations dating from the time of Jack the Ripper himself. According to that story, Jack had been a half-demon who'd made contact with his father. Not that easy when Dad lives in a hell dimension, but I guess an enterprising son can find a way.

According to the lore, the half-demon had made a pact with his father, trading sacrifices for a boon. The nature of the boon varied—invulnerability, immortality, immeasurable wealth—pretty much all the regular wishes. The demon connection, the stories claimed, explained why the killings had been so brutal and why Jack had corresponded with the media rather than commit his crimes in silence. Demons feed on chaos. A demonic sacrifice isn't about bloodletting, it's about the chaos caused by death. This, then, would have been Jack's true offering to his father—not the five lives themselves, but the fear and panic they'd caused.

"Now that one makes the most sense," she said. "Though it is, of course, almost certainly only a story."

"And not . . . really what we're looking for," I said.

"Well, perhaps if you put this into context for me . . ."

I glanced over at Jeremy. He nodded, and I told her what had happened.

For a moment, Anita just sat there, staring at me.

"Jack the Ripper's *From Hell* letter?" she said finally. "As a dimensional portal trigger?"

"I know it sounds preposterous—"

"No, it makes perfect sense."

She slid to the floor, then came out from behind the counter and paced to the far shelf and back, shaking her head.

"Mrs. Barrington . . ." Jeremy began.

"Anita, please. I'm sorry. I'm just . . . exasperated. I knew there was a supernatural story behind that letter. Why else would Shanahan have had it stolen? I haven't been in Toronto long. I came five years ago, when my daughter died and her husband needed help with Erin. But my reputation as a folklorist is impeccable. So, when I heard the infamous *From Hell* letter was here, in the collection of a man known for gathering supernatural oddities, I presented myself to young Mr. Shanahan and requested permission to see it, and learn the story behind it. He—"

Spots of color lit her cheeks and she glanced toward the back room as if remembering her granddaughter listening in.

"He was . . . not accommodating." She paced to the shelf and back again. "It is *so* frustrating. I don't know what race you young people are, and I won't ask, but I hope you don't have any such prejudices to deal with. They can make life quite intolerable at times. Sorcerers and witches—" A sharp shake of her head. "A ridiculous feud rooted in events so far back in time—" Another, sharper shake. "I'm sorry. You didn't come to hear me rage about that. But, yes, I don't doubt that the *From Hell* letter has a supernatural legend behind it, and that Patrick Shanahan knows all about it."

"If he does, we'll get the story from him, and we'll give it to you."

She smiled and nodded. "Thank you, dear." She turned slowly to face me. "I don't suppose— I shouldn't ask but . . . well, at my age, I've learned to pursue opportunities when they present themselves to me. Is there any chance I could examine that letter? Presuming you still have it . . ."

"We do," Jeremy said. "And when this is over, we'd be happy to show it to you. In the meantime, may we contact you if we have questions?"

"Absolutely. And perhaps, now that I know the letter's supernatural link—a portal and dimensional zombies—I might be able to dig up some more stories for you."

The first restaurant we passed had a note on the door, saying that the shop was closed due to E. coli in the city's water supply.

"E. coli?" I said. "So they know what it is? Or is that just a guess? Maybe I should call my newspaper contacts and—"

"And do what? Find out the situation is worse than we thought, giving you one more thing to worry about? Won't get the portal closed any faster."

"Clay's right," Jeremy said. "We need to keep the blinders on and move forward, however tempting it may be to stop and look around."

* * *

We picked up sandwiches and took them to a downtown park, where we could be assured of privacy. With the exception of the occasional late-working office employee cutting through to the subway station, privacy is what we had . . . until a change in the wind brought a now-familiar stink.

"Son of a bitch," Clay muttered under his breath.

"Guess Rose was right," I said. "They *can* find me. Saves us the bother of looking for this one." I inhaled deeper and nearly gagged. "I can barely pick up a scent under that stench. I think it's male . . ."

"You'd be right," Clay said.

He nudged my leg to the left. On the pretext of taking another napkin from the bag, I glanced over and saw a figure almost hidden behind a metal sculpture.

"Shall we try to find a convenient alley?" Jeremy murmured behind his sandwich.

"I know something better." I wiped imaginary sweat from my forehead, made a face and raised my voice above normal. "God, I have to get out of this heat. Can we eat someplace else? With air-conditioning . . . and tables?"

Clay nodded and we gathered up our stuff. I led them to the street corner and across to a looming business tower. We went inside. I smiled at the security guard and waved to a "down" escalator a hundred feet away. He nodded and returned to his reading.

Seeing where I was taking them, Clay stopped. "Is that—?"

"The gateway to hell. Sorry." I took his arm and continued walking, then glanced over at Jeremy. "It's part of PATH, Toronto's underground walkway system. Clay had a bad experience with it last winter."

"Traumatic," Clay muttered. "Still recovering."

"Clay had an early morning department meeting, and I needed to buy him a new shirt," I told Jeremy. "He'd ripped another one."

"*I* ripped—?"

"So I told him to meet me at the Second Cup near the store. Only, he didn't come in that entrance."

"Probably because it was cold enough out there to freeze—"

"It was cold," I continued as we stepped onto the escalator. "So he takes the nearest entrance, not knowing the tunnels stretch for over six miles. The first Second Cup he sees, he thinks, 'This must be it' and sits down. When I don't show, he realizes there might be another one down here."

"Or twenty," Clay muttered.

"Be glad I didn't say Starbucks. Upshot is, if you don't know your way, it all starts to look the same. Of course, the logical solution is to stop and ask for directions."

Clay snorted.

"So what happened next was entirely his own fault."

"Dare I ask?" Jeremy said as we stepped off the escalator.

"Lunch hour. For thousands of office workers. With sub-subzero temperatures outside."

"One minute I was just wandering around, the place practically empty, and then—" Clay shuddered.

"Traumatic, I know," I said, patting him on the back. "But—" I swept a hand around "—much different now."

We stood at the end of a hall stretching a few hundred feet, flanked with coffee shops, bookstores, drugstores and everything else an office worker might need between nine and five. But it was summertime, when no one cared to work later than necessary. The stores had been closed for hours. The walkways were left open only as a convenience for pedestrians.

"Not bad," Clay said as he looked around.

"If our zombie pal wants to make his move, he'll have plenty of opportunities. We just need to watch out for security guards and cameras. There's an even quieter place a block over. We'll head that way."

Before we'd passed three storefronts, hesitant footsteps sounded behind us. Bait taken.

We made sure to turn lots of corners and avoid long straightaways, letting our pursuer stay close but hidden, watching us from behind the last corner until we turned the next. As we walked, I counted the number of attack opportunities we'd given him. When I reached five, I paused at a storefront and pointed to a display of baby sundresses.

"What's he waiting for?" I whispered.

"Same thing his bowler-hatted friend waited for," Jeremy said. "The doe to separate from the herd."

He was right. Unlike Hollywood's brain-dead, brain-munching zombies, these guys weren't stupid.

Before I could even open my mouth, Clay said, "No."

"I—"

"Remember your promise? At my side. At all times."

"I'm not suggesting I lure him away and finish him off myself. Just the luring away part."

"Elena's right," Jeremy said. "We'll be close behind. It's safe enough."

"Good," I said. "Then it's time for me to use the bathroom." I raised my voice. "There's a food court just around the corner. You two can sit and eat while I find a washroom."

When we reached the food court, I put my sandwich bag on a table, then looked around.

"Oh, the bathroom's over there," I said loudly. "We walked right past it. I'll be back in a minute."

I took one last hit of chocolate milk, giving the zombie time to get out of sight.

The bathrooms were down a service hall. As I walked, I tracked the distant pad of footsteps behind me, ready to turn if they got too close before Clay arrived.

I reached the end, only to realize the hall dog-legged. At least this would give Clay a chance to attack the zombie out of sight of anyone passing in the main thoroughfare.

As I rounded the corner, I looked around for security cameras. None. Good. The footsteps behind me sped up . . . and Clay's joined them. I smiled. Easy as—

A shadow leapt from a recessed doorway. I wheeled, but too slow, and a body hit my shoulder, knocking me into the far wall. I kicked. As my foot went up, I mentally slapped myself. Again, the sudden move threw me off balance. As I stumbled, the figure rushed me, hands out, going for my throat. I swung and caught my attacker in the jaw. He flew back with a shriek . . . a very unmasculine shriek.

I leapt onto the falling figure. A face turned to mine—a woman's face, pocked and red. Rose.

"Thought you were done with Rose, didn't you?" she cackled.

My surprise threw me off. She lunged at me, fingers

hooked into claws, aiming for my eyes. An uppercut stopped her hands before they got within a foot of my face. As she fell back, I grabbed her by the throat and slammed her into the wall. Her face twisted, then went slack, and when I let her go, her body slid to the floor and started to crumble.

"Easy to kill," I muttered. "Problem is keeping them that way."

At a noise from the corner, I whirled, hands going up. Clay raced around.

"I heard—"

"Got her," I said. "Again. It was Rose. I could have sworn it was a man—"

"It was." He grabbed my arm and pulled me back toward the main hall. "The same guy I killed at the truck stop."

"Did you—?"

"Started to," he said, now moving at a jog and pulling me along. "Then I heard you and mine got away. Jeremy went after him."

"Let's go," I said, and we started off.

The bowler-hatted man had taken the first exit. We crested the top of the escalator just as Jeremy was stepping onto the down side. He backed off it and led us outside before speaking.

"He crossed the road and I lost the scent in traffic," he said. "Are you both all right?"

"Just another encounter with not-so-sweet-smelling Rose," I said.

Jeremy tensed. "Rose?"

"The zombie we—"

"Yes, I know. You didn't— Did you touch her?"

"Sure," I said. "I had to. She attacked me. But if you're worried about the syphilis, I swear I didn't have sex with her."

Jeremy didn't smile. "Did you touch her lips or any of the sores near her mouth?"

"I don't think so, but—"

His fingers clamped around my elbow. "There's a coffee shop across the road. You need to go into the bathroom and scrub your hands and arms."

He didn't even wait for the light to change, just led me across between cars.

"Jer?" Clay said, jogging up beside us. "I thought you said syphilis was easily treated."

"It is. But it's particularly dangerous to pregnant mothers."

He caught my look and slowed, grip relaxing on my arm. "You'll be fine." A small smile. "I'm overreacting, as usual. The only danger is if you came in contact with the sores around her mouth and ingest the bacterium or transfer it through broken skin. A thorough scrubbing will do the trick. I should have mentioned something last night but . . ."

"Rose was already dead, or so we thought. So what's happening—"

"First, scrub up," he said, stopping outside the coffee shop doors. "Then we can discuss it."

I scrubbed my hands and arms until my skin was red, then washed my face and neck, cleaning off every bit of exposed skin, even parts I knew hadn't touched Rose.

When I went outside, we returned to the escalator

leading down to the PATH walkways, and I found the bowler-hatted man's scent there, but lost it at the street. Between the exhaust fumes and the smog and the stink of a thousand daily passersby, our target's scent had disappeared.

I watched the steady stream of traffic going by. "If we wait a few hours and I Change, it would probably be safe."

Jeremy shook his head. "It's not worth the risk. Killing them doesn't seem to help."

"Either we have an army of zombie clones, or the undead aren't staying dead. Remember yesterday, when Robert was talking about the difference between controlled zombies raised by a necromancer and those created by a sorcerer's portal? He said both kinds are tough to kill. Necromancer ones just won't die, but dimensional ones . . ." I frowned. "Did he say what happened with them?"

"No," Jeremy said. "Because that shouldn't have been relevant. This portal was created over a hundred years ago, meaning any 'controller' should be dead."

"Should be," Clay muttered. "But there's always a catch."

Jeremy nodded. "Time to talk to Jaime and Robert again. And let's see if we can contact that vampire thief tonight. I'll go back to the hotel to make the calls while you two track down Zoe Takano."

Clay opened his mouth, but Jeremy cut him off. "Yes, I know you don't like that idea, but it's the best use of our limited resources. Even if that zombie did circle back and find me, presuming I'd know where the letter is too, they've hardly been difficult to kill so far."

"Rose didn't even have a weapon," I said. "And unless

my nose is wrong, they're coming back a little the worse for wear. Deteriorating."

Clay hesitated.

"You can walk me to the hotel and lock me in, if it makes you feel better," Jeremy said. "After tonight, we won't have this problem with dividing our resources. I'm calling Antonio, and asking him and Nick to come. He still hasn't forgiven me for not summoning them back from Europe when Elena was taken. I don't have an excuse for not bothering them this time."

Clay nodded, and we walked Jeremy back to the hotel.

Zoe

FROM THE OUTSIDE, MILLER'S WASN'T THE SORT OF PLACE I'd wander into in search of a drink. The term "hole in the wall" has never been more apt. The place had an entrance accessible only by a door leading from the alley. The flickering neon Miller's Ale sign made me think that, if the owner had found a Labatt's sign in the curbside trash instead, the bar would have a different name.

There was a single reinforced window beside the door. As I slipped up for a closer look, I realized the window wasn't just reinforced, it was plastered over from the inside.

A shower of gravel rained down. Clay had reached the second-story fire escape landing, but the window overlooking it was barred, which I'm sure would be much appreciated by anyone trapped inside during a fire. The bars were old, though, and Clay snapped them with a sharp wrench. Then he stripped off his shirt and wrapped his hand in it to muffle the noise as he broke the window. No alarms sounded. A place like this, rusted bars were all you got.

Clay looked down through the slats of the fire escape.

"You gonna be okay?" he said.

"Even knocked up, I think I can take on a vampire."

I waited while Clay slipped inside. A moment later, he stuck his head out and gave me the all clear—he'd found a place to watch over me from upstairs.

In the movies, vampires and werewolves are often portrayed as mortal enemies. Not true. There's no gut-level antipathy, no centuries-old feud. I'm just not . . . keen on vampires. Chalk it up to a bad experience.

The first vampire I met tried to befriend me. Nothing wrong with that. I was flattered; who wouldn't be? Then I'd been taken captive by supernatural-collecting psychotic humans. Her response? What a tragedy . . . but, as long as Elena's gone, I might as well help myself to her boyfriend. Clay had told her where to stick it. When I'd escaped, she thought we could pick up where we left off. The lesson I learned from that? Compared to vampires, Clay is downright empathetic.

I shouldn't tar all vampires with Cassandra's brush, but later encounters taught me that with few exceptions, vampires are self-absorbed egomaniacs. Paige says it's self-preservation, because they live so long and watch everyone around them grow old and die. They learn not to form attachments. I can see that. But there's a big difference between understanding a type of person and wanting to hang out with them. When I walked into that bar to meet Zoe Takano, I knew this encounter would take some serious acting skills.

A wave of cigarette smoke rolled over me when I opened the door. Someone was giving a big middle finger to the city's antismoking laws. A glance around, and I knew the owner wasn't in danger of being reported. The kind of people who cared about secondhand smoke issues didn't come here.

A dozen patrons, most of them alone, seemed dedicated to prodding the night into oblivion with beer and third-rate whiskey. A few huddled by the bar, not talking, just drinking, as if being within two feet of another person was as sociable as they could get.

Xavier had said the bartender was a supernatural. He didn't say what kind, and it didn't matter. But it explained why the bartender, and some of the clientele, could see a woman come in here for decades without aging, and not care. The nonsupernatural regulars could probably see a vampire feasting on the guy beside them and only decide they'd had their limit for the night.

Zoe Takano was easy to spot. For one thing, she was the only woman. For another, she was clean—with gleaming black hair, a tight white T-shirt, black jeans and motorcycle boots. And she looked more alive than anything in the bar, which, all things considered, was kind of sad.

She sat at a corner table, reading the *Sun,* her hand wrapped around an icy beer bottle. When I stepped in, she was the first one to look up—the only one to look up. She gave me a slow once-over, then made it a twice-over, her index finger tapping the bottle neck. Sizing up my potential as a more satisfying thirst quencher? Maybe if I played this right, we could skip the whole "small talk" portion of the meeting and get straight to the "invitation into a dark, deserted alley."

This might not be Zoe. Xavier said the bar did attract supernatural criminals looking for a safe place to conduct business. But she was the only vampire in Toronto—a quick call to the council's second vampire delegate, Aaron, had confirmed that. He'd given me a brief physical sketch too. Although Aaron hadn't seen Zoe in years, with vampires, vital stats don't change in two years or two hundred.

She fit Aaron's description, but as I approached, I still ran a sniff test. A vampire's smell is all artificial. I could track Cassandra or Aaron by their particular blend of soap, shampoo, cosmetics, laundry detergent, but underneath that, there was nothing. When you don't have bodily functions, you don't have a smell.

This woman had almost no scent at all, only a faintly chemical odor, as if she used all unscented products. The better to confuse guard dogs.

"Zoe Takano?" I said.

Her gaze slid up me, taking my measure. When she reached my eyes, I expected to see a predatory gleam. Here was a healthy woman, alone and weighted down with child. Mother Nature's version of convenience food—dinner too dumb to keep out of danger's path. Yet her expression was only one of curiosity.

Across the room, the bartender stopped wiping the counter and looked over at us, eyes narrowing. She must have given him some signal because he nodded and returned to his wiping.

"Zoe Takano?" I repeated, almost certain now that she wasn't who I thought she was.

"At your service, ma'am." Her eyes glittered then, in anticipation, but there was no hunger behind it, still only curiosity. "And I presume it is service that you're looking for, a service I can provide?"

"I have a proposition—"

She chuckled. "Exactly what I was hoping."

"It's a job—"

"Ah, business. Too bad."

I hesitated. "You aren't taking clients—"

A tinkling laugh, like wind chimes. "Oh, I'm always taking clients. Don't mind me. It's been a slow week, and when there's little to amuse me, I start to amuse myself. Sit, sit. Get off your feet. That—" a nod at my stomach, "—can't be terribly comfortable. Not in this heat."

"Er, yes. I mean, no, it isn't." I pulled out a chair and sat down. "Thank you."

"A cold drink?" she said. "Something nonalcoholic, I presume?"

"Um, no. I'm fine. I was told—"

"First things first," she said, leaning back in her chair. "Credentials. I presume you come on a recommendation. May I ask from whom?"

I cast an anxious glance around. "I, uh, was hoping we could do this someplace less . . . public."

Another tinkling laugh and she leaned forward. "Does anyone in here look like they could summon the *energy* to eavesdrop, much less the inclination?"

"Er, no, but—" I tried to look nervous. "I'm really new at this and—"

"And you want me to follow you outside, where anyone could be waiting for me." Her smile was brittle now. "I don't know who you are or who sent you—"

"His name's Xavier Reese. He said you don't know him personally but . . ." I could tell by her expression that Xavier's name, if it meant anything to her, wasn't enough to get her outside. "I also spoke to Aaron Darnell, for his recommendation."

A spark of interest behind the caution, but still cool. "Did you? And what did he say?"

"That you were reasonably trustworthy . . . for a thief."

Her dark eyes danced as she grinned. "Ah, Aaron. He tries to be understanding, but he can't shake his disapproval."

She sipped her beer and looked thoughtful, as if even that recommendation wasn't enough. Oh, come on. She was a vampire, impervious to harm. What was she worried about? A very pregnant blond?

She tapped her fingernails against her beer bottle then, gaze still down, gave a tiny "What the hell" smile, and pushed back her chair.

"All right," she said. "Let's go outside and you can tell me what all this is about." I stepped out of the bar first. Zoe paused in the doorway, looking, listening, sensing, then followed me out.

I got two steps into the adjacent alley, turned to ask, "Is this good enough?" and Zoe was already lunging toward me. Her fangs met my fist and she flew into the brick wall with a yelp. She dove for me again. An uppercut to the jaw sent her sailing down the alley.

Not normally the way I'd treat a potential source, but short of lopping off a body part, I couldn't do any lasting damage to a vampire. And, as with any predator, if you plan to establish dominance, you have to do it fast. So before she recovered from the uppercut, I pounced and knocked her to the ground, then pinned her.

"Hope you weren't too hungry," I said.

"Hungry?" She only laughed and stretched out on the ground under me, as if relaxing. "Not at all, but it seemed like the quickest way to get past all that 'I want to talk someplace private' nonsense, and find out what you really want . . . and what you are." She slid her tongue over her split lip, and the skin mended. "Half-demon, I presume?"

"Good guess," I said.

"I don't believe I've ever met one who was quite so . . . physical. Interesting."

I glanced over my shoulder for Clay, and saw him waiting at the end of the alley. As I twisted, Zoe moved. When I swung around, I felt a sharp tug on my hair. I grabbed for her hand, only to find my broken hair band in it. My hair slid over my shoulders, and I gave a small snarl as I tried to flip it back out of the way.

"Sorry, but I just had to do that," Zoe said. "Silver blond. Gorgeous. It's natural, isn't it? Somehow, I doubt that a woman who ties her hair with an elastic band has any use for hair coloring."

Unbelievable. Pinned to the ground by an unknown assailant . . . and she wants to share beauty tips. I guess for a vampire, the phrase "mortal danger" just doesn't pack the same punch.

"I need to talk to you about something you stole a long time ago."

"Business already?"

"It's that or toss you around a bit more."

She paused, as if considering this.

"Business," I said.

A soft sigh. "Oh, all right. Something I stole a long time ago, hmmm? I've stolen a lot of things, and most of them a long time ago."

"I think this object would fall under the heading of unique and memorable. Jack the Ripper's *From Hell* letter."

Her expression didn't change.

"Stolen from the London Metropolitan Police eighty years ago?" I said. "Sold to a local sorcerer's family?"

"You're local too, aren't you? I can tell by the accent."

She laughed. "Or the lack of accent. So why haven't I ever met you before? You certainly haven't been in Miller's. I'd remember."

"How about the letter? Do you remember that?"

"Vaguely." She wriggled under me and put a hand under her head, getting comfortable. "I'd rather talk about you."

I glanced over my shoulder. Clay nodded, and slipped around the corner, guarding the escape route without Zoe knowing he was there yet. He stayed far enough back that she wouldn't sense him.

I moved off her. She stayed on the ground a moment, then sighed, and almost reluctantly sat up.

"Now, what did you say your name was?" she said.

"I didn't."

"I know, I was just giving you the opportunity to correct the oversight." She smiled, teeth glistening in the dim light. "But if you don't want to, I suppose that will give us something to talk about next time."

She sprang to her feet and raced down the alley—the other way, toward an eight-foot fence, moving so fast that she was over that fence before I was on my feet.

Clay raced past me. He reached the fence and jumped, catching the edge, then swung himself up. As he went over, he looked back and saw that I was just nearing the base. He perched on top, waiting.

"No, go on!" I said. "Chasing and jumping, I can't do. Not like this."

"Then we'll track her."

I shook my head even as I grabbed his hands. "Her scent's too faint."

"Doesn't matter." He locked his fingers around my

wrists and hauled me up. "I'm not leaving you alone, re-member?"

He helped me over the fence. We ran to the end of the alley.

"There," Clay said.

We spotted Zoe across the road as she darted into a side street. Clay took my arm and we hurried across. After a few more streets and alleys, we reached a stretch of open land leading to the foot of a wooded hill.

Clay chuckled. "This look familiar, darling?"

I grinned. "High Park."

I used to run here when I'd been going to the University of Toronto. A long hike from the campus, but I'd been willing to make the trek—or pay the subway fare—for the chance to jog away from the city streets. When Clay and I had been dating, this had been "our place" more than any other.

I watched Zoe's white T-shirt disappear into the woods. There was one sure way I could catch her, in a form where my stomach didn't affect my balance.

I lifted my muzzle and took a deep breath, my legs trembling with excitement. High Park. Even in my later days in Toronto, I'd never run here as a wolf. Too many memories, all of them inextricably woven with the one thing I'd been trying to forget. But now we were here, just like in those early days, before the bite, before everything fell apart. Clay here, with me, and all the pieces mended, the new better than the old.

I let out a shuddering sigh and closed my eyes. I could feel the weight in my belly, heavy and warm, alive. Alive. In this form, there was no question about that—no fears.

Everything was simple—my mate, my pup, both safe, all as it should be, the night and the forest laid out before us, ours to enjoy, explore, possess—

A questioning whine by my ear. Clay looked at me, his head tilted, "Still here?" in his eyes.

Oh, right. Before I could enjoy the forest, there was the small matter of a fleeing vampire to contend with.

It had been nine days since my last run, and I paid the price when I tried picking up Zoe's trail. Every other scent, every sound, every sight, even the feel of muddy ground squelching under my pads, was infinitely more enticing than a vampire's scent. The faint smell of wood-smoke said: go check it out. The patter of rabbit feet: dinner, come and get me. A glimmer of light in the trees: go see what that is. Come here, they whispered, forget the vampire . . .

Then I found her trail, and the other voices went silent, drowned under the single overwhelming cry of "prey." An intelligent, humanoid target, not the silly little bunnies I could have anytime. And not only was I allowed to chase her—I had to.

I ran full speed down the path with Clay at my heels. There was no need to take cover. There wouldn't be any other predators here, and if we came upon a person, they'd only catch a flash of fur before we dove into the undergrowth.

Faint though Zoe's scent was, my wolf brain focused on it with a single-mindedness I could never have managed in human form. She was headed for the ravine. Behind me, Clay gave a low growl. I looked up. We'd hit the top of the cliff and there, below, was Zoe's white shirt bobbing along the path. She'd slowed to a brisk walk, certain she'd left the waddling pregnant chick back in the alley.

I stopped at the top of the path, claws digging into the dirt, feeling the ground below me, soft but dry. Good. Sliding down the incline muzzle-first wasn't quite the entrance I had in mind.

I glanced at Clay. His mouth hung open, tongue lolling, blue eyes dancing with "go for it." Hindquarters twitching, I tested my grip for takeoff. A flick of my tail and I barreled down the cliff, picking up speed with every stride.

I was less than ten feet behind Zoe when she finally heard me. She turned. And I got my reward, in that split-second look of "Oh, my God" surprise and, yes, terror. Catch them off guard, and apparently you can even spook a vampire. Nice.

Zoe did what anyone seeing a 140-pound wolf barreling straight at them would do—tried to run. But before she could move, I sprang and caught her in the shoulder. She went down, managing to roll as she fell.

I could have snagged her arm. Could have . . . but chose not to because it had all been too easy. Normally, I don't chase humans. Somewhere along the way, my adrenaline-stoked brain could slide from play mode into hunt, and I couldn't take that chance. But Zoe Takano couldn't be killed, not accidentally and certainly not easily.

My bite couldn't even turn her into a werewolf—Clay and I had discovered that while helping Aaron catch a rogue. So I could toy with her, safely. Even Jeremy would see the value in it, giving her a taste of my strength as a bargaining tool for negotiations.

I let Zoe dive out of the way. Then snarling and snapping, I grabbed for her arm, only grazing her bare skin with my fangs, but making a good show of it. A little reminder that she wasn't completely immune to injury—a good snap of powerful jaws around her wrist or forearm and that was it. Vampires could heal, but if they lost something, it didn't grow back.

When I charged her again, she feinted to the side and then, hallelujah, she started to run.

Frustration

I GAVE ZOE A TEN-SECOND HEAD START WHILE I CHECKED for Clay, then tore after her. I was an above-average runner, as wolf and human, and I started to close the gap right away. She zagged off the path into the bush, dodging trees and ducking under branches with a gymnast's grace.

Clay stayed on the path, out of sight, racing ahead to cut Zoe off if she got away from me. I wove through the forest, getting close enough to be spattered with clods of dirt thrown up by her boots.

She didn't trip or falter once. In the woods, I fell behind. My belly made sharp turns and twists near-impossible.

A car horn blared, and my ears shot forward. The rumble of tires, the stench of exhaust, the faint glow of streetlights. Damn! Another hundred feet and we'd be out of the park. I skidded to a halt, threw back my head and howled. Before the last note left my throat, Clay's answering cry came from southwest . . . and Zoe was heading due south. He'd never cut her off in time.

I roared back into pursuit, scanning the darkness as I

ran. Zoe's T-shirt bobbed to my left, but I already knew she was there. What I wanted was— There, just southeast of us, an open patch.

I flew forward on a southwest angle, coming up to the right of her. Like anything fleeing a predator, she instinctively turned away from me and headed southeast. When she hit the edge of the clearing, I hunkered down, running as fast as I could, counting off the paces between us and then . . . airborne.

I hit Zoe between the shoulder blades. She tripped, and as she fell, she twisted so we ended face-to-face, me atop her.

Zoe looked up and met my eyes. Hers widened, surprised and . . . delighted. A throaty laugh.

"It *is* you, isn't it?" She stroked the ruff on my neck. I growled, but she only smiled. "That hair is unmistakable. I don't know which is more beautiful—the woman or the wolf." Her eyes glinted. "Equally deadly either way, I'll bet."

She buried her fingers in my fur. I snapped. She laughed.

"Tetchy. You prefer the chase to the catch, don't you?" A wicked grin. "We can have another go. You've won this round, so I'll give you your forfeit—tell you what I know about the letter. But if you'd rather play some more before we get down to business, I'm game."

I lifted my head to look for Clay. Zoe brushed her fingertips along the fur at my throat. I snapped again.

"Come now, I'm only curious. I've never touched a werewolf. The only two I've met weren't the sort I cared to talk to, much less touch."

She leaned back for a better look. "A female werewolf.

There can't be many of you around. Shame really. Women make the better predators, I've always said. Or certainly the more interesting ones."

She continued to talk. Being unable to speak gave me a good excuse for not participating in the conversation. Zoe didn't seem to mind, just lay there on her back, pinned by a wolf, chatting as calmly as if we were back in Miller's, having a beer.

About ten minutes after my takedown, the bushes rustled. Clay stepped through, Changed into human form and dressed in sweatpants and an oversized T-shirt. Clothesline pickings.

"Got you some clothes, darling," he said. "Should fit, but probably not well."

He laid them just outside a thicket where I could Change. At the sound of his voice, Zoe had started. Then she looked over at him, and her eyes narrowed. Turning back to me, she said, "I think we can keep this between ourselves, don't you?"

Clay put his foot on Zoe's sternum. I backed off her and loped to the thicket to Change.

"Thank God," Zoe said when I returned. "He hasn't stopped talking since you left."

She glared up at Clay, who stood exactly as I'd left him, his mouth shut, as it likely had been the whole time I'd been gone.

"You can get off me now," she said.

He lifted his foot and walked over to me, hand brushing mine. "I'll scout, make sure we don't have any unexpected guests. You need me, just shout."

"I will."

Clay glanced back at Zoe, then at me. "Have fun, darling."

"Dah-lin'?" Zoe mimicked as Clay walked away. She shuddered. "Please don't tell me that's daddy wolf."

"Don't tell her then," Clay said without turning. "None of her business."

Zoe made a face as she brushed herself off. "Just brimming with southern charm, isn't he? You could do so much better." Her gaze met mine and she stretched again. "No? Why don't we play a little more chase-and-pounce, and see if I can't change your mind?"

"If we play chase-and-pounce again, you're not going to like how it ends. When a werewolf chases, the wolf expects a kill. One frustrated hunt it can handle. Not two."

"Unless the prey can't be killed."

"The predator can sure as hell try."

She threw back her head and laughed. "Touché. As tempting as a chase would be, it clearly won't arouse the kind of frustration I'd care to relieve. I'll surrender my forfeit, then. Tell me more about this letter, and I'll see what I can remember."

So I did, leaving out how we got the letter, how we opened the portal, how we were still in possession of the letter, and focusing instead on the results and what little information we'd gleaned about it.

After I finished, she leaned back and closed her eyes. "The *From Hell* letter? I know I should remember more but . . ." She looked at me and shook her head. "Remembering a job I did eighty years ago is no different than asking a hundred-year-old human to remember a work assignment he undertook at twenty. The letter was historically significant, yes, but the circumstances surrounding the theft were obviously mundane enough that I can barely remember anything more than that I *did* do this job."

"There was a spell cast on the original location. Do you remember that?"

She nodded. "A spell to keep the letter—all the letters—from being stolen by any living being. Presumably someone on the police force was a sorcerer, and cast the spell to protect them. That's why the buyer hired me."

"This buyer . . . do you remember who it was?"

"Of course. He is—or was—a regular customer of mine."

When she didn't continue, I said, "Can you provide a name?"

She met my gaze. "I'd rather you did, and I can confirm or deny."

"And I'd rather *you*—"

"His grandson continues to be a customer of mine, and I don't babble about my clients, past or present, unless there is a very good reason. Granted, a zombie-spewing portal is indeed a good reason, but if you took that letter, as you claim, then you already know the grandson's name."

"Patrick Shanahan."

She nodded. "The original purchaser was his grandfather, Theodore."

"Did Shanahan commission the theft himself?"

"I presume so . . ."

"But you don't remember."

She shook her head.

"Do you remember whether your client wanted this

letter specifically? Or just something from the Ripper files?"

"I believe any . . . no, maybe it was . . ." A sharp shake of her head. "Something snagged there, but it's not coming free."

When I glanced in Clay's direction, she said, "You don't need to call in the muscle to work me over."

"That wasn't—"

"If you want to call your mate over to get his opinion on my sincerity, go ahead, but I have no reason to block you. You've just informed me that my city has an open dimensional portal, leaking zombies. I've lived here all my life and have no intention of leaving, so I'd just as soon see this portal closed."

"That may be so, but I doubt Toronto is about to be sucked into a dimensional portal, and these zombies aren't after *you*."

"That's just because they haven't run across me yet. Zombies don't like vampires very much. Jealousy, I suppose—two kinds of undead, one immune to harm, the other dropping body parts with every sneeze. So I have no incentive to lie about this letter. Let me think about it overnight and I'm sure I'll remember more."

I didn't bother asking about Shanahan. If she knew where he'd run to, she was more likely to tip him off than tell me where to find him.

I gave her my cell number.

"So I leave with a phone number," she said. "Not bad, but it would be nice to have a name attached."

When I didn't respond, she laughed and patted my arm.

"No matter. A smaller challenge before the big one, and something to discuss next time."

She squeezed my arm, shot a look at Clay, then sauntered into the night.

Clay rolled his eyes. "Vampires."

Jeremy had struck out with Robert and Jaime too, leaving messages for both, but having heard nothing back.

"God, I hate running in place," I said, stalking into our hotel room. "This is why we don't have a treadmill. Energy expended and no destination reached. Frustrating."

Clay walked up behind me and put his hands on my hips. "Almost as frustrating as hunting with no catch."

"Or a catch that didn't mind being hunted."

He chuckled against my neck. "I thought you liked hunting willing prey."

"Only one kind. Or, I should say, one specific instance of one kind."

"Well, then, what if that one specific instance offered to compensate for your loss. It's not too late to slip back to the park. Change, hunt and . . ." He nipped my earlobe. "Do as you wish."

I pressed back, felt him hardening against me and shuddered. "The one problem with that scenario. I *can't* do as I wish."

His hands traveled under my shirt and up my sides.

"Or maybe we could try," I said. "Just one more time. A change of position perhaps." I bent forward and thrust back against him. "I know you like it face-to-face, but in an emergency . . ."

A soft growl. "In an emergency, yes, and if you really want to . . ."

I slid my pants down my hips and guided his hand between my legs. "Does it feel like I really want to?"

Another growl, harder this time, as his fingers slid into me.

"Maybe if I just . . . start. Play a bit," he said. "That couldn't hurt."

"Couldn't hurt at all."

I reached behind me, undid his jeans and reached inside. As I held him and arched my hips back to meet him, I closed my eyes, imagined him sliding in . . . and stopping partway.

"Not going to work, is it?" I said.

"I can try, but—"

"Doesn't matter." I looked over my shoulder. "You can try stopping, but once we start, I'm going to do my damnedest to get the rest of it."

He chuckled. "How about we revert to plan A? A jog back to the park, a private hunt, we Change back and you take your forfeit in another way."

"Once we Change, it's only going to get worse. The human side might be able to argue logic, but the wolf knows exactly what she wants. Take me for a run tonight, and it's not rabbits I'm going to want to hunt."

A growling laugh. "Funny, that's what I was thinking earlier, watching you run ahead of me. Had a helluva time remembering you were chasing someone, not running away to tease me."

I leaned over the bed, one hand down to hold myself up, the other reaching between my legs. I found him and tugged him to me. He tensed.

"Don't worry," I said. "I'm being good. Just . . . teasing."

He let out a low growl as I stroked him, still prodding against me.

"Teasing who?" he said. "You or me?"

I grinned. "Both. That's the best kind."

He shifted forward, pushing another half-inch. My eyelids fluttered, and I pushed back. Just another—

"Better stop," he growled.

I slid my hand up his shaft, fixing a stopper for myself, and stroked him from there, letting him thrust just that inch or so, barely parting me, the teasing so exquisite that I had to dig my fingers into the bed to keep from losing my balance.

When it was too much, and I was ready to just let my hand "accidentally" slip off him and let him slip into me, I arched forward onto the balls of my feet, leaning farther over the bed, and slid his shaft down lengthwise along me. Then I held him there, tight against me, and let him thrust.

Didn't take more than a few minutes. Then I slid face-first onto the bed, rolling onto my side as my belly touched down. He crawled in behind me, pressing up against my back, breath tickling the back of my head.

"Getting more inventive," he murmured.

I chuckled. "By the time this baby comes, we'll have figured out all the tricks."

Too lazy to move, I pulled down a pillow, tucked it under my head and closed my eyes. Within minutes, I was asleep.

The next morning we headed straight to the airport to pick up Antonio and Nick, the two remaining members of the Pack.

At five, the Pack was at its lowest recorded size. Changing that wasn't as easy as it might seem. In the past, Packs grew primarily through procreation, with werewolves fathering babies and taking the sons, the gender that carried the werewolf gene. In a modern Pack, with modern sensibilities and a modern Alpha, taking children from their mothers wouldn't happen. Under Jeremy's rule, Pack wolves had two options: surrogacy—and take the child regardless of gender—or joint-custody arrangements with the mother, since by the time a boy had his first Change, he was college-aged and old enough to keep that part of his life from his mother.

The problem was that, until Clay and me, no one in the Pack had showed any inclination to procreate. Antonio was content with one son—Nick—as Jeremy was with Clay. Maybe someday Logan or Peter would have had children, but they were gone now, killed in a mutt uprising five years ago. As for Nick, no one expected him to embrace fatherhood anytime soon, if ever. Although Clay and I were now doing our part, neither of us had any interest in replenishing the ranks by ourselves.

The other method of increasing Pack ranks was assimilation—taking in mutts who wished to join after they proved themselves capable of following Pack Law. Again, this worked far better under previous Alphas. Back in the days when Pack wolves hunted mutts for sport, there'd been no shortage of mutts clamoring for membership.

Under Jeremy, though, the Pack only harassed man-eaters, who certainly didn't qualify for Pack membership without serious rehabilitation. Most mutts who've developed a taste for hunting humans have no interest in being "fixed."

So far, the only candidates had proven disappointing: a closet man-eater hoping to escape detection by hiding in our ranks, one randy SOB hoping that the Pack's communal attitudes extended to communal sex privileges with the sole female werewolf, and a problem gambler hoping the wealthy Pack families would buy his loyalty by paying off his creditors.

Marsten finally seemed serious about getting off the fence and joining the Pack. So our numbers were likely to increase by one. Yet until then, we didn't consider him full Pack, which is why no one had suggested calling him to Toronto with Antonio and Nick.

So, for now, we were five.

I was the first to spot Nick and Antonio, and I hurried over as fast as I could waddle. Bear hugs, kisses and backslaps ensued, and I'm sure anyone watching would've thought we hadn't seen each another in years, instead of just a couple of weeks.

Antonio had been Jeremy's best friend since child-hood. Nick and Clay were also lifelong friends. Both Sorrentinos were dark-haired and dark-eyed. Nick was a half-head taller than his father, with the polished good looks of someone who doesn't think hairstylists, fashion magazines and skin cream are only for women, but who draws the line at manicures and facials.

Normally, Nick would have swept me off my feet and kissed me in a way that wasn't exactly fraternal. Today, though, he stopped short, and settled for a hug and a smack on the lips.

"Am I getting too big to pick up?" I said.

He smiled. "No, I'm just being careful what I do to a pregnant lady in public." He leaned down to my ear. "Wait until later, and I'll make up for it."

"I heard that," Clay said.

Nick grinned. "Of course you did. And you can see it too, if you want. Maybe learn something."

Clay made a comment, and Nick turned to answer, but his gaze snagged on my stomach. A look passed through his eyes as if he still wasn't quite sure what it was, how it got there or, most important, what it would mean.

I grabbed Nick's hand and squeezed it. Our eyes met, and I smiled. He leaned down to kiss me again. I put my hands on his stubble-covered cheeks.

"Couldn't find time to shave?" I teased.

"I'm growing a beard." He tilted his head and posed. "What do you think?"

"Sexy. The gray adds a nice touch of sophistication."

"Gray?" His hand shot to his cheek.

Behind me, Antonio laughed, then caught me up in a hug that *did* lift me off the ground. "You realize he's going to spend the rest of the day in front of the mirror looking for that gray?"

"I think it's sexy," I said.

Nick turned to Clay.

"No," Clay said. "You're not borrowing my razor. You grew it, you get rid of it."

"Troublemaker," Antonio murmured to me.

He kissed my cheek, then leaned back for a better look. The shortest member of the Pack, a couple of inches under my five feet ten, Antonio was also still the brawniest and most powerful. He and Nick had passed themselves off as brothers for as long as I'd known them. Nick had been born when Antonio was a teen, so—combined with a werewolf's slow aging, and Antonio's zeal for healthy living—it had been decades since they *could* have passed for father and son.

"You look more beautiful every time I see you," Antonio said. "Pregnancy suits you."

I made a face. "I'm huge. Getting bigger by the hour."

"You're pregnant. You're not supposed to be getting smaller." One arm still around me, Antonio turned to the others. "So, I hear you have a little adventure for us."

Theories

I SLID INTO THE BACKSEAT BESIDE NICK. CLAY SQUEEZED IN on my other side.

"Hey, Jer?" I said as we shifted around and fished for our seat belts. "Remember when you replaced the Explorer and I suggested buying the model with the third-row seat? Really would have been a good idea."

"That's why I offered to sit back there," Jeremy said from the passenger seat.

"And how would that help? I'm not any wider than you. All my extra load is up front." I bumped Nick's hip. "You've got another couple more inches. Shove over."

"This is fine." Nick put his arm around me. "Nice and cozy."

I swatted him away. "Move."

"Settle down and buckle up, kids, so I can drive," Antonio said, looking in the rearview mirror. He glanced over at Jeremy. "Maybe we should finish raising this generation before we start another one."

Jeremy shook his head.

"I didn't want to bring this up in the terminal," Antonio

said as he turned out of the parking building. "But does *this* have something to do with your problem?"

He handed Jeremy a folded sheet of paper. Jeremy read it, face expressionless. When he lowered and re-folded it, I undid my belt and reached through the open-ing between the front seats. Jeremy hesitated, then handed it to me.

"They gave us that when we got off the plane," Antonio said.

Clay looked over my shoulder as I read: it was a public health announcement, warning of cholera in the munici-pal water supply.

"Cholera?" I said. "I thought it was E. coli."

"So did they, at first, I suspect," Jeremy said. "That would be the natural assumption, given the source and the symptoms."

"What's cholera?" Nick asked.

"It's a bacterium that gets into the water. Overcrowd-ing and poor sanitation are the usual culprits. It's almost unknown in the Western world now, but it was a serious problem in the nineteenth century."

"Victorian England," I said.

Jeremy nodded.

Cholera is an intestinal infection, not unlike E. coli. The main symptoms are diarrhea and vomiting, which can lead to dehydration and eventual death, but only if left untreated. With treatment and fluid replacement, the fa-tality rate is less than 1 percent.

Cholera is transmitted through feces, primarily by food and water becoming contaminated with raw sewage. Jeremy was pretty sure London's cholera problem had been resolved shortly before the time of Jack the Ripper, but sporadic cases had continued, as the problems of overcrowding and poor hygiene continued.

As for how cholera got into Toronto's water supply . . . according to Jeremy it was well-nigh impossible. It shouldn't happen with modern sewage and water systems. Not by any natural means. But by now we were pretty sure "natural means" had nothing to do with the problems Toronto was experiencing.

Opening that portal had let out more than a couple of Victorian zombies. Jaime had warned us about smallpox leaking through that other portal. Somehow these zombies had brought a little of their home with them . . . and all of our modern precautions couldn't protect against it.

"Cholera isn't a cause for concern," Jeremy said. "If it was, we'd be leaving. Tourism will suffer, which the city doesn't need after last year's SARS outbreak, but that's likely to be the extent of the damage. It was caught quickly enough to avoid fatalities or long-term health problems."

When I didn't answer, he glanced back at me. "If you're concerned, go ahead and call your local media contacts."

I made those calls. I'd been dying to since all this started, but Jeremy had wanted me keeping a low profile. He didn't think they could add anything we weren't finding in the papers, and he was right. They did, however, reassure me that the city didn't seem to be downplaying the severity of the cholera outbreak. If anything, after SARS, they were being overcautious. Right now, they were busy trying to clean up the system, which seemed to be far more difficult than it should be, confirming this was no natural outbreak.

We stopped in Kensington market on the way back to the hotel to load up on food. While the guys did that, I stayed in the SUV and listened to the radio. Clay stayed with me, although after five minutes hearing him grouse about wanting fresh air and a leg stretch, I shoved him out, locked the door and let him get his air and exercise pacing around the vehicle and pounding on the windows.

Finding reliable news updates on the cholera situation wasn't easy. The national broadcaster, CBC, paraded a steady queue of public officials, who all repeated the same message: "Everything is under control." As if, by getting enough people to say it, it would become truth.

Then there were the private stations. A talk radio show had a historian on who was giving graphic accounts of Victorian cholera outbreaks. Then I hit a classic rock station located outside Toronto that kept gleefully referring to the situation as a cholera "epidemic," and speculating that it was caused by the city's high population density, congratulating themselves for living elsewhere. Next came a station playing only prerecorded music—I suspected a lone sound technician had lost the straw-draw, staying behind while all his coworkers headed for the hills . . . or at least Barrie.

I'd reached a contemporary station morning show, complete with giggling hosts, when Jeremy rapped at the window. I opened the door and climbed into the back as they loaded the groceries into the rear hatch.

* * *

Back to the hotel. As we walked into the lobby, Nick was telling us about his trip to Cleveland last week, where he'd sat in on labor dispute talks at one of his father's factories.

Clay looked over at Antonio. "What'd he do to deserve that?"

Antonio laughed. "It wasn't a punishment. He volunteered."

I nudged Nick. "So what'd you do . . . that you haven't told him about yet?"

"Ha-ha. I volunteered with no ulterior motive. I told you I'm trying to learn more about the business."

"So how'd it go?"

"It was . . . interesting."

"In other words, boring as hell," Clay said as we passed the lounge. "In Cleveland, no less."

"Cleveland's not that bad—"

"Jeremy!" a woman's voice called.

We all turned, tracking her to the lounge. There, in one of the oversized armchairs, a woman was getting to her feet, hand raised in a hesitant wave, an even more hesitant smile on her face. She wore a yellow sundress that showed off a generous portion of bare leg. Red hair tumbled down her back in that sort of artless, sexy tangle you usually only see on cover models.

"Jaime," Jeremy said, and headed toward her.

She stepped forward . . . and tripped over the suitcase she'd propped at her feet. Jeremy lunged to steady her, and we all hurried forward, except Clay, who let out a small sigh before bringing up the rear.

Jaime regained her balance with mumbled apologies, her face going as red as her hair. She reached down for her suitcase and bopped heads with Jeremy, who was already picking it up. More apologies.

"Hey, Jaime," I said, walking forward. "This is a surprise."

Behind me, Clay made a small noise, as if it wasn't a surprise to him at all. Jaime's gaze swung to mine and, with a soft exhale of relief, she sidestepped Jeremy and hurried over to me.

"Elena. God, you look—"

"Huge?"

"I was going to say 'great.' So how's the baby? Kicking yet? Keeping you up at night?"

"Not yet," I said. "I—"

"What are you doing here, Jaime?" Clay asked.

I glowered at him.

"What?" he said. "If no one else is going to ask . . ."

"I'm sure you're all wondering the same thing," Jaime said. "I had a late show last night, and didn't get Jeremy's message until the wee hours."

"So you hopped on a plane to deliver your reply in person?" Clay asked.

Jaime only laughed. "Something like that. Actually, I'm planning a Toronto show this winter, and I've been meaning to check out potential venues. I hate relying on staff for that—they always get a place that fits all the requirements but . . ." A small shiver. "Well, there are things they can't check. I've done one too many shows in a spook-infested auditorium. Anyway, this seemed like a good time to visit. I can offer my services to you guys while I'm here, and save you some money on long-distance phone bills."

"Great," I said. "Maybe you can contact—"

Jeremy motioned for me to wait before he interrupted.

"Let's take this conversation upstairs, where we can talk privately . . . and get Elena a proper breakfast."

Jeremy bent to lift Jaime's carry-on bag, but Clay and Nick stepped forward, one grabbing the suitcase, the other the carry-on.

"Jaime, you remember Antonio and Nick?" Jeremy asked.

She did. Last winter, the five of us had gone skiing in Vermont at the same time Jaime was doing an appearance at a nearby resort, and we'd spent an afternoon and evening together. As I might have expected, Nick had been keen to get to know Jaime better, but once he'd realized her interests lay elsewhere—and where they lay—he'd backed off.

We laid out a spread of bagels with cheese, blintzes and fruit in Jeremy's room as we talked things over.

"So you guys could probably use some on-scene necro help to deal with the zombies," Jaime said.

"This might be more than you bargained for," Jeremy warned her. "Did you get a notice about the cholera on the plane? That appears to be connected. And the reason I called you last night was to say that these zombies aren't as easy to kill as we thought. This might not be the sort of thing you want to get involved in."

She managed a smile. "Because I have a bad habit of needing rescue every time I *do* get involved?"

"There is that," Clay muttered.

Jaime waved me off before I could jump in. "Clay's right. My track record sucks. I always end up playing damsel-in-distress."

"No," Jeremy said. "You've had some bad luck, but only because your skills made you a target."

"And the bad guys love to pick on the defenseless necromancer. This time, though, I swear I won't get kidnapped or possessed."

The corners of Jeremy's mouth twitched. "All right, then. If you're sure you want to—"

"I do."

"Then I'd welcome the help."

Antonio, Nick and I chimed in with our agreement, but Jaime's gaze swept past us to Clay.

"Long as you're here, you might as well stay," he said. "Hang around and do your stuff until we can use you."

"What Clay means is—" I began.

"Exactly what he said," she said. "If Clayton says I can stay, I feel almost welcome. Now, let's talk about zombies."

"Controlled zombies," she said after I finished. "Don't ask me how that's possible, but that has to be the answer. Remember I said I'd make some calls? Well, I didn't find out much that seemed helpful at the time, but I did learn a few things about controlled dimensional zombies. Like ones controlled by a necromancer, they can't be killed until that control is severed. Instead of just staying alive, though, they disintegrate, and their soul returns to the dimensional holding tank. If the door's still open . . ."

"They walk back out."

"Logically, these shouldn't be controlled zombies. But if it looks like a duck and quacks like a duck . . . It would also explain why that one at the truck stop was so quick to follow you."

"His controller sent him after me," I said.

"Right. The controller must want the letter back, and he's convinced the zombies that getting it will benefit them."

"Would they need that incentive?" Jeremy said.

"It would help. Zombies have to do what their controller says, but they do a better job when properly motivated."

"Like any worker," Antonio said.

Jaime smiled. "Exactly. They still have conscious will, if not free will."

I pushed off the end of the bed and crossed the room to stretch my legs . . . and get another peach. "But we're back to the original problem with the controller theory. The portal was created a hundred and twenty years ago. To still be alive, that sorcerer would need to have found the secret to immortality, which, unless I'm mistaken, is unlikely to the point of impossible."

"Could something like that be passed on generationally?" Jeremy asked.

"Like 'I hereby bequeath control of my zombies to my son'?" She paused. "I suppose it's possible."

I nodded. "If so, then it would also make sense to pass on the portal itself . . . or the device that contains it."

"Patrick Shanahan?" Clay said.

Jeremy nodded, and explained who Shanahan was.

"Shanahan could be it," Jaime said. "If his grandfather commissioned the theft, it could have been to get his own portal back."

"It would be more likely to be a great-grandfather," Jeremy mused. "Or even great-great, given the timing."

"Maybe *he* was Jack the Ripper," Nick said. "The great-grandfather."

I waved my half-eaten peach at him. "So he created the portal, with the zombies, and sent it to the police, knowing it would go into the files. Then, if the police started getting close, he could just release his zombies—"

"Who could destroy the evidence," Jaime said. "The ultimate inside job."

"Only the police never did get close, so he emigrates to Canada. At some point, his son or grandson, Theodore Shanahan, hires a local thief to get the letter back."

"Yes," Jeremy said. "It makes sense, but there are too many—"

"Creative jumps and leaps of faith," I finished. "I know. Regardless of how the portal could have been created, Patrick Shanahan is the best, if not the only possible, zombie controller."

"If there *is* a controller," Clay said. "But no harm hunting the guy down."

"That part you don't mind," I said, grinning as I gave him half my handful of blueberries. "Let's just hope he hasn't hightailed it to parts unknown."

"Can't," Jaime said. "When the zombies are resurrected at the portal, they return to him. Like homing pigeons. So the controller has to stay close by."

"There's our plan, then," I said. "We find one of the zombies, then kill him, and someone waits at the portal to follow him back to his controller."

Rats

KILL A ZOMBIE, THEN FOLLOW HIM OR HER BACK TO THE controller. Sounded simple enough. Or it would be, once we found a zombie to kill.

Jeremy decided we'd wait until nightfall, then return to the warehouse district where we'd found Rose. She'd obviously been comfortable there, so she might return. Even if we couldn't find a zombie, we were pretty sure one would eventually find me.

In the meantime, Jeremy and Antonio would return to Shanahan's house, this time searching for clues not about the letter, but about Shanahan's current where-abouts. Clay, Nick and I would visit the person most likely to have had contact with Shanahan—his secretary.

While Antonio and Nick checked in and unpacked, I helped Jaime do the same. She'd already booked a room, but it was two floors from ours, so Jeremy insisted she switch to the same floor. Changing rooms was easy enough—with the cholera outbreak, the concierge told us half of their reservations had been canceled, and a lot of current guests had decided to cut their visit short.

Clay brought Jaime's luggage over from our room, then left us to unpack. Or he pretended to leave, though I knew he'd stay close, probably in the hallway.

As soon as the door closed behind him, Jaime wilted against the wall.

"Made a complete jackass of myself, didn't I?" she said.

"What do you mean?" I said as I stooped to unzip her suitcase.

"I'll get that," she said. "Sounds like you'll have a busy day. Sit while you can."

When I hesitated, she took the suitcase and shooed me to the bed.

"I do want to do a Toronto show," she said as she took out her toiletry bag. "I wasn't making that up."

"I never—"

She slanted a look my way. "Come on. I show up with some lame story about wanting to check out show venues, and the first thing you all thought was 'Yeah, right.' But it's true. I plan to do a winter appearance, and I need to check out places. I thought this would be a good time to do that if it means I can help you guys with this. Help all of you." Another quick look at me. "Not just Jeremy."

"I don't think you showed up because of Jeremy."

"Well, that makes one of us." She sighed and hung a dress in the closet. "I do want to help, but if it had been someone else? Would I have been on that plane so fast?" She shook her head and took a shirt from her suitcase. "I'm trying to get past it. It's embarrassing."

"Being attracted to someone isn't a cause for embarrassment."

She gave me a look. "Tripping over my feet every time I see him? Tripping over my tongue every time I talk to him? For *three years*? With no sign that he's the least bit interested in return?"

"With Jeremy—"

"I can't expect the usual signs, I know. But he has to know how I feel. Hell, everybody else does."

"If you'd let me ask—"

She waved her hands frantically. "Oh, God. Stop suggesting it or I'm liable to break down and say 'Go ahead.' Can you imagine? It's like in fifth grade, getting your friend to pass a guy a note asking if he likes you."

"It wouldn't be—"

She met my gaze. "Please, don't. I'm not being coy, pretending I don't want you to when really I'm hoping you'll go ahead and do it. Two years ago, maybe I would have. But now . . ." She dropped her gaze to the shirt in her hands, refolding it. "I'm starting to feel like, maybe, Jeremy and I, you know, can still be friends. As cliché as that sounds, it's not so bad."

She took a deep breath, then firmly shook her head and hung up the shirt. "Once I get past that schoolgirl-flustered stage when I first see him, I'm okay, and I can talk to him. Better yet, he listens." A small smile. "Even talks in return sometimes."

"That's a good sign. Listening Jeremy's good at. Talking? Not if it's remotely personal."

"I know. And the stuff I can talk to him about . . ." When she grabbed a handful of shirts, her fingers were trembling slightly. "It's not stuff I normally talk about. I don't feel I have to be . . . I don't know, my showbiz self." She flashed a smile my way. "Who knows, maybe someday I'll even change his mind. Until then, though, it's good."

I wished I could help. I really did. Two years ago, I hadn't been quick to encourage her. I'd liked Jaime well enough, but she didn't seem a good match for Jeremy. I still wasn't sure that she was, but I now thought she deserved the chance to find out.

After Jaime finished unpacking, she took off to investigate potential venues for a future show. Clay, Nick and I got ready for our trip to Shanahan's office. While his administrative assistant wouldn't tell strangers where he was hiding, he or she might be persuaded to divulge a few details to a pair of urban professionals about to have their first baby and looking to make a very large investment to safeguard their child's future.

"I'll play husband and daddy-to-be," Nick said as we walked into the room.

"Yeah?" Clay said. "Well, not to complicate things, but how about the *real* husband and daddy-to-be plays the husband and daddy-to-be?"

"Won't work. You don't look the part. You look like the actor hired to *play* the part."

Clay made a rude noise and grabbed his wallet from the nightstand.

I turned to Clay. "Since when do you ever *want* to play-act anyway? If you do, then fine, but if you're just complaining for—"

"Go ahead," Clay said. "Though I don't see how he looks any more like your husband than I do."

"He doesn't. But if we're about to have our first baby and going to Shanahan for investment advice, we have to look and act like urban professionals. Nick does. I can. You . . . can't. And you'd hate trying. So let's stop arguing. We still need to do a quick bit of shopping. I only have two sets of clothes, and neither screams prospective investment banker client." I picked up my sunglasses, then glanced back at Clay. "Oh, and speaking of disguises, remember to lend Nick your ring."

"Should I wear it?" Nick said. "If I'm wearing a wedding band and you're not, won't that look—"

His gaze went to my hand and he stopped, then grabbed it and lifted the ring finger, complete with both engagement and wedding ring. I'd worn the engagement ring on and off for years, and "on" for the past five, a sign to Clay that I was staying.

As for the wedding bands, while he'd worn his for fifteen years, to show that he considered himself married—whether I agreed or not—my own had stayed in the original case.

"When did you start wearing—?" Nick began.

"When I got pregnant. Though I may have to stop wearing it soon. It's getting tight."

"Ah." Nick smiled and dropped my hand. "Didn't want to walk around looking pregnant and unwed. I'll lay dibs on how fast that comes off once the baby's here."

I reached for the door handle. "It's not."

Clay grabbed the door and opened it for me. Nick jumped forward and pushed it shut again.

"Whoa, hold on. You're going to keep wearing it? Even after the baby?"

"What? You think I'm willing to have Clay's baby, but not wear his ring?" I grinned at Clay. "We're even thinking of making it legal."

"Wha—? Married? What happened to 'not in this life-time, no way, no how'?"

"Did I say that?"

Clay opened the door. "More than once."

"Damn."

"But I won't hold you to it."

"Good of you."

"Wait a second," Nick said. "When did all this—?"

The closing of the door drowned out the rest as we headed into the hall.

Shanahan's secretary wasn't talking, but when we "suggested" taking our baby investment elsewhere, she admitted that he called in daily for messages. We gave her my cell phone number and Nick's. If Shanahan *was* the zombie's controller—and the one giving the orders to kidnap me—then if his secretary announced he'd had a visit from a blond pregnant woman, anxious to speak to him, he might make the logical leap. In fact, he probably would. All the better. With any luck, the opportunity to set up a meeting and catch me would prove irresistible.

Jeremy and Antonio's search of Shanahan's house hadn't revealed anything that would tell us where he was. They'd gathered a few leads—his ex-wife's address, restaurants he liked to frequent, the name of his golf club and such. Chances were that a guy on the run isn't going to pop by the club for a round, but unless we came up with something better, they'd check it out tomorrow.

* * *

After dinner, the Pack headed to the warehouse district where we'd first found Rose. It was barely dusk, but the area was empty enough that we didn't need to wait until nightfall. Jeremy wanted us to try hooking up with Zoe at Miller's again. She hadn't called, maybe because she didn't plan to or maybe because she hadn't remembered anything, but she was now our best source of information on the Shanahan family. First, though, we'd hunt for Rose.

We found her trail easily enough. Found a whole snarl of them, so many that it was difficult to tell whether any of them were fresh.

To untangle the mess, Jeremy split us up into two teams. He assigned Nick, Clay and me the west side of the area.

The second tendril we followed led to the side door of an empty building plastered with yellowed and curling CLUB VERTIGO COMING SOON signs. One look at the building, with its boarded-up windows and spidery cracks in the foundation, and I could have predicted to the hopeful club owners that their dream would never see fruition, buried under a mountain of astronomical contractor quotes. Or maybe the owners hadn't been as enthusiastically naive as they seemed. Schemes for new clubs were great cons for bilking youthful investors.

At the doorway, Clay stopped, then bent for a better sniff of the ground.

"Got an exit trail too," he said. "Been and gone."

I looked around to make sure no one was passing either end of the alley, then crouched and inhaled.

"More than one 'been and gone,' " I said.

"Could be her hideout," Nick said. "Can we get inside?"

Before I could answer, Clay did. "We should get Jeremy and Antonio first."

"Never thought I'd hear you say that," Nick said.

"Gotta be careful these days."

Nick looked over at me—at my stomach—then nodded. "I'll run and grab them."

We stayed just inside the doorway until our eyes adjusted to the dark. The only source of light was the ribbons of moonlight peeking through the planks covering the windows. Even after our eyes adjusted, we could see little more than shapes.

"Should we Change?" I whispered to Jeremy.

He peered inside. "I think it'll be easier to search like this for now."

"Split up, then?"

Jeremy nodded. "We'll stay on this floor. You three take the north side. Meet back here when you're done."

The search was slow-going. Rose's scent permeated the place. Her trails seemed to crisscross in and out of every room, and there were plenty of rooms to crisscross through. From the outside, the place had looked like a warehouse, but in here it was a warren of small rooms, as if it had been converted to offices at some point before its decline. Searching as wolves would have been near-impossible. Turning door handles with your teeth is a real bitch.

We reached a closed door where the floor was thick with scent trails. I stood watch while Nick threw open the door and Clay wheeled through.

A muffled oath. Nick and I both rushed to Clay's aid. My foot hit a rotted board and I pitched forward. Nick lunged for me, and Clay turned, but my ankle twisted and I went down onto my knees before either could grab me.

As I fell, I sent up a cloud of dust that launched a sneezing fit. I pressed my hands over my mouth and nose to stifle it.

Clay knelt beside me. "You okay?"

"Just klutzy," I said. "And that, sadly, I can't even blame on being pregnant." I swallowed an impending sneeze. "Now that I've alerted anyone in here to our presence—"

Something hissed beside me. I turned to see a rat, reared up, teeth bared. Animals smelling their first were-wolf usually run, but city rats can lose their natural fear of predators. This one opened his mouth to hiss again. Clay's foot caught it in the chest, and it flew across the hall and hit the wall with a splat.

"Touchdown!" Nick said.

Clay only curled his lip.

"Never did like rats much, did you?" Nick said.

"Disease-ridden vermin," Clay said. "Worse than scavengers. The room's crawling with them. Must be a nest."

Another rat peered out the partly open door, its nose twitching. Then it charged. Clay drop-kicked it into the wall beside its brethren.

"Next one's mine," Nick said.

"Sorry, guys," I said as I stood. "As much fun as rat-punting might be, we—"

I stopped and inhaled. Another rat appeared in the doorway. Nick drew back his foot. I flew forward and knocked the rat back into the room, then slammed the door.

"What, only Clay gets to punt rats?" Nick said.

Clay shrugged. "With me, it's not animal cruelty. It's my nature. You don't get that excuse."

Nick sputtered and took a swipe at Clay with his foot, trying to hook the back of his knees. Clay grabbed Nick's foot and Nick started toppling backward, but I grabbed him.

"Are you guys trying to make *sure* Rose will hear us if she's here? I closed the door because there's something wrong with those rats. Can't you smell it?"

Nick only shook his head, but Clay walked to the dead ones, hunkered down, sniffed, then made a face.

"Disease-ridden vermin, like I said." Another sniff. "What is that?"

"I don't know, but—"

A floorboard creaked down the hall. Clay let out a silent "shit." Nick automatically reached for the nearest door—the one to the rat room—but stopped before we had to say anything.

Jeremy and Antonio turned the corner, coming down the hall.

"Find something?" Antonio whispered. "We thought we heard sounds of a scuffle."

I shot a covert glare at Clay and Nick, but only said, "Clay found a nest of sick rats. They gave us a start. Sorry."

Jeremy knelt beside the dead pair of rats.

"They smell diseased," I said. "What is it?"

"Nothing I recognize. You said there's—"

Claws scrabbled against the closed door. Jeremy pointed. I nodded. He waved for us to step back, then eased the door open a crack and leaned into it for a better look.

At the base, tiny teeth and claws flashed in the opening. Beside me, Clay rocked forward onto the balls of his feet, tensed, ready to spring if the rodent somehow managed to squeeze through the half-inch crack. After a moment, Jeremy pulled the door shut.

He turned to us. "I'm going to get a better look in there."

Jeremy motioned Clay to the door, to act as rat-punter, then gestured for Antonio and Nick to stand guard on either side of the hallway, in case Rose was still in the building. I backed up Jeremy's nose . . . from the hall.

Clay swung open the door and drop-kicked the first rat that lunged at him. The next two rats fell back, hissing and chattering. From where I was, I caught a glimpse inside—a small room with a blanket and a few boxes. They took two steps into the room, then Jeremy tapped Clay's shoulder, telling him to retreat. A last kick and squeal, and Clay went to close the door, but Jeremy stopped him.

"What's that?" he said, pointing at the floor. "Here, hold them off and I'll grab—"

Clay darted forward and snatched up whatever was there.

"Or you could do it for me . . ." Jeremy said as Clay backed out and slammed the door.

"What is it?" I asked.

Clay held up what looked like a half-chewed cocktail sausage. Then the smell hit me.

"A finger," I said with a small shudder. "A *chewed* finger. Isn't that—" I fought my revulsion and took a deeper breath. "It's Rose's."

"Think the rats got her?" Nick said.

When we all turned to look at him, he said, "What? She smells like she's rotting, right? And rats are scavengers."

Jeremy shook his head. "I think the rotting is what caused the finger loss, not the rats."

"So she's . . . falling apart?" I said.

"The extremities would be the first to go."

"Beyond the 'ewww' factor, this might be something we could use. If she falls apart, does that count as 'dead'?"

"With our luck, it won't," Clay said. "Maybe we should save this. In case we have to find all the pieces and reassemble them before we can close the portal."

"I don't think we want to be found carrying concealed body parts," Jeremy said. "And as soon as we get near a bathroom, I want you to wash your hands—well."

I walked beside Jeremy as we headed down the hall. "Could you tell what those rats have?"

"Not by smell, but there were several diseases commonly carried by rats a hundred years ago that you don't see often now."

"You think that's what it is then? Like the cholera and Rose's syphilis. Something else I released from the portal."

"It isn't your fault, Elena. There's little the Victorian era can throw at us today that we can't cure."

"So far . . ." I said. "But what if the next thing—"

"If we can get this portal closed, there won't be a 'next thing.' Concentrate on that, starting with finding a zombie who can lead us to the controller." Jeremy stopped and looked around. "We'll split up here. I doubt Rose is in the building, but she may return."

Fatherhood

WE FINISHED SEARCHING THE BUILDING, BUT FOUND NO sign of Rose. At eleven, Jeremy sent Clay and me to look for Zoe. This time, both Clay and I went into Miller's. Our entrance caused only the barest ripple of interest from the regulars. One sweep of the bar told us Zoe wasn't there.

"You looking for Zoe again?" the bartender asked.

I nodded and approached the counter. "Has she been in?"

He shook his head. "Might not be, either. You got lucky last night. If she does pop by, I'll tell her you were looking."

I thanked him and we left.

We went back to the warehouse, where we hung out with the others, waiting for Rose. When she didn't show up by two, Jeremy declared the night a bust. That was an understatement. The whole *day* had been a write-off, and we were no closer to finding Shanahan or a zombie or closing the portal than we had been when we woke up. Shanahan hadn't even called me back about the investment.

A jab in the stomach woke me the next morning, and I started awake, hands flying to my belly, twisting to tell Clay that I'd felt the baby move, I'd finally—

"Sorry," Nick mumbled.

I wasn't surprised to see Nick sleeping beside me. I'd have been more surprised if he hadn't been. When the Pack was together, shared sleeping arrangements were common . . . which isn't as kinky as it sounds. Our goofing around does push the boundaries of platonic pretty hard sometimes, but Clay and I are monogamous, fanatically so, as Nick often grouses. A wolf thing, one mate for life and all that.

"That was you? The jab?"

"Yeah." Nick blinked and rubbed his hand over his face. "Stray elbow. Next time, tell Jeremy you need a king-size bed—" He stopped. "Oh, you thought it was the baby kicking. Shit. I'm sorry."

"Don't be," I said, turning before he saw my expression. "It's this guy's fault." I prodded Clay, who was sprawled over two-thirds of the mattress. "Bed hog."

"It still *could've* been the baby. He could be practicing his rat-punting in there, and you're just passing it off as indigestion."

I leaned over to kiss his cheek. "Thanks."

I looked back at Clay, whose face was buried in the pillow. I laid my hand between his shoulder blades, and felt his back rising and falling in soft, steady snores.

"He's wiped," I whispered. "Too many nights worrying about me. We should let him sleep."

Nick nodded and we grabbed our clothes, then slipped into Nick's room to shower and dress.

We were checking out the room service menu when the door swung open and Clay wheeled in, wearing only his jeans, his curls mussed, eyes bleary but dark with worry that vanished as soon as he saw me.

"Whoops," Nick said, snaking a hand around my waist. "He caught us. We were about to get food without him."

I forced a smile. I knew why Clay had come bursting in. For ten years, anytime he'd gone to bed with me and woken up alone, there'd been a good chance that I wasn't just in the next room.

It had always happened like that. We'd get back together for a while—days, maybe weeks—then one morning, I'd wake and see him beside me, and my brain would scream, "What the hell are you doing? Have you forgotten what he did to you?" and I'd run.

Since I'd accepted that I wanted to stay, we'd had our spats, but I never took off. Yet sometimes, if I wasn't beside him in the morning, he wouldn't so much as use the bathroom until he knew where I was.

"You sleep okay?" he asked, still standing in the doorway.

I nodded. He nodded. Silence thudded down.

After a moment, he waved to the room service menu. "Go ahead and order."

"Glad we have your permission," Nick said.

Clay made a face and started to retreat.

"Hold on," Nick said. "Since you're up, we might as well eat someplace with tables. There's a restaurant across the road. Elena and I'll head over. You can catch up."

Clay hesitated, but he couldn't very well refuse, not without implying that Nick couldn't protect me.

"I'll shower and be right there."

We loaded up plates, then headed to the sidewalk patio to eat. Although it was lunchtime, the only other patrons were one couple who'd stayed inside, out of the late morning heat, so we had the patio to ourselves.

I ripped the top off my orange juice. "So you're going to be an uncle. Think you're up for it?"

When Nick murmured something and picked up his bagel, I laughed. "Oh, I'm kidding. We don't expect you to—"

He shook his head. "I *want* to be an uncle, Elena. A 'drop the kid off and I'll spoil him rotten' kind. I'll have fun teaching the little guy everything that'll drive his dad crazy. Payback time."

"Good. I just thought . . . well, you haven't seemed very happy about it. I understand that. Your friends are going to be parents. Things will change—"

"Sure, but it wasn't like you guys were out partying with me in the first place. Hell, I had to twist Clay's arm to get him out to a club even when he was single, and then it was a couple of drinks, no girls and home by midnight for a run or a hunt, because that was his idea of boys' night out. You coming along was a godsend, because at least he'll socialize a bit for your sake. But fears that our wild partying days will be curbed by a new baby?" He snorted a laugh. "If anything, a baby might drive you guys out of the house more often, and I'm not complaining about that."

"True. But a baby will mean Clay and I will have to be more careful, take things easier."

Nick lifted his brows.

"A bit easier."

"I'm not worried. I'm thrilled for you guys. And I'll love being an uncle. That's the role I'm cut out for. Uncle-hood."

A shadow crossed his face, but he hid it behind a quick swig of coffee.

"That's it," I said softly. "You're thinking about yourself. Fatherhood."

"Can you see me being a father?"

"Do you want to be?"

A sharp shake of his head. "Never really thought about it before."

"Before Clay and I started talking about it . . . and talking about it, and talking about it." I shook my head. "Three years of 'should we or shouldn't we.' Must have driven everyone crazy."

"You had a lot of stuff to consider. But now that the baby's coming . . . My father . . . He's even more excited about it than I am."

"He loves kids."

A nod as Nick dropped his gaze to his coffee cup.

"Is that it? You feel like you should give him one? A grandson?"

"Shouldn't I? Hell, what else do I give him? I'm forty-three, never left home, piss around his company pretending I'm working . . ." He cut himself off with a snarl of disgust. "And I can't even bother bringing him home a grandson?"

"Do you think he cares? My God, Nick, if you think

your father expects you to have a son for him . . . Antonio would *never*—"

"Of course, he wouldn't. He doesn't expect anything of me. And he's never disappointed."

I leaned forward and moved my leg against his. As I opened my mouth, he moved back fast, gaze flying over my shoulder.

"Clayton's coming," he said. "Don't—"

"I wouldn't."

"And . . . forget I said a thing, okay?" He leaned back and made a face. "I'm just . . . in a mood these days. You've got enough to worry about—"

"I can always use a distraction. I won't forget it, whether you want me to or not."

I looked over my shoulder and called to Clay, "Better hurry. I've been eyeing your bagel."

Clay walked up to the table and put his hand on my shoulder. "It's yours, darling. You two divvy up my plate. I'll get more."

I smiled up at him. "Thanks. Oh, and if you could—"

"Yeah, I'll top up your coffee." He took my half-full mug, but waved off Nick's. "You're not pregnant. Get your own. You can move that table over here too. Jeremy and Antonio are on their way."

"Are they bringing Jaime?" I asked.

Clay shrugged, as if it didn't matter to him one way or the other. That was no bad reflection on Jaime. Clay might not have been particularly interested in Jaime as a person, but he didn't dislike her either, which was, with Clay, about as much as an outsider could hope for.

* * *

Jeremy *did* arrive with Jaime . . . and with news. Cholera cases were still trickling in—either unreported incidences from the original outbreak or secondary contamination.

"The hospitals are scrambling," Antonio said, "but it's under control. The problem now is convincing people of that."

"Like SARS," I said. Just a year ago, the WHO had issued an advisory against traveling to Toronto *after* the outbreak had been contained, and the city was still reeling from the effects.

"The memory of SARS only serves to magnify the panic," Jeremy said. "As with that Walkerton water contamination case. People are understandably nervous and, apparently, many have decided to squeeze in an unplanned week at the cottage."

"Traffic jams on the 400 northbound instead of south this morning, I'll bet. I'm afraid to ask: anything . . . new?"

Jeremy hesitated, as if as reluctant to say anything as I was to hear it. "Reports in two papers about an outbreak of rat bites in the downtown area, but it pales in comparison with the water contamination problems."

"So far," I muttered. "Any signs of things spreading beyond Toronto?"

He shook his head. "Everything appears to be contained to the city, and primarily the core."

"It's likely to stay that way too," Jaime said, her first words since we exchanged good mornings. "The effects are usually localized."

"So—"

The ring of my cell phone cut me off. An unfamiliar local number appeared in the display.

"Shanahan?" Nick mouthed.

"Let's hope so," I said before I pushed the talk button.

"Good morning," sang a chipper female voice. "I'd ask to speak to someone specific, but I don't have a name. I suppose I could ask for the lovely lupus I met the other night."

"Hello, Zoe," I said. "You got my message?"

"Message?"

I told her about my visit to Miller's.

"Ah, no. Message undelivered. I didn't stop in last night and Rudy can be a bit protective, so he didn't phone me to say you'd called. Here, let me give you my number, in case that happens again."

I jotted it down. "You remembered something?"

"After a night of mind-clearing thievery and a morning of mind-settling yoga, I do believe the memory files are creaking open. I'm just running off to the library right now, but perhaps we could meet for lunch?"

"Which library?"

"At the uni. Getting a head start for my fall classes. Got to keep the mind sharp. At my age, it's the first thing to go." A tinkling laugh. "Or, with vamps, the *only* thing to go. Are you familiar with the campus?"

"York or U of T?"

"U of T."

"Very. Give me a place and time, and I'll be there."

Professor

WE'D BEEN AT THE UNIVERSITY ONLY FIVE MONTHS AGO, when Clay had done a stint of lectures, filling in for a hospitalized colleague. We hadn't come to this particular cafeteria, though. I'd avoided it, sometimes going several buildings out of my way rather than grab a drink or snack at this one. Clay knew why, though we never discussed it. When Zoe suggested this cafeteria, I'd been tempted to insist on someplace else, but hadn't. I needed to get past this.

This was the cafeteria I brought Logan to the first time I'd met him, and the one we'd always used when he came to the university to see Clay and me. Logan, my Pack brother, the best friend in those years when I'd fought my ambivalence about the Pack, about being a werewolf, and about the man who'd made me one. Logan, dead five years now.

Five years. My breath caught when I even thought about it, as if unable to believe so much time had passed when the pain was still so sharp, when I could look down the hall, see those empty tables and see him there.

"I can grab Zoe," Clay murmured, his breath warm against my ear. "Bring her outside instead."

I shook my head.

"Can you grab us some cold drinks?" Clay asked Nick, with none of his usual mock-bullying bluster. He even reached for his wallet, but Nick waved him away.

Logan's relationship with Clay had been an uneasy friendship even before I came along. They were too different for anything more. After Clay bit me . . . well, they'd never been close after that. Clay hadn't been able to control his jealousy of my friendship with Logan when I was often barely on speaking terms with *him*. Logan had never forgiven Clay for biting me, not after he'd sworn he'd never hurt me.

I remembered the first time Logan saw Clay after he bit me. I'd finally asked Jeremy to revoke Clay's banishment, and a week later, Logan had come to Stonehaven. He hadn't known Clay was back, and we hadn't known Logan was coming. At the time, I'd been out grocery shopping with Nick while Antonio and Jeremy had gone to Syracuse.

When Nick and I came back, we found Clay and Logan on the back patio. I can still see—no, I can *hear* it. That's what I remember—hearing the dull thwack of fist hitting flesh.

We'd raced to the back door. There was Logan—good-natured, easygoing Logan—beating the hell out of Clay. And Clay? Clay just let him—just took it, his face already swollen and cut, his shirt bloodied, blood flying from his mouth.

In the years that followed, I'd thought of that scene, and I would tell myself that Clay had staged it, that he'd let Logan whale on him because he'd wanted me to see him taking it, like a little boy getting a whupping he thinks he deserves.

I knew better, even then. Clay was incapable of plotting and carrying out a ruse like that. He'd taken the beating because he'd thought he deserved it, and because he'd thought Logan deserved to be the one to dish it out.

Clay cleared his throat. I looked over at him.

"I've been thinking," he said. "I know you don't want to talk about names . . . for the baby, I mean. And this probably isn't the time, but I've been thinking about it for a while, and maybe you wouldn't want to, but if you did, if we have a boy . . ." He shrugged. "Logan's a good name."

My throat constricted, and I couldn't answer.

After a moment of silence, Clay looked around the almost empty cafeteria. "I don't see—oh, there she is."

I smiled. "Don't sound so thrilled."

"I don't know why she needed to do this in person." He looked over at me. "No, I *do* know. I just wish she could have saved us the bother."

I performed introductions.

"My, my," Zoe said, checking out Nick. "You boys don't come in ugly, do you? It's a good thing I wasn't born a werewolf, or I might have had some serious conflict."

Nick grinned, that easy grin of his that makes women's stomachs flip, and the most blatant come-on sound almost sweet. "If you do start feeling conflicted, I can help."

"Oh, I bet you can," she said with a lilting laugh. She laid a hand on Nick's arm. "I appreciate the offer, but I worked it out long ago." She flashed a smile my way. "I'm willing to extend the same offer to anyone who hasn't."

I touched my belly. "I think I've worked it out too."

Zoe started to respond, but was cut short.

"Dr. Danvers," a voice called from halfway across the cafeteria.

Clay didn't turn. Maybe he was intentionally ignoring the hail. More likely, he was so unaccustomed to the form of address that he didn't recognize it.

A heavyset young man appeared at our table, smiling at Clay, his hand extended. Clay hesitated—he hates physical contact with outsiders—but the pause lasted only a second before he took the student's hand in a firm, if brief, shake.

"Are you teaching next term?" the young man asked. "I didn't see your name on the schedule."

"Just visiting."

"Damn. I didn't get a chance to tell you how much I enjoyed your lectures. That's exactly what I'm interested in, and I've read all your—" He stopped, flushed, then laughed. "Sorry. Academic fan boys—what geeks, huh? Anyway, I wanted to thank you for the comments you made on my paper. I really appreciated the encouragement."

Clay's gaze slid my way. I only smiled.

"Oh, and it's Mrs. Danvers, right? I remember you from class." He looked down at my stomach. "Don't remember that, though. Congratulations."

"Thanks," I said. "And I read your paper too. It was great. Clayton will have some competition in a few years."

The young man blushed again, thanked us, then hurried off after imparting a warning to be careful. "Not a good time to visit Toronto," he said. "Weird things happening."

When he was gone, Clay looked at me.

"Comments on his paper?" he said.

"You said it was very good. Damn good, and he shows a lot of promise. So I wrote it down—without the damn."

"I gave him an A. That's not enough?"

"Comments help."

"Comments won't get him into grad school."

"Hard-ass."

Zoe had followed our volleys with a half-open mouth. When we stopped, she said, "*Doctor*? Please tell me he was kidding."

"He was kidding," Clay said. "Now, you called us here—"

"You're a professor? In . . . what?"

"Phys ed. You called us here—"

She sighed and waved for us to sit. Clay and I grabbed drinks from Nick's tray. There were two left.

Zoe laughed. "Didn't want to be rude, I see."

"I wasn't sure," Nick said. "Do you . . . drink?"

She took a bottle. "If it's cold, I will. It gets terribly uncomfortable in the summer when you can't sweat . . . and when your food only comes warm."

Clay made a noise in his throat.

"Oh, stop growling. I'm getting to business." She paused. "Weren't we supposed to be doing this over lunch?"

"We just ate," Clay said. "Besides, you don't."

She waggled a finger at him. "Don't be racist. Vampires are civilized beasts, just like you—" She looked over at Nick and me. "Like you two. As such, we enjoy social customs such as shared meals . . . even if we can't actually share them."

"This is a cafeteria." Clay pointed at her water bottle. "Consider that lunch."

"Come on," I said. "We'll start walking, see if we find someplace to eat."

We headed out to University Avenue.

"Theodore Shanahan *did* commission the theft himself, directly through me," Zoe said as we walked along the shaded sidewalk. "And it was for that particular letter. He was very specific. No substitutions allowed."

She took a sip of her water before continuing. "I remember that because I always ask. If I arrive on the site and realize that the piece they want isn't accessible—has been removed, etcetera—I want to know whether the buyer will accept a second piece from the same collection, at a discount, of course."

"Shanahan said no."

"Emphatically no. It was the *From Hell* letter or none at all. That stipulation almost made me turn down the job. Traveling to England was hardly an overnight jaunt in those days. Imagine getting all that way only to discover they'd pulled the letter from the file. When I raised that concern, Shanahan promised that if that happened, he would cover all my travel expenses and pay me for my time."

"So he *really* wanted that letter. What—"

"El—Darling?" Clay cut in, nudging me.

When I glanced over, he flared his nostrils. Sniff. I did, and caught the faint scent of rot on a crosswind, coming

from the southwest—behind us and to our right, probably across the road.

"Knew they'd take the bait sooner or later," I said.
"Zoe? One of my zombie stalkers has caught up with me,
so we need to cut this conversation short. Can I call you
later?"

"Is that a subtle 'get lost'?"

"If you glance to your right, you'll probably see someone seriously overdressed for the weather."

"Oh, I'm sure you were telling the truth about the
stalker. I meant the part about telling me to take off."

"Natural antipathy or not, this one wants me. But if he
does go after you, we'll get him."

"That's very sweet, but antipathy works both ways."
She flashed her teeth. "Been a long time since I met a
zombie."

"Forget it," Clay said. "If we need more from you, we'll
call."

"Oh-ho, so that's how it works, professor? I give, you
take?"

"No, you give us information, we give you a zombie-
free city." Clay jerked his chin at Nick and me. "Come
on."

I offered an apologetic shrug and half-smile to Zoe,
but like Clay, I had no desire to let a stranger join our
hunt. Even Nick's murmured "sorry" was halfhearted.

"How long has it been since you actually lived in
Toronto?" Zoe called as we started to walk away.

I turned and frowned.

"A few years, I'll bet," Zoe continued. "And this—" she
waved a hand across the scene before us, construction
zones everywhere, "—probably doesn't look very familiar.

But it is to me. This is where I make my living, and I know every back alley, every shortcut, every hiding place."

"We'll manage," Clay said, fingers closing around my arm.

"With your superhuman sense of smell? Works great in the forest, I'm sure. Or in a quiet neighborhood. But here? Take a good sniff, professor. Smog, exhaust, roofing tar. It would help to have someone who doesn't need scent to track."

I looked at Clay, but his gaze had moved on, scanning the street. He was considering Zoe's words but, even more, looking for the zombie, knowing that every moment we stood here arguing was a moment in which our pursuer could decide this wasn't a good time or place to attack.

"Do what you want," he said finally. "Just stay out of our way."

The problem now was where to lead the zombie so we could kill him. We were downtown in the middle of a workday. I suggested returning to the university campus.

"Too open." Clay squinted up the street. "The museum would be good. An enclosed building, probably not too busy with this cholera thing. There'd be lots of quiet places for you to lure him into."

"But then you have the problem of admission," I said. "I doubt he carries much walking-around money."

"If that's the only problem, you're in luck today," Zoe said. "All the cultural centers are offering free admission for the rest of the week. A tourism bonus in light of the water problems. I was going to visit the art gallery this afternoon, to check out a few business opportunities."

"The museum it is," Clay said.

We headed for the Royal Ontario Museum, just a block up University. As we walked, I called Antonio and told him we had one of the zombies in our sights. He and Jeremy would hightail it to Cabbagetown to await delivery.

I hung up as we reached the front steps, then I realized Clay was no longer beside me, but a dozen feet back, glowering at a construction board.

He waved at the board. "What the hell are they doing to the museum?"

"A total overhaul," I said. "Creating a revitalized cultural and architectural landmark for Toronto."

"Overhaul? From that picture, it'll look like it was hit by a goddamn glacier."

"I know," Zoe said. "Isn't it gorgeous? Did you see the front? They're going to have the dinosaurs right there, so you can see them from the street. Wonderful. Although, if they're going to put artifacts in the window, I'd personally prefer something more portable."

Clay shook his head and strode up the museum steps.

Once inside, we split up. Past experience told us our zombie friends wouldn't come out while I was surrounded by bodyguards, though Clay would stay with me for as long as possible.

We'd barely made it to the second-floor landing when my phone vibrated. I checked the display. Nick.

"She's coming," he said when I answered.

"She?"

"Think so. Zoe says it's a she. Hard to tell under all that clothing."

"Be on the lookout for her partner then," I said. "They've played this game with us before."

"Tag-team stalking."

"Exactly."

When I hung up, Clay said, "Rose?"

I nodded.

"Shit." He glanced at the exit, frown deepening to a scowl.

"You'd prefer a knife-wielding thug to an aging hooker?"

"Hooker with syphilis. Remember what Jeremy said?" He looked around, scouting the territory. "Change of plans. I'll be the bait. She's seen me with you enough to know I'd be just as good a source for that letter. If I'm easier to nab than you—"

I shook my head. "Unless her brain's rotting with the rest of her, she's never going to think you'd be easier to nab than me. I'll be careful. You know I will. I'll avoid her mouth and scrub up afterward. Better yet, I'll knock her down and wait for you. Minimal contact."

After a moment, he nodded and we headed for the stairs.

We bypassed the busier second floor—home of the kid-friendly dinosaur and natural history displays. In the third-floor Islam gallery, we settled in for some museum browsing, which was one act I didn't need to fake. Fifteen years with an anthropologist has made me a bit of a museum geek.

Clay always finds an artifact that catches his eye,

usually with a great story attached. When we visit a city, Clay will snore through opera and jazz concerts, stake out a bench in the art gallery, even fall asleep during eardrum-shattering Broadway musicals . . . but don't ask him to leave town before he's visited every museum.

I used to wonder how a guy who wants little to do with humans can be so fascinated by their history. I understand now that the two attitudes aren't mutually exclusive. Human society is foreign to Clay and, therefore, all the more fascinating, if only from a scientific point of view. Like an anthropologist studying apes, he finds the structure intriguing, but he has no desire to join it.

We wove through the Islam gallery, through Rome, and back to the Greek areas in the southwest corner. There, we split up a few times, one of us wandering off to look at something, conveniently rounding a corner and getting out of the other's sight. Yet Rose didn't strike. Nor did Nick phone to say she'd backed off. Every once in a while, I detected a whiff of rot on the air-conditioning, confirming she was nearby. There was no sign of the bowler-hatted man, though.

We wove through a forest of armless, legless, emasculated marble male torsos. I stopped in the corner, behind a raised scale model display of the acropolis of Athens.

"Either she's waiting for her partner or she's waiting for us to give her a better shot," I said. "You know the place as well as I do. Where's a safe place to take someone down?"

As his eyes half-closed, I could almost see the floor plan of the museum flipping past them, his brain ticking off every place he could kill someone or hide a body. A discomfiting skill, but I knew it came from that part of his brain that instinctively assessed danger and mapped out escape routes in any new environment. When it came to randomly killing strangers and stashing the bodies, there were few werewolves less likely to do it than Clay.

"That's the public areas," he said after he'd recited the list. "You want the labs and stuff too?"

"Uh, no, that's okay. Just don't ever invite me to the museum after we've had a fight, okay?"

He snorted. "I think *I'd be* the one more likely to be knocked over the head and stuffed in a sarcophagus."

"Never," I said. "They're all behind glass. Lousy place to hide a body. But there's a really big vase over there that might work."

He growled and swung to grab me. I sidestepped just as a mother and two kids walked in.

"Speaking of sarcophagi," I whispered. "I think it's time to move on to the Nile."

Clay nodded and followed me out.

Pursuits

WE CHECKED OUT THE EGYPTIAN WING, BUT DECIDED IT was too busy for Rose, so we crossed the floor to the Samuel European Gallery, and walked through the rotunda, then turned right.

The south wing was semidark, with tasteful spot lighting illuminating decorated rooms from various periods. A corridor about ten feet wide wended through the gallery, with lots of twists and curves, so you couldn't see more than two or three glassed-in rooms at a time. Alcoves and doors were everywhere. Even on the busiest days, the wing was quiet. Today, it was empty. Perfect.

We stopped by a well-marked emergency exit near what looked like a large storage closet. Even a zombie had to recognize an ideal kidnapping opportunity when she saw it. Then it came time to separate. If Rose was looking for that ideal opportunity, we were going to give it to her, making sure she knew Clay was leaving, and might be gone for a few minutes.

Clay asked for my cell phone.

"Gotta call work," he said, speaking just above a normal conversational tone. "See how that department meeting went."

I handed him my phone. He didn't have one—a cell phone presupposes a desire to communicate with the outside world.

He hit the buttons, pretended to listen, then grunted, looked at the display and said, "No signal."

"It's these old buildings," I said. "The walls are too thick. Try moving closer to the stairwell."

Before he left, he circled his lips with his finger, then pointed the finger at me, reminding me to stay away from Rose's mouth. I nodded. He walked away, head down as he redialed. I turned to examine a room done in French Regency, all gilt and ornate tapestry. On a pedestal stood a bust of a toga-wearing man who, judging by his expression, had lived in a time that predated laxatives.

Behind me, Clay circled the first corner. "Yeah, it's me. How—?" He muttered a curse. "Hold on." His voice drifted farther. "There? Can you hear me now? Christ, the echo in this place. How did the meeting go?"

A split-second pause. "Hold on. I've lost you. I'll move . . ."

As his footsteps headed in the direction of the rotunda, his voice faded under the soft strains of piped-in classical music. Okay, Rose, it's not going to get any better than this. Here, I'll even bend over to read this placard, so you can—

A growl, half-anger, half-surprise off to my left. The clatter of the cell phone dropping and skating across the hard floor.

Even as I turned and ran for Clay, my brain told me I was overreacting, that he'd probably just bumped into something or someone. But my gut knew better.

As I ran, I heard a thump, then a grunt. Another thump—harder, like a body hitting the floor. I rounded two corners, then saw Clay pinning a figure to the floor beside twin display cases of silver tableware.

It was Rose. She held a knife in one hand, but he had her by the wrist, so the weapon was useless. His other hand reached for her head, to snap her neck.

"The swords!" a child's voice shrieked. "I want to see the swords!"

Running footsteps sounded at the mouth of the gallery. Arms and armor were on the opposite side, but Clay hesitated, listening. As he turned, he saw me. I motioned for him to wait.

The footfalls screeched around the corner, heading our way. The child's parents tried calling him back, but he was too far to hear or too excited to care.

Clay pulled back and looked around, still holding Rose's knife hand, but his attention was elsewhere, searching for a place to move her before the child came racing around the corner.

"There!" I hissed, pointing at a gap between two displays. "I'll head off—"

Rose bucked. The knife flashed and, although Clay still held her wrist, he instinctively dodged, loosening his grip just enough for her to wrench free. As she scrambled up, I raced around to cut off her escape route. Clay dove for her. Then two kids, no more than seven or eight, turned the corner and stopped dead, gazes fixed, not on us, but on the knife-wielding woman rising before them, her face like something out of their most macabre comic books. One screamed.

Rose raced past me. Clay tore after her.

"It's—we were rehearsing," I said quickly. "A play. She's dressed up."

I wanted to say more, but once Clay realized I wasn't behind him, he would stop chasing Rose. And, to be honest, I wasn't sure I wanted to be around when the parents found their terrified children. So, with a weak smile, I scooped up my cell phone from the floor and hurried after him.

I caught up as Clay reached the stair landing. He'd stopped there and was looking back, ready to return for me. I waved him on, but he didn't move until I'd caught up.

Rose was hurrying down the stairs, disappearing then reappearing from behind the huge Haida and Nisga'a totem poles that rose up the center of the circling stairs. I touched Clay's arm.

"Hold back," I whispered. "Let her think she's lost us."

He nodded, and let me nudge him back into the shadows, but kept his gaze fixed on Rose as she descended.

"She ambushed me," he whispered.

"Guess her brain *is* rotting after all."

"Or she was getting me out of the way first. Learning our routines."

"Possible. Where the heck is her partner?"

"Don't know, but I'm keeping my eyes open."

I touched his forearm, to tell him we could start forward. When I pulled back my fingers, they were wet with blood. I grabbed his arm for a better look, but he pulled away.

"Just a scratch."

"She stabbed—?"

He shook his head as he propelled me to the steps.

"Her nails." He swiped away the blood, then started down the steps.

Rose hit the second-floor landing. I expected her to carry on down the stairs and run for the exit. Instead, she hurried toward the museum's most popular exhibit: the dinosaurs.

Clay let out a soft snarl of frustration. The dinosaur gallery was right under the European galleries, but U-shaped, guiding traffic in one end, then around and out the other, with no possible side trips.

I looked at Clay. We were both thinking the same thing—we had a surefire shot at catching Rose here . . . if we split up.

A moment's hesitation, then Clay nodded and motioned for me to cover the exit.

I watched him stride through the exhibit entrance, then ducked in the exit and stopped to get my bearings. In any other gallery today, this would have been a simple matter of looking down the empty hall for the first sign of life. But there were quite a few other people here, most under the age of five, as if parents were taking advantage of low attendance at the museum to give their preschoolers as much face time with dinosaur bones as they could want.

Children raced along the corridor, under the snouts of the looming beasts as their parents sat or stood in twos and threes, chatting and laughing. The noise level, replete with choreographed booms and shrieks, made listening for Rose impossible. Sniffing was also out of the question—the old and well-loved gallery was overpoweringly ripe. So I had to look for her . . . which would have been much easier if the lights weren't cranked down to simulate primeval darkness.

I walked down the center of the hall, my gaze drifting from side to side, only registering life-forms four feet and taller, which cut the prospects dramatically.

I hit a stroller barricade and murmured an "excuse me," my gaze still focused ten feet ahead. Someone caught my arm, and I swung back, hand balling into a fist ... then realized I was about to deck a smiling woman holding a baby.

"Sorry," I murmured. "Excuse me—"

"When are you due?" she asked.

"Due?"

She motioned to my stomach. I looked down, and for a split second stared at my jutting stomach, wondering "where did that come from?" before my brain slammed back on track.

"Oh, ummm, soon. Excuse—"

Another woman in the group let out a squeak. "Oh, my God. See, I'm not the only crazy one." She laid her hand on my arm. "Lee was just reminding me about *last* August when I was—" She motioned to my stomach. "That huge, and whining about the heat."

"I warned you, never get pregnant at Christmas," the third woman said. "As romantic as it might seem, it isn't nearly so nice eight months later, when it's baking hot and you're carrying an extra twenty pounds." She looked at me. "Am I right?"

"Er, uh ..." I struggled for something to say, something other than: excuse me, I have a homicidal zombie to catch.

The women were all beaming my way, ready to welcome a temporary addition to their clique, and I realized just how much I was not going to be "moms and tots" playgroup material. Had I already doomed my child to life as a social misfit? A father who'd never coach Little League . . . a mother who'd never host PTA bake sales . . . an entire family whose idea of an exciting summer getaway was chasing down zombies? Which reminded me . . .

"Excuse me—" I began.

"Oh, speaking of warm, show her the sweater set."

The first woman, the one with the baby, lifted a paper from her stroller and held it out. On it was a picture of a matching knit sweater, booties and hat.

"That's . . . cute," I said, scanning over their heads for Rose. "Great idea for winter. Maybe I'll buy one. Now if I could—"

"Buy one?" The second woman laughed. "It's a pattern. For knitting. Old-fashioned, I know, but it's a great way to relieve stress."

Knitting? I stared in horror at the outstretched pattern, mumbled my excuses and finally squeezed through, hurrying back to less terrifying pursuits.

I rounded the corner at the same time as Clay came barreling around the other side. We stopped, twenty feet apart, looked at each other, then searched the gap between us, our lips forming a silent curse—probably the same curse.

We strode forward and met in the middle.

"She didn't get past *me*," I whispered.

"Me neither. It's not crowded or dark enough to have missed her circling back."

I looked for potential hiding places, but the layout was simple—too simple to misplace an entranced toddler, let alone a woman. Then I remembered the stroller barricade.

"I was stopped," I said. "Back there. The hall was

blocked. Maybe, when I got through, if she was right on the other side, in the shadows or something . . ."

"You could have missed her. Probably not, but . . ."

"We should check."

The strollers were still there, the women now talking to a pair of preschoolers. Their faces lit up when they saw me again.

"Oh, is this your husband?" one said. "Lucky girl. I can never get mine anywhere near this place."

"We were with another woman," I said as I reached them. "A friend. We've lost her. Did anyone come back this way?"

"No one's been by since you, hon," said the oldest. "It's dead in here today."

As I thanked them and turned to go, the one with the baby grabbed the sweater set pattern and thrust it out.

"Here, take this. I have a copy."

Clay glanced down.

"Isn't it sweet?" she said. "I'm making one for Natalie." She looked at me. "You'll love knitting. It's so relaxing . . . and you're going to need all the relaxation you can get soon."

As the women chuckled, Clay grabbed the pattern.

"Knitting?" He looked at me. "Yeah, I can see that."

He thanked the woman and stuffed it into his pocket.

As we strode away, I muttered, "When that page leaves your pocket, it better be headed straight for a trash can."

"You heard the lady. You'll need relaxation. Knitting would be—" His lips twitched. "—fun."

"You ever buy me knitting needles, and I'll show you a whole new use for them."

"I'll remember that." His grin vanished. "Now where the hell did—"

He stopped as our eyes traveled in the same direction . . . and reached the same destination. An exit door, concealed in the back wall.

"Shit."

Clay jerked his chin at me. Not much of an instruction, but I understood it. Stay and watch while he opened the door.

I did, he did, and we slipped through the doorway and into a narrow service hall. There was no one in sight, so I dropped into an ungainly crouch and took a deep breath.

When I caught the scent, we set out, jogging quietly along the back hall. Patrons weren't the only ones avoiding the museum that day. Only once did we hear footsteps echoing through the maze of corridors, and they turned off before getting anywhere near us.

At each doorway or branching hall, I stopped, dropped and sniffed. The trail stuck to the main passage. Did Rose know she was being followed? Or had her near-death upstairs spooked her into picking a back exit?

When we hit a flight of service stairs, the trail went down. She hadn't stopped at the first floor, but had kept going, into the basement. All the better. I pulled out my cell phone and turned it on. Despite its tumble, it still worked. I called Nick and told him to meet us downstairs. As I hung up, I almost missed a step. Clay caught my arm. As he moved, I caught the scent of blood. I grabbed his wrist. He looked down at the dripping "scratch" and snorted, as if it was a cause for annoyance not concern.

"It's deeper than I thought," I said.

He shook his head. "Probably nicked a vein or something. No big deal. Jeremy will take care of it—later."

"Maybe I should check—"

"Keep walking. I'll fix it."

He stripped off his T-shirt and tore a few inches from the bottom. I tried to get a better look at the scratch, but then we hit the bottom step and he swung around me to take the lead.

Hull

THE TRAIL ENDED AT A DOOR LEADING BACK INTO A SEMI-
dark construction zone. It was an obstacle course of
construction materials—piles of drywall and lumber,
sawhorses, tarps and rubbish. A room full of places to
hide.

Clay cocked his head, nostrils flaring—listening, looking and sniffing.

I squinted to let my eyes adjust, and counted the exits.
The farthest, an open doorway, led to what looked like
another hall.

A shape passed that distant door, and I tapped Clay's
arm, redirecting his attention. He nodded, and we split
up again, heading for that far door.

I made it there first and glanced around the doorway to
see a figure obscured behind a sheet of opaque plastic
hanging from the ceiling. Clay tensed but, after a deep
breath, I shook my head.

"Nick," I mouthed.

I cleared my throat, so I wouldn't startle him. Zoe
pulled back the plastic and waved us over. Nick was on
her other side, hunched down, trying to pick up a scent.

"Don't bother," I said. "She went down this hall. I can smell her already."

"So can I," he said. "It's the other one I'm trying to pick up."

"We were wondering when he'd show up."

Nick shook his head. "I don't think it's a zombie. I didn't smell the same—"

"That's because we've only killed him once so far. He's not as ripe as she is."

Clay waved us to silence. "Let's concentrate on the one we have—the one that's getting away as we stand here."

We followed Rose's trail to a door that opened into an outdoor construction zone. This site was empty, someone having apparently decided current events were sufficient grounds for a mass personal day.

Tarps flapped in the breeze, against the distant roar of the streets. Clay tapped my arm and gestured to a security van parked off to the side. I nodded as he alerted the others.

Zoe shook her head and whispered, "There's no one here. I can tell."

I bent to pick up Rose's scent, winnowing it out from all the others. Once I found it, I started forward, weaving around piles of building material.

Within ten feet, we hit a spill of some kind, as if someone had dumped building chemicals—hopefully by accident. The trail became indistinct, the smell of rot more apparent on the air than the ground. Clay and I headed around the piles of material in one direction, while Zoe and Nick took the other.

I finally picked up Rose's scent again, but only got about twenty feet more before I lost it behind trailers stacked with lumber. When I bent, Clay waved me up.

"You shouldn't be bending so much. Can't be comfortable. I'll take a turn."

As he crouched, I heard the crunch of stones underfoot. I motioned to Clay, but he'd already stopped, head tilted, following the noise. He grabbed the edge of the trailer and swung onto it. I followed . . . with more heaving and clambering than "swinging."

By the time I was atop the trailer bed, Clay was on the lumber pile. He looked over the other side, then helped me up. As I scrambled to the top, a fair-haired head bobbed from behind a truck. A man stepped out. Thirties, maybe nearing forty, and small, though that was probably the fault of my vantage point.

The man was dressed in slacks and a dress shirt. An office worker cutting through the empty construction yard. Then I noticed his pants were an inch too short and his shirt was too large in the collar and long in the sleeves. Not as ill-fitting as the bowler-hatted man's clothes, but enough to make me take a second look. In that look, my gaze slid down the overlong sleeve . . . to a semiconcealed knife in his hand.

"Zombie?" Clay mouthed.

I took a deep breath, but he was downwind.

"Can't tell," I whispered.

He was below us—about a dozen feet away. Decent positioning for a jump. As Clay crouched, neither of us moved or said a word, but the man stiffened, and his gaze swung up and around. He caught Clay before we could backpedal.

The man's face paled and his eyes widened. I shifted,

and the man's gaze shot my way, as if he hadn't noticed me there before.

"Oh, thank God," the man murmured in a soft, British-accented voice. "It's you." He lifted a hand to shield his eyes as his gaze turned to Clay. "Yes, yes, of course it is. I should have recognized you as well, but—" His eyes closed and he shuddered. "Dear God, my heart. When I saw you up there, I was certain I'd run straight into a trap, that you were another of those—" He shuddered again. "—those things."

"Things?" I said.

"That . . . Those . . ." He faltered, as if he couldn't find a word. "The man and the woman. They—" He took a deep quavering breath. "I'm sorry. Just give me a moment."

He lifted his hand. The knife blade flashed. Clay dropped, ready to leap, and the man nearly fell backward, arms going up to ward Clay off.

"D-don't— I mean you no harm. Please—"

"Drop the knife," Clay said, his voice a nearly unintelligible growl.

"The—?" The man's gaze dropped to his hand. "Oh, oh, yes, of course. I'm sorry." He stooped and laid the knife down, then gave a small, nervous laugh. "I can't blame you for being wary. I know they've been after your wife, which can't be very pleasant." His gaze slid to my stomach. "Particularly considering her delicate condition. But I believe—" He swallowed. "That is to say, I *hope* I can help you."

"Not interested."

As Nick and Zoe approached, I could see that my assessment of the man's size hadn't been skewed by our position—he wasn't much bigger than Zoe, in height or weight.

Zoe stopped and looked at him, head tilting as if puzzled. Nick was downwind, so I motioned for him to sniff the air. He did—twice—then shook his head.

"Hello," the man said, his head bobbing in greeting. "I was just speaking to your friends. I saw you together earlier. I was following you. That is to say, I was following her, that . . . thing. The woman. She led me to you, and I continued on here, in hopes of getting an opportunity to speak to you. But before I could go inside, the other one cut me off."

"The other one?" I said.

"The man. Her partner. He saw me and—" The man swallowed, his gaze tripping around the construction site. "I hid, and I thought I lost him. Then I heard noises. I was preparing to run when I saw you."

"Who are you?" I asked.

Clay grunted, telling me not to engage him.

I leaned closer and whispered, "He's not a zombie."

Clay's expression didn't change. "Don't care."

"I'm not one of them," the man said, then hesitated. "Or, I should say, I do not believe I am. It's all very . . ." He shook his head sharply. "It doesn't matter. My name is Matthew Hull, and yes, I did come through that . . . whatever it was. I could use your help, and in return, can offer my own."

I glanced at Clay, but he was staring at Hull as if he could bore into his thoughts and read his intentions.

Hull continued, a near-pleading note in his voice. "My perspective is one you're not likely to have, or be able to find elsewhere. A firsthand account, so to speak."

Clay's scrutiny was obviously making Hull uncomfortable. He shifted from one foot to the other, glanced over his shoulder at Zoe and Nick, then took a sideways step, as if preparing for a quick escape.

"Perhaps we could speak in someplace more . . . public," he said. "We passed a park south of here. When I was following you. The road appeared to circle around it."

"Queen's Park," I said, as Clay tensed, ready for the leap. "Fine, but we have someone else who'd like to speak to you, and he's not here right now, so why don't I give him a call . . ."

I took out my cell phone. A momentary distraction that worked better than I expected because, as I lifted it to my ear, the man stared at me in confusion. The perfect opportunity for Clay to take him down. When he didn't, I looked over to see him staring out over the construction yard. There, on the other side, a man was creeping around a dump bin. While I couldn't make out his features, I recognized his form and his stance, slightly stooped. The other zombie.

Below, Hull had noticed our attention wander. I motioned to Nick, telling him to go after the zombie and leave this one to us. He slipped away. Zoe hesitated and glanced at me for instructions. When I didn't give any, she followed Nick. The man watched them leave.

"They—they're still here, aren't they?" he stammered. "Those . . . things. Perhaps I should leave this to you—"

"Don't move," Clay said.

"We could still meet in the park," the man said, gaze darting about for the clearest escape route. "Shall we say, dusk? At the north end?"

Clay leapt just as Hull bolted. A second sooner, and he would have landed atop him. As it was, he hit the ground about five feet behind the already running man. As I moved forward to jump down, the toe of my sneaker snagged on an exposed nail. Any other time, that would have just meant an embarrassing stumble and quick recovery as Clay sprinted away, leaving me to catch up. But the moment Clay saw my shadow stutter, he stopped, turning fast, arms going up as if I was about to fall headfirst off the trailer.

"I'm fine!" I said. "Go!"

He hesitated until he saw that I was indeed okay. Then he continued the pursuit, but slowly now, as if my stumble had reminded him where his priorities lay. As the gap between Clay and Hull widened, I knew that the only way we were going to get him is if I caught up—and fast. So I concentrated on forgetting the twenty-pound weight on my gut and the sweat streaming into my eyes.

As I sprinted forward, something jumped from behind a pile of lumber. Out of the corner of my eye, I caught only a furry brown blur, and my brain screamed "wolf." I backpedaled so fast I tripped and thudded down on my backside, letting out a whimper as I felt the jolt slam through to my stomach. I jerked forward into a semi-seated fetal position, protecting my stomach.

Something hit my shoulder, teeth catching in my shirt. A strangled snarl from Clay. A high-pitched squeal of rage from whatever was clinging to my shoulder, then the thump of flesh hitting wood as it flew off. I caught a whiff of my attacker then, and knew what it was even as I turned to see it lying dead beside a pile of boards.

"A rat?" I said. "In daylight?"

"Elena?" Clay's voice was oddly quiet, with that same strangled note I'd heard in his snarl. "Don't move. *Please*, don't move."

I started to ask "why?" then realized speaking probably

fell under the heading of "moving." Instead, I moved only my eyes, following Clay's gaze up to the pile of boards beside me. There, perched on top, were four rats, all staring at me. Their mouths were open, lower incisors revealed. The fur on their foreheads was flattened, their ears rotated forward. They let out short hisses and the occasional squeak. Definitely not a display of welcome.

Clay's gaze slid to the other side of me, where I remembered seeing a pile of bricks. I couldn't look that way without moving, but a crosswind brought more rat stink, and I knew I was surrounded by them.

I tried to relax. Reminded myself that as nasty as rats were, even a dozen of them were no match for two werewolves. But the crosswind brought another smell—that smell of disease we'd picked up on the rats in the warehouse.

Diseased rats. Out in the daytime, when rats normally seek shelter. Aggressively confronting, not just a human, but a werewolf.

The rats started to chatter, teeth snapping and grinding, needlelike incisors flashing, eyes blazing with rage, as if the disease had driven them mad and only the faintest shreds of sanity were keeping them from jumping down and ripping into me. As they hissed and squeaked, I could see those sanity shreds stretching thinner, ready to snap.

I didn't look at Clay, knowing if I did, the panic in my eyes might panic *him*. He was trying to think up a way to get me out of there, and didn't need any distractions.

"Inch toward me," Clay said, his voice just above a whisper. "When you're close enough, I'll grab your feet and pull you out of the way. Just move very, very slowly."

Before I could "inch" anywhere, I needed to get my

hands on the ground. I hated uncovering my stomach, but there was nothing else I could do to move forward. I started with my left hand, easing it down toward the ground. The largest rat lunged for the edge of the wood pile.

I froze, heart thudding, knowing they'd sense my fear and fighting to control it. The big rat paced along the edge of the pile, as if struggling to resolve warring fight-or-flight impulses. Behind it, the others jostled for position. The sharp scrabbling of claws on wood underscored their chatters and hisses as two more rats joined them.

"Clay?" I whispered. "It's not going to—"

"I know."

"If I jump up fast and—"

"No."

"I have to. They won't wait much longer. If you cover me—"

"They'll attack before you get your hands down."

"Maybe if I can push off . . ." I knew even as I said it that I couldn't. My stomach was too big for me to jump from a sitting position without using my hands.

"I'll—" My throat dried up and I swallowed before starting again. "I'll just have to move fast. Put my hands down and—"

"Clay!" Nick's loud whisper cut through the construction yard. "There you—" He stopped at Clay's shoulder. "Holy shit."

A quick confused glance at Clay, as if to say "Why are you just standing there?" then Nick leapt forward. Clay's hand slammed into the middle of his chest, stopping him.

"Spook them and they'll attack."

"What's—" Zoe began as she came up behind Nick.

She saw me. "Good lord. Don't move. They must be rabid—"

"It's something else," Clay said. "Some disease from the portal. Elena? I'm going to jump in there. When they go for me, get out."

I shifted my gaze to the pacing rats. The biggest one was perched on the edge, as if calculating the distance to my belly, snapping at the others as they jostled him.

"Elena?" Clay said. "I'll be okay. I can handle rats. Better me than you right now."

I hesitated, then nodded. Clay slowly lowered himself to a half-crouch, ready to jump. Then something hit his shoulder. Zoe, knocking him out of the way. Before anyone could react, she raced toward me.

"Run!" she said.

The king rat jumped, the others flying behind him in a stream of brown fur. One hit my side. Another my head, claws catching in my hair as it scrambled for a hold. I was already up, barreling forward. Hands clamped around my arm. Clay yanked me out and passed me to Nick, then dove past me.

I turned to see Zoe covered in rats, at least six of them, hanging off her arms and clothes as she swung wildly, trying to get them free. More attacked from the ground, lunging at her legs. Clay kicked the nearest one, bones crunching as his foot made contact. He grabbed one off Zoe and whipped it into the brick pile.

Nick steered me out of the way, then ran back to help. By then, the rats were already dispersing, hissing and squeaking as they ran for cover. Nick snatched the last one off Zoe's back. The rat twisted around to bite him, but Clay's fist knocked it out of Nick's grip, and it hit the ground, convulsing as it died.

I hurried over to them. Zoe was shivering, eyes wide and wild, as she looked herself over.

"They—they're gone, right?" she said, teeth chattering. "Oh, God. That was—" She rubbed her hands over her arms as the bites healed.

"Thank you," I said.

A weak smile. "Not much of a sacrifice. Give me a couple of minutes, and I'll be good as new. Wounds heal and, whatever they carry, I can't catch. These clothes are garbage now, though."

"Doesn't look like they ripped anything," Nick said.

"That's okay. They're still going in the trash." She wrapped her arms around herself and gave a hard shudder, then shook it off. "Well, now that I've revealed myself to be a total wimp . . ." She waved off our protests. "I can talk the talk, but as a predator, I'm a washout."

She looked at Clay. "Thanks. I know you were just getting them out of the way before they went after Elena, but thanks. I was about ten seconds away from doing my Jamie Lee Curtis impression and screaming like a total sissy-girl."

"I was about five seconds away from it myself," I said. "Psycho killer rats. That's a new one for me. Whatever disease they're carrying must be making them—" I stopped, my head jerking up. "Clay? Nick? Did you get bit—"

Clay put up his hand to stop me as I sprinted over, ready to check him myself. "They only got Zoe." He glanced at Nick, frowning. "You didn't—"

"You didn't leave any for me, remember? Deprived again."

"Left you one."

"Which *you* killed."

"Are you sure everyone's okay?" Zoe said. "I smell blood."

Clay lifted his arm to check the bandage. It was soaked with blood.

"Shit," he said. "That must be what the rats smelled."

"Here," I said. "Let me—"

He waved me off. "Got a few more strips on this shirt. You work on picking up a trail. I'm guessing if Nick circled back, he lost the zombie, right?"

Nick nodded. "We both did, so we came to grab Elena to see if she can pick up the trail. There's roofing tar over there, and I can't smell a damned thing except that. Where's—"

"Lost him too," I muttered. "So much for our bird in the hand. Come on."

We made it just to the other side of the trailer when Clay's head jerked up, gaze going north, following something. A second later, running footsteps thundered through the construction yard. A young man in a security uniform raced around the corner, a sandwich in hand. The absentee guard, returning to his post, he hoped, before anyone noticed he'd been gone.

Clay swore. Zoe stepped closer to Nick and motioned for us to head toward the road. The guard saw us, lips parting as if to call out. Zoe waved with one hand and gripped Nick's arm with the other, then she motioned to the far road. Just two couples taking a shortcut through an empty construction site. The guard nodded and waved us on. We'd have to pick up the trail off the site.

* * *

Logically, there had to be a trail. Three, in fact—Rose's, the bowler-hatted man's and Hull's—but we couldn't find them.

Twice I caught that whiff of rot that told me one of the zombies had been by, but after following them for a few feet other scents got in the way. Hull was even tougher, lacking that special zombie odor. His story might be complete fiction, but if he *did* come through that portal, that was why we hadn't picked his trail up at the site.

After twenty minutes, the blood seeping from Clay's arm had soaked through a third bandage. We decided—or I insisted and Nick backed me up—to take Clay back to the hotel so Jeremy could have a look.

Not wanting to walk down the road trailing blood, we stopped in an alley to apply a fourth bandage while I called Jeremy and told him not to expect that Cabbage-town delivery, but to return to the hotel for Clay.

"There goes another shirt," Clay said as he handed me the remains of his T-shirt.

"Here," Nick said. "Use mine."

"No, mine's garbage already."

As I tore a strip for the bandage, I couldn't help noticing Zoe . . . hovering. All three of us turned to look at her, perched on a trash bin, leaning toward Clay, gaze fixed on his bloodied arm.

"The answer is no," Clay said. "Yeah, it's going to waste, but it's not teatime, so stop drooling."

"Ha-ha. I was just considering whether I should offer to help."

"By sucking up the rest of it?"

"No, by drooling. You must be used to that, Professor, students drooling over you." She hopped off the trash can. "In this case, though, it might be more welcome than I suspect it usually is. I could stop the bleeding."

"How?" I said.

"Vampire saliva stops blood flow. Keeps our dinner from bleeding out once we're done feeding. I can do that here."

"Do I wanna ask *how*?" Clay said.

"Normally, I'd lick the affected area, which I know neither of us wants, so may I suggest some discreet expectoration onto that bandage?"

I looked at Clay. He nodded, grunted a thanks and I handed Zoe the bandage.

Zoe's saliva did the trick. Ten minutes later, as we walked down Bay Street, Clay's bandage was still white. But while that meant he wasn't strolling downtown wearing a bloodied bandage, he was still half-naked. With each honk or whistle, Clay's hands jammed deeper into his pockets and he stepped a little farther into the shadow of store awnings.

We'd been searching for a taxi since leaving the museum but, like everyone else, they seemed to have taken a personal day.

"I could take off my shirt too," Nick said.

"There's an idea," Zoe said. "Wait, let me grab my lip liner. I'll write 'Meet us at Remingtons' on your backs." She grinned. "Bet they'd get a crowd tonight, cholera or no cholera."

"Leave your shirt on," Clay said.

Zoe looked at me. "We could take ours off too. In a show of solidarity. It's legal here."

"It is?" Nick perked up. "Why have I not seen a single topless woman the whole time I've been here?"

"Because, outside of beaches and concerts, you probably won't. And if you do? They won't be anyone you *want* to see topless. Every time I see one, I thank God for eternal youth. But, still, it is legal." A sly look my way. "So, if you want to take your top off . . ."

"Trust me, these days, I fall into that category of women no one wants to see topless."

"I wouldn't complain."

Her gaze rolled over to Clày, expectantly. He just turned to watch a taxi zip around the corner, then swore when he saw it was occupied.

Zoe sighed. "Not even going to rise to the bait, are you, Professor?"

"Show me bait; I'll rise."

"Oh-ho. So you think just because I'm a woman—"

"Didn't think that at all. Doesn't matter."

"Well, you may be prettier right now, but don't forget who's the one with eternal youth. In a few years, that six-pack of yours is going to look more like a collapsible cooler bag."

"Yeah, probably."

Another sigh. She started to say something else when a trio of young women ogled Clay, tittering as they passed.

I waved toward a variety store with a rack of tourist T-shirts in the window. "Want one?"

"Please."

"I couldn't resist," I said as I handed him the folded shirt.

He shook it out and laughed. It read "Had a howling

good time in Toronto" above a picture of a mutant wolf with fangs as big as walrus tusks. Typical tourist wear—drawn by someone in a distant country who'd never actually seen a wolf, but was certain Toronto must be teeming with them, running alongside the Inuit, moose and polar bears.

Clay shrugged it on. "How does it look?"

"God awful," Zoe said.

Nick waved a finger at me. "The joke will be on you five years from now, when he's still wearing it."

"That'll bother you more than it'll bother me." I reached into the bag and pulled out chocolate bars. "I heard stomachs growling."

I produced a bottle of water for Zoe.

"Ah, nice and cold," she said as she took it. "You're so sweet." She glanced over at Clay and sighed. "And so wasted."

"Damned shame, isn't it?" Clay said through a mouthful of chocolate.

"Criminal."

At the hotel, we left Nick and Zoe in the lounge. Upstairs, Jeremy popped his head outside his room almost the moment we stepped off the elevator.

"There you are," he said. "I was about to go out searching for you."

"It's just a scratch," Clay said.

Jeremy ushered us into the room. He gestured to the bed, and had the bandage off before Clay even finished settling. A frown, then he reached down to an already-prepared basin of warm water, took out the cloth, squeezed it and carefully sponged off the blood. As the wound came clean, Jeremy's frown grew.

"It does appear to be—" he began.

"Just a scratch?" Clay finished. "Told you."

"But why did it bleed so much?" I asked, drawing closer for a better look.

"It's a deep scratch," Jeremy said. "It looks as if it nicked a vein."

Clay looked over at me. "Right again. I'm a genius."

"No," Jeremy said. "You've been hurt so often you can't help but recognize the signs."

"What about . . . ?" I began, then paused. "It was Rose."

"She's worried about syphilis," Clay said.

Jeremy shook his head. "Don't be. Unless she bit him, that isn't a concern."

Jeremy cleaned it well, then plastered it up and told me to let him know if it started bleeding again or bothered Clay. No sense expecting Clay to tell him. To him, as long as the limb was still attached, he was good to go.

Once Clay was bandaged again, Jeremy and I both breathed easier, and I could tell Jeremy what had happened at the museum.

"So the zombies are catching on to our plans," I said.

Jeremy nodded. "Meaning our chances of catching one, without serious risk, are rapidly diminishing. Time to take a break and focus on Shanahan."

"I'll talk to Zoe. See if she'll be more forthcoming about him now." I turned to Clay, who was picking up the tourist shirt. "Hold on. I'll grab one of yours."

"I like this one."

I rolled my eyes and helped him into it. "As for this Hull guy, his mannerisms suggest that he is what he claims to be—a refugee from the Victorian portal—but Clay thinks he's working with the controller, maybe an actor hired to get close to us."

"Explains how he just happened on the scene," Clay said. "Better than 'I was following the zombies.' "

"So what do we do about this supposed meeting?" I said.

"Let me think about it. For now, go back to Zoe."

We started for the door.

"Oh," Jeremy said. "Anita Barrington hasn't called you, has she?"

I double-checked my cell phone, then shook my head.

"She called me here, at the hotel," he said. "Something about digging up a story we'd probably like to hear. I called her back and left a message asking her to phone your cell or Antonio's, but she hasn't returned my call . . ."

"We'll swing by there after we talk to Zoe."

We had the lounge to ourselves, so there was no need to take our business to a more private spot.

I explained our suspicions about Shanahan, and why we needed to find him.

"Patrick Shanahan as a zombie-controlling madman?" Zoe said, her finely drawn brows raised.

"Madman . . . debatable," I said. "But the zombie-controlling part seems a good guess. As for why he's controlling them or why the portal was embedded in that letter or what he hopes to gain by getting it back, we're still working on all that."

"As motivations go, I always liked world domination myself. Or perhaps this is just metropolitan domination.

Patrick never was the type to think big. Never struck me as zombie lord material either, but I can't say I know him well. It's a working relationship, and a sporadic one at that. Most of my jobs for the family were with his grandfather, and he wasn't chummy with the hired help either."

"Which means you won't be able to give us much insight into Shanahan."

"Next to none. But I know someone who can. A client. Randall Tolliver. He grew up with Patrick."

Fake

IN A CITY LIKE TORONTO, WHICH, AS FAR AS I KNEW DIDN'T even have a Cabal satellite office, the supernatural community is small. I'd lived here, on and off, for ten years after I became a werewolf, and never knew it existed. Zoe said there were only a few sorcerer families, so the community was tight—many of them knowing each other from birth, as Patrick Shanahan and Randall Tolliver did.

Although Zoe claimed to know Tolliver much better than she did Shanahan, she'd say little about him—protecting another customer.

We had a heck of a time finding Tolliver. His office either didn't have his exact schedule, or was reluctant to provide it, so we ended up canvassing a list of places he was expected to visit that afternoon. We stopped at a low-income housing complex, then an AIDS hospice, both times being told he'd come and gone.

Those places gave me a pretty good idea what Tolliver did for a living. An investment broker of another kind . . . the sort who buys bargain-basement housing, turns it into something barely livable and reaps the benefits of government assistance. Typical sorcerer.

"Let's pop by his office," Zoe said. "I'll see if I can sweet-talk the receptionist into paging him for me."

Clay swung a look my way that begged for something more active than trailing Zoe across town.

"How about we catch up with you after you find him?" I said. "We've got another stop we can make in the meantime."

"Erin?" Anita said as we walked into the bookshop.

The girl popped up from behind a display where she'd been unpacking books.

"Can you watch the store, dear? We'll be in the back."

Anita ushered us through the beaded curtain into the back office.

"We'll have to step out back to speak freely if a customer comes, but that's unlikely. We haven't seen anyone since noon. Now they're just phoning about charms and whatnot—afraid to even leave the house. Complete nonsense, of course, like wearing those hospital masks during the SARS outbreak."

"You said you have more information for us?" Clay said.

I resisted the urge to glare at him. I suspect it didn't matter how rude Clay was—Anita would get to the point at her own pace.

First, she had Clay haul out three folding chairs. Then she set up bottled water and cookies on a box of books, insisting I at least have the water to avoid dehydration.

She finally settled into the empty chair. "I managed to dredge up a Jack the Ripper story with a portal angle, though it doesn't mention the *From Hell* letter."

The story seemed to be an embellishment on the one

about a half-demon making a deal with his father. In this version, the killer had been only partway through fulfilling his obligation to his demon father when he'd been caught by a band of sorcerers, who'd imprisoned him in a dimensional portal.

"The legend goes that the sorcerers then lost the portal device, and it's out there somewhere, waiting to be accidentally triggered, whereupon the monster will, once again, be unleashed on the world, rendered insane by his long imprisonment, driven only by the need to fulfill his unholy obligation." Anita grinned, eyes twinkling. "Rather sounds like a campfire story, doesn't it? Something for our children to spook their supernatural friends with."

"It does. I suppose there could be a nugget of truth buried in there . . ."

"Well, it's not the part about sorcerers playing world saviors, I'm sure." She shook her head. "Uncharitable of me, but I suspect they would have been negotiating to share the demon's boon instead."

We discussed the story for a few minutes, then Anita asked about our progress, and I brought her up to date. When I told her about Hull, her eyes widened.

"He came through the portal?"

"Well, he says so. But he isn't a zombie, so I doubt—"

"Oh, but that doesn't prove anything. Only those who were sacrificed come out as zombies. If they were alive when they went in, they'll be alive when they come out."

"Like in the story," I said. "If Jack the Ripper was imprisoned in a dimensional portal—"

Clay snorted. "That guy is not Jack the Ripper."

"And how do you know—?"

"It *is* just a story," Anita said. "At most, as you said, it may contain distorted elements of truth, as most folklore does. But still, if this man came from Victorian London—"

"He claims," Clay said.

"But if he did, I would love to speak to him. The historical wealth of information, combined with his circumstances . . . Why, it would be supernatural folklore in the making."

My cell phone rang.

"Zoe," I said. "Hopefully she found Tolliver."

She had. "He's at Trinity Church. Are you still over on Yonge? I can swing by and meet up with you."

I told her where we were. A moment of silence. Then, "Hmm, that's a bit farther out of my way than I thought. How about I just meet you there?"

According to the plaque outside, the Church of the Holy Trinity was built in 1847, on what had then been the outskirts of Toronto. Looking around, it was hard to imagine this had ever been on the outskirts of anything. The small church stood incongruously cheek-to-jowl with the sprawling Eaton Centre shopping center—an urban shopping mall in the heart of downtown. As if having a house of spiritual worship standing beside a monument to material worship wasn't ironic enough, the church also served as a walk-in center for the homeless.

As we waited for Zoe, I read the homeless memorial list posted outside. The list of names was dotted with

Jane and John Does, those who couldn't even be properly immortalized on their own memorial.

Clay glanced over my shoulder as Zoe approached. She tensed, her face going rigid.

"What?" he said.

"Go ahead. Say it."

"Say what?"

"Ask how many of those—" She waved at the list. "—were mine."

Clay gave me a "huh?" look, but said only, "I was going to say something. Like 'hello.' Or 'about time you showed up.'"

Zoe nodded, obviously relieved. A few of the names on those lists undoubtedly had been her victims. A vampire doesn't kill every time she feeds, but she does need to drain lifeblood once a year to retain her immortality. Most pick someone like the men and women on this list. Choosing a victim from the streets lessens the ripple effect, affecting fewer lives than, say, killing a suburban mother of four, and drawing less public attention. Still, however much has gone wrong with a life, it is still a life. I suppose vampires realize that, at least some of them.

As we headed for the front doors, Clay said, "So what's up with Anita Barrington?"

Zoe blinked. "Why? What did she—?"

"You heard where we were, and suddenly didn't want to meet us," he said.

"No, I—" She paused, then shook off the denial. "I'm sure there's nothing wrong with Anita Barrington. She's quite new here, but from what I hear, a nice lady. It's just . . . well, she's an immortality quester."

Zoe looked across our blank faces. "An immortality quester is—"

"A supernatural trying to find the secret to immortality," Clay said. "Yeah, we know. Ran into a couple of vampires doing that a few years back."

"Edward and Natasha." Zoe nodded, then lowered her gaze for a moment before continuing. "Well, even vampires can catch the bug. But those questers who aren't vampires sometimes develop an . . . unhealthy interest in our kind, the semi-immortals."

"So Anita's bothered you—"

"No, no. Never met her. But I had an . . . experience with an immortality quester years ago. It just taught me to avoid them."

Clay studied her face, then grunted. "Let's get inside. Before this Tolliver guy takes off."

We climbed the steps to a set of tall, narrow green-painted wooden doors, propped open to welcome daytime visitors. Inside was a reception area, staffed by a volunteer at a table with guides and history booklets. To our left, a huge framed antique coat of arms hung over recycling containers. On the right, tarnished brass memorial plaques hung above a bulletin board covered in flyers for antiwar demonstrations, AIDS clinics and missing-person notices.

Zoe led us to the left, where the pews were. They were arranged to form a three-sided box that faced a table in the middle. Above the western entrance doors were colorful banners for social justice, peace and cultural diversity. Beneath them, a young man slept on a green sofa.

Zoe headed toward two men talking near an interior door. The younger man, probably in his early forties, turned and started walking briskly down the aisle.

Dressed in jeans and a T-shirt from the Metro-Central YMCA, he was fit, average height, dark-skinned with a short beard and distracted eyes. In one hand he carried a black bag that looked like an old-fashioned medical satchel.

He almost smacked into me, as if I'd materialized from nowhere. With a murmured apology, he started going around me.

"Randy," Zoe called after him.

He stopped, and turned. "Zoe?"

"Hey, Doc. Do you have a minute? We need to talk to you."

A discreet glance at his watch, then at Clay and me, as if curiosity was warring with an insanely busy schedule. Without a word, he nodded and waved us to a hall on the east side of the church. We went down a few steps, then out a single door into a courtyard.

Brightly painted red and blue metal chairs and tables were arranged around a small fountain. Every chair was empty, but Tolliver still led us around the fountain, to take a table at the far side, where the noise of the falling water would mask our conversation.

He gestured to the chairs. There were only three, and he seemed ready to give them to us, but when Clay took up position at my shoulder, Tolliver turned the third chair around to face ours, then sat.

"So . . ." he began. "What's this about?"

I told him the story. A version of it, that is. Zoe had suggested we remove the part about stealing the letter ourselves. If that would bother Tolliver, it seemed a little hypocritical, considering he engaged Zoe's services often enough to be on a first-name basis. But she'd advised us to stick to a variation on the truth—that we were interracial council delegates investigating the portal and trying to close it.

I also left out the part about suspecting Shanahan of being the zombie controller.

When I finished, Tolliver looked at Zoe.

"You know that these two are council delegates? For a fact?"

She laughed. "Why else would they be investigating this? It's hardly the kind of thing people volunteer for."

"I can think of one group who would, particularly if they could use this portal to their advantage."

"A Cabal?" Zoe waved at me. "Does she look like a Cabal goon?"

"No, which would be a perfect way to convince us she isn't. It would also explain why Patrick is missing. They likely took him into custody themselves."

"Yeah?" Clay said. "Then why would we be looking for him? That's what we're doing here. Trying to find him, hoping he can close this thing."

Tolliver's expression didn't change. "If you *are* on the council, then tell me this. Who's the sorcerer delegate?"

"Trick question," Zoe muttered.

"No," I said. "If Dr. Tolliver does know the current council, then it's a trick question within a trick question. There is no sorcerer delegate. Never has been. However, one other delegate is married to a sorcerer who does help with our investigations, though he doesn't participate in matters of policy."

Tolliver met my gaze. "You know him?"

"Of course. And he knows us. Call him up and ask, about either us or the investigation. He's aware of it, and has been helping with background."

Tolliver hesitated, then nodded, but didn't move. I suspected he didn't know Lucas well enough to have his number, though he might be able to get it if he made a few calls. I reminded myself to ask Lucas about Tolliver. He hadn't known Shanahan, but he was more likely to know a supernatural doctor, at least by reputation.

Tolliver finally put his medical bag on the ground and relaxed into his chair. "I can tell you this much. Whoever said Patrick's letter is responsible for this portal is wrong."

"Right," Clay said. "So the fact that this portal opens on the same night his letter is stolen, and spews out Victorian zombies and cholera is . . . a coincidence?"

Tolliver blinked. "This portal is responsible for the cholera?"

"Nah, it's just a coincidence."

Tolliver ignored him and turned to me. "Is there anything else?"

I hesitated, then said, "Possibly something with the rats, but we aren't sure yet."

Tolliver let out a quiet curse. "Typhus, probably. I've been dealing with rat bites all day."

"Typhus? How . . . bad is that?"

"Treatable with antibiotics if it's caught. People haven't started showing symptoms yet. I'm just dealing with the bites, far more than normal. Typhus will be a concern, if that's what it turns out to be, but at this stage, I'm more worried about infection from the bites. The rats seem to be more aggressive than normal."

"We found that out. They're attacking in daylight too. Is that from the disease?"

"I don't know enough about typhus to say." He leaned back. "First, cholera. Now this. No wonder I'm so busy."

Clay looked at him. "So, getting this portal closed might not be such a bad idea."

"I never said it was. Cholera and typhus notwithstanding, I completely agree that it needs to be closed, but I'm not convinced that finding Patrick will help. Yes, it seems impossible that this is a coincidence, but I find it very hard to believe his letter is to blame. It's a fake."

"That may be," I said, "but whether Jack the Ripper wrote it or not—"

"No, I mean it wasn't a real portal device. It was a fake. That's what Mr. Shanahan—Patrick's father—always said."

As he looked across our faces, he must have seen our confusion, and continued, "Geoffrey Shanahan was what you'd call an affable drunk. Normally, he barely said two words to me, but when he'd been drinking, he liked to talk, especially about his father's collection. He'd take Pat and me in there and regale us with the stories behind the pieces, what they were supposed to do, who had exposed them as fakes—"

"Fakes?" I said.

"Of course." Again, Tolliver looked at us, then Zoe. "You must know this, Zoe. You put some of those artifacts in that collection yourself."

She shook her head. "Theodore Shanahan placed the order and I filled it. Half the time, I barely even knew what I was stealing."

"Not surprising, I guess. He was an arrogant old bugger. Like most men who get their money from shady dealings. If you act like you've been born to it, no one questions where the money came from."

"So it's a collection of . . . fakes?" I glanced up at Clay, remembering the files we'd found in the house, where we'd thought he'd cleverly documented his artifacts as counterfeits. "Supernatural curiosities."

Tolliver nodded. "All of them, including that letter."

"So it supposedly *did* contain a portal," I said. "One that was believed to be fake."

"I don't remember the exact story behind it, but Patrick will have it on file."

"File's gone," Clay said.

Tolliver nodded, as if neither surprised nor indignant that we'd searched Shanahan's house.

"Can you remember anything about it?" I asked.

He paused, then shook his head. "I'll think on it some more, but that piece never interested me. Neither did Jack the Ripper in general." A small laugh. "Even as a child, I think I was offended by the suggestion that a doctor might have been responsible. Patrick would know more. The letter was one of his favorite pieces."

"Which brings us back to square one . . ." Clay said.

"Finding Patrick. I agree that the portal needs to be closed, and quickly. Even if I don't know how much help Patrick can be, I'd be happy to help you locate him . . . if I could."

"Why can't you?" I said.

"Because, while Patrick and I were close as boys, we've barely seen one another since college. He only calls now and then to see whether I've come to my senses and taken up a more profitable branch of medicine . . . with profits he could help me invest. When he learns I haven't . . ." Tolliver shrugged. "That's the end of our contact until the annual Christmas card. I can try—"

Tolliver's cell phone rang. He answered. As he listened, he closed his eyes, suddenly looking very tired. "Tell them I'm on my way," he said, then hung up.

"There's a small outbreak of intestinal upset at a nursing home I cover, and they're worried it's the cholera. More likely food spoilage from the heat, but I need to check it out immediately. As I said, I'll think about the letter some more, and Patrick as well, and see what I can come up with."

I took out a piece of paper, jotted down my number and gave it to him. He was out of the courtyard before I got to my feet.

Zoe made us promise to call and update her. In the meantime, she'd try to track down more on the story behind the letter.

The five of us went to dinner before the meeting with Matthew Hull. Jeremy had decided we'd go—that the potential reward outweighed the risk.

We found a sit-down restaurant and a quiet table. Easy enough now—in the wake of the cholera "epidemic," they were all quiet. The city still hadn't cleaned the water supply. They'd taken every step—multiple times—but the problem persisted. As long as the portal remained open, the cholera was here to stay.

While Jeremy and Antonio updated us on their dead-ended investigations, Clay kept casting anxious glances at me as I picked at my dinner.

When it was our turn and I asked Clay to tell them what we'd learned, he leaned my way.

"What's wrong?" he murmured.

"Noth—"

"You've barely touched your meal."

"It's just the heat."

"You look pale," Jeremy said. "I thought it was the lighting, but—"

"It is. I'm fine."

"You're probably dehydrated," Antonio said. "Finish your milk and we'll order you another."

I lifted my hands. "Enough. The pregnant woman is fine. Not terribly hungry tonight, that's all." I felt Clay's gaze boring into me, and sighed. "Okay, maybe a little tired, but no more than everyone else, I'm sure. It's been a very long day."

Clay pushed back his chair and stood. "Come on. I'm taking you up to our room."

"Before I finish my dinner?"

That gave him pause, but only for a second. "We'll ask for takeout."

I shook my head. "Yes, I am tired, probably from the heat, but the sooner we get this done, the sooner I can go home and really rest, in my own bed. Now sit down and bring everyone up to speed on what Randy Tolliver said." I looked up at him. "Please."

Sorcery

"SEE?" I SAID AS JEREMY LEFT OUR HOTEL ROOM. "DIAGNO-
sis: just tired."

"Exhausted," Clay said as he handed me a bottle of water. "And dehydrated."

I took the water and made a face. "Oh, that's just
Jeremy."

"He's right, though, about tonight. You need to rest,
not run off again in a few minutes."

"Notice how he tossed out that 'suggestion,' then
bolted, leaving you to handle the fallout?" I shrugged off
my shirt, which, despite a morning shower and liberal
applications of deodorant, smelled faintly of body odor.
"Can you hand me that one over there?"

"We haven't even discussed it yet, and you're already
changing to go out. You need to rest, Elena."

"And I will. Right after that portal is closed. If Hull is
working with Shanahan, then this meeting might be—"

"The end of it? How many times have we said that in
the last few days? Just steal the letter, and it's done. Just
kill the second zombie, and it's done. Just follow the
zombie back to Shanahan, and we're done." He wrapped

his hand around my other forearm and faced me. "Forget the meeting. I'm pretty certain Hull has no intention of showing up. Even if he does, he found us today, so he can find us again. Right now, it's *this* I'm worried about. You and the baby. You need—"

He jerked his left hand back, and blinked.

"What is it?"

"Your stomach. It—"

"Oh, please. Jeremy said I'm fine, so don't go trying to convince me something's wrong."

His mouth set. "You think I'd do that? I was going to say I felt—" He stopped, anger falling away in a quick grin. "There. Give me your . . ."

He took my hand and put it on the side of my stomach.

"I don't feel—" Something jabbed my hand. "Oh, my God. A kick! That's a kick."

"Or a punch," Clay said, still grinning. "If it's our baby, it's probably a punch. Trying to fight his or her way out already." He steered me across the room. "Here, look in the mirror. You can see it."

After a minute of watching, a lump poked from the lower right of my belly, then disappeared.

"Can you feel it?" Clay said.

I nodded and realized that Jeremy was right. I *had* been feeling the baby moving for weeks now, though never this obvious. Even this didn't feel so much like a kick as a stomach gurgle. I don't know what I expected— I guess when someone says "kick," I think of something hard enough to hurt.

A knock at the door. Clay leaned over to open it.

"I didn't hear shouting," Jeremy said as he walked in. "Have you come to an agreement already?"

"The baby's kicking," Clay said. "You can feel it."

"And see it," I said, grinning like an idiot.

And so, for a few minutes, all thoughts of our meeting with Hull were forgotten in the simple excitement of a baby's kicks. When he or she stopped bopping around and settled, though, the question still needed answering. By then, Clay wasn't in the mood to argue, and even Jeremy had to agree that I looked much better, having gotten my second wind.

We decided to walk. It was a bit of a hike, but if this was a trap, the zombies might start tracking us from the hotel. The sooner we smelled them, the sooner we could catch them.

Not a single whiff of rot came my way, though, and when we arrived at the park, Hull was already there. Antonio and Nick stayed out of sight, watching and patrolling the perimeter.

Hull was under a tree, scanning the growing dark. He started when he heard footsteps, and once again, he seemed relieved when he saw it was us.

"Expecting someone else?" Clay said as we approached.

A weak smile. "Fearing, I would say. Though I suppose I'm only a minor threat. For now, they're much more interested in—" He met my gaze, then looked away, as if naming the target would be rude.

"We know who they're after," I said. "The question is why?"

"A question we're hoping you can answer," Jeremy added.

Hull looked over at the new voice. "Oh, you're not—I

thought it was—" A nod to Clay and me. "—your friend from earlier."

"He has other business to attend to," I said.

Hull cast another look around the park, as if he knew darned well what the "other business" might be.

"You said you had information for us," Jeremy said. "A firsthand account, I believe, was the phrase you used."

"Yes, of course." He hesitated. "I'm not sure where to start . . ."

"Try the beginning," Clay said.

Hull nodded. "Before all this, back when I was . . ." The sentence trailed off.

"Alive?" I said.

Dismay flashed across his face. "Oh, no. I'm still alive. That is, I think I am. I didn't die. I'm certain of that."

"Let's move to that bench." Jeremy nodded at me. "She should get off her feet."

"Yes, of course," Hull said. "I should have insisted. My apologies."

As we moved to the bench, Hull relaxed.

"Now," Jeremy said. "As you were saying . . ."

Hull nodded. "Yes, right. Well, I was employed as a bookkeeper, as I had been for many years. At the time, though, I only had one client." He gave a small laugh. "That doesn't sound very good, does it? As if I couldn't find enough work, but this particular gentleman gave me more than enough, and the remuneration was excellent, so I'd temporarily given over my other clients' accounts to my business partner. This man—my client, not my partner—had recently arrived from Ireland, with sizable holdings to transfer and invest, and therefore required my undivided attention. His name was Edwin Shanahan."

He looked at our faces, waiting for a reaction. When no one obliged, he continued. "Yes, well, I suppose you guessed that this device originated with the Shanahan family, where it has apparently remained. As I was saying, Mr. Shanahan was my only client and, being a widower, without a wife to complain about such things, he conducted most of his business from his home. I was there much of the time, my presence forgotten, as employees often are. I quickly learned that some of Mr. Shanahan's business was . . ."

He flushed. "It wasn't my place to judge. My father always said a bookkeeper's responsibility was to protect his client's assets, not to question the source of those assets. Yet with Mr. Shanahan, it wasn't just the source of his money. Some of his associates were less than savory characters. One in particular. He called himself a surgeon, but he and Mr. Shanahan would laugh when he said it. When this business in Whitechapel started—"

Hull swallowed. "I . . . heard things, between Mr. Shanahan and his friend. I tried to tell myself I was wrong. Then one night this friend brought over a woman. A . . . paid companion, but not the sort you'd expect a man like Mr. Shanahan or his friend to consort with. I was supposed to be working late in the offices in the south wing, but I was curious, so I crept over to the main quarters. Nothing seemed particularly amiss. They were laughing and talking in the dining room.

"I was about to leave when I heard a scream. A dreadful scream. I stood there, frozen in my nook. Before long, Mr. Shanahan and his friend came out. They were talking about needing to 'procure' one more. As Mr. Shanahan escorted his friend to the door, I snuck down and peered into the dining room, expecting to see the poor woman dead on the floor. She wasn't there.

"The table had been moved aside, and there were strange patterns on the floor, drawn in some fine powder, like salt or sand. And there were other things . . . Objects of . . . devil worship. That reminded me of something I'd overheard before this Whitechapel business began. They'd been talking about his friend's father, of asking him for a boon and, when they spoke of him, they called him a demon. At the time, I thought they were simply being disrespectful to the old man. But after seeing that room, I had cause to wonder.

"A couple of weeks later, Mr. Shanahan seemed very agitated. He gave the staff the night off, and encouraged everyone to leave early. I pretended to leave, then returned. After dark, Mr. Shanahan's friend arrived. Again they retreated to the dining room. I could hear bits of conversation, primarily Mr. Shanahan reassuring his friend that 'it' was ready, and he'd be safe there. At the right time, he would release the servants who would prepare things for his friend's return, then they would carry out the final phases of their plan.

"Next, I heard Mr. Shanahan speaking in a strange tongue. I summoned my courage and cracked open the door. I peeked in just as Mr. Shanahan's friend disappeared. One moment he was there. He took a step . . . and vanished. I was so startled I stumbled back. Mr. Shanahan heard me. I tried to flee, but he worked some sorcery on me. He dragged me into the dining room and flung me on that same spot where his friend had vanished. The last thing I remember was him saying, 'We can use a third servant.' Then all went black. When I awoke, I was stepping onto a street in another time . . . your time."

We looked at one another.

"So," Clay said, "what do you want from us?"

Hull stared at him. He'd just relayed the fantastical tale of his brush with demons, sorcerers, black magic, notorious serial killers and over a hundred years of suspended animation. Why weren't we speechless with horror and amazement?

"You told us earlier you wanted something from us," Clay said. "What is it?"

Jeremy shook his head at Clay, telling him to be patient.

"So you believe you were pushed through that portal while you were still alive, which explains why you aren't a zombie," Jeremy said.

"A zom—? Oh, yes, I see. I suppose that's what they are." Hull shuddered. "No, I'm quite certain I'm not one of those. Neither is he, though, and he is our main concern."

"*He* being Jack the Ripper," I said.

"Jack the—? Yes, he did call himself that once, didn't he? Is that the name they kept for him? Suitably macabre, I suppose."

"And you believe this friend of Edwin Shanahan, the real Jack, came out of that portal with you?"

"No, he didn't." Hull swung to his feet, trembling with agitation. "That's what they're trying to do. The rite, the one they need the letter for."

"How do you know that?" Jeremy asked.

"It's obvious, isn't it? I know they want that letter. When I was hiding from them yesterday, I overheard the man say something to the woman about getting it back."

"To free this killer? They said that?"

Hull's brows knitted as he looked at Jeremy. "No, but that must be the reason, mustn't it? That's their purpose, to act as his servants. This killer can't have come through yet or they would be serving him, not Mr. Shanahan's grandson."

"Great-grandson, presumably," Jeremy murmured.

Hull nodded. "I suppose it *has* been that long, hasn't it?" He went silent, eyes downcast.

"If he isn't through yet, then we really need to close that portal," I said. "As quickly as possible. So how do we do that?"

Hull looked at me as if I'd just asked him how to turn off the moon. "I—I have no idea. I thought you knew how to close it. That's why you're still here, isn't it? Trying to close it and set things right?"

Clay made a noise deep in his throat. "In other words, you're just here to warn us that yet another catastrophe might strike if we don't fix this damned thing."

"Perhaps I can do more than that. If I could lure in a zombie, would that help?"

"You still haven't told us what you want in return," Clay said.

"I was hoping for your assistance."

"With what?"

Hull spread his hands and gave a tight laugh. "Anything. To me, just days ago, I was a bookkeeper in London, under the reign of Queen Victoria. Now I'm here, and I'm not even sure where *here* is. What little money I have on me is useless. Since I've arrived here, I've had to . . ." He flinched. "Steal to eat, to clothe myself—"

Jeremy took some bills from his wallet. "This will be

enough to find a place to stay tonight and buy food. We'll meet with you again tomorrow, in case we have further questions."

"Did anyone else get the impression he was hoping we'd take him with us?" I asked as we left the park.

Clay snorted.

"It would be the humane thing to do," Jeremy said. "If his story is true. But if it isn't . . ."

I nodded. "If he's working with Shanahan, he'd like nothing more than to go back to the hotel with us."

"You think he's full of shit, then?" Clay asked.

Jeremy shook his head. "I have no idea."

"We could skip the wrap-up," Clay said as he held open our hotel room door. "Let Jeremy bring the others up to date, while we get an early night."

"No, I want to—" I stopped, seeing the bed across the room, so inviting, and feeling lead seep into my bones at the thought of heading out again. "Yes, I *want* to be there, but . . . sure, let's call it a night. They don't need—"

Clay had moved to the middle of the room, and was slowly turning, scanning the room, nostrils flaring. "Someone's been here." He strode to the work desk. "I left this drawer open when I grabbed my key card."

He dropped to a crouch and inhaled. A pause and a frown, then another sniff, his head dipping almost to the carpet.

I walked over. "Maybe the maid service popped in—"

"Someone's been here. I can't smell anyone, but my papers—" He gestured at a stack of notes he'd brought on the trip. "Someone's flipped through them, and straightened them up."

I pulled open the dresser drawer I'd been using for my clothes. They were still haphazardly stuffed in, but the piles were separated, neater, as if someone had rifled through, and made some effort to cover his tracks.

I walked to the door, dropped to all fours and sniffed. I did the same at the connecting door into the next room.

"Our scents, and the cleaning woman's from this morning. That's it."

As Clay did a quick check of the room, I picked up the phone and called Jeremy's number. There was no answer. When I went to try Antonio's room, Clay shook his head.

"I'll find them." He strode to the connecting door and opened it. "Nick?"

A muffled answer from the bathroom.

"When you're done, get in here," Clay called. "Stay with Elena for me."

I grabbed the door from Clay. "Go on. I'll wait in there."

Clay left. I stepped into Nick's room, then realized I had a call of nature of my own to answer. A word to Nick through the bathroom door, then back into our room.

The bathroom door was half-closed. Hadn't I just watched Clay shove it open, glancing inside as he'd checked the room?

I crept closer to the door and inhaled. Nothing. Another step, and I could see into the bathroom. Empty and still no scent.

Okay, now *I* was getting paranoid.

I walked in, and pushed the bathroom door shut behind me. Out of the corner of my eye, I caught a blur through the mirror. I started wheeling, fists flying up, but an invisible force hit me with a werewolf-strength upper-cut to the jaw. As I fell, my head cracked against the toilet and I blacked out.

My eyelids fluttered, and I saw a figure hunched over me. I punched, but a hand closed around mine before I could make contact.

Still dazed, I struggled to get up and throw my attacker—

"Elena."

That voice slapped me to my senses. I focused and saw Jeremy over me, his hand still gripping mine. Clay was behind me, cradling my head.

"What happ—?" I tried to jump up, but Jeremy's grip held me back, letting me rise slowly until I was sitting on the bathroom floor.

"Someone hit—" I looked around. "Did you catch—?"

"He's gone," Jeremy said.

"I heard you yell," Nick said from behind Jeremy. "I ran in here, but he was already in the hall. I took off after him, but all I saw was . . . I don't know. Like a blur, I guess. I probably should've chased him but I was worried about you . . ."

"The right decision," Jeremy said.

"Is there a trail?" I asked. "Maybe we can track—"

"No trail." Antonio's head popped through the bathroom doorway. "I checked to the elevator and the stairs. This floor is practically empty, and the only strong trails are ours."

"No scents in here. No scents out there. That's not possible—"

"Shanahan," Clay said. "Potion or spell to cover his

scent. A knockback spell to hit Elena. A blur spell to escape."

"So he knows what we are. Damn it. But if he was here—either lying in wait for me or looking for the letter—I bet his zombies are nearby. And no potion or spell can cover their stink."

I pushed my feet, wobbled for a second, then steadied myself.

"Can we Change?" I asked Jeremy.

He nodded.

We Changed inside an empty loading dock near the train tracks.

When I was done, I stuck my muzzle out and inhaled. An explosion of scent hit me, so complex and strong that I almost reeled back. Clay's nose brushed my shoulder as he pushed out for a sniff of his own.

Cities smell foreign. There's no better way to describe it. As a human, the smell of the city conjures up many emotions and connotations, some good, some bad, but all . . . normal.

As a wolf, though, I'm assaulted by a combination of incongruent scents. With the forest, I know what to expect—flora and fauna, all earthy, musky, natural smells. Here in one whiff, I picked up dirt and asphalt, mouse droppings and sewer gas, leaves and fresh paint, sweat and cologne, rotting roadkill and fresh cut fries. None of it seemed to fit together, but the incongruence, while jarring, was like a wonderful puzzle for my brain, picking apart the scents and trying to identify each.

Nick nudged my hindquarters. When I didn't move,

he nipped my haunch. I swallowed a snarl and settled for flicking my tail in his face before sliding out.

I went only far enough to stop blocking the way, then glanced around. The look was more habit than necessity. If anyone was here, I'd smell him.

Once all four of us were out, we split up. Antonio and Nick took the side streets while we'd search the ground behind the hotel. That meant their territory was tougher to cover, but ours was far more vast—instead of circumscribed paths along sidewalks and back streets, we had train tracks, open grassland and parking lots.

I started with the tracks, which ran along the rear of the hotel over to Union Station. After five minutes of that, Clay bumped my shoulder, telling me to give it up. He was right. The stink was too much—creosote, diesel fuel, pesticides and whatever else decades of use had dumped into the soil.

We headed for the maze of sidewalks, green space and covered walkways that linked the SkyDome, CN Tower and convention center. The wind whistled around the empty buildings, the distant clomp of a security guard's boots was the only sign of life. Here we became canine scent vacuums, loping back and forth over the open areas, noses to the ground.

We eventually ended up down a small hill, in a desolate piece of wasteland that earned a tidy sum as a parking lot during baseball season. As we crisscrossed the lot, I found what we'd been hunting for—zombie rot.

I let out a doglike bark, calling Clay over. He snuffled the ground between my forelegs, then grunted. We split up, Clay tracking the scent one way, me the other. When I realized my trail headed away from the hotel, I doubled back and took over from Clay.

Once out of the parking lot, the tracking was slow going—too many other people's scents joined the zombie's . . . and it was the male zombie, who didn't stink as bad as Rose.

When headlights flashed behind us, Clay bumped me into the shadow of an advertising sign, and we huddled there while the cars disgorged by a red traffic light zoomed past. Coast clear, I headed back to the sidewalk . . . and couldn't find the trail. It was so faint and overlain with other scents that I had to backtrack to pick it up. Half a block later, it vanished again.

As we stepped away from the streetlights to let more cars pass, Clay nudged me and gave a slow shake of his head. With the trail this faded, it probably wasn't recent. True, but it was the only one I had, so I veered around Clay and kept following it.

The longer I insisted on following the trail, the more incensed Clay became. By the time we neared the hotel, Clay was furious, growling and jostling me as hard as he dared. Several times he strode off, but when I didn't follow, he came back, mood fouler. When he nipped my haunch, I spun on him, ears back, snarling. He returned my snarl and we faced off, growling and snapping until footsteps sent us both diving for cover.

A couple passed on the distant sidewalk, laughing, arms around each other. As we watched them go, a sigh shuddered through Clay's flanks. He looked over at me and gestured, asking me to just leave the old trail for a while, and we'd come back if we couldn't find a better one.

I lowered my nose to the ground and inhaled. Yes, it was the bowler-hatted zombie's trail, but at least four

others crisscrossed over it . . . and there couldn't have
been that many people across this grassy patch since
dark.

As I lifted my head, I caught another sent. Faint
but . . .

I strained, my nose twitching. I gestured for Clay to
follow, continuing in the same direction the bowler-
hatted zombie had gone.

He growled, patience evaporating. I smacked the bottom of his muzzle with mine, directing his nose. His eyes
widened as he caught Rose's scent.

I bumped his side, snorting a "See, I was right." He
swatted me with his tail, then, as I turned on him, tore
off after Rose's scent, leaving me to catch up.

We slowed as we entered a service road. From up ahead
came the clicking of nails on pavement. I sniffed, then
let out a sharp yip. Clay circled me, tail swishing, eager
to be off now that we might have a target.

I was about to yip again when Antonio slipped from
the shadows ahead of us, with Nick at his heels. I made a
show of sniffing the air. He dipped his muzzle in a nod,
and signaled left. I followed him. Within twenty feet we
hit Rose's trail, which they'd already been following.

I snuffled along it for a bit, back and forth, then looked
up at Clay. He grumbled deep in his chest, eyes doubt-
ful. This trail was stronger than the bowler-hatted zombie's, but didn't seem any more recent.

When I motioned I wanted to follow it, though, he
grunted his agreement. We were about to set out when
Antonio stepped in front of me. I backed up, presum-

ing he wanted to lead. Pack hierarchy can be a tricky thing. Technically, as Jeremy's "spokesperson," I outrank Antonio. Yet he was my senior—and the stronger wolf— so the distinction was questionable. In a hunt, Clay and I followed Antonio's lead.

When I fell back, though, he snorted, and gestured for me to lead, but cautiously. He must have seen or smelled something up ahead earlier—probably people. So we proceeded in a single file down the empty service road, clinging to the shadows in case someone appeared.

As we reached the end, my pulse quickened. Rose was here. I could smell her in the air. Just around that corner—

A gentle nip at my hind leg. Antonio. I stopped and took a deep breath. Other scents fluttered past, woven with Rose's stench. Other people. Close by.

I hunkered down, crept to the corner and peered around it. It opened into an alcove, maybe the size of a bedroom. And that's what it was being used as—a bedroom. Four kids—none older than twenty—slept on the bare pavement.

One twitched in sleep, and I jumped. I steadied myself, then took a careful look around. In the back corner lay a dark pile. That seemed to be where Rose's smell was coming from . . . on the far side of the four sleeping teens.

I backed up so Clay and Antonio could take a look. Then I waited for Antonio to make the decision. After a quick look, though, he walked behind me, sat and started nipping at a burr in his coat.

I glanced at Clay. He peeked around the corner, then pulled back and gave a soft "hmmph"—your choice.

Again, I checked with Antonio, but he was studiously working at that burr, leaving the decision to me.

I set Clay and Nick on watch duty, then crept into the alcove, rolling on my foot pads so my nails wouldn't click.

I picked my way through the sleeping bodies. My focus stayed on my goal, relying on Clay and Nick to warn me if the kids woke. I was passing the final sleeper when Clay grunted. I stopped, one paw still in the air. The boy beside me shifted. He flung out his arm, knocking against my hind leg. My heart thudded as his fingers brushed my fur. Then his hand fell to the pavement, and the deep rhythmic breathing of sleep resumed.

I eased my back legs over his outstretched arm and crossed the final few feet to the pile in the corner. Rose's stink was evident, but her heavy clothes must have stifled the worst of it or those kids would never be sleeping so close.

The coat Rose had been wearing was pulled up over her.

I maneuvered as close as I could, leaned in to take the coat's edge between my teeth, then thought better of it. I didn't want my lips anywhere near Rose. So I stepped on the hem, catching the edge under my nails, and gingerly peeled it back.

Behind me, one of the kids muttered and I froze, still stretched over Rose, but Clay didn't sound a warning, so I waited until all went quiet, and tugged the coat off the rest of the way. As I did, I realized the stench came from the garment. The underside was dotted with sloughed skin and bits of rotted flesh. I looked over to discover that I'd uncovered a pile of crushed cardboard boxes. I stifled a snarl of frustration and headed back to the others.

* * *

We followed Rose and the bowler-hatted zombie's trails for a while, but soon I had to admit that Clay was right. They were old tracks—probably from earlier in the day or even the night before. So we headed back to the hotel and packed. I suggested the hotel beside Trinity Church, where we'd been that afternoon, and Jeremy agreed.

Time-Out

CLAY MADE SURE I SLEPT IN THE NEXT DAY BY KEEPING THE curtains drawn and the room cool and quiet. He even un-plugged the bedside clock, so when I groggily awoke and glanced over to see what time it was, there was no glow-ing LED display chastising me.

When I did wake, probably midmorning, I found a food court breakfast buffet within arm's reach. Muffins, croissants, bagels, fruit and fresh-squeezed orange juice. Enough variety to guarantee I'd find something tempting.

Even as we ate in bed, Clay was quiet, stretched out beside me, reading and drinking orange juice as I munched my banana-nut muffin. When my stomach was full, there was nothing to stop me from lying back down and drifting off, so that's what I did.

When I awoke again, Clay was still reading. I reached out and touched his arm below his bandage. I expected the bare skin to be cool from the air-conditioning. In-stead it was warm, almost hot.

"Morning, darling."

He rolled onto his side and let his book slide to the floor. I moved my fingers to his chest . . . which was cool.

"Your arm's hot. Where she scratched you. Jeremy should—"

"Yeah, I know. I'll have him check it when he gets back." He flexed his arm and made a face. "Who knows what crud that thing had under her nails?"

"You think it's infected?"

"Maybe a bit." He brushed a strand of hair from my face and frowned. "I'll have him check you too. You still look tired."

"I've had enough sleep." I stretched and shuddered, trying to throw off the numbness. "Too much sleep. What time is it?"

"Almost one."

"In the afternoon?" I sat up. "Where is everyone?"

"Out looking for Shanahan. Nick just called."

"I didn't hear—"

He lifted my cell phone from the bed. "Vibrate. Nick set it up before he left. They're stopping back before the meeting with Hull."

I jumped up. "That's right. I have to get ready."

"We're not going."

"Don't start this again."

He pushed himself out of bed, snarling a yawn. "It's not me. Jeremy's orders. It's a daytime meeting in a public place, so he's taking Antonio and Nick. We're supposed to stay here and rest up for tonight."

"What's tonight?"

He shrugged. "No idea, but I'm sure Jeremy will think of something."

* * *

When Jeremy got back, he checked me over and declared I needed more rest. Clay's arm was the bigger concern. It was showing signs of infection, despite Jeremy's thorough cleaning the day before. Being scratched by a rotting corpse isn't exactly sanitary.

Once he cleaned the wound, dosed Clay with antibiotics and rebandaged him, Jeremy had to leave for his meeting with Hull.

"Is there anything we can do here?" I asked as he put away his medical supplies. "Phone calls to make? New questions to research?"

"I believe we've exhausted all those avenues. Just take it easy and rest for tonight."

"What's tonight?"

I could tell by Jeremy's expression that he didn't know.

"Well," he said finally. "Jaime did suggest a séance—"

"Great. With whom?"

"She wants to attempt to contact the people from Cabbagetown who went through that portal, to make sure they're still there and are all right."

"Oh. I guess that would be something . . ."

"Yeah," Clay said, pitching our muffin wrappers into the trash across the room. "A waste of time."

"I think her real goal is to see whether there's anyone else in there," Jeremy said.

"Now that's a good idea."

Jeremy looked at me. "Asking Jaime to conduct a difficult séance so she can make the acquaintance of a notorious serial killer?"

I crossed the room and grabbed my half-finished orange juice from Clay before he dumped it. "But it *would* tell us how true Matthew Hull's story is."

"Perhaps, but I'm hoping to get a better sense of that this afternoon."

For lunch, we met up with Jaime and walked over to the mall. Just through the doors was a newsstand. The headline on one paper caught my eye: KILLER CHOLERA? RAMPAGING RATS?

"Killer?" I said, veering toward the papers. "Has it killed—?"

"No," Clay said, snagging my arm. "Someone in a nursing home died yesterday, but the other papers say it wasn't related."

"What about the rampaging rats? Have they—?"

"Attacked someone and torn them to shreds?" Clay gave me a look. "I told you we watch too many horror movies. But if you want to go home . . ."

"No. Jeremy's right. Avoid tap water and rats. I can handle that."

We headed down to the food court. The mall was so quiet you could hear Jaime's heels clicking as we walked down the corridor.

We bought lunch at the little market where Jeremy had bought my breakfast earlier. I suggested we take it outside to Trinity Square, but Clay headed for a forlorn patch of empty tables. I shook my head to Jaime, and followed.

"What's that?" I said, seeing Clay pick up a leaflet from a table.

When he didn't answer, I grabbed one from another table. On the poorly printed leaflet, someone had listed the recent problems plaguing the city, and likened them to the signs of the Apocalypse, entreating the reader to make his peace with God, because the end was near.

"What bullshit," Clay said, snatching my leaflet and balling it up. "Did they even bother to read Revelations? Killer rats as one of the signs?"

He waved us to the mall corridor, apparently having changed his mind about eating indoors. We walked down the other side of the mall, cruelly raising the hopes of a fresh batch of bored sales clerks. As we passed one kiosk, I noticed a hastily hand-drawn sign.

"Home filtration systems," I read. "Guaranteed to kill cholera, E. coli and all other waterborne pests. Oh, and they have animal repellent spray for rats. Figures. Start an apocalypse, someone else cashes in."

"You should ask for your share," Jaime said.

"No kidding. You know what I really feel like doing, though? Climbing to the top of the CN Tower, busting out a window and shouting 'I'm sorry. I'm really, really sorry. I apologize unreservedly.'"

Jaime laughed. "And you hereby undertake not to repeat any such apocalyptic actions at any time in the future?"

"Wasn't your fault," Clay said. "*I* squashed the mosquito."

"Kill a bug, launch the apocalypse," Jaime said. "Now that's serious karma."

"I had a backlog," Clay said. "Now let's move. We're starting to attract attention."

"Let's sit over there in the shade," Jaime said. "By the waterfall."

To call the water flowing into the concrete pond to our right a "waterfall" was being generous. It was a spout coming out of a wall, with a constant high-pressurized rush of water. It was supposed to be an industrial-style fountain, but every time I saw it, I couldn't help but suspect that the building's owners had found an ingenious way to dispose of waste water and call it art.

We sat on a bench overlooking a vast empty patch of weeds and dead grass, a solitary squirrel cavorting through it.

"What the hell is that?" Clay said.

I squinted at the sign, which showed barefooted people happily wending their way through a large maze of green grass.

"A labyrinth," I said. "Looks like they forgot to water it. And weed it. And . . . pretty much do anything at all with it."

"Where's the labyrinth part?"

"See those dark paths, where the grass is browner than the rest?"

Clay shook his head. "And I thought our yard maintenance was bad."

"That squirrel's having a blast, though," Jaime said, laughing through her veggie wrap. She chewed, then swallowed and said, "So about tonight . . . I talked to Jeremy about a séance—"

My cell phone rang.

"Nick?" Clay asked as I checked the call display.

"Anita Barrington."

He snorted. "Probably got another story for us. Tell her—"

I motioned him to silence as I answered.

Yes, Anita had more information for us. When I tried to

get her to relate over the phone, though, she insisted it wasn't safe.

"I'll call back from a landline," I said. "Just give me five min—"

"No, dear. You don't understand. This is— I really must see you."

Clay shook his head emphatically.

"Actually, I'm sticking close to the hotel today. Doctor's orders—"

"Then I'll come there. Erin's gone to my sister's. Getting her out of the city during all this seemed wise. I'll close the shop early and head over. Oh, and I can take a look at that letter while I'm there. You still have that, don't you?"

Clay frowned and shifted closer to hear better.

I told her I had the letter, and she was welcome to examine it.

"Excellent. Now where are you staying?"

I glanced at Clay. "The same hotel we gave you the phone number for."

"Oh? You're still there? Yes, of course you are—"

"No, I'm sorry. Completely forgot. We moved last night. We're at the Marriott over by the Eaton Centre. I'll meet you in the lobby."

"The letter's right there on the table," I said as we brought Anita into our hotel room. "There are gloves beside it."

She headed straight for it. I collapsed onto the bed.

"Tired, darling?" Clay asked.

"Too hot," I said, then looked at the nightstand. "Where's the bottled water?"

"Finished it. I'll run down and grab some more."

"No, get juice. Do they have cranberry?" I pushed up from the bed. "Here, I'll go with you. Anita—"

"I'm fine, dear," she said, head still down as she examined the letter.

Two minutes later, Anita Barrington opened our hotel room door, slipped out and nearly barreled into Clay, planted in the hallway. She spun and saw me blocking the other side.

"Oh, you're back," she said. "That was quick. I was just—"

"Leaving . . ." I waved at the tube in her hand. "With our letter."

A small laugh. "Oh, dear, this doesn't look good, does it? But I wasn't leaving. I was coming down to see you, and it didn't seem safe to leave this in the room."

As she spoke, Clay opened the room door. I waved Anita in. She hesitated, looking across our faces, then went inside.

"Now," she said as the door closed. "About that story I brought—"

"Don't bother unless it's the real one," Clay said.

I grasped the end of the letter tube. She clung to it for a second before letting go.

"She's right, though," I said to Clay. "We need to be more careful about this. Someone could break in and ransack our room looking for it."

He nodded. "Someone who knew where we were staying."

"Because that person specifically asked for our hotel phone number. Someone who must have figured out what we are, so she knew she needed a potion to cover her scent when she broke in."

"Someone who can cast blur spells, knockback spells, probably cover spells too . . . which is why we didn't see her in the bathroom."

Anita looked from Clay to me. "I don't think I follow. Did someone break in—"

"Earlier, you asked me where we were staying. You knew we had a reason to move last night."

She laughed. "No, dear, I have a very poor memory. I completely forgot that you told me which hotel—"

She lunged for the letter, slamming Clay with a knock-back spell. I dove to cut her off, but her fingers wrapped around the tube as she cast another spell. Her form blurred and, for a second, she seemed to disappear.

"Elena!"

Clay sprang to his feet. A blur appeared at my shoulder. I spun out of the way as fingers grazed my side. The blur faltered, thrown off balance. She hit the nightstand, sending the lamp crashing to the floor. I lashed out, but missed. The blurred form raced for the door. Clay ran at her and threw himself down in her path. Anita tripped over him, reappearing as she struck the floor. I raced past her and grabbed the dropped letter.

"Elena!"

I wheeled as Anita's hands flew up in a knockback spell. Our eyes met and she faltered, giving Clay time to roll up from the carpet. He charged, grabbed her by the back of her blouse and threw her over his shoulder. She hit the floor lamp, taking it down with her. Clay stalked over. She tried to scramble backward, out of his range, but he kept coming. Finally he was above her. Her lips parted in a spell, but she was shaking too badly to get the words out.

"Clay," I murmured.

He hesitated, then backed off. I stepped into his place.

"Playing games doesn't go over well with us," I said. "We take them seriously."

I reached down and helped her up.

"Sit there," I said, gesturing at the chair. "Then tell us the real story behind the letter—the one that has something to do with immortality."

She still tried to protest and sidetrack us, but finally told us the letter's history, the one she'd known before she'd approached Shanahan to see it.

The story went that a sorcerer had created the portal. He'd been finishing work on an experiment, one that promised a form of immortality. A common enough type of experimentation, but something about this one made other supernaturals think he may have actually hit on a way to do it. Some wanted to steal his research. Some wanted to stop it. So he created the portal to hide, and put the trigger in the paper used to make the *From Hell* letter.

When Anita was done, I told her Hull's version of the tale.

She frowned. "That seems like a blending of the two stories—the half-demon one and the immortality experiment one. Perhaps that campfire tale bears more truth than one would imagine."

I said nothing. After a moment, she continued.

"The demon's boon may be immortality. Or the secret to it. The sorcerer only created the portal—it was the half-demon Jack the Ripper who hid inside."

"And will be unleashed to wreak unholy terror on an unsuspecting world," Clay drawled. "He's doing a half-assed job of it so far."

"Maybe he's just warming up."

Two hours later, Jeremy walked into our room, looked around and sighed.

"So much for resting," he said as he righted the broken floor lamp.

"It wasn't us," I said. "Anita Barrington stopped by and all hell broke loose."

Another sigh.

"You think I'm kidding? Seems Shanahan wasn't the spellcaster who broke into our room last night."

We told him what had happened.

"And after all that—plus nearly giving me a concussion last night—she had the gall to ask again if she can speak with Matthew Hull."

"Probably hoping he knows more than he's saying, which, after speaking to him today, I doubt. But as for the letter, I can't imagine what she hopes to learn from that."

"Our theory? She's hoping to use it as leverage with Shanahan. If the zombies seem to want it back, what better offering to the man she believes may hold the secret to immortality."

"Did you confront her on that?"

I shook my head. "It seemed better not to. Not yet."

"Good. She may still prove useful."

Our lunch having been interrupted, we ate a delayed one with Jaime, Nick and Antonio in the hotel restaurant. The restaurant was bright and open, with huge windows and market umbrellas—the feel of eating on a patio without the bugs, heat and smog.

According to Jeremy, Hull had scored about 80 percent when he'd quizzed him on the geography and minor current events of 1888 London—the kind of things it would be hard for a nonresident to answer, but equally hard for a resident to get perfect.

Jeremy had even mentioned that we had a source who might attempt to contact Jack the Ripper through the portal tonight, to see how Hull reacted, but he'd been all for it, and even offered to help, making no attempt to retract or change his story.

The server appeared with our plates before he could continue.

"So," Clay said after the server left. "He seems legit. But besides winning the sympathy vote, can he do anything for us?"

Antonio opened his mouth to answer, but Nick cut in. "He thinks he can lead us to Shanahan. He says he can feel a pull or something, like Shanahan is trying to control him. He's offered to try following that pull tonight."

Antonio swirled a french fry through his ketchup puddle, gaze down.

"You aren't buying it," I said.

"It felt like when a middle manager books a meeting with me, shows up and swears he can get some big industry name on board for a joint project because his third cousin married the guy's niece. He might have convinced himself he has an in, but all he's really doing is trying to find an in with me, to get the attention of the guy whose name is on the sign outside. Hull might think he feels some connection to Shanahan, and he'll probably try his damnedest to make it work, but what he really wants is some connection to *us,* to make himself seem useful so we'll help and protect him."

"Parasite," Clay said.

Antonio nodded. "A harsh way of putting it, but yes. Still, can you blame the guy? He's lost and alone in a strange world. All he wants is a little of our time."

I glanced over at Jeremy. "So are we going to give it to him tonight?"

"Yes, but only because it's a lead, and we don't have many else to follow."

"You do have one more," Jaime said, then looked up from her salad and met his gaze. "Dimensional portal fishing, courtesy of your very underworked necromancer."

After eating, we switched hotels . . . again. Dealing with Anita Barrington was a complication we really didn't need.

Notorious

JAIME STOPPED AT THE END OF THE PORTAL ROAD. "THIS is it?"

"It's not going to be easy, is it?" I said.

"Jeremy warned me it was a residential area, but I figured, being downtown, that meant high-rises, walkups, busy roads . . ." She scanned the empty street. ". . . people. We're going to be a tad obvious, conducting a séance at dusk, in the middle of the road."

"If it's not going to work—"

"There are two ways we can do this. One, come up with a plausible story to explain why we're hanging out on a sidewalk for an hour or so."

"The other?" Clay said.

"I play me—flaky celeb spiritualist trying to contact the souls of those who disappeared."

"Option A," Clay said.

"I thought you'd say that. Let's get some props then."

We bought an inexpensive camera and a notepad, and Jaime assigned us our roles. Clay would play photographer.

I'd do the note taking. Jaime would be our boss, gathering source material for a proposed television special on recent events.

We'd still attract attention. If it was too much, we'd have to abort.

Clay and I wandered up the road, taking notes and pictures. I knew Jaime wouldn't accept help if offered; she didn't even allow onlookers when she was doing the setup work. I guess even seasoned performers can get stage fright, particularly when they aren't comfortable in a role.

Once Jaime was ready, she called us over and began peeling back the dimensional layers, looking for our lost souls. Less than ten minutes later, she had one: seventy-eight-year-old Irene Ashworth.

Only Jaime could hear Irene, so the conversation was pretty one-sided. After a few minutes of confirming her identity, based on some basic facts we'd gleaned from the newspaper, Jaime was about to let her go.

"Not yet," Clay said. "Gotta be sure."

"Sure of what?" Jaime said, whispering so Irene wouldn't overhear. "You don't think this could be Jack? But she's a wom—" She shook her head. "Of all people, I should know better. There's no reason Jack the Ripper couldn't be a woman. But she answered the questions right."

I shook my head. "If she had contact with the real Irene Ashworth in that portal, that wouldn't be hard. You have to ask her something only someone from our time could answer, like what the Internet is or a DVD."

"DVD?" Jaime's voice rose as she laughed. "At her age,

we'd be lucky if she knew what a VCR was." Jaime froze, then turned. "Oh, y-yes, of course you could hear that."

Pause.

"No, you're not deaf. I didn't mean—"

Pause.

"Well, yes, I'm sure the Internet is great for online brokerages and, yes, you're right, voice-over-Internet protocol must be a cheaper way to talk to the grandkids . . ."

Strike missing person number one off the list.

"There's another one already," Jaime said. "I wish trolling for ghosts was this easy. Okay, here he comes . . . Got a male. Midthirties. He's almost here . . ."

While the description sounded promising for Jack the Ripper, it also matched that of the second missing person, Kyle Belfour, the thirty-six-year-old systems analyst who lived one block over and had vanished while jogging. Initial probing suggested the spirit *was* Belfour, but Jaime ran into some difficulties with the questioning.

"We just need your name and some basic—"

Pause.

"To confirm your identity—"

Pause.

"Why do we need to confirm it?"

She looked back at us for help. I murmured a suggestion.

"Right," she said. "Because, when we pull you out of there, we need to be sure it really is you."

Pause.

"Who else could it be? Er, well . . ."

"Just tell him to answer the damned questions," Clay said. "Or we'll leave him in there."

Jaime started to respond, then stopped. "Government conspiracy? Uh, no, this isn't—"

Pause.

"No, it's not part of a military test either."

Pause.

"Well, yes, I suppose sending enemies of the state into a dimensional holding cell wouldn't be such a bad idea, but neither the CIA or the mil—"

"CSIS," I said.

She looked over her shoulder at me.

"In Canada, it's not the CIA. Remind him that if this was a Canadian intelligence or military operation, it would have to have been dreamed up by CSIS and funded with our military budget."

She did.

After a moment, she said, "Well, yes, I suppose that is kind of funny."

Pause.

"No, no, don't apologize. You've been under a lot of stress. Now, if you could just tell us—"

Pause.

"An American-designed-and-funded experiment? Using hapless Canadian citizens?"

She looked back at us. Clay rolled his eyes.

We never did get Belfour to admit to his name. It didn't matter. After ten minutes of spouting a conspiracy diatribe on the growing U.S. military power under Bush, sprinkled with references to CIA mind control experiments, *The Manchurian Candidate,* and even an *X-Files* nod, we knew our guy was from the twenty-first century. We gave him the same reassurances we'd given Mrs.

Ashworth, then let him slide back to his dimensional holding cell.

By that time, we'd started to attract notice from the neighbors. I'd fielded a few questions while Jaime had been listening to Belfour, cutting off the onlookers' approach before they got close enough to hear her arguing with herself. After she sent Belfour back and started trolling again, Clay and I took our show on the road, taking pictures as I played reporter and asked questions of the curious. Ask the right questions, and you can get rid of people pretty fast. Once the first wave had retreated to their homes, I slid over to Jaime.

"Any luck?" I whispered.

"I'm . . . not sure. I'm picking up one more presence, and I think it's male . . ."

"Could be our boy. Is he playing shy?"

"Seems more confused."

"Not surprising if he's been in there for over a hundred years."

"I'm trying to lure him over. There— He sees me. He's coming this way. Yep, it's a man, maybe late fifties . . . Here he comes. Showtime."

Lyle Sanderson, sixty-one, claimed to have been walking his dog the evening before when "everything went black." Very suspicious . . . except that he'd answered all our test questions about the twenty-first century with flying colors. A quick query to the next onlooker who'd popped from her house confirmed that a man named Lyle Sanderson lived just down the road . . . and that a neighbor had found his dog running free last night.

* * *

Jaime continued hunting for another person inside the portal, but finally, she shook her head.

"Empty," she said.

"So Hull's lying."

"Or Jack the Ripper is somewhere else. But he's not here, and that means he's not getting out."

I glanced at the hairline crack in the road, where everything started. "The door going the other way is still open, though, isn't it? More people can go through. Like Lyle Sanderson."

"It's not easy. You have to hit just the right spot, at just the right angle. Think of how many people have walked across it in the last few days. Only three went through. You could probably stroll over there and dance on it, and nothing would happen." She looked at the crack again. "Though I wouldn't recommend it . . ."

Clay shook his head and walked toward the sidewalk.

"They won't . . . remember any of this, right?" I said. "Being in the portal, talking to you . . . ?"

"Nada. Just like that Hull guy. He only remembers going in and coming out, which makes me think *that* part of his story is true."

"And the rest?"

She shrugged. "I haven't met the guy, but this business about feeling a 'pull' from the zombie controller?" She shook her head and adjusted her oversized purse. "I told Jeremy I think that's bullshit—if Hull didn't die, then he's not a zombie, so he has no connection to any controller. But, like Jeremy said, it can't hurt to try."

"Time to call and see how it's going."

* * *

"Hold on," I said to Jeremy. "There's a police car whipping up Yonge. I can't hear you."

He waited a second, then said, "We're over—"

"Wait, got another one."

"I can hear the sirens. How much trouble did you three cause?"

"Very funny."

"We're near Bay and Gerrard if you want to take a cab over."

"It's close enough to walk. How did it go with Hull?"

Silence.

"He's standing right there, isn't he?" I said. "Did he lead you on a wild goose chase?"

"So it would seem."

"We'll be right there."

I called Rita Acosta, a reporter I'd known at *Focus Toronto*. She now worked at the *Sun*, and we still traded the occasional lead. Now, though, I needed to check on Lyle Sanderson, make sure he was really missing.

"Sanderson, you said?" Her fingers clicked away on the keyboard. "Got him. No missing person report yet, but it's only been a day and if he lives alone, that's not unusual. A third person missing in the neighborhood would be a helluva story to break. I owe you on this one."

"No problem. Can you call me back after you check it out? It's yours to break, but I might see if I can sell it as a tidbit south of the border. Count the trip as a write-off."

She laughed. "Smart girl. How much longer are you in town for? We should— Oh, hold on, someone's here."

She put me on hold. A minute later, she came back on.

"Gotta run," she said. "Just got a tip. Working girl killed over on Yonge Street."

"Just now? I heard the sirens."

"Well, if you're in the area, hustle your butt on over." She rattled off an address. "It's a knifing, and a nasty one. First guy that found her lost his dinner. Sounds good. Could be my ticket to the crime desk." A pause. "Gawd, that sounded awful, didn't it? Time for a new job." A rustle as she grabbed her purse. "Will I see you there?"

Prostitute? Knifed? Mutilated? With Jack the Ripper not in his portal cell where Hull swore he should be?

"I'll be there."

A half block from the crime scene, a cab pulled up beside us. Nick got out, then Antonio, while Jeremy paid the driver. Hull was still with them.

"Mr. Hull is concerned," Antonio said. "If this could be our—" A quick look at the crowded sidewalk. "—notorious friend, he doesn't feel it would be safe for him to be alone."

"Tell him to stay clear," Clay said.

I'd never been at a murder scene. At least, not while it was an active crime scene. I'd always stayed away from crime reporting. I'd have a hard time talking to a victim and just taking the story, without wanting to do something about it. Maybe that's because I'm a werewolf or maybe it's just me.

This victim wasn't talking, but everyone else was.

That's what struck me first—the swell of voices as we turned the corner. So much for respect for the dead.

The body had been found in an alleyway near an intersection popular with urban nightlife—the sort that did a brisk trade without the benefit of a business license. It seemed everyone within blocks had heard about it, and they'd all converged on the site. Police had erected barriers across the sidewalk on either side, but that only forced the crowd onto the road.

We split up to cover as much as we could. Clay and I stood on the edge of the crowd, trying to eavesdrop, hear what they knew.

"Elena?"

A short woman with dark curly hair waved and strode my way. Then she stopped dead and stared in feigned shock at my stomach.

"Holy Christ. Where'd that come from?" She gave me a hug that nearly toppled me over. "Congratulations." She reached for Clay's hand. "Rita Acosta, we met a couple of years ago."

Clay shook her hand and murmured a greeting, which for him was downright friendly.

Rita waved at the crowd. "Not a hope in hell of getting a firsthand look, although, in your condition, you probably shouldn't."

At a high-pitched squeal from the alley, Clay turned sharp, eyes narrowing.

"Is that—?" I began.

"Rats," he said, lip curling.

Rita nodded. "They've got animal control in there now, but it's a real mess. They must have come out the minute they smelled blood. I heard that the first cops on the scene had to beat the suckers off. Apparently, that's why the rookie puked. They were feeding—"

She stopped, gaze dipping to my stomach. "Sorry. Anyway, point is you can't get near the crime scene, and you don't want to. Come over here, and I'll fill you in. Unless . . ."

She looked at Clay, as if checking to be sure that murder details would be okay, considering my "condition."

"It's fine." I patted my belly. "All is quiet—it must be nap time."

She laughed. "I'll keep my voice down so I don't give the little guy nightmares."

Contact

THE YOUNG PROSTITUTE HAD BEEN TENTATIVELY IDENTI-
fied as "Kara," last name still unknown. Her throat had
been slashed, a deep left to right cut that seemed to have
been done from behind, and she'd died quickly, a blessing considering what the killer had done next.

She'd been cut open from sternum to pubis. Rita had
heard that several organs had been removed, though that
wasn't confirmed. The coroner was still working on the
body, and not about to talk to reporters. What didn't need
to be confirmed were the facial mutilations, which had
been seen by witnesses before the police arrived . . . including a few who had snapped pictures with their cell
phones. According to Rita, Kara had sustained multiple
deep cuts to her face, splitting her nose and severing part
of her right ear.

I tried not to jump to conclusions.

"That's exactly what you're gonna read on the front
page of the *Sun,* so don't you dare scoop me," Rita said.

I struggled to smile. "Wouldn't know how."

Jeremy caught my eye. Rita noticed, and her gaze traveled over him.

"Friend of yours?"

I nodded, but wasn't about to introduce him to a human acquaintance if I could help it.

She kept looking at Jeremy, sizing him up. "Single?"

I was about to say something noncommittal when Jaime saw Rita looking, and shifted closer to Jeremy, her hand moving up behind him so she seemed to be resting her hand against the small of his back.

"Guess not," Rita murmured.

Clay made a noise between a snort and a laugh. Rita's photographer waved to her.

"Gotta run," she said. "About that other lead, the missing man? I'll follow up on that, and give you a call."

When we got within ten feet of Jeremy and Jaime, I said, "Better wait here. They're arguing about something."

Jaime's face was taut, her eyes flashing as she spoke. Jeremy leaned back with his arms crossed.

"Doesn't seem like much of a fight," Clay said.

I stared at him.

"Yeah," he said. "For Jeremy, I guess that's a fight."

We tried not to eavesdrop, but that's tough for werewolves.

"I can sense her," Jaime was saying. "She hasn't crossed over—"

"Which doesn't mean you need to speak to her."

"Doesn't it? If I can get a firsthand account—"

"From a victim, firsthand accounts are often unreliable. That's particularly true with the ghost of someone who's just been murdered. You've told me that yourself. You've also told me how difficult it is to contact them, and how traumatic—"

Jaime crossed her arms as Jeremy uncrossed his. "I never said traumatic."

People moved between us, and Jeremy stepped away to avoid being overheard. A few minutes later, Jaime wheeled on him and strode off. Jeremy hesitated, then walked over to us.

"That's the problem dealing with nonwerewolves," I said. "They lack that critical 'you are Alpha, you are right' gene."

"Very inconvenient," he said wryly.

He turned and watched Jaime pace along the far sidewalk and, for a second, I thought I saw something more than friendly concern flicker behind his eyes.

"You know, she's right," I said softly. "You can offer your opinion and advice, but it's her choice."

Jeremy nodded, but he didn't make a move in her direction. I knew he was thinking the same thing I was—wondering whether Jaime thought it *would* help or she was just desperate to make the effort, to show us that she could be useful.

"If she's going to do it anyway, at least we can be grateful," I said.

Jeremy exhaled, brushed back his hair, then nodded.

"I'll go tell her she's allowed to do it," he said.

As he turned to go, I touched his arm. "Jeremy?"

"Hmmm?"

" 'Allowed' is probably not the best word choice. The whole 'not a werewolf' thing?"

A small smile, then he headed over to her. They spoke for a minute, then Jaime headed for the alley. When Jeremy started to follow, she hesitated, glancing back at him. He caught up and, without a word exchanged, they headed into the alley.

"She's letting him help her set up?" Clay said.

"Looks like it."

"Huh."

About ten minutes later, Jaime popped her head out from the alley and motioned us over as Jeremy left, presumably to round up Antonio and Nick.

"We only get one shot at this, so the more brains we have, the better questions we can ask." Jaime stopped halfway down the alley. "Her spirit's still here, so what I need to do is coax her over—kind of like what I did at the portal site. Then I'll be doing something a little different. I want you to hear her answers directly, so I'm going to channel her. That means she can speak through me, but can't hear or see you guys, okay?"

"Got it."

Jeremy approached. I looked behind him and saw that Antonio and Nick had taken up position at the end of the alley. Two couples sneaking into the dark depths of an alley wasn't that unusual in this neighborhood, although hearing them *talking* might be a little odd. But with an active crime scene right across the road, we weren't likely to attract much attention.

"I was just telling them how this'll work," she said to Jeremy. "I'm not going to introduce you guys—no need to make this more complicated. As far as she'll know, it's just me and her."

"This . . ." I began, then faltered.

Jaime nodded for me to go on.

"Is she going to remember this?" I asked. "Any of it? If she's seen the crime scene, seen what happened to her . . ."

"Wiped clean when she crosses over. Postdeath amnesia, which is why we need to get to her now. She'll forget what happened, and this conversation."

"So you're like a . . . psychic? Like those people on TV?"

A small laugh. "Exactly like that."

"Have you ever been on TV?"

Jaime hesitated, but at a nod from Jeremy, she told the young woman who she was, and the woman knew her TV spiritualists well enough to be impressed and, maybe, for a few minutes, to forget what had happened to her.

"Okay," she said finally, taking a deep breath, like a child steeling herself to do her best. I wondered how old she was . . . then realized I probably didn't want to know.

Jeremy started the interview, keeping it slow, easing her into it by asking what she'd done earlier that evening, who she'd spoken to, the sort of police-type questions that wouldn't help us, but were more humane than jumping straight to "so, how'd you die?"

We did get to that question, although, of course, Jeremy didn't word it quite that way.

"It was a guy," Kara said, then gave a squeaky giggle. "Guess I don't need to say that, huh?"

"He approached you on the street?" Jeremy asked.

Jaime relayed the question.

"Yeah, only I was kinda off near the alley. I had to, uh, go, you know, and the bit— old bat in the store on the corner won't let us use her bathroom unless we buy something. I was coming out of the alley, and this guy stopped me, wanted a blow."

"Did you get a look at him?" Jeremy said.

"Uh, kinda . . . but not really. It's dark right there. I

know he was a guy. Dark hair. Kinda skinny. Looked okay. That's all I really noticed—that he wasn't, you know, gross." She paused, then hurried on. "If he'd wanted me to get into a car or something, I'd have made him get out into the light. I'm pretty careful, but it was only a blow, and he didn't want to go anywhere, just the alley, so I figured it was safe . . ."

Her voice trailed off. Jeremy stopped the questioning for a few minutes, giving Jaime time to talk to Kara, make sure she was ready to continue. When she was, Jeremy skipped the "what happened next" part, which I'm sure would have fulfilled anyone's definition of "traumatic," and instead asked whether the man had said anything or done anything that might help us find him.

"Uh-uh. It happened pretty fast, I guess. He took me in there and I thought everything was okay. I heard someone else, down the alley, in the dark. A woman. I thought it was another girl, with a guy, but then she seemed to be talking to my guy. I was gonna tell him it'd cost him extra for that—doing it in front of his girlfriend or whatever. Then I smelled something. Something awful."

Through Jaime, I asked her to describe the smell, if she could.

"It was like when this cat died at a place I was staying at and everyone thought it ran away and we were gone for a week and came back and—" She made a gagging noise. "It was real rude. Never smelled anything like that before . . . until tonight. Then I saw a shape move at the end of the alley and then—" She shook her head. "That's it. He must have . . . done it then."

Jaime let her go after that, with an herbal mixture she hoped would send her to the other side. We could have pressed for more, but we already had our answer. Rose had been there, and probably the bowler-hatted man was in the shadows with her. According to Jeremy and Clay, Patrick Shanahan could never be mistaken for "kinda thin," meaning someone else had been with the zombies. Their true master, the one they'd been killed to serve.

"He's out," I said.

Jeremy paused, as if struggling to find another explanation. Then he gave a slow nod.

"I hope you don't mean—" Clay looked at us. "Ah, shit."

We decided to try tracking the zombies from the crime scene, hoping "Jack" was still with them. Even if he wasn't, this might be our chance to try the "kill a zombie and follow him to the controller" ploy.

Great plan . . . except that this block had been so heavily trodden in the past few hours that even when I looped around to the other end of the alley, Rose's stink was almost covered.

"We have to Change," Clay murmured as he, Nick and I walked the crime scene perimeter.

"I know."

"Jeremy isn't going to like that," Nick said.

"I know." I glanced back to where the others were waiting with Hull. "Let me talk to him."

Jeremy agreed with surprisingly little resistance. I think, by that point, he was as frustrated as the rest of us. If we were spotted, what was the worst that could happen? Giant wolves in Toronto? Hell, why not—they already had zombies, killer rats, dimensional portals and, now, Jack the Ripper.

"Circle wide around—" he began.

"Where are they going?" a voice to our left asked. Hull.

"They're going to scout the perimeter," Jeremy said. "In case the killer stayed nearby."

"Is that—" Hull hesitated, clearly uncomfortable. "Is it safe? It would appear, as you've said, that she"—a nod my way—"is this madman's target . . ."

"No, we believed she was the zombie's primary target—and only because she must have seemed the easiest of us to capture. Yet they seem to have abandoned that plan."

"Probably because they have a more important goal now," I said. "Fulfilling Jack's contract."

"Fulfilling . . . ?" Hull's brows knitted.

Jeremy surreptitiously motioned for Clay, Nick and me to slip off, while he dealt with Hull.

As we turned to go, I caught a glimpse of a familiar silver braid through the crowd.

"Jer?" I whispered, directing his gaze to Anita.

"What the hell's she doing here?" Clay said.

"Who?" Hull raised onto his tiptoes, trying to see over the crowd. "Is it the zombie woman? Dear God, I hope they aren't—"

"They aren't." I turned to Jeremy. "Her bookstore's barely a block away, and her apartment's over it. She probably heard the commotion and came down. One look at this and she'll know—"

Anita turned, surveying the crowd. Her eyes met mine.

"Shit," Clay muttered. "Still time to get away?"

"Better to cut her off at the pass," Jeremy murmured. "Matthew, come with me, please. Elena—"

"Got it."

While Jeremy hustled Hull out of the way, Clay and I headed toward Anita. A mob of newcomers, jostling to get close to the crime, cut between us and her. When one knocked hard against my stomach, Clay shouldered him back with a glare.

"Hey—" the young man said, letting out a stream of alcohol fumes strong enough to knock any Breathalyzer well over the limit.

"Hey, yourself," Clay growled. "Watch who you're mowing down."

He gestured at my stomach. The young man scowled down at it.

"Yeah? Well, if you're really worried about your baby, pal, you'd get your wife out of the city. Haven't you heard the bulletins? Pregnant women are advised to leave the city—"

"Thanks," I said, taking Clay's arm and propelling him forward. "We didn't hear that."

By the time we made it through the crowd, Anita was nowhere to be seen. Nick and Antonio met us on the other side, having seen the confrontation and hurried to help. We gave them a description of Anita and set out, weaving through the crowd. I was circling a police cruiser when I almost bumped into another familiar body—Jeremy.

"We lost her," I said.

"And I lost Hull," he murmured.

"Oh, shit."

Panicked searching ensued, and Jeremy was about to

take Antonio and head over to Anita's bookstore when Hull came flying along the sidewalk, face white.

"Oh, thank God," he said, panting as he drew up beside us. "They're here. The zombies. I smelled that awful stench, and I turned to tell Mr. Danvers, but he was gone and—"

"Where are they?" Jeremy asked.

Hull gestured wildly, taking in half the surrounding block.

"Did you see them?"

"No, I only smelled them. But they were close. I think they were coming for me. I ran into a crowd and that seemed to scare them off."

Hull led us to where he'd smelled the zombies. They had indeed been there—both of them—along a side road. Jeremy and Jaime took Hull aside then, luring him with the promise of a drink to calm his nerves. Before they left, though, Jeremy changed his mind about our search—we'd do it as humans.

We found the zombie trails easily enough. As for Jack, it was impossible to lift a decent suspect trail. I had no idea what he smelled like, and at least a dozen other trails in that alley were recent enough to be his. So I did my best to commit all of them to memory. When I found more of the zombies' trails, I could match up my memories with any human scents following theirs.

Yet after three streets, it became obvious this wasn't as easy as it sounded. No single human trail intertwined with that of the zombies for more than half a block. We could only guess that the stench was too much for Jack, and he'd taken another route. That left us following the zombies, and we did that for an hour, but kept losing the trail as it crossed roads.

When we checked in with Jeremy, he decided that was enough. What he'd hoped for was a scent signature for the killer, and if we weren't going to get that, we'd be better off getting some sleep.

Trust

JEREMY DECIDED TO TAKE HULL BACK TO THE HOTEL WITH
us. Hull obviously wanted that—the poor guy was convinced Jack the Ripper and killer zombies were on his
tail. We were more worried about Anita Barrington coming after him and trying to "trade" him to Shanahan, but
either way, it seemed wise to keep him close.

While some of us wanted to discuss the night's events
before turning in, Jeremy refused, feigning exhaustion,
with Antonio backing him up, as if they hoped a few
yawns would convince us *we* were tired too. I certainly
wasn't. That's the problem with sleeping until early afternoon: twelve hours later, I was still raring to go.

So after we tossed our suitcases into the corner of the
room, Clay and I left as Nick made a phone call. We
headed into the hall, looking for a diversion . . . and hoping Jeremy and Antonio might reappear after they were
certain Hull had retired.

No such luck. Even after pacing past their door three
times, talking loudly, they didn't come out. As we wandered along the hotel corridor, Clay spotted a communal
balcony. The sign on the door warned that it was locked

after eleven. But when Clay tried the handle, it opened . . . though I'm sure his extrahard twist helped.

The balcony was about the size of a hotel room, with a brick railing overlooking the streetscape. There were two lounge chairs—one nearly hidden by the wall, the other on the far side, as if the people who'd used them last had been strangers, and had intended to stay that way.

Clay stretched out in the shadow-shrouded lounger. I walked to the railing and looked down at the city.

"Do you think we did it?" I asked.

"Did what?"

"Let him out. With Jaime's séance."

"And none of us noticed him strolling out of that portal?"

I nodded. "You're right."

"Timing's off too. Even if he jumped out the moment Jaime started doing her thing, there's no way he got over to that corner, met up with his zombies, picked out a girl and killed her, all before we finished. Your friend said the 911 call came in almost an hour before she got the news—while we were still in Cabbagetown."

The door slid open behind me. I turned, expecting to see Nick. A slight figure hovered in the doorway. Hull. I nodded, but didn't extend an invitation. He still walked in—right past Clay without seeing him there in the dark—and took a spot beside me at the railing.

"Nice night," Hull said, gazing out at the city.

I nodded.

"It's all very . . ." He looked around. "Different. It's hard to believe how much can change in a hundred years." He gestured at the side of the hotel. "Hardly a common roadside inn."

A stab of guilt raced through me. Any other time, I'd

have been fascinated by Hull's situation, but here I was unable to muster more than a twinge of empathy.

Granted, empathy and I are not close friends, but I can usually put myself in someone else's shoes, imagine his situation and feel the appropriate response. Yet, with Hull, there was nothing. Not even curiosity. Maybe I had a lot on my mind, but I should make the effort.

"This must be . . ." I began, then shook my head. "I can't imagine what it's like. Did you have a family? Wife, kids?"

He shook his head. "My work took up much of my time, I'm afraid."

I managed a few more questions, but his answers were simple, none opening the gate to anything approaching spirited conversation.

I glanced over at Clay, but it looked as if he'd fallen asleep. No rescue there. Hull just watched me, as if waiting for the next question. I struggled to think of one, but under that blankly polite gaze, any spark of interest I could manage sputtered out. It was like being cornered by the most boring person at the party.

"This must be very difficult for you as well," Hull said after a moment. "In your . . . condition." He sidestepped closer. "I don't mean to be rude but, all things considered, I'm surprised your husband is putting you through this, dragging you here and there, trying to catch these monsters—"

"Her husband doesn't drag her anywhere," Clay drawled, appearing at my shoulder. "She goes where she pleases; he just tries to keep up."

Hull jumped at the sight of Clay. "My apologies. I didn't hear you come in."

"That's because I didn't."

Clay nodded at the lounge chair.

"Oh, oh, yes, of course. I should have known. You're quite . . . attentive."

"You could say that," I murmured.

Hull searched for something to say, but under Clay's steady stare, he wilted. With a murmured good night, he hurried out the door, closing it behind him.

"Scared off another one," I said. "No wonder I don't have any friends."

"You have me," Clay said, leaning beside me. "What more do you need?"

"You really want me to answer that?"

"And you have Nick."

"Doesn't count."

"Bet he'd be happy to hear that."

"You know what I mean. Pack brothers don't count."

"Okay. You have Paige."

"To your everlasting dismay."

"No, it just confirms that you still haven't forgiven me for that biting thing."

I laughed and leaned into his side.

"Paige is okay," he said. "Same as Jaime, and anyone else you want to befriend except Cassandra."

"Had to slide that one in, huh?" I stretched, and stifled a yawn. "About Hull . . . was that just a general 'get out of my face, human' warning, or something more specific?"

"Seemed like you were in danger." He met my gaze. "Death by boredom."

I sputtered a laugh. "That's not nice."

He shrugged. "I didn't like him hanging around out here when he thought you were alone, so I wanted to make sure he knew you *weren't* alone. Maybe I'm paranoid, but I don't trust him."

"You don't trust anyone."

"Sure, I do," he said, sliding his hands around my waist and turning me to face him. "I trust Jeremy."

I swatted him. "Thanks a hell of a lot."

"Oh, I trust you . . . in ways. I trust you not to run off with some other guy. Trust you not even to *think* about running off with another guy. Trust you to watch my back in a fight. Trust you to watch my back more than your own, no matter how much I tell you otherwise. Trust you not to smother me in my sleep. But do I trust that you'd never throw me off this balcony, no matter how much I pissed you off? Uh-uh. I'm not stupid."

"More a lack of complacency than a lack of trust, then."

"Exactly."

I laughed and leaned over the railing. "It's only three floors down. You wouldn't die."

"You say that like it's a bad thing."

When I didn't answer, he growled, scooped me up and kissed me, teeth nipping my lip. I groaned and pressed into him . . . well, pressed the protruding part of my body into him, which really wasn't all that sexy.

"Damn," I muttered. "Even making out is getting tough."

"Just a matter of ingenuity. And repositioning."

He hoisted me up, putting my legs around his waist, and my arms around his neck, then moving against the railing. With his hands behind my back, he leaned me over the edge. I turned my head to look down at the cars passing below.

"You trust me?" he said.

I met his eyes. "Absolutely."

He leaned over and kissed me hard. Still awkward, but

after about three seconds, I forgot that. I tried to forget too how much more fun this would be without the clothing barrier. That one was tougher, but you take what you can get, and this was pretty damned fine, feeling him hard against me, tasting him, hearing his low growl of—

A deep sigh. "Figures."

I glanced over to see Nick carrying an ice bucket of drinks and an armful of snacks.

"Don't ask me to leave," he said. "You have sex in public, you get an audience." He squinted over at us. "You're . . . still dressed. Great method of contraception, buddy, but I think it's a bit late."

Clay pressed his lips to my ear as he straightened me up. "You have my permission to throw *him* off the balcony."

Nick continued, "Elena getting shy in her maternity? Won't let you do it in public anymore?"

"It's not in public." Clay lowered me from the railing. "It's in a public place. There's a difference."

"Hey, if you were working up to the clothing-ripping part, go right ahead. I'll just sit back and enjoy the show. I have snacks and everything."

"Unfortunately, until this is over," I said, waving at my stomach, "making out is all you're going to see."

"You mean you can't have—?" He sputtered a laugh. "Damn, that's tragic."

I looked at Clay and jerked my chin toward the railing. "You want to take his arms or legs?"

"Oh, come on," Nick said. "So you can't have sex for a while. No big deal. Even I've gone without sex for a few weeks."

"Four months," I said.

Nick looked up from his lounger. "What?"

"If I go to term, I have four months left."

"Four . . . ?" He looked from Clay to me. "Good luck with that."

Clay smacked the top of his head as he walked over to pull out the second lounger and motioned for me to join him on it.

"Better make sure it doesn't have a weight restriction first," Nick said.

I seconded Clay's smack.

Nick rubbed the top of his head. "Hey, don't take it out on me. I'm not getting any either. Of course, I'll be home soon, and then that'll change, unlike some of us . . ."

He ducked before either of us could smack him again. I settled in beside Clay. As I laid my head back onto Clay's shoulder, my cheek brushed his.

"You're warm," I said, lifting a hand to his forehead.

"Better than being cold. Got enough dead people wandering around this city."

"I'm serious. You're . . ." I tried with my other hand. "No, I guess it's not too bad. I'll get Jeremy to check you before bed. He should have another look at your arm too."

"Sounding more like a mother every day," Nick said. "Scary."

Medical

I DREAMED THAT THE PORTAL CAUSED A CITYWIDE BLACK-out, and I was down in the PATH system, running through the hot, stuffy corridors, searching for the bathroom while the bowler-hatted zombie chased me, and I couldn't fight him when I had to pee so badly I could hardly see straight.

Then I awoke, sweating and clawing at the heavy covers. Sunlight seeped through the crack between the drawn drapes. Nick was sleeping against my back, his hand on my rear. I realized I did have to use the bathroom. Badly. A quick look around reassured me that the zombie part of the dream, at least, had been imaginary.

I wriggled out of the tangle of limbs. As I climbed over Clay, I felt the waves of heat coming off him. He gave a low moan, almost too low to hear. Then his arm flew out, narrowly missing my head.

I scrambled up and turned on the bedside lamp. Clay's color was high, the hair around his face plastered down with sweat.

Nick lifted the pillow from his head. "Wha—?"

"I'm getting Jeremy."

I pulled on my pants, then grabbed the nearest shirt—Clay's—and yanked it on as Nick rose from the bed, still blinking back sleep.

"Elena."

Clay lifted his head from the pillow.

"I'm okay," he said. "Just the fever coming back."

He started to sit up, then stopped and wobbled, face going ashen with the sudden movement.

"I'm getting—" I began.

"No, let Nick."

Nick nodded and brushed past me, scooping up his pants. I hesitated, then nodded and grabbed the bucket of melted ice water as Nick went to get Jeremy.

I was mopping icy water onto Clay's forehead when Jeremy got there, his feet bare and his shirt undone. Clay started to sit up, but I pushed him back down, and he settled for rolling his eyes at Jeremy.

"She's overreacting," he said. "I have a fever. Just let me pop some Tylenol—"

Jeremy popped something else in his mouth—a thermometer. Clay grunted and sank back onto his pillow with a martyred "I'm surrounded" look.

"How high is it?" I asked when Jeremy checked.

"High."

Clay started to reach for the Tylenol, but Jeremy shook his head. He dumped the capsules into his own hand, and held them to Clay's lips. Clay rolled his fever-bright eyes at me, then opened up and let Jeremy tend to him.

Nick returned with a fresh bucket of ice, and I wrapped some in my wet towel.

"Enough," Clay growled. "Give the pills a chance to kick in."

Jeremy was checking Clay's arm.

"How bad—?" I began.

"Do you have the number for that doctor?" Jeremy asked quietly. "The sorcerer you met the other day?"

"I don't need—" Clay began.

"It's your right arm, so we aren't taking any chances." He glanced at me. "Get the number, Elena."

I called Zoe. The phone rang five times. When the machine answered, I hung up and hit redial. This time, she grabbed it on the second ring.

"Hello, there," she said before I could say anything. "About time you called. I was beginning to feel—"

"I need Randall Tolliver's number," I said quickly.

A pause. "Are you okay?"

"It's Clay. His arm. It's—"

"We'll be right there. Tell me where you are."

When Tolliver arrived, he cleared Antonio and Nick out of the room, and only let Jeremy stay when it was clear he wasn't leaving. I couldn't blame Tolliver for not wanting an audience of supernatural strangers hovering over him, making sure he did his job right.

"It's infected," he said, after a quick examination.

"How badly?" I asked.

A nervous glance my way, as if I might pounce if I didn't like his answer. "It's . . . progressing."

"Gangrene?" Clay said, pushing himself up.

A look crossed Jeremy's face, and I knew he'd been wondering the same thing.

"Gangrene?" I said. "No, it can't be, not from a scratch. That's all it was. A scratch."

"From a decomposing corpse raised by supernatural means," Jeremy said.

"Which likely explains the acceleration and the refusal to respond to cleaning," Tolliver said. "But it isn't gangrenous. Not . . ." A glance my way, and he shut his mouth.

"Yet," Clay finished for him.

A slow nod from Tolliver. "We should still be able to get it under control. Stronger antibiotics is one way to go. Or we can remove some of the infected tissue. The latter would be more likely to work, but would cause scarring—"

"I don't care about looks," Clay cut in. "Just function."

Tolliver hesitated. "It's . . . in a bad spot. If I needed to go deep, it might damage the muscle. It shouldn't have any lasting effect on fine motor skills, like writing."

"It's larger motor skills I'm worried about."

Tolliver nodded, as if this didn't surprise him.

"If it would stop the spread of infection—" Jeremy began.

"Last resort," Clay said.

He met Jeremy's glance with a look that said he'd give in if pushed, but begged Jeremy not to push. I knew what Clay was thinking. If mutts found out Clay was no longer in peak fighting form, there'd be trouble.

Clay met my eyes. "Rather not take that risk." His gaze dropped to my stomach. "Not now. Antibiotics will be fine."

"Do you know what can happen if gangrene sets in?" Jeremy asked.

Clay nodded. "It'll have to come off."

"Off—?" I sputtered. "What will have to come off?"

I knew the answer, but my brain refused to process it. That couldn't be what they meant, not with Clay so calm and decisive, as if they were discussing cutting off his hair.

"And even that might not work," Jeremy said, his gaze locked with Clay's.

"Are we talking about—?" My voice squeaked and I couldn't finish the sentence. "From a scratch? It's just a scratch!"

Clay reached for me, but I backed away.

"That is what we're talking about, right?" I said. "Losing his arm? Losing his—his life?"

"No, no," Jeremy said, coming toward me, face stricken. "I didn't mean—"

I turned to face Tolliver. "That is what they mean, isn't it?"

"Yeah," Clay said, pushing himself up. "That's what we mean, darling. Jeremy's talking worst-case scenario, just so I know what *could* happen. It's me he's trying to spook, not you."

Jeremy waved me over to sit down. "I didn't mean to scare you. You don't need that, not now. I'm sorry. I only wanted—"

"It's okay," I cut in, cheeks heating. "Of course, I know that could happen with a bad infection. Amputation, I mean. But I didn't think—everything seemed fine—"

"It will be fine," Clay said. "If antibiotics can still fix this, then I want to let it play out a bit longer. Keep an eye on it. If things get worse? I'll take the surgery. I lose some function? I'll compensate. But unless we're at a critical stage already, I don't want to jump into that."

He glanced at Jeremy, waiting for his verdict, but Tolliver beat him to it.

"It's not critical yet. I'll dress it and give you some antibiotics. If that doesn't clear it up in twenty-four hours, we'll move to debridement—removing the damaged tissue."

We looked over at Jeremy. He hesitated, then nodded.

"Good," Clay said. "Let's get me cleaned up, dosed up and ready to go."

When Tolliver finished, he checked Clay's temperature.

"The Tylenol seems to have knocked the fever," he said. "At the very least, the antibiotics should slow the infection." He glanced at Jeremy. "Is that normal? For your kind? Susceptibility to infection or swift progression once it sets in? I know accelerated healing is a hallmark—"

He cut himself off. Jeremy stayed stone-faced.

Tolliver started repacking his bag. Without looking up, he continued. "I should probably keep my mouth shut and pretend I haven't figured out what you are. But as a doctor, it would help to know what I'm dealing with." Before anyone could answer, he shook his head. "No, I do know what I'm dealing with, so I'm going to take the chance and admit it. After I saw you with Zoe the other day, I had my suspicions. I've . . . heard things. I made some inquiries, more to confirm the council connection than to confirm who—or what—you were."

"Accelerated infection isn't normal for us," Jeremy said.

"It's connected to the zombie then. I don't have any experience with their kind, and my experience with werewolves isn't much broader. I ran into one of you a few years back, in Europe, and helped him recover from an injury . . . though it wasn't help freely given."

"I hope you know it's not like that this time," Jeremy said. "If Zoe gave that impression—"

"She didn't."

"I fully intend to pay you for your time, as much as you'd charge for any emergency call, and whatever extra is appropriate for asking you to be available, on call, should the problem worsen."

Tolliver shook his head and hefted his bag onto the bed. "That's not necessary. I know you're trying to fix this portal mess, so consider this my contribution to the cause."

He fingered the straps on his bag. "I may be able to do more. I would have called later today. I have an idea where Patrick is hiding."

"Where?"

"I'd prefer to check it out myself. Patrick and I may not be close these days, but I still consider him a friend. If he's going to be brought in for questioning, I'd like to do it myself."

We looked at each other.

"That may not be the best idea," Jeremy said slowly. "We think he might have a larger role in all this than simply owning the letter."

"If you knew Patrick— Well, it's unlikely he has any involvement in this. But, as I've admitted, we're no longer close, so I have to also admit that I may be mistaken. What I'm asking is that you allow me to bring him to a location I deem safe, with myself present at all times—including during questioning—to ensure that he has a representative there, and everything proceeds as it should."

I bristled. "Proceeds as it should? If you're suggesting we're going to work this guy over—"

Jeremy cut me short. "If we saw clear evidence that Patrick Shanahan is responsible for this portal, and refused to help us close it, then we would indeed exercise methods of persuasion. No one's arguing that. People have disappeared, one person has died and more are at risk. We'll do what we need to, within reason, to close this portal."

He stared hard at Tolliver, who finally dropped his eyes and nodded.

"Understood. If I can find Patrick, he's yours—so long as I'm present for the questioning."

Before Tolliver could leave, Jeremy said, "There's one other thing I'd like you to do. A brief examination." He nodded toward me.

"I'm fine. The baby's kicking and—"

"Let him take a look," Jeremy said, then lowered his voice so Tolliver couldn't overhear. "You'll feel better with a second opinion."

Tolliver checked me out, then asked, "How far along are you?"

"About twenty-three weeks," Jeremy answered.

Tolliver blinked, then nodded. "Yes, I suppose that wouldn't be unexpected. What's a wolf's gestation period?"

"Nine weeks," Jeremy said.

Tolliver took a tape from his bag, did a few measurements, asked me some questions, then leaned back on his heels. "Everything looks fine. This is the time, though, when you really need to be careful. I know, under the circumstances, easier said than done, but you're well into your third trimester, or the equivalent of it."

"Th-third trimester?"

"It's impossible to tell for certain, but I've handled prenatal obstetrics at a few shelters, often with women who aren't quite sure how far along they should be. I'd estimate you only have a few weeks left to go, but you're healthy, and they're doing fine—"

"Th-they?"

"The babies."

I swung an accusing glare at Jeremy. "Bab*ies*?"

Jeremy rubbed at a small smile. "I thought I detected more than one heartbeat, but I didn't want to say anything until I was sure. All things considered, a multiple birth wouldn't be unexpected . . ."

"Multiple? How . . . multiple?"

"Two," Jeremy said quickly. He looked anxiously at Tolliver. "It is just two, isn't it?"

Tolliver nodded.

"So I'm having . . . twins. *We're* having—"

I looked around for Clay. He was out of bed and standing at my shoulder, grinning.

"News to you too?" I said.

He only nodded, still grinning, then pulled me into a hug. When I didn't return the embrace, he looked down at me, eyes dimming.

"That's okay, isn't it? It'll be extra work, but—"

"It's okay," I said as my heart thumped double-time. "Just . . . I think I need to sit down."

Clay sat me on the bed while Jeremy grabbed juice from the minifridge. Tolliver probably thought we were all mad, but had the grace to just wait without comment.

Finally Jeremy asked, "But everything is all right, isn't it? With the pregnancy? No obvious problems?"

"Nothing I can see. My only concern would be the timing. The less stress she has now, and the sooner you can get her home—" He stopped. "But I'm sure you know that already, which is why you're so anxious to end this business. With twins, the possibility of early labor increases." He looked at me. "Do you know the signs of labor?"

"We do," Jeremy and Clay said, almost in unison.

I gave a small laugh. "They'll fill me in."

Missing

JEREMY INSISTED ON WALKING TOLLIVER OUT. AFTER PROM-
ising Clay I'd stick close to Jeremy, I tagged along, using
the excuse of grabbing breakfast so I could speak to
Jeremy without Clay overhearing.

When we reached the lobby, Tolliver stopped to answer his cell phone, and we stepped aside to give him privacy.

"I can see Antonio from here," Jeremy murmured to
me. "Go get something to eat. I'll see Dr. Tolliver off."

My cell phone buzzed. Rita calling to say that she'd confirmed Lyle Sanderson's disappearance.

"Three people missing from one neighborhood," she
said. "Something's going on. When I mentioned it in the
newsroom, we laid bets on how long it takes someone to
connect these disappearances to our dead girl from last
night."

I stopped walking. "You think there's a link?"

"Hell, no. I'm taking criminology classes at the uni—
figured it can't hurt, right?—and from everything I've

learned there, and working here, I can't imagine a connection. On the one hand, you have people disappearing without a trace. No letters or calls to the press. Not even ransom notes. Then you've got this ballsy SOB who not only displayed his work in public, but did it within screaming distance of people. You could argue that he killed the others and didn't enjoy it enough, so he went public, but that's a big step to take so quickly. My opinion, at least."

"Can I quote you on that?"

She laughed. "Like to see you try. Speaking of tips, I've got a few you *can* have. The crackpots are really coming out of the woodwork on this one. Just this morning we had a guy report seeing a walking corpse downtown."

"The core is pretty dead these days."

Rita snorted a laugh. "Unbelievable. Take a heat wave, add a health scare and people's common sense takes a holiday. Zombies, killer rats, signs of the apocalypse . . . I'm just waiting for someone to say they've spotted sasquatches on Spadina. Or vampires in the Don Valley."

I glanced over at the table, where Zoe was sipping a mimosa. "I'd believe vampires."

"I'm sure you would. Listen, someone's waving me into a meeting. Give me a call later. I want to get together before you leave town." Her hand went over the mouthpiece as she yelled a muffled "hold on," then came back to me. "Gotta run. You take care. And watch out for those vampires."

"I will."

As I hung up, I sensed something, and turned to see Clay coming up the steps.

"Back up to bed," I said. "You heard the doctor."

"Yeah, and he also said to eat. At this rate, I'd have starved before you brought breakfast."

"Clay, please . . ."

He stepped beside me, hand dipping to mine. "I'll go nuts in bed, darling. You know that. I'll just take it easy."

I hesitated, then nodded, and we headed over to the table, where everyone was laughing as Jaime regaled them with a story.

"—and I've seen fake tears before, but these were so bad the entire crew was snorting, trying not to laugh. So the woman's wailing her heart out, practically rolling on the stage, and the ghost says—" She saw us and stopped.

"Is everything okay?" she asked Clay. "You *look* okay."

"I am," he said, pulling out a chair for me. "Just an infection. Fever's gone; doc dosed me up. I'm fine. But we need to get this woman food." His grin broke through. "Seems she's eating for three."

Congratulations ensued, infused with shock from all but one person at the table, though he tried to feign it.

I turned to Antonio. "You knew, didn't you? Jeremy told you."

A small smile. "He said he suspected—"

I waved off the rest. "Payback for the conspiracy later. First, food."

I looked at Nick's plate.

He moved it out of my reach. "It's a buffet. All you can eat, no waiting. I'll even get it for you." He pushed his chair back. "Just don't touch mine while I'm gone."

I reached for Nick's plate, but Clay beat me to it, snagging two pieces of bacon and handing me one as he sat down.

"Jaime was just telling us about a show she did last

month." Zoe poked the back of my hand. "You were keeping her hidden from me, weren't you?" She caught my look. "No, I don't mean *that* way. I meant—Jaime Vegas, spiritualist extraordinaire."

"Zoe's a fan," Nick said as he set a heaping plate in front of me.

"Big fan," Zoe said. "I was telling her that I know someone who's an even bigger fan. Producer friend of mine. I used to do some work for him when he was starting out in Toronto—needed equipment but couldn't quite afford to pay retail. He's in L.A. now, and he just got the go-ahead to do a TV special next year. They're going to try to contact Marilyn Monroe, find out how she died. Huge, splashy production." She looked at Jaime. "It'd be a blast. You know it would."

Jaime laughed. "Cheesy as hell. Right up my alley."

"So is that a yes?"

"It's a maybe."

We brought Zoe up to date on the killing the night before.

Zoe tapped her nails against her champagne flute. "You know, I might be able to round up a witness for you. Not sure how much good it would do, but if you're waiting around for Randy to call back anyway . . ."

"A witness? Working girl?"

"No, a supernatural who haunts—and hunts—in that neighborhood."

Nick leaned forward. "I thought you were the only vampire in Toronto."

"This isn't a vamp. Or a were. She's . . . well, we're not quite sure what she is, but—"

A cell phone rang. At the first note, Jaime, Zoe, Nick, Antonio and I all jumped, ready to grab ours. Clay rolled his eyes and muttered something about electronic leashes. As the tone began, I said, "That's mine."

"Never even got the damned thing back in your pocket."

"It's . . . oh, it's Anita Barrington."

Clay growled and went to pluck the phone from me, but I pulled it out of his reach.

"Don't answer—" he began.

Too late. A minute later, I hung up.

"Let me guess," Jaime said. "She has urgent information and wants to come over right away."

"Nah," Clay said. "She's back to wanting us to go there."

"But it is urgent, as always," Nick said, sneaking a wedge of cantaloupe from Clay's plate. "She did sound pretty freaked out, though."

"How did you guys—?" Jaime began. "Oh, enhanced hearing, right? Nice trick."

"Just be sure you never whisper anything in front of them," Zoe said. "So what's up with Anita?"

"She won't say. Just that it's *extremely* urgent this time, and she has critical information we absolutely must have right away, because we're making a very big mistake."

"Uh-huh. So, when you said you'll be there, you were just blowing her off, right?"

"That's up to Jeremy. And here he comes now, with Matthew Hull in tow."

Zoe sipped her mimosa. "If you want, we can pop by Anita's place on the way to visit that friend of mine. She lives near there."

"Thought you wanted to steer clear of Anita Barrington," Clay said.

"Steering clear of a curious old woman is one thing.

But an immortality-questing witch who's obsessed enough to tackle werewolves? Time to put a face to a name before I end up on the wrong end of a binding spell."

Jeremy sent us to see Anita, but with Antonio and Nick in tow for backup. When we arrived, the beaded curtain was still drawn over the front display, the sign proclaiming the shop closed. We knocked there, rang the bell for the apartment and even found—and banged on—the rear door. No answer.

Antonio broke open the back door.

"Do you want me to wait out here with Elena?" Zoe whispered.

Clay shook his head. "Nick?"

"I'll stay with the ladies."

Ten minutes later, Clay and Antonio came out.

"She's gone," Antonio said. "We found traces of blood—"

I pushed past Clay and went inside. Clay waved Nick around to cover the front, while Antonio stayed and watched the back door. Zoe came in with us.

The shop was dark and quiet. I flipped on a light.

"Tiny place," Zoe said, checking behind the counter. "Where's the—?"

She inhaled and turned, following the blood beacon over to a display table. Beside it was not "traces" of blood, but a pool of it, covering several tiles. To the left was a sneaker print—large and wide, probably male.

As I crouched beside the blood, I bumped heads with Zoe.

"Sorry," she said. "Just getting a better look."

I sniffed, then looked up at Clay. "It's hers." I turned to Zoe. "Would that much blood loss be . . . ?"

"Fatal?" She studied the pool. "It's probably only a pint. Not fatal, but . . . well, you don't lose that much with a paper cut."

As I pushed to my feet, I saw another bloody print a couple of feet away. A small handprint, almost certainly not belonging to the same person who'd left the footprint. To the left of the print was what I thought was a smear. Then I got closer and saw it was a line, drawn by a bloody finger. On one side of the top was a diagonal, as if someone had started drawing an arrow, then been interrupted.

We followed the direction the arrow was pointing— the same as the outstretched handprint.

As Zoe surveyed the overstuffed bookshelf, she swore under her breath. "Let me guess, there's a clue in one of those hundred books."

"Forget it," Clay said. "No time for games."

I examined the shelf. "How about a quick round of 'what in this picture doesn't belong?' "

I reached down and took Anita's cookie plate off a stack of books. A folded piece of paper tucked under it fluttered to the floor.

"Clever witch," Zoe murmured.

I unfolded the note and read it with Clay looking over one shoulder, Zoe peering around the other.

Elena,
I know I should have delivered this message in person,
but I don't dare. I'm an old woman and if I can't find

the answers I seek, the least I can do is preserve what little time I have left. Patrick Shanahan has been here. He didn't get what he wanted, but he won't give up so easily. You need to know that—

The ink smeared there, the pen sliding across the page. Then, below it, a hastily added line, the handwriting cramped and rushed.

You are the key to the ritual and Patrick will say— do—anything to get to—

The note ended there.

We called Jeremy. After much discussion, he agreed Clay and I should push on and still visit Zoe's contact. He'd bring Jaime over to the bookstore, meet up with Antonio and Nick and see whether Jaime could figure out what had happened to Anita.

Zoe led us along a shortcut behind a three-story walkup. Clay walked behind, on the lookout for rats. As we wove through the bags of garbage, steaming in the midday heat, I clapped my hand over my mouth and nose.

"Sorry," Zoe said. "That must smell even worse to you. It'll be better inside." She paused. "Well, 'better' might not be the word. But it won't smell of garbage. Will you be okay?"

I nodded. We came out on a street that straddled Cabbagetown and Regent Park. Like the portal street, this one was lined with Victorian homes, but these houses were like withered old ladies, traces of their former beauty still visible, but only if you strained to see past the signs of deterioration and decay.

Good bones, a Realtor would say. Farther down the road, the process of gentrification had already begun, putting a pretty face on the old gals to entice urban professionals who dreamed of owning a historic home without the inconvenience of hissing steam radiators and push-button lights. Here, though, no such process had begun. These old gals sat tight, comfortable in their squalor and decay, glaring down the road at their uppity neighbors.

"Here," Zoe said, swinging open a rusted gate that led into a yard of weeds.

"So this woman . . . it's a woman, right?" I said as we trekked through the yard.

"Umm, we think so."

Zoe led us to the back of the house. She went to move an overloaded trash bin out of the way. Clay reached around and gave it a heave.

"Watch your arm," I said.

Zoe slid into the space left by the bin.

"So this . . . woman," I said. "What is she?"

Zoe knelt in front of a locked hatch. "We think she might be a clairvoyant. She seems to have some clairvoyant abilities, and the madness certainly fits that profile."

"Madness?"

Clay shrugged at me, as if to say, after dimensional portals, zombie servants and half-demon serial killers, he wouldn't have been surprised if Zoe was leading us down a hole to visit a white rabbit.

"Clairvoyants," I continued. "They can't see the future,

right? More . . . lateral sight. Seeing things that are happening in other places right now."

"You got it." She undid the first combination lock on the hatch.

"And what they see drives them crazy. But . . . how crazy are we talking?"

Clay looked at me. "How crazy? They can't figure out her gender, darling."

"Okay, stupid question. Does she have a name?"

Zoe opened the second lock. "I'm sure she did. Once. We call her Tee. It's—" Her gaze dropped with her voice, as if embarrassed. "It's an abbreviation. Not my idea."

The wooden hatch door was at least two feet by three, and when she tugged at it, she had to dig in her heels, her tiny frame straining with the effort. Clay leaned in and yanked it open.

"Thanks, Professor. Quite the southern gentleman today, aren't you?"

She tried to sound like her usual jaunty self, but didn't succeed.

A narrow set of stairs led down.

"She—Tee has the basement apartment?" I said.

Zoe shook her head. "She owns the whole place. Elena, you come first. I'll help you down and Clayton can—"

"Elena shouldn't be stooping to climb down rickety stairs," Clay said.

"This is the only way in. The doors are bricked over."

"I'll be fine," I said.

The moment I reached the bottom step, I gagged. Clay knocked his head on the low ceiling frame in his rush to get to me.

"I'm okay," I said, trying to speak without swallowing or

closing my mouth. I motioned for him to wait, hurried up the steps and spat outside. When I came back down, the gag reflex kicked in again and I hesitated on the lowest step.

"Come on," he said, taking my arm. "We're getting out—"

"No."

I pried his fingers free, then walked into the room, taking shallow breaths, acclimatizing myself to the smell. As for what it smelled like— I pushed back the thought as the bile rose again.

"I can talk to Tee," Zoe said. "You go outside, get some fresh air, maybe something to settle your stomach—"

"I'm fine. Just give me a moment to . . . get used to it."

I peered around the room. It was midday and sunny outside, but only a faint glow shone through the window above, illuminating a scant few feet of dust motes. As my nose adjusted, my eyes did too, and I could see that we were in a hallway, barren except for neatly stacked crates. The hall was tidy, clean even. The smell seemed to come from a closed door down the hall, opposite the stairs leading up to the second level.

"No lights, I suppose," I said.

Zoe shook her head. "Sometimes I bring a flashlight but . . . it's better this way."

"She— Tee doesn't like the light?"

"Umm, not so much her . . ." Zoe slid off the crate and headed for the stairs.

Labyrinth

ZOE LED US UP THE STAIRS, WHICH ENDED AT A LANDING. To the left was the back door, which was indeed bricked over on the inside.

We followed Zoe to the interior door. She did a fast patterned knock. As I waited for an answer from within, Zoe eased open the door just enough for her to slide through sideways. I grabbed the handle to push, but the door didn't budge.

"Uh, there's no way I can fit—" I began.

"Hold on." She grunted, as if moving something. Another grunt, and the door opened.

I stepped in to see her restacking a pile of books.

"Hope that was right," she murmured. "Tee hates them out of order. Is the smell better in here?"

The horrible smell from downstairs was now overpowered by another sort of rot. Mildewed paper. I edged in, banging my stomach on a stack of books.

"Hold on," Zoe whispered. "Give your eyes a second. It's a bit of a maze."

Clay was breathing down my neck, but I waited, blinking a few times to adjust to the dimmer light. The windows had been boarded up, again from the inside, behind the blinds. To a passerby, it would look as if the shades were always drawn.

When my night vision kicked in, I found myself in a labyrinth of books, some stacked taller than me. A narrow passage snaked into the room. Zoe had disappeared ahead of us.

"Just follow the path," she called. "It only leads one way. Pretty easy."

I'm sure it was easy—for those who could turn without adjusting like a transport driver for swing room. After banging my stomach into another stack, I walked with my hands over my belly. By the time I caught up to Zoe, my knuckles were scraped.

"Stay close," she said. "We're almost there."

"Good," Clay grunted behind me.

Another few steps and the maze opened up into a second book-lined room. I tripped. Clay caught my arm, and I looked down to realize that the floor was carpeted with open books.

"Just brush them aside as you walk," Zoe whispered.

A small noise to my left drew my attention. There stood what looked like a giant white nest. Moving closer, I saw that it was a pile of pages ripped from books. It was at least three feet high and twice that wide. Somewhere at the bottom, a happy mouse squeaked and burrowed deeper.

I squinted at the stack of dismembered book spines beside the pile—everything from cookbooks to popular fiction to history texts to automotive manuals.

"The answer is in there," a voice whispered somewhere behind me.

I spun, but saw only books and darkness.

"It's there," the voice said, as harsh and scratchy as sandpaper rasping against metal. "I haven't found it, but it's there. I know it is."

I stared down at the pile of papers, but the voice said, "It isn't in those pages. That is, I don't think it is. It's hard to tell, isn't it? How do you know if you've found the answer, when you aren't quite certain of the question? Better to keep it all, just in case."

I followed the voice to a shadow-wrapped corner. Something moved, then reared up, long, thin appendages unwrapping, like a praying mantis awakened from sleep. A face appeared in the darkness, a tangle of white hair nearly hiding the gaunt oval beneath. The head swayed from side to side, bobbing, weaving and snuffling, as the skeletal arms waved. Male or female? I couldn't tell if it was even human, this insectlike *thing*.

I knew then what "Tee" stood for, and why it embarrassed Zoe. T for thing. Someone's cruel idea of a joke.

Zoe stepped forward, as if to speak, but the thi— woman's gaze was fixed on me.

"Oh, oh my," she breathed. "Yes, yes, I see. It is indeed. Or so it . . ." Tee's head cocked, sunken dark eyes darting to an empty spot beside her. "Are you quite sure?" She squinted at me again. "No, of course it isn't. I know a wolf when I see one, and that is a woman—" She paused, then hissed. "Yes, of course. I see that now. Human form. I was confused. No need to mock me."

"Tee?" Zoe said.

A scrabbling noise. Tee's head moved higher, looming above ours, jutting forward and sniffing the air.

"Zoe?" she said. "Yes, yes, I can see. I'm not blind. I know my Zoe. Did she bring me something?" A wet, smacking noise. "A sweet morsel from my sweet Zoe?"

"Straight from me, if that's what you'd like, Tee. I have a favor to ask of you."

More smacking, then a nauseating gurgling sound. Tee's face moved back and forth, as if she was rocking.

"Oh yes, yes. You're good to me, Zoe. You never try to trick old Tee. Give and take. That's the way the world works. Give and take."

"That's the only way to do it, Tee. Now, I'm here—"

A cackle from Tee drowned her out. "Oh, I know why you're here, Zoe. Yes, I do. Been waiting for you. As soon as it came, I knew my Zoe would be here."

"It?" Zoe said.

Another cackle. "The gate opened, and out it came. Now it'll come for sweet Zoe, and she needs protection. But it's not big bad vampires this time, is it?"

Clay opened his mouth, but Zoe cut him off.

"Something has come out of that gate, Tee, but I'm not the one in trouble. It's—"

"The bitch." A high-pitched, spine-grating giggle, and her gaze flicked to that empty spot at her side. "Oh, I know it isn't nice to call our poor momma wolf that, but she forgives Tee, doesn't she? Knows she's just having a little fun. Momma wolf needs a little fun right now. All that trouble closing in, and the other wolves keep circling around her, leaving no one to watch out for my Zoe. No one except Tee."

Tee's head jerked, eyes narrowing as she stared at that empty space. "Sheep? What sheep? I'm talking about wolves. Don't confuse— Stop that. You're—" Her head whipped around, eyes going wide. "No! Not you. I said I won't talk to you." Her gaze darted about, then her head pulled back into the shadows. "I won't— I'm busy, can't you see that? No! Stop!"

Her long arms wrapped around her head and she crouched, cradling herself. An eerie noise, somewhere between keening and humming, filled the room.

"Should have known it was going too well," Zoe muttered.

The noise rose, and Zoe motioned us into the mouth of the book labyrinth, where the stacks insulated against the sound.

"Maybe if I try—" I began.

Zoe shook her head. "She's gone. I might be able to pull her out again, with the proper motivation." Her gaze skipped to a crate near the door. On top of it, beside a few dark blotches, lay a penknife. "But it'll take some time. Better to give her a rest and try again. Let's get out of here, get some air and a cold drink, and we'll try again."

We walked a few blocks in the bright sunlight and found a café patio. Clay ordered while I called Jeremy. I phoned Nick's cell first, but Jeremy was back at the bookstore with Jaime. I wondered why Antonio and Nick weren't with them, but found out as soon as I got hold of Jaime.

"Matthew's clinging like a barnacle," she said. "He was terrified of being left behind at the hotel, and Jeremy agreed it might not be wise, so we took him along, and sent him with the guys for a coffee while I worked here."

"What have you found?"

"Nothing. Either her spirit has already left or the wound wasn't fatal but . . ." A small pause. "I think she's gone. Jeremy's been trying to pick up a recent trail of hers leading out of the apartment or the shop, and there isn't one."

"Meaning she was probably carried out."

"Maybe to dispose of the body . . . or maybe because they've figured out you guys have a necro working for you. Either way, I'm useless here, I'm afraid. How'd Zoe's lead go?"

I told her what was happening, leaving out the less palatable details of our encounter.

"A clairvoyant?" Jaime said. "Now *that* I can help with."

"I think Zoe has things under—"

"No, seriously. I've had experience with older clairvoyants. There's one Lucas knows—used to work for his dad—and I've visited her a few times. Great old gal, but she . . . has her problems. I'm used to stuff like that. My Nan . . . well, it happens to necros, too, and I've been around a lot of them, so you learn the tricks. Same things work with clairvoyants."

"I'm not sure—"

"Is she catatonic?"

"Umm, no, not exactly . . ."

"That's okay. I'm sure I could get her to talk. Faye— that's Lucas's friend—her nurses say no one can get through to her like I can."

Beside me, Clay shrugged and said, "Can't hurt." I wasn't so sure.

"She's pretty far gone, Jaime," I said. "It's not . . . it's not something—"

"Too much for the celeb necro to handle?" She laughed, but an edge crept into her voice. "I know, you guys are looking out for me. And I appreciate that. Really I do. Been a long time since anyone didn't just want to get whatever they could . . ." The sentence slid off into silence.

"Here's Jeremy," Jaime said. "Let me run it by him, and I'll phone you back."

Twenty minutes later, we were back at the hatch, with Jaime. Zoe had gone ahead to check on Tee.

Jaime stepped into the basement. "Dark, huh? And it smells . . . kind of like my apartment when I run off for a week and forget to clean first. Only this place is cleaner than mine, which is pretty sad. We should speak to this Tee about relocating. I'm sure that Dr. Tolliver has some connections. He could probably get her into a decent nursing home."

"Um, maybe," I said.

At Tee's door, I paused. This wasn't right. I had to warn her.

"About this—" I began.

Jaime jumped and clutched my arm. A small laugh, and she released her grip, and patted my arm in apology. "A little tense, I guess. Seems there are a few spooks here. Old houses. Always a few, it seems."

"Oh? Maybe you shouldn't go in then—"

"It's okay. Oddly, they don't seem to be interested in me."

She reached around me and opened the door.

I led her through the maze of books, with Clay once again bringing up the rear. Jaime took in her surroundings with the occasional "hmm," but didn't comment.

Finally we found Zoe, talking to Tee, who was still hunched in her corner, enshrouded in shadow.

"Zoe," I said as I walked in. "Here's—"

But Zoe's gaze was fixed behind me, brow furrowed in concern. I turned. Jaime was still in the mouth of the maze, with Clay barely visible behind her. She was rigid and pale, her gaze flitting about the room. Then she flinched, as if a bird had swooped toward her.

"Jaime?" I said.

"Sh-she's not a clairvoyant," Jaime whispered.

As she spoke, her eyes never stopped moving, landing and focusing on one thing, then another, then another. Ghosts. A room filled with ghosts.

"Shit," I murmured as I swung around. "Let's get you out—"

"N-no. They aren't interested in me. Not while there's a stronger necromancer around."

Stronger? Oh, God. I hadn't brought Jaime to see a mad clairvoyant; I'd brought her to a mad necromancer.

I frantically motioned for Clay to grab Jaime's arm, yank her out if necessary. As he reached for her, though, she darted out of his reach and around me.

At a rustling from the corner, Jaime stopped dead.

"Yes, yes, I see," Tee's voice rasped out, barely above a whisper. "A timid thing, isn't she? Afraid of ghosts perhaps?" A cackle of a laugh. "Come in, sister. They won't bother you."

Tee's face moved forward, but it was too dark for Jaime, who kept squinting. I moved up beside her, blocking her from getting a closer look.

"Who are your people, sister?"

"P-people?" Jaime said.

An exasperated growl. "Your kin. Your family. What line are you?"

She stopped, the pale oval of her face tilting up as she listened to what I'd thought were voices in her head, and now realized were ghosts. "Really? Don't tease. It cannot be."

Her face swiveled back to us and craned forward, her body still wrapped in her long limbs. "Oh, yes, yes, I see it. I do see it. Molly O'Casey's granddaughter. Poor Molly. What must she think, having such a timid girl?"

Some of Jaime's fear fell away and she edged closer.

"You knew Jaime's grandmother?" I said quickly.

"Knew? Yes, yes. I haven't seen her in—" A pause, as she looked to her right. Then a sharp hiss that sent Zoe, Jaime and me all jumping backward. "Gone? Gone? You lie. Molly O'Casey is not—"

She stopped, face swinging in the other direction. Then she started to keen, a razor-edged howl that had all three of us backing up again, until Jaime and I both bumped into Clay.

"Lost," Tee wailed. "Oh, the fool. I tried to warn her. Tried. And now she's lost. A slave for eternity."

Tee reared up then, limbs unwrapping, as she moved out of the shadows. Jaime got her first real look at the necromancer, and let out a whimper, stifled fast, but her face white with horror and disbelief that this . . . thing had been human, let alone one of her own kind.

"You'll listen to me, won't you, girl? You won't stop up your ears to the truth."

Tatters of clothing hung off her larvae-pale body, limbs so thin and white they seemed bone not flesh.

"They tell us we'll be free after they die," she whispered, "but it's a trick. The great lie. We think we are slaves in life—bending to the will of others, hounded by the living, hounded by the dead? It's nothing compared to what happens when we pass over." She waved her spindly arms over her head, as if shooing off flies, lips twisting in a guttural snarl. "No, I won't listen. You lie. I know you lie. You want to trap me. Trick me into your world. But I know the secret. I know how to stay alive until I've found the answer."

Her skull-like face dove toward Jaime's. "Do you want to know the secret, Molly's girl?"

"No," Zoe said, leaping between them. "I . . . I don't think she's ready, Tee. Better wait until she—"

Tee swung an arm at Zoe, who ducked and darted to the side. Then she advanced another step toward Jaime, the smell of her so strong I gagged again.

"I will tell you, sister, but I don't think you're strong enough to do it."

Jaime stiffened, eyes blazing, mouth opening.

Tee cut her short with a cackle. "Don't like that, do you? Maybe there is some of your grandmother in you. Tell me, sister, if you wanted the key to long life, where would you look?"

"I . . ." Jaime paused, obviously thinking, not wanting to appear the fool in front of this woman. "In the ancient texts—"

Tee's laugh roared out on a blast of breath so foul even Jaime blanched.

"Closer, sister. Look closer." She waved an arm around. "In this very room we see long life—two kinds of it—do we not?"

"Vampires and werewolves," Jaime said.

"What do they have in common?"

Jaime looked from Zoe to me. "Um, they both . . ." Her

eyes widened as she made a connection. "They hunt. Hunt their prey."

"And what do they hunt?"

I could see where this was going, and I took hold of Jaime's arm. "I think—"

"Vampires hunt people," Jaime said. "But werewolves only hunt . . . well, I guess some of them hunt—" Her face paled. "People."

"That, sister, is the key. Imbibe the flesh of the living, and ye shall live." She stretched her neck out, voice lowering to a whisper. "It's quite simple. You take a knife, and slice off a strip of—"

I coughed. In hindsight, a silly and useless thing to do. No sudden noise would drown out Tee's meaning. But I had to do something.

Tee only cackled and reached out her hand, her bony fingers caressing my arm. I fought to keep from pulling away, and lifted my head. My gaze met hers and I saw something there, something human and almost tender. Her bloodless lips twisted into a smile.

"Momma wolf's tummy is a bit sensitive, isn't it? We'll speak no more on that, then." She looked at Jaime and lowered her voice. "Come to me later, and I'll tell you the rest."

With that, she retreated, scuttling backward to the safety of her corner.

"About the . . . what we came here for?" Jaime managed. "This killer. The one who came through the portal. You said you know something about that?"

"Something?" Tee sounded offended. "Everything. My friends tell me everything."

"Then we'd like to know—"

"Smoke," she spat. "Smoke and mirrors. Sound and fury. Signifies nothing. Do not waste your time."

We looked at one another.

"Perhaps," I said. "But still we'd like to catch—"

"The killer?" Tee made a rude noise. "Foolishness. Another spirit crosses over? It happens every second. Happening now, all around you. Will you catch all their killers too? Cancer and rage and loneliness? Catch those and lock them up?" She turned her head and spat into the darkness. "Foolishness, and you have no time for it." Her eyes peered at mine. "Your babies have no time for it."

"If it's connected, though—"

"Smoke and mirrors. Sound and fury," she grumbled. "You want to stop him? Why bother me? Ask her." Tee waved one arm at Jaime. "Or do you tell me Molly O'Casey's granddaughter doesn't know how to call a zombie?"

"Call?" Jaime said. "Summon a zombie, you mean? Sure, if I raised a zombie, I'd know how to call it to me, but these aren't my—"

"Oh, so it's beyond you, then, sister, is it? Not so simple as chatting with ghosts." She flapped her arms, mumbling to herself. "No, no, you're right. Wouldn't help. They aren't the problem. Smoke and mirrors. Sound and fury."

My cell phone vibrated, spooking me enough to jump. I pulled it out, thinking—hoping—it was Jeremy.

"Elena? It's me. Rita."

"Oh. Um, Rita. Right. Can I call you back?"

"If you do, you'll regret it. There's been another murder."

That stopped me. "You mean from last night? They found another—?"

"Body. And this just happened. Broad daylight. Downtown, a few blocks from the last one. Near Regent Park."

For a second, I couldn't speak. Then I thanked her and hung up.

"Another one," Clay said before I could speak. "Right here. Right now."

"Maybe it's a coincidence—"

"It isn't. It's a message."

Tee had completely retreated, pulling herself into her cocoon and going silent.

"We should check it out right away," I said after telling Jaime and Zoe about the call. "While it's still fresh. Maybe see if we can pick up a scent this time."

Jaime nodded. "I'll stay here—" A quick look over her shoulder, into Tee's corner. "See if I can get her talking . . ."

"We'll need you there," I said. "In case the victim's ghost is still around."

Relief flooded her face. "Yes, of course. I'll come."

"I'll work on Tee," Zoe said. "I still need to—" Her gaze flicked to the crate with the penknife. "—give her what I promised. If I get anything from her, I'll call you."

Negotiation

CLAY HAD INSISTED ON MEETING THE OTHERS HALFWAY,
mumbling something about being careful with his arm.
In other words, if it was a setup, he didn't feel comfortable protecting me alone.

I took Jeremy aside and told him what happened with
Jaime.

"I'm really sorry," I said. "If I'd known this woman was a
necromancer—"

"You couldn't have. Even if you had, I doubt we could
have dissuaded Jaime. She's—" He brushed back his
hair. "She wants to help, and the uglier it gets, the more
insistent she becomes. I'll speak to her. The rest of you
continue on to the crime scene."

Fifteen minutes later, we were huddled a half block from
the crime scene, waiting for Jeremy, having seen and
heard all we needed.

"I'm sorry," Hull said as we huddled to the side of the
scene. "I've tried to keep quiet, but I cannot. This—" He
waved an agitated hand toward the taped-off alley. "Surely,

I can't be the only one who sees this for what it is. The girl in there, the pregnancy, the physical resemblance—"

"We saw," Clay said.

"Then you understand the significance—"

"I said—"

"We understand that it's a message," Antonio said slowly.

"Could it not be more than that? The resemblance, the location, the timing." He looked at Clay. "If Shanahan sent this beast here, on orders, knowing your wife was near, and he saw that young woman, is it not possible that he mistook—"

My knees buckled, and only my grip on Clay's hand kept me steady. What if that woman died—her baby died—because I'd been near, only a block away?

"Enough," Antonio said, voice hard.

"I'm only saying she should be kept safe. If Shanahan gets hold of her—"

"No one needs to remind me of that," Clay snarled. "I'm taking care of my wife and—"

"But you're injured, are you not? If you can't protect her—"

Antonio caught Hull's arm and propelled him backward, out of Clay's reach. Clay didn't move, though, just fixed Hull with a look that said he wouldn't waste the energy on him.

"I think—" I began, then noticed a familiar face bobbing through the crowd. "Oh, here comes—"

I didn't even get Jeremy's name out before Hull had wriggled out of Antonio's grasp and was scampering across the road to his protector.

"Where's Jaime?" I asked as Jeremy reached us.

"She went back to the hotel. She insisted on coming to

the end of the road, but when she found the victim was—" A quick glance at Hull, as he realized he had to be careful what he said. "—gone, I persuaded her to head back for a rest."

My cell phone went off. I glanced at it and saw a hospital name flash across the screen.

"Hold on," I said. "It could be Tolliver."

A moment later, I returned to the group.

"It's him," I said.

"And?" Jeremy prompted.

"He has Shanahan," I said, and handed Jeremy the phone.

"You cannot be serious," Hull said, staring at Jeremy as if he'd just announced plans for a mission to Mars. "After—after this?" He waved in the direction of the crime scene. "You cannot negotiate with these people. They aren't people at all. They—they're monsters. In league with Satan. Go to that meeting if you must, but I pray to God it's to kill them."

"If it comes to that, yes," Jeremy said. "But we gave our word to Tolliver that we would negotiate in good faith."

Hull's eyes bulged. "Faith? You're a good man, Mr. Danvers, but creatures such as that will never act nobly. They will lie to you, and cast magics against you. Negotiation? Annihilation is the only way to treat such beasts."

"Antonio, please call a taxi for Matthew. I want to be sure he arrives back at the hotel safely."

Hull shook his head. "No, if you go, I go—"

"*That* isn't open for negotiation. This is dangerous

business, and you need to keep out. You deserve to live long enough to enjoy your new life."

Antonio left to hail a cab.

"But that madman could come after—" Hull began.

"Me," I said. "That's what we just finished discussing, right? That this murder suggests I'm still the primary target. So you'll be a whole lot safer at that hotel than hanging out with us."

Hull looked from me to Jeremy, openmouthed and wide-eyed. "Surely you don't plan to take her to this meeting? After what just happened? If you need any further proof that she's in danger—"

"I don't," Jeremy said. "And I didn't before. But the safest place for her is with us."

Jeremy had wanted a private, wide-open place, to avoid the possibility of being ambushed by the zombies. Tolliver still insisted that Shanahan wouldn't know how to control a zombie if someone handed him a user's manual, but he'd suggested a small community center where he coached an after-school soccer program. It was closed for the summer, but he had access.

The community center was indeed tiny—little more than a gymnasium, changing rooms and a meeting room. The property was a decent size, though, with basketball courts, soccer fields and a thickly wooded strip in the back. When Jeremy saw that small forest, he was much happier with Tolliver's choice. If things went bad, we could get Shanahan to *our* turf quickly.

The ball courts and field were community property, but in late afternoon, with the summer sun cranked on full, no one much felt like playing ball. The empty court and field added an insulating layer of emptiness between the building and the surrounding town houses.

We didn't break into the community center. No qualms about B&E, but there was always the chance that Tolliver and Shanahan were watching, or had set up a sorcerer security alarm. If we were seen going inside, that could suggest we'd gone in to prepare a trap, which would be grounds for canceling the meeting. So we settled for peering through windows and mapping out our plans that way.

As we circled the block, getting a wider lay of the land, Jeremy and Antonio took the lead, discussing the final details. Nick started in the rear with us, but when his few attempts to start conversation failed, he jogged up to Jeremy and his father.

"You okay?" I whispered to Clay.

His tanned face was flushed, eyes brighter than usual. When I reached for his forehead, he shook his head, then jerked his chin at Jeremy.

"He doesn't need to worry about that right now," he said. "I took some pills. They'll kick in before the meeting."

I nodded and we walked in silence the rest of the way.

Once at the community center, we watched from the woods. Tolliver and Shanahan arrived ten minutes early. They went straight in the main door.

Nick loped across the field to watch them through the hall window. Antonio followed at a distance. Once Nick was done, he headed back to us while his father stood watch.

"The doctor checked the meeting room and the bathrooms," Nick said. "Just flipping on lights and taking a look. Then they went to the gym."

"So no sign that they're setting a trap or casting spells," Jeremy said. "Good. Let's go then."

We entered the gym, Antonio in the lead, followed by Jeremy and me, with Clay and Nick covering our backs. As we approached, Shanahan looked anxiously at his friend, but Tolliver laid a hand on his arm and whispered something that seemed to reassure the bigger man. If Tolliver was nervous, he gave no sign of it, not even when his gaze traveled over the five of us. Of course, he may have known that they had reinforcements too—two zombies and a serial killer.

Antonio veered to Jeremy's left. I stood on his right, and Clay moved up to flank me. Behind us, Nick turned around to watch the exit.

Shanahan began to speak even before we stopped moving. "Randy told me—"

Tolliver cut his friend short with a squeeze on his forearm and a look that said they'd discussed earlier how they'd proceed.

"I've updated Patrick on the situation," Tolliver said. "Both with the zombies, the disappearances and yesterday's killing."

"The first of *two* killings," Jeremy said. "We were at the second crime scene when you called. A woman, killed in the same way, in a nearby neighborhood. A young, blond, *pregnant* woman."

Shanahan's brow furrowed, then his gaze shot to me. He paled.

"Christ, no— I'd never. A pregnant—? You can't think—"

Tolliver squeezed his arm again, but this time,

Shanahan shook him off. "No, I know you want to stay calm and present our facts, but this is ridiculous. I can set this whole thing straight myself, starting with this Jack the Ripper nonsense. That letter—"

The lights went out, plunging us into darkness. I swung around to cover Jeremy, but his hand closed on my arm first. Clay caught my other arm, and they hustled me to the exit.

Nick pushed open the heavy gym doors. Jeremy propelled us all the way to the main entrance. Then he propped the doors open and waved for Nick and Clay to take a look outside.

A banging erupted from inside the gym. Antonio strode to the gym doors and swung them open.

Shanahan's voice was shrill. "I told you it was a trap."

"You!" Tolliver's voice boomed. "Tell your boss to open this door immediately, because if he doesn't, I have two Cabals on speed dial—"

"Jer? They're at the rear exit," Antonio called. "They can't get the door open."

Motioning for me to follow, Jeremy returned to the gym entrance. In the dim light, I could see Tolliver and Shanahan whaling on the exit door.

"It must be jammed—" Jeremy began.

"It wasn't jammed when we got here," Tolliver shouted back. "I checked it."

"Tonio?" Jeremy murmured. "Go help Clay get that door open. Send Nick back in." He caught his friend's arm before he left, and lowered his voice. "Be careful."

"I suspect we're going to find it's been spell-locked, not jammed," Jeremy called to Tolliver.

"Spell—?"

"The same thing I believe responsible for the black-out," Jeremy said. "Either that or we have a zombie in the basement who tripped the breaker. Not quite so dramatic as a spell, but equally effective."

As Nick came up behind me, I could hear someone yanking on the outside door.

"You think I turned off the lights?" Tolliver said with a tight laugh. "On werewolves? Who can see in the dark? And I locked myself in with them?"

"We can't see in complete darkness," Jeremy said. "No more than you can. As a doctor, I'm sure you figured that out."

Clay's footsteps thundered down the hall. His face was red, as if he'd run six miles instead of feet.

"It's not jammed," he said, breathing hard. "Doesn't seem locked either. Antonio can snap the hinges . . ."

"Not yet," Jeremy murmured. "Tell him to stand by."

"It's spell-locked," Jeremy called to Tolliver and Shanahan. "A backup plan to distract us when the power outage didn't do the trick, I suspect. You have two choices. Either we relocate this meeting—quickly—or I will make that Cabal call for you, to Benicio Cortez, whom I suspect will handle this in a much less diplomatic way."

Tolliver was silent.

"Quickly was the key word in that offer," Jeremy said, voice still calm. "In sixty seconds, I'm going to declare this a potential ambush and instruct—"

"There's a room down the hall. A meeting room. Smaller than this, but it has windows. It'll be light enough to talk."

Truth

WHILE I WASN'T DISCOUNTING TOLLIVER AS THE SOURCE of the power outage, my money was on Shanahan. His "horrified innocent" act didn't work with me. I'd seen too many mutts pull the same routine. We'd show up at their doorstep and they'd stand there, stammering and wide-eyed at the very notion that they would be hunting people, denials pouring out on breath that reeked of human flesh.

Tolliver paused at the meeting room door as if expecting a wolf to lunge out from behind it. When Antonio closed the door behind them, Shanahan jumped, fingers flying up in a spell.

"If you finish that cast, this meeting is over," Jeremy said.

As we moved to the center of the room, Clay whispered weakly, "Nicky?"

Nick started—surprised by Clay's tone, the childhood nickname or both, so out of place here. Clay's face was

still as flushed as when he'd come running in from outside, and now neither heat nor exertion could be blamed.

"You're—" I began.

Clay silenced me with a meaningful nod at Jeremy.
Frowning, Nick moved up beside Clay.

"Watch Elena, 'kay?" Clay whispered, voice hoarse as
if speaking cost more effort than he could afford.

"Are you—?"

"No, I'm not. So watch her. Please."

Jeremy caught my eye, but Clay had turned away, as if
still talking to Nick. Jeremy waved me up beside him. I
glanced at Clay again, but his eyes warned me to stay
quiet.

Jeremy began, "I'll presume Dr. Tolliver has told you
what's happened this week, and your suspected role in
it."

"I—" Shanahan said.

"Then you know the charges are serious. These negotiations are equally serious. If you claim to have played no
role in these events, and I discover otherwise, I will claim
justice as our jurisdiction, to be decided by me—"

"But—"

"A member of my Pack is under direct threat, and neither the interracial council nor the Cabals will deny me
justice if I demand it."

Shanahan swallowed. His gaze shot to Tolliver, who
said nothing.

"If you admit to your role in this," Jeremy continued,
"and help us close this portal, you will be turned over to
the Cortez Cabal or the interracial council—your
choice, but you have my word that I will attend any pro-
ceedings, and ensure that your cooperation here is noted
and considered."

"And if I played *no* role in any of this?"

"Then you'd be well advised to tell us anything that will help exonerate you, and anything that will help us close this portal . . . and to pray that we don't find out you've lied."

Shanahan pulled himself straight and met Jeremy's gaze. "I played only one role in all of this." He enunciated each word as if such gravity would prove his sincerity. "And that is as the original owner of that letter. If I failed to properly safeguard it, then my only defense is that I had no reason—absolutely no reason—to believe it wasn't what my grandfather claimed."

"A fake?" Jeremy said.

"Not a fake. A dud. A failed experiment. A supernatural curiosity with an interesting story attached. That's what my grandfather collected: stories."

Jeremy's gaze veered toward the windows, and his nostrils flared. The windows were closed, and he gave a slight head shake, as if the sniff had been instinctive. All I could see was the empty basketball courts.

"And the story behind this particular artifact?" Jeremy said. "You called it a dud."

Shanahan nodded, emphatically, as if seeing a sign that his story was being believed. "It *is* supposed to be a portal. A holding cell."

"For the man known as Jack the Ripper."

"No, there's no—"

"We'll get to that," Tolliver said. "Back to the letter and its intended purpose."

They told us a story very similar to the one Anita Barrington knew, with the sorcerer creating a portal to hide from those wanting to take or stop his immortality experiment.

"Only either he wasn't as good as he thought he was, or he rushed the last few steps while his enemies were closing in . . ."

"And the portal failed," Jeremy said. "The sorcerer couldn't get inside in time."

"That wasn't the problem. He—"

Shanahan went rigid, then stumbled back, hands going to his stomach. His mouth opened as if to scream, but no sound came out, just a wisp of something gray, like smoke, and he collapsed backward to the floor.

Tolliver shot forward. Nick pulled me back. Clay tried to lunge for Jeremy, but it was more of a lurch, his face shiny with exertion. Antonio spun on Tolliver, and the sorcerer flicked his fingers in a knockback spell, but Antonio grabbed his hands before he could finish.

Jeremy rushed to Shanahan, who was writhing on the floor, letting out what was probably a howl of pain, but came out only as a mewling whisper carried on a stream of breath that stunk of burnt flesh.

"Let me help—" Tolliver said, struggling against Antonio.

"Help what?" I said. "Finish him off?"

Tolliver's eyes shot to mine, blasting me with cold fury. I walked over to him, Nick sticking so close his arm brushed mine as we moved.

"Are you going to blame us for that too?" I said. "Maybe we could flip off a power breaker, but we sure as hell can't do that. That's magic, and there are only two magic-makers here. Was he about to say something you didn't want us to hear?"

"You think *I* did this?"

Shanahan had gone still, eyes open and blank. As

Jeremy closed Shanahan's eyes, Tolliver let out a roar and started struggling again.

"You just let him die? I could have—"

"Helped?" Jeremy said, voice deceptively low. "No one could have helped him . . . by curing it or hastening it along. But I'm sure that's no surprise to you."

"I didn't—"

"I don't know very much about magic, but there's nothing else that would do that—burn a man from the inside." He walked over to Tolliver. "He was about to tell us something about the portal spell, something you didn't want him to say. What—"

A shout from outside cut him short. We all froze. When Tolliver opened his mouth, Antonio clapped his hand over it.

Another shout came, then a laugh, followed by the *slap-slap* of a ball hitting the pavement. Teens setting up for a game of hoops.

"How close?" Jeremy murmured as I slipped over to the window for a look.

"Too close."

"Nick? Clay? Move Shanahan," Jeremy said. "Elena? Find them a place to hide his body. We'll meet you in the gym."

"The gym?" I said. "It's still dark in—"

"We're only using the exit."

The hall closet door was locked, but I broke it open and cleared a place inside.

Clay moved in to help Nick drag Shanahan to the closet, but he was barely able to stand without toppling. Nick waved him back.

"Is it just the fever?" I said. "What about your arm?"

He hooked his left arm over my shoulder in an awkward, furnace-hot embrace. He leaned in to me, lips going to my ear. I could feel the heat radiating from him.

"Don't—don't worry 'bout me, 'kay?" he whispered. "Get this done, I'll be fine. Keep going. You need cover? Tonio and Nicky, 'kay?" A small sound, like a choked growl. "Not me. Can't count on me."

"I'll cover her," Nick said. "You know I will."

Clay motioned for us to get moving to the gym.

Using a skipping rope, we bound Tolliver's hands to prevent spellcasting. He fought like someone seeing the end coming. But he was no match for Antonio, who just heaved the taller man off his feet, ignoring his kicking and flailing.

We took him into the forest.

Jeremy sent Nick, Clay and me ahead to look around. Out of Jeremy's sight, Nick and I sat Clay down on a fallen tree, never going so far that we couldn't look back and make sure he was still okay. When we found a small clearing a safe distance from the path, we collected Clay, and returned to the others.

Antonio sat Tolliver on the ground and we surrounded him.

"Think about this," Tolliver said, struggling to keep his voice calm as a vein in his forehead pulsed. "How could I possibly be responsible for all this? I haven't seen Patrick in years. The letter was in his possession, then it was stolen and this portal—" His head shot up. "You think I stole the letter and activated the portal?"

"No. We know who stole the letter."

"Then why aren't you questioning—?" His gaze flicked across our faces, and the vein started pulsing again. "*You* stole it? Let me get this straight. You stole the portal letter. You activated that portal. And somehow this is all our fault?"

"The theft of the letter had nothing to do with the portal," Jeremy said. "The person who wanted the letter had no idea what it supposedly contained—"

"And you believed that?"

Jeremy's voice stayed even. "Yes, we do. It was a separate matter, with a human purchaser interested only in the letter's historical value. We did steal it, in return for information that helped us to stop another set of crimes."

Tolliver's dark eyes still fumed.

Jeremy continued. "Perhaps Shanahan did believe that the portal was a failed experiment—in fact, I'll wager he *did*. But when those zombies came to his door, looking for their master, he saw an opportunity. He knew the story behind the letter, that his great-grandfather had created it and trapped a killer within, a killer whose work was pivotal in those immortality experiments."

"Jack the Ripper?" Tolliver's lip twisted. "Don't you get it? There is no Jack the Ripper." He shook his head sharply. "Yes, I'm sure there was one, once, but he has nothing to do with the letter. That's what Patrick was trying to tell you. I stopped him because I didn't want to go off on an unnecessary tangent. Whoever killed those young women is *not* Jack the Ripper."

Jeremy studied Tolliver's face, and let him continue.

"The whole *From Hell* thing was a ruse used by the

sorcerer who created that portal. *He* wrote the letter. He arranged for it to be sent, with the kidney, to the . . ." A sharp shake of his head. "Whoever it was sent to. It's all in the file. I don't remember—"

"Where's the file?"

Tolliver hesitated, then said, "I can take you to it. Patrick showed it to me this morning, and we put it someplace safe. If you let me take you—"

"Not now. So this sorcerer—Patrick's great-grandfather—"

"Maybe," Tolliver said. "There's nothing in the file about the creator being a Shanahan, but if that's what you heard, okay, we'll go with that. Whoever this sorcerer was, he created the portal as a holding place, as Patrick said, to escape supernaturals who wanted to steal or stop his experiment—an experiment unconnected to Jack the Ripper. He sacrificed two petty criminals to create the portal, then put the portal trigger into a piece of paper. At the same time, the police are investigating a string of homicides in Whitechapel. Letters are flowing in, claiming to be from the killer, all being carefully collected and stored in the police station. So he uses the paper to write a fake letter, figuring there's no safer place in London than that police file . . ."

Tolliver continued explaining, but Jeremy's gaze had swung out over the forest, eyes narrowed, nostrils flaring as he tried to catch a breeze. He saw me watching but, instead of waving it off as nothing, he motioned Tolliver to silence.

"Antonio?" Jeremy murmured. "Take over. Elena, I need your nose. Clay?"

Near-panic crossed through Clay's eyes, as he realized

Jeremy wanted him to cover me, leaving Nick behind with Antonio.

"Keep him talking," Jeremy said to Antonio, not noticing Clay's hesitation. "We'll be right back."

Clay's mouth opened, probably to suggest Nick go in his place. First, though, he looked at me. I shook my head, jerking my chin toward Antonio and Tolliver. If Clay stayed behind, he'd be the only one protecting Antonio, whose attention would be on questioning Tolliver. Better to have Nick doing that.

Clay followed us into the forest.

Deal-Breaker

CLAY WALKED BEHIND ME, AS MUCH TO KEEP HIS DISTANCE from Jeremy as anything. Any other time, Jeremy wouldn't have needed to see Clay to know something was wrong—he'd just know, in that uncanny way of his. But right now, he was too preoccupied.

I crept up beside Jeremy and whispered, "Was it something you heard?"

He hesitated, as if not certain himself, then shook his head. "Not heard . . ."

"Give me a direction, and I'll get upwind."

He scanned the forest, but his eyes were unfocused. He hadn't seen, heard or smelled anyone. He'd sensed them, the same way he often did when we were hurt or in danger.

"There," he said, pointing east. "We'll loop around to the south. I don't want to get too far from the others."

We'd gone only about twenty feet when I caught the smell, not because our target was upwind, but because we were so close.

I took a few slow steps. A shape moved through the

trees only twenty feet away. As Jeremy touched my arm, I recognized the scent.

"Oh, I don't believe it," I muttered, shrugging off Jeremy's hand and striding forward.

"Ele—!"

A grunt cut off Jeremy's cry. I turned to see him knocked off his feet. Clay ran forward, but stumbled midway. As I dove for him, someone caught me by the shirt and yanked.

With a growl, I swung my elbow back to knock my attacker flying. Metal flashed, and I felt a prick—a small but sharp jab—not at my chest or throat, but in the side of my stomach.

I heard a whimper, and felt it bubbling up from my throat.

"Stay where you are, Mr. Danvers," a voice behind me said.

The tone, from that voice, was so unexpected that my brain blanked out.

I forced my gaze from the knife, expecting to see Clay ready to leap to my rescue. But Clay was on the ground, crumpled face-first, not moving. Jeremy's gaze shot down to Clay's prone body. Fear darted behind his black eyes.

Was Clay breathing? Oh, God, I couldn't tell.

Jeremy's gaze swung to the knife at my side. His fists twitched at his side, body tensing as he rocked onto the balls of his feet—

"You know that isn't a wise idea, Mr. Danvers," Hull said behind me, the meekness gone from his voice. "You may be able to save her, but this knife will go into her belly the moment you move. I'm sure you understand what that means. No grandbaby to dandle on your knee. I mean grandbab*ies*. I did overhear that correctly, didn't

I? Twins?" A bark of a laugh. "I must have done some-thing right in my life—pleased some demon or deity—to give me so rich a boon. Two full-blooded werewolf babes."

Clay let out a guttural moan.

"He's dying, you know," Hull said. "Zombie scratches—nasty things. Only way to help him now is to kill the zombies. I could help with that." Another small laugh. "After all, they are *my* zombies."

That's what Shanahan had been saying just before he died—that the sorcerer *had* made it into the portal.

My hair prickled as I remembered Shanahan, convuls-ing on the floor, dying almost instantly. Oh, God, if Hull could do that—

Wait. According to Paige, the problem with casting a strong spell was that it drained your power. The stronger the spell, the greater the drain, which is why Hull had only used a simple knockback spell on Jeremy.

And if Hull could do that to Shanahan, why hadn't he just used a spell against Clay to grab me earlier, like out on the balcony last night? Something was making him cautious. Maybe, after a hundred years in a dimensional portal, he was out of practice, or his spell power was still recharging.

"So you've been controlling them all along," I said, hoping to give Jeremy time to think. "You came out of the portal after they cleared the way."

Hull laughed. "Cleared the way? I was out only min-utes after my first zombie. You were too engrossed in fol-lowing him down the road to even notice. So I followed you. It seemed strange—humans pursuing the man in-stead of calling for help. So I cast a little spell, and discovered my good fortune. A pregnant werewolf had opened my portal."

"You weren't after me for the letter at all," I said.

"The letter has served its purpose. You're the vessel of value now."

"I am not exchanging Elena for—" Jeremy began.

"You don't need to exchange your dear girl for anything. That's the beauty of my offer. You will get both her and your boy back, healthy and sound. I'll even relinquish control of my zombies, so you can kill them and close this portal. Like the letter, they were useful enough, but they've quickly become more of a hindrance. Take them with my blessing, close the portal, heal your boy there . . . everything you want."

"In exchange for . . . ?" Jeremy said.

"No," I said through my teeth.

Hull chuckled. "You already know what I'm going to ask for, don't you? I wouldn't be so hasty with your refusal, though. After all, I could take what I want now, with no deal . . . leave the portal open, let your mate die, let you die with him . . ."

"What do—?" Jeremy began.

"No!"

Hull turned the knife. At the movement, Jeremy's gaze dropped to my belly, and he paled.

"A fair exchange, don't you agree? Two lives for two lives? It's a simple enough matter to take the babes out early. You fancy yourself a doctor, don't you, Mr. Danvers? Or perhaps, if that other one isn't too upset with you, he'll undertake the task."

"They—" Jeremy swallowed, as if his mouth was too dry to form words. "The babies aren't far enough along. They wouldn't live."

"No matter. I don't need them alive. Even if I take them that way, they won't stay that way for long."

I didn't think. Couldn't think. I just reacted, howling, twisting, my elbow going up to smash—

The knife dug into my belly.

As I froze, I heard Jeremy's voice, distant, barely piercing the roar in my ears, begging me to stop, to hold still.

I stood shaking and gasping for breath. Hull laughed, but I ignored him and forced myself to look at Jeremy. Again he mouthed something, and this time it was clear: "Wait."

As Hull stopped laughing, a small crackle cut through the silence of the forest, too soft for Hull to hear.

Gaze still locked to mine, Jeremy dipped his chin, telling me yes, they were coming. His eyes were clear and calm, panic gone. Seeing that, I felt my own fear drain.

"Why offer this deal?" Jeremy asked. His voice was even again, as collected as it had been when negotiating with Shanahan and Tolliver. Time to distract, stall . . . and wait. "If, as you pointed out, you can take Elena and the babies now . . ."

"Too messy." Hull was equally nonchalant, even as blood trickled down my side. "I like things tidy. That's why I tried to resolve this without confrontation. Had you let her return to the hotel with me, you'd have saved yourself much unpleasantness. I'm sure Mr. Shanahan would have preferred that. Now, I'll settle for an offering freely given—" He repositioned the knife again, and I bit back a snarl. "—with the promise of no retaliation to come."

I could smell Antonio and Nick now, coming closer.

"But why the—" Jeremy faltered, then continued,

voice as casual as he could make it. "The babies. What do you need them for? Surely not the experiment you were working on back in England."

Hull laughed. "That would be rather coincidental, wouldn't it? No, they aren't for that—though, thanks to you, I may have found the final rare ingredient I need. This, however, is a simple matter of economics. Had I ever considered the possibility of arriving here, a hundred years late, in another time, another country, I would have made financial arrangements. No matter. Providence interceded, and I arrived to find a woman pregnant with full-blooded werewolf twins. Some things never change, and such babes would be a sorcery ingredient of untold potency, as rare as the mythical unicorn's horn. On the black market? Priceless. One alone would be enough to keep me in great comfort."

"If one would be enough . . ." Jeremy said.

I stiffened, but he met my gaze, reminding me he was only stalling.

"In the mood to negotiate now, Mr. Danvers? That's the spirit. Perhaps—"

The bushes exploded behind Jeremy. Hull jumped, startled. I hit the knife away from my stomach, but the blade caught the back of my hand, slicing it open. As I dove to grab the falling knife, Hull kicked my legs from under me. I fell, twisting to protect my stomach.

Hull's hands sailed up, knocking Jeremy back with a spell, then Nick, as he burst through the bushes behind Jeremy. Intent on Nick, Hull didn't see Antonio slip from the woods on the other side.

As I scrambled up, Antonio leapt at Hull, and they went down. Another crash in the forest, and I glimpsed something that made my gut go cold.

The bowler-hatted zombie burst from the woods, Rose
lurching behind him, cutting Nick and Jeremy off from
Hull, Antonio and me. Hull cast a spell. Something like
an electrical bolt hit Antonio, and he fell, gasping. I
started for him, then saw the knife, just inches from my
hand. I stretched to grab it, but it flew out of my reach,
sailing back toward Hull, propelled by some spell.

I struggled to my feet, my hand throbbing, my ankle
blazing as if I'd twisted it. I stumbled forward, nearly
blind with dizziness. Had I hit my head? I couldn't remember. Couldn't worry about that. Not now. Had to
get—

A familiar jab in my belly, and I went still. Hull
grabbed the back of my shirt.

"Walk," he said.

When I resisted, the knife dug in. I walked then, letting him push me as I tripped and staggered, my ankle
giving way with every step, the world around me swaying
and dimming, threatening to go black, the sounds of
struggle fading as we moved deeper into the woods.

"You ought to have accepted my offer," Hull said. "Had
the operation gone smoothly, surely there would have
been more babes to come."

I tried to growl, but only managed a rasp.

"Perhaps you still held out hope for escape. It would
have done you no good. Your blood opened my portal. As
long as you live, I can find you, wherever you hide. You
carry the treasure of a lifetime in your belly. I would have
tracked you to the south pole if I had to."

As I trudged in silence, I struggled to think of a plan,
but my brain kept shorting out, throwing up images of
Clay prone on the ground, Antonio falling back, hit by

God-knew-what, Jeremy and Nick fighting off the zombies . . .

Hull kept talking. Rambling in a happy monologue, so pleased with himself. After a moment, I could hear the sound of distant traffic. Then an odd rhythmic thumping. A train? No, running paws, beating against hard ground. Who could Change that quickly?

The answer came even as the dark blur flew from the undergrowth beside us. I twisted, putting every bit of energy I had into getting away from that knife. The tip of it scratched along the side of my belly. Then the knife flew up as Jeremy caught Hull's arm in his teeth.

Hull cast a spell, snarling the words. But nothing happened. Jeremy swung Hull around. As the sorcerer flew off his feet, he cast again, flicking his fingers. A simple knockback spell, but it worked. Jeremy lost his grip on Hull's arm.

As Jeremy stumbled back, I clumsily dove to protect him. We both hit the ground. I turned to see Hull's back disappearing into the forest.

Jeremy went after him, but a moment later the squeal of tires and horns told me Hull had reached the road. Jeremy couldn't follow him there.

I paused for just a second, then raced back to Clay.

I remember that headlong rush as a blur, tree branches whipping my face, vines grabbing my feet. Nick and Tolliver were crouched beside Clay. His eyes were still closed.

A cold nose pressed my palm, as Jeremy moved up beside me. As I swayed, I reached for him, my fingers deep in the fur around his neck, grabbing him for balance as my knees gave way and everything went dark.

If

ON THE TRIP BACK, I CAUGHT SNATCHES OF CONVERSA-
tion. I struggled to follow it, only to hear the words that
would let me fall back to sleep. At last they came: Clay
was alive. Still unconscious, and burning up with fever,
but alive.

I drifted back to sleep.

When I awoke, my first thought was that I was in a hospital bed. The sheets were cool and crisp, the air around
me equally cold, blinds drawn, lights out, room blan-
keted in the eerie hush reserved for those who are recovering or dying, the only sounds the whir of the
air-conditioning fan. The only thing lacking was the stink
of disinfectant and overcooked food.

As I roused myself, I dimly heard Jeremy's voice in the
next room, urgent and frustrated. I jumped up. My whole
body screamed in protest and I froze, hovering there.
Had I been hurt? No. There was a cut on my hand, but
the protest was from pure exhaustion, my body having

tasted rest and screaming for more. I started sinking back into the covers—

Clay.

I scrambled up. A hand closed on my bare arm.

"It's okay," Nick whispered from beside the bed. "Lay back down. Rest."

"W—where's Clay?"

"He's fi—" Nick stopped himself, as if unable to force the lie out. "He's . . . okay. Jeremy's looking after him. And that doctor, Tolliver."

I tried to get up again, but Nick's grip tightened.

"Tolliver?" I said. "How can we be sure—?"

"That he won't take revenge?" Nick finished. "Because Jeremy trusts him. And Jeremy's right there, watching every step. If anyone can help Clay, it's Tolliver. He has every kind of medicine Clay could need. That's what Zoe does for him—steals supplies so he can give them to shelters and stuff."

"I want to see—" I began.

"He's okay, Elena." Nick's gaze met mine. "Would I say that if he wasn't?"

I searched his eyes and saw worry, but not panic.

"If he's okay, why can't I see—?"

"Because you'll get upset and Jeremy has enough to worry about right now."

I blinked, not sure I'd heard right. Those words and that tone didn't sound like the Nick I knew. He slid closer, arm going around me.

"I'm right, aren't I?" he said. "You walk in there and see Clay lying on the bed, unconscious, medical stuff all over, you're going to get upset. You know they're working on him, but if it doesn't look like it—if they just seem to be standing around talking—it'll drive you nuts. Same with Clay if it was you lying in there."

"And that will only upset Jeremy more," I said softly.

"Because he'll want to do something. Do more. You're in here with me because Tolliver wants you in bed. Off your feet. What happened today, out there . . . that's too much for someone so close to having a baby." A small smile. "Babies."

I swallowed. He was right, but there was another, more immediate danger to my babies now: Hull, who could find me, find us, wherever I went. Who was probably outside the hotel right now, watching and waiting—

I shook it off, and turned to the adjoining door, straining to hear Jeremy's voice.

I longed to race to Clay's side, but I had to trust that Jeremy would do everything in his power to help Clay, and that was as certain as the sun rising tomorrow morning.

"What—?" My throat was dry and I had to clear it before trying again. "What exactly is wrong? Is it the infection? Are they going to—?"

Nick pressed a glass of water to my lips.

As I drank, he answered. "It *is* the infection. Or, right now, it's mostly the fever caused by the infection. They got the fever down enough so it's not dangerous, but it's not going away."

"Did he wake up? Is he conscious?"

Nick hesitated.

"Nick, please," I said. "Whatever you tell me, it's not going to be as bad as what I can imagine. I'm only going to get more worked up if I don't know."

"He . . . he was delirious for a bit. They had to sedate him. He'd started to Change and the noise . . . they had to do it. Now the fever's down, and Jeremy wants to wake him up so he can have some say in what they decide, but they're afraid if he does wake up and he's still delirious—"

"Have some say?" I cut in. "In what they decide about his arm. That's what you mean, isn't it? They're thinking of amputating."

Someone knocked on the hall door before Nick could answer me. It was Jaime.

"Oh, geez, I'm sorry," she said when Nick opened the door and she saw me. "I wasn't sure which room . . . It's the next one, right? I needed to speak to Jeremy."

"Come through here," I said.

She nodded and took a hesitant step toward the foot of the bed. "How are you? I mean, I know you must not be— I was just going to talk to Jeremy. I had an idea . . ."

"He's right in there," I said.

Nick grabbed the adjoining door. As he swung it open, Antonio turned sharply. He must have been covering it, in case Nick failed to persuade me to stay put. I lifted a hand, and he managed a smile, his face drawn and pale, then ushered Jaime in and closed the door.

I crawled back into bed and pulled up the covers. Nick hovered, as if expecting me to resume our conversation about Clay. I patted the spot beside me and he climbed on, lying atop the covers, back against the headboard. I reached up for his hand. Holding it, I turned onto my side, as if ready to fall back to sleep. Then I closed my eyes and strained to hear the conversation in the other room.

"—idea for catching Matthew Hull," Jaime was saying.

She was still right on the other side of the door, her voice clear.

"Catching . . . ?" Jeremy's voice was muffled, then it came closer, as if he was walking toward her. "Oh, yes. Hull. Thank you, Jaime. I'll . . . I'll talk to you about this later. If you need a lift to the airport, Antonio can—"

"Sure," Antonio cut in. "Whenever you're ready to go. We should be leaving in a couple of hours ourselves, as soon as Clay's fever breaks. I can run you over now, or you can wait and catch a ride out with us."

"You're . . . you're leaving?" Jaime said. "But . . . you can't. You need to catch Hull. Not just for Elena. To fix Clay. Close that portal, and Clay will get better."

"No," Jeremy said, his voice low, words clipped. "I said that's what Hull *claimed*. I'm sorry, Jaime. I don't mean to be short with you; I'm just angry with myself for letting it go this far. I'm taking Clay and Elena back to Stonehaven, where they should have been all along."

"But if Hull's the controller and if you kill him—"

"And if I could wave my magic wand—" Jeremy cut himself off and made a noise almost like a growl. "I'm sorry, Jaime. I don't want to snap at you. But I've had enough of these magical 'ifs.' Do this, do that, and everything will be better. From the start, Clay wanted to take Elena back to Stonehaven, batten down the hatches and protect her. We stayed because I thought it was best. Just do this one last thing, and she'll be safe. But she isn't. And now he isn't. And I'm not playing the 'magic wand' game anymore. What will cure Clayton is medicine, and what will protect Elena is her Pack. We're going home, where I can do that."

In the silence that followed, I knew Jeremy had moved off again, returning to Clay's side. Discussion over. My fingers dug into the mattress as my stomach flip-flopped. Home? We couldn't leave. Not now. We weren't safe.

Clay. Our babies. Pain ran through my abdomen. A cramp? Oh, God, no. Please no. I had to keep them inside me, where they were safe, until I could make sure it was safe for them out here.

If I went home, I'd only take the danger with me. Our house wouldn't be a safe haven, but a fortress. Clay would lose his arm, and with it, his place in the world. No longer able to protect his Alpha, his Pack, his mate, his children . . .

"We can end this now." Jaime's voice, on the other side of the door, so perfectly echoed my thoughts that I jumped.

Nick squeezed my fingers, his free hand patting my shoulder, lulling me back to sleep. I forced myself to relax and listen.

"I think I can catch one of those zombies," Jaime said. "If I catch one, she or he can probably lead me to Hull, the controller."

"Think . . . if . . . probably . . ." Antonio said. "Jaime, I'm sorry, but Jeremy's right. We've had enough ifs. If you really thought you could do this, you would have mentioned it sooner—"

"I didn't know it sooner. That—that woman Zoe took me to. The necromancer. She said something to me about calling a zombie, and I finally figured out what she meant. If a zombie is dead, then all I need is some artifact from one and I can use that to call the zombie, just like a spirit—"

"Jeremy's going home, Jaime. He can't help you—"

"I don't expect him to. You come with me. Or Nick. Leave Jeremy here with Elena and Clay, and let him get ready to go home. I can find Hull. You or Nick can kill him. Done. Without bothering Jeremy."

Antonio's sigh rippled through the door. "He won't go for it, Jaime. With Clay sedated, Elena wiped out by exhaustion and Hull out there waiting for his chance, Jeremy wants all hands on deck. He's even called Karl Marsten to meet us at Stonehaven. Demanded his help fortifying the battlements, or he can forget about getting into the Pack. Now for Jeremy to do that—"

"He's serious. I know. But—"

"Why don't you come back to Stonehaven with us? If you have the time, and you feel safe enough being there, come with us and talk to Jeremy in a day or so, when everything's under control. He'll listen then."

A few more murmured words, but I didn't listen because I knew *they* wouldn't listen, not Antonio, not Jeremy, their only concern being getting us out of this hotel before Hull made his move. When the door opened and Jaime stepped back into our room, I shot up.

"How's Clay?" I said. "Any change? Have they decided anything?"

"Uh . . . no. I—I didn't really . . ." She turned, as if to go back in and ask.

"No, don't," I said. "They probably won't give you a decent update anyway. Nick?"

He shifted in the bed. "If anything changed, they'd let me know, Elena."

"Please?" I looked up at him. "Just check. Jaime's right here. She can watch me for ten seconds while you check."

He shook his head, but climbed out of bed and headed for the adjoining door. When he went through, he left it ajar behind him. I motioned Jaime over. She hesitated. I gestured urgently, my other hand pointing at the open door. She crossed to the side of the bed.

"Meet me outside," I said. "Under the terrace. Ten minutes."

She frowned and opened her mouth, but Nick's return cut her short.

"So you're coming back to Stonehaven with us?" I said to her.

She paused, then nodded.

"Good."

"I—" She looked over at Nick. "I guess I'll go pack then."

I nodded and waited for her to leave, then let Nick give me the non-update.

There were two ways to get past Nick. Prey on his trusting nature and trick him, or clock him over the head and run. I picked option two. Less cruel. I've tricked Nick before. More than once. Given the choice between betrayal and a potential concussion, he'd pick the latter.

So, when he wasn't looking, I grabbed my hairbrush. As he turned, I hit him. He hesitated, and for one terrible moment I thought it hadn't worked. Then he slumped to the bed.

I checked his breathing and his pupils, making sure the blow hadn't been *too* hard. Then I lifted him into the bed and stuffed the pillows under the covers beside him, making a human-sized figure. It wouldn't trick Antonio when he came to collect us, but it would probably pass muster if he just glanced in the door to check.

Next: shoes and cell phone. Then I was out the door.

Summoned

I WALKED OUT INTO THE NIGHT. JAIME WAS WAITING UNDER the hotel terrace, tucked between two half-dead spruce trees. When I approached, she didn't move, as if wondering whether she was well enough concealed just to stay there and avoid me.

"I need you to help me find Hull," I said.

She nodded, no surprise in her eyes.

"You said you can call a zombie if you have something of hers. Would a finger work?"

She only stood there, worrying her rings, trying to avoid my eyes.

"We can't do this, Elena," she said finally. "I can't. I know you want to, but you're not thinking clearly and—"

"Not thinking clearly?"

I strode up in front of her. Jaime stepped back, eyes widening in alarm. The second I saw that look, I stopped and stared at her. In her eyes I saw more than alarm. I saw fear.

"You're worried about what Jeremy will say," I said.

She shook her head. "No. Well, yes. But that's not my

main concern. Not really a concern at all. It's pointless anyway."

She looked so sad then, so deflated, that a twinge of conscience pierced my determination. I shouldn't drag her into this. But I couldn't find Hull on my own. Or could I?

"Stay here." I started to walk away, hesitated, then said, "No, come with me. It's safer."

When she hesitated, I strode off. No time to cajole her. After a moment, I heard her footsteps jog up behind me.

"What are you doing?" she whispered.

"Scouting the perimeter."

"For Hull?"

"More likely a zombie."

I paused at the corner and knelt by a scent trail. Hull's, but an old one. I pushed up and kept moving.

"What'll you do if you find one?"

"I'll grab it. Make it lead me back to Hull."

"But you can't fight Hull, Elena. Not by yourself. Not in your—"

"Condition? Trust me, right now, my condition is what's going to make me damned sure I can kill him. He won't even have time to try negotiating."

Her hand clamped down on my arm. As I wheeled, I swallowed a snarl, but she must have seen it. Fear darted behind her eyes, but she didn't let go of my arm.

"What about time to cast a spell, Elena?"

"He won't kill me like that," I said. "He said he doesn't care if the babies are dead or alive, but he's lying. That's why he was so eager to make a deal instead of just killing me. It makes a difference. Dead, he'd have to sell them fast, before they—" My throat seized up, images flipping past, images I really didn't want to see, didn't want to consider. "Better if they're alive. Then he has time to find a good buyer. I'm not saying he won't kill me—if it comes to that—but he won't be *quick* to kill me."

I circled the building twice, and found only old trails from Hull, including one that intersected with the scent of the bowler-hatted man, who'd must have stopped by earlier to get his orders. How stupid had we been? Searching for the zombie controller when we had taken him into our "protection."

He had to be out here, somewhere, watching for our next move. But "out here" was a downtown block. He could be hiding in any of the darkened offices overlooking the hotel or on top of those buildings or in the parking garages—anyplace where he could see us if we tried to make a run for it.

If I had to, I might be able to find Hull, but my best bet was still the woman jogging behind me, her sandals catching in the roots and holes of the hotel gardens.

"The abandoned building where we found the fingers is about three kilo— two miles over," I said. "We'll slip down the block behind the hotel and get a taxi."

"Elena. I . . ."

I turned. "You don't want to do this? Twenty minutes ago, you were begging Jeremy to let you have a go at it. So it's one thing to fly to the rescue and win Jeremy's gratitude, but going behind his back and doing it is out of the question? Sure, it might save my life, my babies' lives, Clay's life . . . but if that's not what matters, then it's hardly worth the bother, is it?"

Her eyes flashed. "This isn't about impressing Jeremy."

"No? Then—"

"Prove it?" A small laugh. "Nice trap, Elena, but I'm not falling for it. Yes, I offered to do this same thing with Jeremy. Or with Antonio. Or with Nick. But not with an eight-months pregnant—"

"Five months."

Her eyes met mine. "According to Jeremy, you're the equivalent of at least eight months along, so don't split hairs. You are in no condition to fight a sorcerer and his zombies, and when it comes to fighting, I'm useless. If I let you do this, then I'm just what you accused me of being—a desperately infatuated, self-centered twit who'll put your life at risk for the faint hope of impressing a man."

"No, Jaime, *I'm* the one who's desperate here. Yes, I'm running on instinct and adrenaline, but it'll take me where I want to go. You have a cell phone, right?"

"Sure, but—"

"If, at any point, you decide I'm in over my head, all you have to do is use it. Hell, once you've delivered that zombie, you can use it to call a cab. No one even has to know you were involved."

"I wouldn't do that."

"But you have the option. You have other options too. You can go back upstairs and pretend you never spoke to me. Or you can tell Jeremy what I'm doing, which might earn you some brownie points . . . until Clay loses his arm and my babies are put up for sale on the black market and Jeremy realizes he's made a horrible mistake. Or, you can slip back up there, grab your bag and come with me."

"I don't need to."

"No, you're right, you don't need to come with me—"

"No." She hoisted her purse. "I mean I don't need to go

back upstairs. I didn't think you were asking me to take a moonlight walk."

"Good. Let's go then."

Yesterday Tee had chastised Jaime for not knowing how to call a zombie. At first, Jaime had chalked that up to Tee's madness—that she was confused and had forgotten it wasn't Jaime who'd raised the zombies. But the comment had gnawed at Jaime.

Zombies were ghosts inside dead bodies. If necromancers would summon ghosts, did it matter which plane—or form—they were in? While we'd been meeting with Tolliver and Shanahan, Jaime had been making calls, trying to track down instances of necromancers calling zombies they hadn't raised.

It had taken a lot of digging to come up with anything. Not surprising. If you can raise your own zombies, why steal someone else's? What she did find were a couple stories of incompetent necromancers who didn't have the skills to raise their own, trying to "buy" zombies—pay a better necro to raise them, then take them over. And it *had* worked . . . in a fashion.

In one story, the necromancer had been trying to recruit cheap farm labor. He'd hired someone else to raise a half-dozen zombies, successfully summoned them to his home and handed them their picks and shovels. And, industrious zombies that they were, they immediately set to work using those tools . . . to beat him to death. Then they went on a rampage of neighboring farms, leaving a swath of dead bodies as they tried to find the necro who'd raised them and could set them to rest. The second story was a variation on the first: yes, the summoning worked, but then you were left with the problem of *controlling* the zombies, which you apparently couldn't do if they weren't yours.

According to these stories, then, it *was* possible to summon another necro's zombies. And I wanted to believe it. We both did. But, like so many other stories passed down through the generations—like the one about the sorcerer's portal accidentally unleashing a demon or most of the stories in the Pack Legacy or even Jaime's *Pet Sematary* encounter—it smacked of didacticism. Humans tell fairy tales to warn children not to talk to strangers or wander into the dark woods. We impart our own story-lessons to our youth—the lesson being simple and universal: don't mess with forces you don't understand.

"Jaime?"

A muffled oath behind me. I backtracked to find Jaime kicking the wall.

"I—have—rat—shit—on—my—foot," she said, punctuating each word with a kick.

"Then wipe it off."

A scowl, as if I was being funny.

"Here," I said, trying not to growl. "Let me—"

"It's off."

"You're only going to step in more. This isn't a sandal-friendly excursion."

"It was these or heels. At least I can jog in these."

I strode down the hall, weaving around the patches of feces.

"Rat shit wipes off," I said. "Worry about the rats

themselves. I don't smell any—they're probably out hunting—but be careful. Now, we were right over here . . . There. Clay put it up—"

I stared down at the empty ledge.

"It's gone. Goddamn it!" I felt along the ledge, though I could see well enough to know it wasn't there. "Who'd take a rotting finger?"

"Maybe it's the wrong ledge."

I bent to sniff the ledge. Yes, I could smell blood and rotting flesh. Even found a fleck of it on the wood. I scooped it up on the end of my finger. Too small for Jaime to use.

"Maybe a rat managed to knock it down and carry it off," Jaime said. "You said she was staying here, right? There has to be something else. Maybe a blanket she used, or a piece of her clothing."

"A piece of her would be better. If a rat got it, maybe I can track—"

As I dropped to an awkward crouch, I saw a spot of white in a small pile of debris below the ledge. I picked up two white bones, still connected by rotting cartilage.

"That was easy. Rat must have had to eat and run." I held it up. "Will this do?"

The woman who had been dodging piles of rat poop now reached for the bones as if I were offering her something as innocuous as a pen. She took the bones, rotting flesh and all, and turned it over in her hands.

"Perfect," she said.

When she called me over to say she was finished, I resisted the urge to shout "Did it work?" We'd been gone an hour. By now, unless something had happened with

Clay's condition to distract Jeremy, he'd know I was gone. Then he'd find Jaime missing and figure out what had happened.

How long would it take him to realize that the best spot to find something belonging to the zombies was here? Where Rose had been living? Not long enough.

"She'll follow you, right?" I said, pacing the small room as Jaime packed her supplies. "We don't have to stay here."

"It'll be easiest for her if I'm close by, but we can move on."

"Good," I said, and headed for the door.

We relocated to the building across the road, where we could spot Rose or the others when they showed. Forty-five minutes passed. No sign of Jeremy or Rose.

"We can't wait much longer," I said. "Can we move someplace else? We'll need to take a cab, to cover my trail, but if we can get to another location, could you try the summoning again?"

Jaime peered out the filthy window. "I could . . . but if I summon her twice, from different locations, she might get confused. Let's wait a bit longer. She can't be far."

I resumed pacing from one window to the next, watching for any sign of movement outside.

"I wish I could get in touch with Eve," Jaime murmured as she undid her sandal strap and rubbed her foot.

"Eve?"

"Savannah's mother—"

"I know who you mean. You've had contact with her, haven't you? From the other side. Could she help with Rose?"

Jaime shrugged. "I don't know. At this point, I'd be willing to try anything. Eve's been helping me out some. An exchange of services."

"Like a spirit guide?"

She forced a tired smile. "More like a spirit guard dog. She scares off the spooks that don't take no for an answer. I do some work for her in return."

"Why can't you reach her?"

"No idea. For a few months, she'll be there whenever I need her, then she's gone, popping by now and then to check on me, maybe get my help, but I can't summon her—"

Jaime's gaze shot to the corner window, overlooking the east side. "What's that?"

I hurried over, but saw nothing.

"Someone was there," Jaime said, standing on tiptoe, trying to see over my shoulder.

I stepped aside. "Where?"

"Someone came around the corner of that building. I saw a shape. Moving fast."

The street was empty.

"One shape?" I said.

She nodded.

One person, darting around in the shadows, now hiding.

"Rose," I said.

Dupe

"OH, GOD," JAIME WHISPERED BEHIND ME, VOICE MUFFLED as her hand flew to cover her nose and mouth. "What is that smell?"

"Decomposing zombie."

No wonder Rose had taken so long to get here. Smelling that bad, she'd have to take side streets and alleys all the way.

I peeked out the door. A dark shape emerged from behind a garbage bin, hesitated, then scuttled back behind it. A moment later, she popped out her head again, trying to find Jaime.

"You wait here," I said, closing the door partway. "When I have her down, I'll call you."

Jaime shook her head. "I might not be any help against a powerful sorcerer. But this I can handle."

"No."

"Elena, she's a half-dead zombie. What's she going to do? Rot on me?"

"You're right. She'd probably just scratch you. Like she did to Clay."

Jaime paled, then shook her head. "I still want to help—"

"Stay," I said. "Please. One less thing for me to worry—"

Something hit the door, whacking it against my palm. An angry squeal set my hairs rising, and I looked down to see a rat's head through the crack, teeth flashing.

I slammed the door so hard I should have decapitated the rat. But it wouldn't shut. A throng of rats were throwing themselves at the door, bodies thumping, claws scrabbling on the wood as they climbed on each other, trying to get in.

Another head appeared over the first, then a third, teeth gnashing, squirming and wriggling to squeeze through.

As they shrieked and squealed, the smell of blood drifted through the opening, as if they were so desperate to get inside that they were tearing each other apart.

"They must smell Rose," I called to Jaime.

The door handle jolted in my hands. It was Jaime, throwing herself backward against the door, trying to help. Yet even her body weight wasn't enough for me to push it shut—not with rats jammed in the opening.

When I lifted my foot to kick the bottom one out, Jaime grabbed my arm.

"No! Jeremy said—"

"If I don't touch that one, we're going to be touching a whole lot more when they break the door down."

"Switch places."

I shook my head. "You're wearing sandals. They'll gnaw your—"

She grabbed a plank from the floor and brandished it. "Now switch. On my count. Three, two, one."

I went sideways, throwing my back against the door. Jaime flew into my spot and whacked the head of the top rat. It squealed but kept trying to wriggle through.

"Not taking the hint, are they?" she said through her teeth as she kept hitting.

"They won't. You're going to have to—"

She heaved back the plank for a home-run swing. It hit the top rodent with a skull-splitting splat.

"I'm going to feel bad about this in the morning," she said, taking a swing at the second one.

When the opening was clear, I slammed the door shut. We ran to the back of the building, searching for another way out, but found only boarded windows. As Jaime dragged over a wooden crate, I pried the boards off a window, ignoring the splinters.

"Go," I said.

"You first."

I glared at her. "We can't waste time arguing—"

"Then don't. Get moving, and I'll cover you."

She helped me out the window, then crawled through just as the rats broke down the front door. They didn't follow—they just wanted inside, away from the unnatural creature coming their way.

We found a building a half block down. Then I persuaded Jaime to stand guard inside while I flushed Rose out.

I don't think I'd be exaggerating if I said the entire city block reeked of Rose's rot. Like Jaime, even humans would notice it if they got within fifty feet. Hell, they'd notice if they drove by with the windows rolled up and

A/C on. Fortunately, it was past midnight and the streets were empty.

Rose had ducked behind the bin right across the road. I moved behind a bin of my own to look and listen. After a moment, she appeared from a new hiding spot, her face a pale, indistinct oval under her shawl. A slow look around, and she came out.

Rose took a staggering step, then jerked backward. Another stagger, another jerk. Being pulled in two directions? Was Hull trying to summon her too?

That stagger-jerk dance took her to the edge of the sidewalk. Something moved down the alley behind her. I tried picking up the scent on the wind, but Rose's rot overpowered everything. I stared at the spot where I'd seen the movement. Nothing.

My brain cycled through the possibilities. Too big to be rats. Jeremy or Antonio? They wouldn't be skulking in shadows.

Could it be Hull? Or the other zombie?

Rose appeared to be Hull's backup zombie. He'd let her be killed three times. That made sense. Give a nineteenth-century sorcerer two zombie servants, one a male criminal, one a female whore, and which will he let hang out to dry? So, when Jaime summoned Rose, I expected Hull wouldn't be around to notice—he'd keep as far from her rotting corpse as he could.

But what if I'd guessed wrong?

If Hull or the bowler-hatted man was down that alley, then I might be able to skip a step in my "get Rose to take me to Hull" plan, but I wasn't ready for it. Not nearly.

I backed up into the building.

"Jaime?" I whispered. "Get upstairs. Watch that alley across the road, where Rose was. If anyone comes out of it—or anyplace else—get down here. I'm bringing Rose inside."

I looked around. There was a rusted filing cabinet against the wall that was big enough to hide me. I'd just have to remember that if I moved forward, it would be my stomach, not my feet, that could give me away.

I hurried behind the cabinet. After a moment, I picked up the clomp of footsteps, heavy and oddly spaced.

A shadow crossed the door. I pulled back, then tried to peek through the crack between the cabinet and the wall, catching only a sliver of the room.

The streetlight coming through the open front door cast a yellowish glow on the floor. A shadow crossed it, jerking and rocking, as if Rose was still following the steps of her strange dance, pulled between opposing forces.

A low gurgling filled the room, then a muttering, words unintelligible. Fabric rustled as Rose started forward again. A moment later, the hem of a long skirt appeared under an almost-equally long overcoat.

Rose staggered, as if losing the war against balance. She swung her other foot up, boot clomping down. So that was the problem. Balance, not the opposing pull of supernatural powers. Something must have been wrong with her leg—

As her far foot lifted for another step, I stared. Beneath the hem of the long gown, there wasn't a boot, just something long and white, like a cane. Her lower leg bone, no foot attached, strings of dirty flesh hanging off it. The bone came down to meet the floor. A second's pause as she struggled to get her balance, rocking forward, then back as she launched her good foot up and over, then rested her weight on it.

402

Dear God, how much willpower did it take to walk like that? But she had to. She'd been summoned, and had to obey.

When her face turned my way, I nearly gasped, biting my lip at the last second to stifle the sound. Her nose was a blackened cavity above another hole that had been her mouth, her teeth bared in a permanent skull-like grimace, her lips gone. Bloodied bone shone through her chin and cheekbones.

As I tried not to whimper, I told myself I was being ridiculous. I'd seen worse. Bodies torn apart by mutts. *But they were dead!* my brain screamed. Not walking around, living, breathing, *conscious*—

I pulled back before she saw me, but I moved too fast, and my elbow clanged against the file cabinet. The sound rang out as loud as a gong.

Rose let out something between a roar and a squeal, and started thumping in my direction. I wheeled out from behind the cabinet, and she flew at me, hands up, hooked into claws—bone claws, most of the flesh gone, half of her fingers missing. I veered out of her path, but she kept coming, lurching and lunging, faster than I would have thought possible.

As I backpedaled, one of those bony claws sheered my way. I acted on instinct, hitting the bottom of her arm with an uppercut. Her arm flew up with the blow, then fell limply to her side. Yet she kept coming, her good arm clawing at me.

As I dodged her blows, her limp arm seemed to be slipping . . . sliding from the sleeve.

Had I knocked her arm off? With a simple blow? Then how the hell was I going to subdue her? If I threw her down, I was liable to rip her in half.

She kept coming, eyes rolling with rage.

"Rose!" I yelled.

She didn't stop coming at me, stumping forward, good arm clawing the air. When I called again, her gaze met mine, telling me she was still capable of hearing and processing words.

I let her get less than a foot away, then scampered to the other side of the room, leaving her yowling in rage.

"I can keep this up all night, Rose," I said. "You can't get me and you know it."

She only snarled and flung herself toward me. I side-stepped past her. Just walked. Once across the room, I perched on the side of an old metal desk, as if making myself comfortable.

"I can give you what you want, Rose," I said.

Her lipless mouth opened. Her words came out garbled, but I could make them out. "Good. Then come 'ere."

"Still got a sense of humor? Pretty soon it'll be all you have—"

She lunged. I pulled my foot back, caught her in the stomach and shoved as hard as I dared, knocking her to the floor. She didn't rest for even a second, just struggled to rise on her good leg. As her body jerked with the effort, her severed arm slid to the floor. Seeing it, she let out a howl of rage and frustration.

"I didn't mean to do that," I said. "If you can still think as clearly as I believe you can, you know that was an accident. I have no interest in making things any worse for you than they are. All I want is to get Matthew Hull."

Her eyes rolled up to mine and I knew she recognized the name. Had there been an inkling of doubt in my mind that he was the controller, it evaporated. She stared up at me, unblinking. She couldn't blink. She didn't have any eyelids. I forced my gaze away as my stomach rolled.

"What has he promised you if you catch me?" I asked.

"That it'll stop," she mumbled.

"So you can die in peace."

Her body went rigid. "No. Not—can't die. I'll go to 'Ell." She shuddered. "This is better. Close the gate. No more . . . it'll stop."

"The rotting you mean."

"It'll 'eal."

"Heal? Is that what he told you? Maybe so, but is he planning to regrow all those parts you've lost? Your foot? Your lips? Arm? Nose? Eyelids? What you really want is peace, isn't it? To die and go someplace peaceful, where you'll be whole again. I can make sure that happens."

She made a hiccuping noise that, after a moment, I realized was laughter.

"You don't believe me? I have someone here who can help. The one who summoned you. She can make sure you cross over."

"And go straight to bleedin' 'Ell," she snarled. "After all I've done, where else would I go?"

She had a point. Then I remembered Jaime talking earlier about Eve . . .

"I wouldn't be so sure of that," I said. "I can't tell you what's on the other side. No one can. But there's more redemption than vengeance. I'd say you have a shot at some peace in the next life. Especially if you finish this one doing some good."

"She's right," said a voice behind me. "I don't know what's over there either, but I know plenty of spirits who expected to end up someplace far worse than they did."

Jaime stepped forward. Her gaze lit on Rose and if she

felt any revulsion or horror, none of that showed. Not even pity. She just walked over to stand beside me.

"Just lead us to Hull, and we'll take it from there," I said. "You'll be free."

Rose looked at us with her horrible lidless eyes.

"You don't still feel some obligation to him, do you? Maybe you did, when you first realized he'd given you a shot at another life, but I hope you don't forget he ended your first one. You're a servant. A zombie slave, put in that portal to serve him. And serve him you have, haven't you? He used you up, and let you die, and die again—and still threw you into our path. Who cared if you fell to pieces? He had a backup. A man. You don't see *him* rotting this badly, do you? Did you think that was just luck?"

"Will you kill 'im?" she asked. "The wizard or whatever 'e is?"

"That's the surest way to close the portal. And something tells me Hull isn't going to get one of those 'get out of Hell free' cards."

Her face contorted in a hideous smile. "Good."

Betrayed

AS IT TURNED OUT, HULL DID HAVE SOMEONE WATCHING the hotel: Rose. I don't know how he expected her to stop us if we'd tried to leave. More likely, Hull had been giving Rose a near-meaningless assignment to keep her rotting corpse away from them. Guarding us hadn't been a high priority. Even if we left, he could find me.

But what could have been so important that it diverted his attention—and his primary resources—away?

Rose knew only that Hull was "getting something" related to his ongoing experiment, the one whose completion he intended to finance with my children . . . and the one that had landed him in dimensional limbo in the first place. Seems the only lesson he'd learned from that experience was that he'd better hurry and finish his work before someone else in the supernatural community learned of it.

Although she didn't know where he'd headed, she could find him using a gut level sense that worked as well as any homing device. Yet we couldn't pop Rose in a taxi, so we had to walk, at her pace, staying on side streets and skirting all signs of activity.

"Gettin' close," she mumbled an hour later, as we cut through a narrow service lane between buildings.

"Watch—" Jaime said, waving at a swath of broken glass.

I steered Rose out of the way of the glass, resisting the urge to shudder as her bone fingers clamped into my side. My arm was hooked around her, under the stump of her right arm, and her good arm was around my torso, which made her trip a little easier, and mine a little less so.

We'd hobbled two-thirds of the way down the long lane when that broken glass crunched behind us. I tensed, but forced myself to keep moving. Jaime slanted a "What's up?" look my way.

"My back," I said. "The baby . . . Hunching over like this . . . Could you maybe take a spell?"

"Sure," she said.

As I disengaged from Rose, I tried to get a look behind us.

"You okay?" Jaime said.

I made a show of stretching my back, nodded and waved them on. Stop too long, and whoever was following us would know I'd heard him. I listened and sniffed, but both senses were useless. After an hour of walking beside Rose, I could fall face-first into one of these trash bins and still smell nothing.

If I turned around, our pursuer would know he'd been spotted. Even a second excuse to stop would tip him off. Or would it?

I moved up beside Jaime. "I have to go."

She frowned at me. "Where?"

I pressed a hand to the bottom of my belly. "My bladder. It—"

"Ah." She gave a small laugh. "We interrupt this life-or-death situation for a pregnancy pee break. Don't see that in the movies, do you?" She looked around. "I can't remember the closest restaurant, but we can go back—"

"No time. Just . . . keep walking. I'll catch up."

"Ah. Okay, then. Do you need tissue?"

"If you have some."

As she dug for tissue, I surveyed the lane, but whoever was following us must have taken cover. When Jaime and Rose moved on, I took cover of my own, backing into a gap between two stacks of cardboard boxes. They didn't reach my head, but that was okay. I had an excuse for crouching.

Now all I needed to do was wait for Hull or his zombie to get his butt over here and attack me. Only it wasn't happening. The lane had gone silent.

Finally, I heard the faintest shuffle of feet on dirt. Silence fell again. Was he hiding? Oh, great. Two of us, in our separate cubbyholes, each waiting for the other to make the first move.

I did my own dirt-shuffle, as if I was trying to crouch comfortably and not having much luck. All stayed quiet.

Great. Just great.

As I looked around, my gaze snagged on the long fire escape stretching overhead. I checked my outfit. Wine-colored T-shirt. Maternity jeans. Navy sneakers. All dark. Good.

I lowered a box from the stack on the far side. It was solid and heavy, marked "recycle," probably filled with newspapers or magazines. I laid it on the ground, then stepped on top and grabbed the fire escape. A quick tug to test how well it was affixed to the wall, then I pulled myself up. Not so easy with twins on board.

Once up, I crouched there, listening and looking. Nothing moved in the lane.

I bounced on the balls of my feet, testing the fire escape for stability and squeaks. Seemed fine.

I shimmied forward, stopping every few inches for a look-and-listen sweep. All stayed silent and still. I'd almost made it to the end when a scent wafted past.

It smelled like . . . No, that couldn't be.

I looked down to see Nick glaring up at me, arms crossed.

"Does that seem safe to you, Elena? Crawling on a rusted fire escape?"

"You—you're—"

"Supposed to be sleeping soundly, knocked unconscious by a blow to the head?" He snorted. "At least you didn't trick me this time."

"I'm sor—"

"Get down from there."

His voice was stern, but he helped me down. As he brushed me off, I tensed, realizing if Nick was here, that meant—

"Jeremy and Antonio," I said, looking around. "Where are they?"

"Back at the hotel. Hopefully, still busy with Clay and thinking we're down in the bar, getting some food into you before we leave for home."

"So I didn't—?"

"Knock me out? No, I tricked you this time. Seemed fair enough."

He took my elbow and led me out into the lane. I balked, knees locking, certain he was about to drag me back to the hotel, but he started heading the way Jaime and Rose had gone.

"But how'd you—" I began.

"Know you were going to take off? Come on, Elena. Clay's in danger of losing his arm—or worse—and you're both in danger of losing your babies, but you can stop both things by killing Hull. Only Jeremy wants to go home. You overhear that, and overhear Jaime saying she can track down Hull. Then you find an excuse to talk to Jaime alone. You don't need a college degree to know how to add two plus two."

We reached the end of the lane. Still holding my arm, he steered me south. I dug in my heels.

"I can't go back, Nick. I'm sorry but—"

"If I was taking you back, do you think I would have let you hit me in the first place? My sense of smell isn't as good as yours, but I can still track that zombie, and she went this way."

He paused, looked around, then started striding down the quiet road. From the smell, I knew we were indeed following Rose.

"If Clay was awake, this is what he'd want," Nick said. "Well, no, letting you go after this guy is *not* what he'd want, but if he could have done it himself, he'd have made the same choice you did—stopping Hull instead of running—so I guess that's what we should do."

"Nick, I don't want you—"

"Don't. I'm pissed off enough that you never trust me enough to tell me what you're planning—" He cut off my protest with a wave. "I know, it's because you don't want to lead me into something dangerous, but I think I'm old enough to decide that for myself. Point is, I'm pissed off already, so don't make it worse by telling me to run along home. I'm here, I'm staying. You need me."

I looked up at him. "Thanks."

He nodded, then waved down the street. "There they are. Let's get moving and find this bastard."

From the look on Jaime's face when I arrived with Nick, she was too relieved to question. Probably happy to have someone else on the assault team . . . someone more capable than a necromancer, a pregnant werewolf and a zombie who was shedding body parts at an alarming rate.

Nick took the burden of Rose, and we carried on.

"Almost there," Rose cackled as she disengaged herself from Nick's arm and fairly scampered toward an alley. " 'e's down there. I can feel 'im now. Right down there."

I paused at the head of the alley. It looked . . . familiar. Halfway down it, I stopped and stared down at the marks in the dry dirt. Footprints showing a brief scuffle. My own footprints, plus a second pair. Boots—short black boots. I could see us there, only a few days ago, me pinning Zoe in the alley.

My stomach flip-flopped. I blamed it on the babies, and told myself this was a coincidence. No, not a coincidence. Danger. Zoe was in danger. Hull had fixed his sights on the one "team member" left outside the circle.

I grabbed Nick's arm.

"He's after Zoe," I said. "The bar where she does her business is right down there, around the corner. She must be inside. He's got to be waiting somewhere."

"If he's waiting for her, he won't be expecting us."

I nodded.

"Wot are you waiting for?" Rose said. "You—"

I shushed her.

"But 'e's right 'round this corner a ways," she said.

"We need a plan of attack."

"Plan? There's three of you—"

I clapped my hand over her mouth. A last resort—believe me. Her lidless eyes glared at me, but when I pulled my hand back she only limped away to lean against the wall.

"Before we get too far with our plan, we should find out exactly where he is."

"You think so, do you, luv?"

Shaking her head, she hobbled to the end of the alley. She peeked out, then pulled back. Another mutter. Another check, leaning farther out. Then she came back to us.

"I thought 'e was right 'round that corner, but there's an ale 'ouse back there. 'e's inside."

"Inside?"

I looked at Nick.

We headed up the fire escape Clay had used earlier. Once inside the second floor, I followed his trail to find the vantage point he'd used to watch Zoe and me below. We ended up at a trapdoor over the bar. Prop the door open a crack, crouch down and you had a pretty good view of the patrons below.

Crouching was easier for Nick, so he looked through. When he glanced up again, I knew our fears had been confirmed.

"She's there with Hull, isn't she?" I whispered.

He nodded.

"Talking to him?"

Another nod.

"Not being coerced, not held against her will . . ."

I tried not to be surprised. I really did. Yet, in my gut, I still felt betrayed.

It was almost laughable. Given four potential allies, we'd batted zero for four. First, Shanahan, whom we hadn't trusted from the start, who'd turned out to be as innocent as Tolliver had claimed—and as innocent as Tolliver himself. Then Hull. Never trusted, but ignored. His story believed; his presence tolerated; his threat overlooked entirely. Now Zoe. Of all four, this one hurt the worst.

"What do we do?" Nick whispered.

"Don't fight her unless you have to. She'll heal faster than you can hit. Disable her if necessary. She doesn't have any special powers except her fangs. If she gets those into you, she can knock you out. Otherwise—not a threat. We disable her and hand her over to Cassandra for trial."

He nodded, obviously relieved that I wasn't going to suggest we behead her ourselves. That wasn't our place . . . and even if it had been, I wasn't sure I could do it.

"I think they're getting ready to leave," Nick said, scrambling up. "Hull's standing and Zoe's talking to the bartender."

"There's only one way out," I said. "Get back into the alley we came in through. Shoo Jaime and Rose someplace safe, then find a spot as far down as you can."

"What about you?"

"No way I'll get down that fire escape fast enough." I prodded him toward the exit, still talking. "There's a window around the corner. I'll watch from there. Don't attack if you don't absolutely have to. We'll follow them for a bit."

He swung through the window onto the fire escape.

I grabbed his shoulder. "If we have to fight Hull, re-member what I said. Stay out of sight for a bit. Let me draw his fire, wear his spell power down. He won't kill me."

Nick hesitated—I knew he didn't like the idea—but he nodded and left.

Control

I FOUND MY WINDOW AND CRACKED IT OPEN, NOT SO much so I could hear—I'd hear through the glass just fine—but so I could yank it open and jump through. A second-story leap was easy enough for a werewolf. It wasn't something I cared to do when I was pregnant, so if I had a choice, I'd return to the fire escape.

Nick barely made it to a hiding place before Zoe and Hull turned the corner. As they headed into the alley, Hull slowed, chin going up as his nostrils flared. Damn! The alley would still smell of Rose.

After a moment's hesitation, though, he kept walking. Rose's stink must have been faded enough that he just dismissed it as a stray "bad smell." He'd ordered Rose to stay at the hotel, so that's where she'd be.

"I should call," I heard Zoe say. "Let them know we're on our way."

A shiver raced up my spine. Them? Oh, God, there were more supernaturals involved. Of course there were. Zoe had a whole network of contacts here. When Hull promised to let her in on the "deal," she'd probably offered the services of others.

Did this mean those others already knew about the babies? I fought a prickle of panic. Handle the immediate threat first.

I'd missed Hull's response, but it must have been something like "Don't bother calling," because she took her cell phone from her purse and waved it at him.

"This little box?" she said. "Great modern invention. Means I don't even need to stop walking. No time wasted."

"Do you really think they need any disruptions right now? Why else would they have sent me?"

Sent him? Was Hull working for someone else?

A figure appeared at the end of the alley. The bowler-hatted man, coming up behind them.

Zoe stopped. "Why send someone at all? Why not just phone?"

Hull shrugged. "Perhaps they couldn't find your code . . . your numbers. They don't tell me such things. Now, please, we have to hurry—"

When Zoe still didn't move, Hull sighed and turned to her.

"This is hardly the best place, but you're going to be difficult, aren't you? No matter. I take my opportunities where I can find them, and I can't ignore a chance at my last ingredient."

It hit me: Zoe thought *we'd* summoned her, using Hull. Why wouldn't she? The last time she'd seen us, he'd been in our care.

I remembered Tee telling Zoe she was in danger.

The rare ingredient. The one Rose said Hull had come to collect.

As I grabbed the window sash and threw it open, the

bowler-hatted man strode toward her, a huge butcher's knife in his hand.

"Zoe!" I screamed.

At my shout she turned, but too late. The zombie swung, and the knife cleaved into her throat. She wobbled, eyes wild. Then she fell.

The zombie yanked the knife out of Zoe's neck, then looked around. Dimly I realized I'd given myself away. I stumbled back from the window, getting out of his sight, my gaze still fixed on Zoe. She lay on her back, head almost severed, held on only by her spine. My nails dug into my palms as I watched her, and willed that torn flesh to mend itself. It didn't.

In the woods, Hull had crowed about his luck, how he'd happened across not only me, but that rare final ingredient for his immortality experiment. A semi-immortal vampire.

"You might as well come out, Mrs. Danvers," he called.

It took a moment to realize he was speaking to me. I crept to the side of the window, where I could see out without being seen.

"Hiding is useless," he said. "All I need to do is cast a spell, and I can find you. Better come out now, while I'm in a good humor, buoyed by my success with your little vampire friend."

When I didn't answer, pique flickered across Hull's face. He didn't cast a spell, though, probably because he didn't want to waste his spell power. Instead he motioned for the zombie to start searching for me. I weighed my options. I could jump down, surprise Hull and leave the zombie to Nick. Or I could search for a window farther down the alley, slip out, collect Nick and get someplace safer, where we could talk strategy.

The zombie walked in Nick's direction first. Excellent. All I had to do was wait until he was close enough for Nick to grab, then jump out—

Nick lunged at the zombie. His aim was perfect. As he knocked the zombie off his feet, he sent the butcher knife flying. When they hit the ground, Nick grabbed him by the hair and smashed his skull into the ground. Not as clean or foolproof as snapping his neck, but it did the job.

I moved to act, to take advantage of Nick's distraction. But the zombie was already crumbling, and Hull had recovered from his surprise. His hands were going up in a spell—

My mouth opened, the scream still burbling up through my throat, hands still reaching for the window to swing through as Hull launched his spell. My blood turned to ice water, certain Hull had launched a fatal spell, taking Nick out—

Hull's fingers flicked and Nick stumbled back. Stumbled hard enough to trip, but that was it. A simple knock-back spell.

The air whooshed from my lungs, nearly doubling me over with relief. Hull advanced on Nick and I recovered, taking hold of the window again—

"If you get up, I will pick a spell that will keep you down," Hull said, looming over Nick.

I scrambled back, out of sight. Hull wasn't going to kill Nick. Not yet. Magic was all Hull had, and a lethal spell would drain his power.

My gaze traveled to the knife. It lay in a heap of garbage about ten feet away. Hull ignored it, probably knowing that if he went for it, Nick would do the same, and in a hand-to-hand fight, Nick could kill Hull before he could cast.

"Where is she?" Hull said.

Nick glared.

Stones crunched at the end of the alley. Hull slowly turned toward the sound, his face creasing in a smile.

"Ah . . ." he murmured. "Perhaps I don't need that tracking ritual after all."

Another crunch of gravel, the noise still small enough to be a mistake, someone shifting impatiently. Jaime was drawing Hull's attention away from me.

Perfect. Without Hull's zombie servant, he'd have to go after "me" himself, turning his attention from Nick.

But he didn't budge. Instead, his voice rang out, echoing along the alley.

"Mrs. Danvers. Earlier, you refused to consider my offer to spare your life and your mate's in return for your babes. I trust you'll be more flexible in the matter now."

No, no, no! I'm right down that alley. Can't you hear me? Knock Nick out, then come after me. I'm right there!

"I'm sure you can see, from your nook, that I have your friend. Do I even need to articulate my exchange? I think not. I will say, though, that it comes with a time limit. I am a patient man, but I have waited so long—so unbelievably long—and the end is right before me. A vampire to complete my experiment, and a black-market treasure to allow me to make the final preparations at my leisure, unhurried by want of funds. Seeing these things, so close . . . it would try any man's patience, would it not? You have five minutes. At the end of that, I kill your friend and come after you."

"Elena," Nick said, his voice a low growl. "Get out of here."

"Oh, come now," Hull said. "Do you really think—"

"My choice, Elena," Nick continued. "Do you remember that? I make my own choices."

Hull's fingers flew up, the spell cast too quick for me to even move. Another knockback spell, this one harder, sending Nick flying into the brick wall. A dull crack, and he slumped. I didn't breathe until I saw the steady rise and fall of his chest.

I clenched my fists, fighting the urge to attack. *Okay, Hull. Now Nick's not a threat. And you know where I am, where you think I am. No reason not to just stroll down there and take me—*

"Mrs. Danvers!" he called. "The clock is ticking. Your friend is sleeping away the last minutes of his life."

I balled my fists. Hull didn't care that he could get me easily. He wanted me to turn myself over. He wanted control.

There was only one thing to do. Give him that control. I had to do what we should have done back in the woods. Let Hull take me, get him away from my family and friends, bring this down to us—him and me and my un-born children—and pray that once he thought he'd won, I could somehow turn the tables. I went numb even thinking about it, but that's what I had to do.

"I'm here," I said, moving to the window.

His gaze swung along the alley, then up, following my voice. Seeing me, he smiled.

"Very good. That's the first step. Now, come out—slowly. If there is anyone with you, please remind them I still have your friend, only a spellcast away."

I knew Hull wouldn't let me retreat to the fire escape. I

crawled backward out the window, lowered myself as far as I could and dropped, bending my knees as I fell.

A deep breath, and I turned around.

"Excellent," Hull said. "Now, I'm afraid our departure will be delayed while my zombie makes the journey from the portal. An inconvenience, but I'm not about to leave my vampire corpse just lying about where anyone can find it."

As we waited, I struggled against the urge to plot, to plan, to use the delay and find a way to end this, right now. I couldn't. I had to get Hull away from Nick and Jaime.

At the thought of Jaime, my gaze stole down the alley. Was she still there, watching helplessly? Or had she gone for help?

A flicker of hope at the thought, doused as I realized that was what I *didn't* want. I'd already endangered—and killed—enough people trying to escape Hull. Time to bring it down to the two of us. No rescue. No backup. Just us.

After a couple of minutes, Nick mumbled something, and I jumped. Hull spun, hands rising to cast. Nick settled again, still unconscious, but for how long? Maybe I should distract Hull, end this here before Nick woke.

"You killed Anita Barrington, didn't you?" I said. "She saw you at the crime scene. She knew you were a sorcerer. That's what she wanted to tell me. But you got to her first."

Hull laughed. "Ah, yes, the poor witch. Always innocent, aren't they? Yes, she recognized what I was . . . and begged me to help her, promised to deliver you into my hands in return for immortality. Pathetically desperate. Cried about her poor granddaughter, who'd be all alone if she passed, but the truth is that she saw death in the mirror every morning, and would do anything to stop it from coming." He smiled, showing his teeth. "So I helped."

"You killed her. After you made her finger Shanahan—"

"Enough of this, Mrs. Danvers. I'm not fool enough to fall for distraction tactics. You can talk, if it makes you feel better, but it won't help."

Distant running footsteps sounded before I could answer. The bowler-hatted man? I sampled the air to be sure.

After his second death, he was ripening nicely. Not falling apart—if he could run—but decay was setting in. Kill him a third time, and he'd skid into living death, like Rose. Good.

The footfalls slowed at the end of the alley. Then they stopped. Hull frowned, and opened his mouth to call out. The zombie turned the corner. The skin around his mouth and nostril had blackened and that left arm seemed to swing a little too freely as he moved.

"There you are," Hull said. "A little the worse for wear, but we'll get that fixed up soon enough. Now, I want you to harvest a few items from the vampire. Then we'll hide the corpse, so I can return later and take more. I hope you remember your anatomy lessons." Hull chuckled. "Seems they'll be useful for more than playing . . ." He cocked his head and looked at me. "What did they call him? Ah, yes, Jack the Ripper. Nasty fellow, I'm sure. But I owe him a debt of thanks. He's been most helpful, whoever he was."

That's why I hadn't found a third scent with the zombies after the Ripper-style killing. There hadn't been one. As I'd guessed from Hull's words in the forest, it had been the bowler-hatted zombie, following the recipe of a long-dead killer.

A hundred and twenty years ago, Hull had used Ripper panic to safeguard his portal letter. Now, he'd used it again, to try to panic us and convince us that I was the target, and needed to be taken off the streets and secreted away with him while the others tracked this new threat.

The zombie had stopped in front of Hull, head drooping and swiveling. Was something wrong with his neck? He looked confused, almost lost.

Hull sucked in his breath and glared down at Nick's unconscious form. "Had to hit him in the head, didn't you? If—"

The zombie lurched forward, like a stalled motor jumping to life. He walked over to the knife and scooped it up.

"Good," Hull said. "That's it. She's right over there, behind you."

The zombie turned. He looked at Zoe's body, but his brow knitted, as if confused by what he was seeing.

"Yes, that's her. Now—"

The zombie turned back to Hull, head bobbing, brow still furrowed.

Hull let out a hiss of frustration. Something moved at the far end of the alley. Jaime had come out and was standing with her back against the wall. I gestured for her to get back before Hull saw her, but her eyes were closed, squeezed shut. Her face was ashen, almost glowing in the moonlight, shiny with sweat. Eyes closed, concentrating so hard she was sweating . . .

My gaze swung back to the zombie, who was tottering

there, confused. Confused by a conflict of commands. A conflict of control.

But that couldn't be. According to the stories, a necromancer couldn't control someone else's zombies.

The zombie lunged at Hull, knife flying. Hull fell back, already casting. Casting a spell at the zombie. Protecting his own life. Mine forgotten. Nick's forgotten.

I saw my chance . . . and waited. Attack now, and all he had to do was redirect the cast my way. The last words left his mouth and the zombie fell back, then I flew at Hull.

I hit him in the side. As we fell, I grabbed for his hands. I caught the right one, but my fingers only brushed the left. He cast a knockback spell, the best he could manage when he was low on power. It still hit me like a blow to the solar plexus. Any other time, I wouldn't have let go, but my brain screamed "the babies!" and my hands shot to my stomach.

Before I could grab Hull again, he backed up, putting distance between us as his hands lifted, starting a fresh spell.

The bowler-hatted zombie struggled up, knife in his grip. Hull looked from him to me, hands hovering, spell uncast. Only enough power to repel one of us. Which to choose—the knife-wielding zombie or the pissed-off werewolf? Before either I or the zombie could take advantage of his hesitation, Hull made his choice . . . and bolted.

Cover

HULL GAVE THE ZOMBIE A HARD SHOVE AS HE RAN PAST. AL-
ready unsteady, the zombie fell. I raced after Hull.

"Elena!"

I stumbled as I wheeled back to Jaime. "Stay with
Nick."

"But I can—"

"Please."

She hesitated, then nodded. "Once I wake him up,
we'll be right behind you."

I'd seen Hull turn right, onto a side street, but there
was no sign of him. I jogged along the sidewalk, sniffing
and listening. When I reached the first corner, I peered
around a building to see Hull fifty feet away, casting a
spell at a door. An unlock spell.

I rocked on the balls of my feet, holding back until he
was inside. Then I stole down the sidewalk. At the still-
closing door, I paused. All was silent within. I grabbed
the handle before the latch caught, then eased the door
open.

Inside the small, dark vestibule, there were stairs

leading down to my left. So Hull had taken refuge in a windowless basement, probably with one exit. I smiled.

The stairs stopped at a landing, then doubled back. I peered over the railing into the gloom. A dim security light at the bottom illuminated a time-card rack and punch on the right wall, and an open doorway to the left.

Down the steps, stop and look. A cavernous room opened before me, so big that in the near dark, I couldn't see the other three sides.

As my night vision kicked in, I could see enough to know where I was. The room—at least fifty feet square— was filled with cheap office tables, arranged like pews. On each desk was a row of telephones and headsets. A telemarketing pit.

I'd worked in telemarketing at fifteen, too young for something better and needing more pay and hours than a fast-food job would provide.

There were two exits, not counting the one I'd come in. One opened into a small room with a curtained glass wall. The supervisor's office. The other led to a hall— lunchroom and supply closets if this setup was anything like my old workplace.

Which had Hull picked? Office or hall? Or was he still here, huddled behind a table, waiting to slam me with a knockback spell when I passed? I went still, sniffing and listening. His scent was here. *Been* here or *still* here, it was impossible to tell.

Something clattered in the back hall. I hurried forward. At the hall entrance, I paused and peered through. It was a short corridor, no more than fifteen feet, with two closed doors to my left and one open doorway to my right.

Hull's scent hung in the air, giving me no directional

clues. I considered bending to check for a trail, but these days I couldn't fly up from a crouch. Better to stay standing and rely on my other senses.

The open doorway led to the lunchroom. I could tell by the stink—food that probably smelled just fine on its own, but when combined and left to mellow, was enough to revolt the hungriest stomach.

Edging against the door jamb, I glanced inside. It could have been a carbon copy of my old lunchroom— little bigger than a walk-in closet with a sauce-spattered microwave, a Goodwill rescue dinette set and an ancient refrigerator.

No hiding places even for a small man like Hull. Well, there was the fridge, but he'd need to clear out all the condiments and unwanted food.

The first closed door was locked. I checked the second. Also locked. Back to the first. I twisted the handle hard and fast, snapping the simple key-lock.

I turned my back to the wall, then threw open the door. The stink of cleaning chemicals hit me. I peered inside. Just a closet—so jammed with janitorial equipment even Hull couldn't have squeezed inside.

As I closed the door, something rustled in the main room. Had Hull somehow retreated there while I'd been checking the other rooms? But how? He couldn't get past without—

Witch magic.

I cursed under my breath. Unlock spells were simple witch magic, and most sorcerers never bothered to master more than that, but they *could* learn stronger witch magic, like cover spells. I could have walked right past Hull and not known it unless he'd moved or I'd bumped into him.

I scanned the main room. All had gone silent. Of course it had. Hull had found a new spot, and cast his spell again. So why change places and risk making noise? Because he wanted me to hear him, to know he was there, and to keep searching.

Hull hadn't "accidentally" backed himself into this basement. He lured me in, and now he was teasing me while his spell power recharged enough to take me down—kill me if necessary, here in an empty basement where he could take what he wanted from me without fear of interruption.

My hands shot to my stomach. I had to get out of here. The impulse surprised me. Any other time, I'd have been hell-bent on showing this bastard he couldn't beat me, that I wouldn't be a victim. But now "showing him" didn't enter my mind.

I made my way slowly across the room, each step deliberate, gaze swinging from side to side, nostrils flaring as if searching, but my focus fixed on that exit doorway.

Footsteps clomped onto the stairs. Heavy footsteps, coming down. Nick? My heart leapt. With Nick I wouldn't have to run. We could flush out Hull and finish this—

The footsteps faltered as if he'd tripped and caught himself before falling. I hurried forward. If Nick was still hurt, then we were both getting out of here.

I rounded the doorway before I noticed the heavy stink of rotting flesh. I looked up to see the bowler-hatted zombie staggering down the stairs, knife in hand.

My heart sank, but I shook it off. This would do. Get the zombie in here, and I could run for reinforcements while he kept Hull busy.

"He's in here," I said. "He's using magic to hide, but he's here—"

The zombie's eyes met mine. I leapt aside just in time, as he barreled down the final steps, knife raised like a bayonet.

I backpedaled into the main room. The zombie faltered, as if still struggling under dueling orders. Then he shot forward. I backed up and smacked into the first table. As he came at me, I swung onto the table top, sliding across the slick surface and nearly tumbling off the other side.

"Elena!" Jaime's voice, from the top of the stairs.

"Down—"

The zombie's knife arced my way. I shimmied back along the tabletop, out of the knife's reach, then pushed to my feet. I turned, planning to leap to the next table. Then I saw Hull, across the room, face drawn in concentration as he warred for the zombie, the effort too much for him to continue casting the cover spell.

Our eyes met. He lifted his hand in a knockback spell, which would send me sailing right into the zombie. I kicked fast and low, keeping my balance. My foot connected with the side of the zombie's head just as Hull's spell hit me. The zombie went down. So did I—the spell sending me flying over him, so fast that I could barely protect my stomach.

I hit the floor in an awkward tumble, teeth clamping down on my tongue. As I scrambled up, Hull raised his hands in a second cast, his lips forming the words. Then he stopped, face darkening, lips forming a silent curse.

"Not quite able to muster enough juice, hmm?" I said, spitting as I tasted blood. I swiped my hand over my mouth.

Hull restarted his incantation.

"I hope that's nothing stronger than a knockback spell," I said as I advanced on him. "Or it's not going to work. Witch magic is tough on sorcerers, and you've already OD'd. But you know that, don't you? You can feel it."

Hull's lips twisted in a humorless smirk, but he said nothing.

"Maybe a hundred years ago, you could have done it, but you're still recuperating from an unexpectedly long incarceration. An incarceration that proves you're far from perfect . . . and too dumb to realize it."

He snarled, and lifted his hands. Then he stopped before even beginning the incantation. I was now within fifteen feet of him. Just a little closer . . .

Hull looked over his shoulder.

"No escape there," I said. "It's a dead end."

I charged. Hull's hands went up, lips moving, but he'd never have time—

A jolt struck me, and I flew off my feet, body going rigid as if I'd been hit by an electrical shock. I tried to land in a roll, but my limbs wouldn't obey. I crashed down and lay there, mentally struggling to get up, body refusing.

Hull's face appeared above mine. "It's called an interrupted cast. I cast part of the incantation . . . then wait, so I can launch it at a moment's notice."

I fought to move, but my arms and legs only twitched randomly.

"I tried to make this easy," Hull said, kneeling beside me. "I really did. But you'd have none of it. Now, we have to do it the hard way."

His hands wrapped around my throat. I swung my

head to the side and chomped down on the underside of his forearm. Then I ripped my head back, a chunk of flesh still between my teeth, his blood dribbling into my throat. Hull howled and fell back, clutching his forearm as blood spurted.

I pushed up and fell on him, my arms and legs little more than deadweights. My teeth sank into his flesh—any flesh—tearing, spitting and biting again, mind blank, spurred on by the instinct to use whatever I had to stay alive.

Hull's screams echoed through the room. Across the room, the zombie rose up and started lurching toward us. Hull's head lifted, gaze going to the zombie, relief and hope filling his eyes. His lips parted. I swung my head down, teeth clamping on his throat, and ripped. He screamed, a high-pitched death shriek that turned to a gurgle as blood filled his throat.

I pushed off him, some feeling finally returning to my limbs. Swiping my hand across my bloodied lips, I wobbled to my feet as the zombie drew closer.

"Uh-uh," said a voice across the room. "This one's mine."

A figure rounded the doorway—a tiny, dark-haired figure. Zoe—her throat still cut, the edges open, her voice wheezy and garbled.

She staggered a little, then rushed at the zombie, who turned at the last second to see an iron rod swinging into the side of his head. He fell. Her dark eyes glittering, Zoe leapt over him and swung again, with more force than seemed possible for her tiny frame. When she pulled back for a third swing, he started to crumble, and she stopped, rod still raised, waiting until he'd disintegrated.

"Glad that worked," she said. "I sure as hell didn't want to have to bite him."

"You're—" I said, still staring, as I had been since she'd come in.

"Alive, I hope," she said. "Or as close to it as I can get."

At a noise, she turned toward the stairs, swiveling her whole body, as if she didn't dare try to turn only her head.

"Oh, thank God," Jaime said, running in. "You *are* down here. I called, but I didn't hear an answer, then I couldn't summon that damned zombie. I tried and tried—"

"You did great," I said. "You controlled someone else's zombie. That's amazing."

She nodded and swallowed, face pale, as if she still wasn't sure how she'd done it. Then she saw Zoe.

"You're—"

"Alive," Zoe said. "Or so I hope. I am alive, right? Not a zombie. Not a walking ghost. Just my usual undead self?"

"Looks like it to me," Jaime said, smiling.

"Thank God." Zoe's dark eyes lit up as she tried to grin, then she winced, hand going to her throat. "God, that's gross. Please tell me it's healing."

"It looks like it," I said.

A small wheezing laugh. "Neck cuts are the worst. I'm always up for a new experience but this—" She shuddered. "This one I could have skipped." She looked down at the scattering of dust. "At least I got my payback. As vampires go, I'm not much of a predator, but that was one time I made an exception."

"Nick! Oh, God, where's—?"

"Back in the alley," Jaime said, taking my elbow and helping me to the stairs. She glanced back at Hull's body.

"You guys go on," Zoe said. "I'll handle cleanup duty. Done it before."

When we got back to where Nick still lay, Rose stumped her way toward us, face fixed in the horrible grimace that passed for her smile.

"'e's gone," she said. "I can feel it. A real weight off my mind, let me tell you."

I scrambled over to Nick and shook his shoulder. His head lolled to the other side.

"Mmm, still tired, baby," he mumbled. "Gimme a couple minutes. I'll make it worth your wait."

"He's fine." I laughed.

"'e might be," Rose said. "But I'm not. Now get yourself over 'ere and give me what you promised. I can't do it myself."

"Right."

I turned to Rose, but hesitated. As hideous as she looked, I couldn't forget that there was a person in there. Someone who had—until made a better offer—been ready to kill me and yet . . .

"'op to it, girl," she said. "I 'aven't got all day. While you're standing there gawkin', I'm turnin' to mush."

I bit back a laugh. "Okay. Um, how do you want to do this? Snapping your neck is fastest—"

"Fast? Gawd's sakes, girl, you could 'ave 'ad it done by now. You did it fast enough the last time. Now 'op to it or—"

I grabbed her neck and snapped it before she finished the sentence, and hopefully before she saw it coming. As she crumbled, I took a deep breath, my heart tripping.

"She's better off now," Jaime said softly. "No matter where she went, it's better than where she was."

Price

I GOT NICK AS FAR AS THE SEMICONSCIOUS "WHERE AM I? What am I doing here?" stage, then left him to Jaime while I took the next step—one at least as terrifying as any that had come before it.

"A—Antonio," I said into the phone. "It's me."

"Elena?" His voice boomed loud enough to make my head rock. "Where the hell—?"

"We're okay. Nick's fine. I'm fine. Jaime's fine. Hull's dead. The zombies are dead. The portal should be closed. Is—" I swallowed, knowing if I could feel red-hot fury from Antonio, it was nothing compared to the icy blast that was coming. "Is Jeremy there?"

"He's with Clay. I'm outside, searching for you two. Or three, I suppose, if Jaime went with you. I thought she was in her room." A growl of a sigh. "Whatever you did, Elena, whether it killed Hull or not, it was stupid—"

"I know."

"And risky as hell—"

"I know."

Another sigh, softer. "And probably the right thing to

do, but that doesn't mean I'm ever going to admit that to Jeremy. Understood?"

I gave a small smile. "Understood."

"Now get your asses back here pronto."

"We still have one more thing to do," I said. "Hull didn't disintegrate like the zombies. Zoe said she'd clean up but—"

"I'll be right there. But *you're* coming back. Get yourself and Jaime into a cab."

Somewhere on my headlong run up the hotel stairs, Jaime disappeared. She must have decided this was one family scene she didn't care to join.

I took a deep breath and knocked. Seconds ticked past. Then Jeremy opened the door. For a long moment, he just stood there and looked at me, face impassive.

A few years ago, getting a "welcome" like this would have crushed me. But now even if he stood there as calmly as if I'd returned from a coffee run, I could see the warring emotions in his eyes—as if he wasn't sure whether to hug me, congratulate me or scream at me. In the end, he just nodded and waved me in as he held the door. When I passed, his free hand went around my shoulder, an awkward half-embrace that slid into a gentle prod as he directed me where he knew I really wanted to go, to Clay.

I saw Clay and faltered. The room was dark, quiet and empty. Tolliver was nowhere to be seen, but the room was still littered with medical supplies, as if he'd just left. Clay lay on the bed, asleep.

I don't know what I expected. Not for him to be at the door, back to normal, furious and ready to wring my neck for taking such a risk. Nothing would have pleased me more, but that wish had been only a fleeting fancy. Still, I had hoped to find him . . . awake.

"The drugs, I guess, huh?" I said. "You probably had to dose him pretty good—" I stopped as my hand touched his forehead, then quickly looked at Jeremy. "He's still warm."

"The fever broke, but he's still fighting the infection."

"Infection? But—" I looked at the bandages on his arm. "Have you checked—?"

"Yes, it's still there."

Jeremy walked over to me, close enough to touch, but just standing beside me.

"Okay," I said. "But that's because the portal isn't completely closed, I bet. It probably takes some time. We should send Nick and Antonio over, see whether anyone's come back through. Then we'll know it's closed."

Jeremy nodded, gaze down, and motioned for me to sit beside Clay while he took the chair. I made the call. Then all we could do was wait.

An hour later, Nick phoned. They'd returned to the portal site to find a growing crowd of media, police and on-lookers. The three missing people had appeared shortly after Rose's death, unharmed and dazed, remembering nothing.

So the portal was closed.

And still Clay slept, still feverish, still infected.

The others returned. They checked on Clay, but there had been no change. Jeremy told them to make ready to head back to Stonehaven. When they left, I stood clutching Clay's warm hand.

"It didn't work, did it?" I said.

He shook his head.

"You knew it wouldn't. You knew Hull was lying, that closing the portal wouldn't cure Clay. There's no magic here, is there?"

He walked up behind me, very gently kissed the back of my head and whispered, "No."

My knees wobbled, and I grabbed the side of the bed, but Jeremy caught my arm to steady me.

"He'll be fine, Elena. Randall is coming back to do the debridement—cut away the infected area—"

"But that means— Tolliver said— It'll be permanent, won't it? Muscle damage?"

"Possibly." He hesitated. "Probably. His arm won't be perfect, but he'll still have it. Right now, those are my priorities. First, that he keeps the arm. Failing that, that he keeps his life."

I lowered myself onto the bed.

Jeremy put his hand on my shoulder. "Matthew Hull is dead. The portal is closed. Your babies are safe. You're safe. Yes, Clay might lose muscle. Possibly even his arm. But you know what he'll think about that?"

I looked up at Jeremy.

"That it was a small price to pay, considering what he could have lost."

When you live in a world of magic, you come to expect magic. You can fight that, try to concentrate on what's real, but deep down, you still hope that the flick of a wand can make everything better and everyone will live happily ever after.

Clay's cure did come—at the hands of a doctor.

Tolliver cut out the infected tissue, and found clean flesh below it. So it was over. A price paid but, as Jeremy said, a relatively small one. I only hoped Clay agreed.

He woke up later the next day, when the drugs wore off. Groggy at first, he just lay there, listening as I told him that Hull was dead. He was too weak to manage more than muttering, "You took a stupid risk, Elena."

Then Jeremy explained what they'd done to his arm, that some of the muscle had been damaged. While he'd have plenty of physiotherapy to undergo, he'd never get his full strength back in that arm.

He took it all in, unblinking. I tensed, waiting for the dismay, the rage that this had happened, all because of a letter I'd insisted we steal. As he turned to look at me, I steeled myself for what I'd see.

He met my gaze. "Ready to go home, darling?"

News

TWO WEEKS LATER, I WAS SITTING ON THE WEIGHT BENCH
in the basement at Stonehaven reading the Toronto papers Jeremy had brought me. Clay was battling the
punching bag, starting the long process of training his
brain to favor his left arm. I was reading the news
aloud—at Clay's request. Not that he cared about the aftermath of events in Toronto, but my reading distracted
him.

As Jaime and Robert had predicted, once the portal
closed, things had started getting back to normal in
Toronto. It wasn't instantaneous—no magic-wand solu-
tions there either. But the city's efforts to clean the water
had begun working, and the rats—though still infected—had stopped rampaging. Like Clay, the city had
begun the long road to recovery.

As I reached for the *National Post*, I rubbed my abdomen.

"Still bothering you?" Clay said, stopping.

"Just uncomfortable."

I'd been "uncomfortable" since last night, unable to
sleep and restless, an intermittent dull ache in my groin.

Since our adventure in Toronto, I'd been feeling the pregnancy more—weighed down, tired and generally ready to get it over with. Nothing alarming, but Jeremy and Clay panicked every time I mentioned a stray twinge . . . so I'd stopped mentioning them.

I opened the paper. "The *Post* is blaming the provincial Liberal government for—"

A sudden gush of liquid between my legs made me jump up, those horrible miscarriage dreams zooming back from their hiding place. No, probably just another bladder leak—I'd been experiencing the joys of mild incontinence all week. Yet I hadn't laughed or sneezed or any of the other things that normally set it off. When I inhaled, I smelled something that wasn't blood or urine . . . something I didn't recognize.

"Shit!" Clay said, turning so fast the ricocheting bag hit him in the back. "Your water broke."

"My—?"

I looked down at the wet stain down my legs, and was still staring, not quite comprehending, when Clay started yelling for Jeremy.

So it began.

When I'd first become pregnant, Paige had offered to be my midwife. She'd done it several times when she'd still lived with her Coven. Yet when Jeremy had suspected, early that morning, that my labor had begun, he'd put off calling her. Savannah had started school, and Lucas was out of town, finishing that investigation they'd been on last month, as he tried to find the shaman a local lawyer to handle his legal case.

So Paige couldn't throw together a bag and leave for

what could be a false alarm. Jeremy postponed the call until he was sure. By then though, judging by my dilation, the babies would be here before Paige would, meaning we had to settle for a long-distance midwife.

My "discomfort" solidified into recognizable contractions. They were intense, but a few minutes apart— hardly debilitating. While Jeremy prepared tea from the brew Paige had sent, I prepared for our new arrivals.

We'd cleared out Malcolm's old room, but hadn't started decorating yet, so my room would stand in as a temporary nursery.

I put bottom sheets on the bassinets, shook out baby blankets, gathered sleepers and opened the package of diapers. Clay kept trying to figure out my next move so he could beat me to it. He got in the way more than he helped, but I didn't even snap at him. That hour seemed almost surreal, me calmly laying out tiny diapers and bath towels, unperturbed by Clay—and later Jeremy— as they tried to persuade me that none of this needed to be done now. When a contraction hit, I'd just wait it out, breathing deeply, then carry on. Maybe it was a sudden nesting urge, but I was probably in shock.

Then, all of a sudden, the contractions progressed from "that's not so bad" to "holy crap!"

When it came to childbirth, being a werewolf gave me a few advantages. First, I was used to going through "holy crap!" pain, the kind that makes you vow never to do something again. As with Changing, this pain had a reward at the end, so I concentrated on that. And when that promise of reward no longer worked, well, the guys were used to seeing me in a cursing, shouting temper, so they handled it remarkably well.

Jeremy acted as midwife while Paige coached over the

speakerphone. When the time came, I started to push. Baby number one slid into position . . . then I realized, with sudden clarity, that I was about to shove a baby out of a hole usually used by something much smaller. I panicked, and I was about to scream, "I can't do this," when I couldn't help giving a last push and . . .

"We've got . . . a boy!" Clay said, grinning.

He was about to come to me, then stopped, as if uncertain where his attention should be. Jeremy finished cutting the umbilical cord, then passed Clay the baby—wiped down, but still bloodied.

Clay handed him to me and for a second, I was lost in those big unfocused eyes. I nuzzled the top of his head, inhaling the scent of him, a new smell with the barest whiff of the scent that marked him a werewolf. It didn't smell the same as a mature werewolf, but I expected that—Jeremy said it would be subtler.

As I kissed his head, I remembered this wasn't done.

"Better take him," I said to Clay. "The first impression he gets of his mom shouldn't be cursing and screaming. He'll hear enough of that later."

Clay took him, and juggled him around a bit, trying to figure out a safe hold. The baby only whimpered, eyes wide and unblinking, taking in his new world.

"Shouldn't he be . . . louder?" I asked. "Squalling?"

"It'll come, I'm sure," Jeremy said.

Clay grinned. "And if it doesn't, you won't complain, right?"

"True."

"Elena?" Paige said through the speakerphone.

"I'm still here."

She laughed. "Good, because you're only half done. Do you feel the other one coming yet?"

I did. And we started all over again. This time was better. The way had been cleared and I knew the end would come fast. In what seemed like minutes, I had another baby.

"A girl!" Clay looked over at me, his grin as wide as the first one. "We have a daught—"

His words were drowned out by a squall so loud even Jeremy started.

"I think you have your screamer," Paige yelled over the phone as Clay passed our son back to me.

Getting this baby cleaned up and ready for presentation wasn't nearly so easy as her brother. She screamed and kicked and flailed so much that I could tell Jeremy was worried something was wrong. But when he handed her to Clay, she fussed only a moment, as if getting comfortable, then snuggled in.

When she'd settled, we traded babies. Our son only wriggled a bit in complaint, but she howled, face red, enraged at the disturbance. Again, after she was nestled in—to my arms this time—she quieted.

As I held her, I bent to kiss the top of her head, and inhaled deeply. I blinked. Was that—? No, it shouldn't be. The genes didn't pass to daughters. I took a deep breath of room air, then tried again. There seemed to be . . . No, I couldn't tell. It didn't matter. Either way, it didn't matter.

"Do you have names picked out?" Paige asked.

I looked up. "Um, pretty much."

We'd decided if we had a girl, we'd name her after my mother. And yet, looking down at the baby in my arms, "Natalya" just didn't seem to fit.

"Paige?" I said. "What's your middle name?"

"My—? Um, Katherine . . . with a K."

I glanced up at Clay. He nodded.

But there was still one more question. We hadn't settled on a surname, not because we'd been arguing over it, but because neither of us really cared whose name the babies bore. As Clay said, Danvers wasn't even his name, so if I wanted Michaels, he didn't mind. And yet . . .

I looked over at Jeremy. Danvers might not be our name, but it was the name of this house and this family. Clay slid onto the bed beside me. I smiled up at him.

"Logan Nicholas Danvers and Katherine Natalya Danvers."

About the Author

KELLEY ARMSTRONG lives in Ontario with her family. Visit her website at www.kelleyarmstrong.com.

Kelley Armstrong introduces readers to
an all-new heroine who is completely
of this world. . .
Coming soon,

EHIT STRATEGY

is an all-new Kelley Armstrong series
you won't want to miss.

Here's a special preview:

EXIT STRATEGY

Coming soon

Mary

Mary Lee pushed open the shop door. A wave of humid heat rolled in—another hot Atlanta night, refusing to give way to cooler fall weather.

Her gaze swept the darkened street, lingering enough to be cautious, but not enough to look nervous. Beyond a dozen feet, she could see little more than blurred shapes. At Christmas, her children had presented her with a check for a cataract operation, but she'd handed it back. Keep it for something important, she'd said. For the grandchildren, for college or a wedding. So long as she could still read her morning paper and recognize her customers across the store counter, such an operation was a waste of good money.

As for the rest of the world, she'd seen it often enough. It didn't change. Like the view outside her shop door tonight. Though she couldn't make out the faces of the teenagers standing at the corner, she knew their shapes, knew their names, knew the names of their parents should they make trouble. They wouldn't, though; like dogs, they didn't soil their own territory. As she laid her small bag of trash at the curb, one of the blurry shapes lifted a hand and waved. Mary waved back.

Before she could duck back into her store, Mr. Emery

stepped from his coffee shop. His wide face split in a Santa Claus grin, a smile that kept many a customer from complaining about stale bread or cream a few days past its "best before" date.

"Going home early tonight, Miz Lee?" Emery asked.

"No, no."

His big stomach shuddered in a deep sigh. "You gotta start taking it easy, Miz Lee. We're not kids any more. When's the last time you locked up and went home at closing time?"

She smiled and shrugged . . . and reminded herself to take out the garbage earlier tomorrow, so she could be spared this timeworn speech. She murmured a "good night" to Mr. Emery, escaped back into her shop and closed the door.

Now it was her time. The customers gone, the shop door locked, and she could relax and get some real work done. She flipped on her radio and turned the volume up.

Mary took the broom from behind the counter as "Johnny B. Goode" gave way to "Love Me Tender." Crooning along with Elvis, she swept a path through the faint pattern of dusty footprints.

Something flickered to her left, zipping around the side of her head like a diving mosquito. As her hand went up to swat it off, she felt the prick at her throat, but it was cool, almost cold, a sharp pain followed by a rush of heat. At first, she felt only a twinge of annoyance, her brain telling her it was yet another hiccup of age to add to her body's growing repertoire. Then she couldn't breathe.

Gasping, her hands flew to her throat. Sticky wet heat streamed over them. Blood? Why would her neck be—? She noticed a skewed reflection in the metal rack. A man's face above hers. His expression blank. No, not blank. Patient.

Mary opened her mouth to scream.

Darkness.

* * *

He lowered the old woman's body to the floor. To an on-looker, the gesture would seem gentle, loving, but it was just habit, putting her down carefully so she didn't fall with a thud. Not that anyone was around to hear it. Habit, again. Like unplugging the security camera even though there was no tape in the recorder.

He left the wire embedded in the old woman's throat. Standard wire, available at every hardware store in the country, cut with equally standard wire cutters. He double- and triple-checked the paper overshoes on his boots, making sure he hadn't stepped in the puddle of blood and left a foot-print. Not that it mattered. The boots would be gone by morning, but he looked anyway. Habit.

It took all of thirty seconds to run through the dozens of checks in his head, and reassure himself that he'd left nothing behind. Then he reached his gloved hand into his pocket and withdrew a square of plastic. He tore open the plastic wrapper and pulled out a folded sheet of paper within. Then he bent down, lifted the old woman's shirt and tucked the paper inside her waistband.

After one final look around the scene, he walked past the cash register, past the bulging night-deposit bag, past the cartons of cigarettes and liquor, and headed out the back door.

Chapter One

I twisted my fork through the blueberry pie and wished it was apple. I've never been fond of blueberry, not even when the berries were wild and fresh from the forest. These were fresh from a can.

Barry's Diner advertised itself as "home of the best

blueberry pie in New York City." That should have been the tip-off, but the sign outside said only "Award-winning home-made pie." So I'd come in hoping for a slice of fresh apple pie and found myself amid a sea of diners eating blueberry. Sure, the restaurant carried apple, but if everyone else was eating blueberry, I couldn't stand out by ordering something different. It didn't help that I had to accompany the pie with decaf coffee—in a place that seemed to only brew one pot and leave it simmering all day. The regular coffee smelled great, but caffeine was off my menu today.

A man in a dirt-encrusted ball-cap clanked his metal lunchbox onto the counter beside my plate. "He got another one last night. Number four. Police just confirmed it."

I slanted my gaze his way, in case he was talking to me. He wasn't, of course. I was invisible . . . or as close to it as a non-superhero could get, having donned the ultimate female disguise: no makeup and thirty-five pounds of extra padding.

"Who'd he get this time?" the server asked as she poured coffee for the newcomer.

"Little old Chinese lady closing up her shop. Choked her with a wire."

"Garroted," said a man sitting farther down the counter.

"Gary who?"

The other man folded his newspaper, rustling it with a flourish. "Garroted. If you use something to strangle someone, it's called garroting. The Spanish used it as a method of execution."

I glanced at the speaker. A silver-haired man in a suit, manicured fingernails resting on his *Wall Street Journal*. Definitely not the sort you'd expect to know the origin of the term "garroted." Next thing you know, his neighbors would be on TV, telling the world he'd seemed like such a nice man.

They continued talking, but I ignored them. The old Nadia Stafford would have been right in there, following every media blip, debating motivation, second-guessing the investigation, searching for the crucial missing clue or over-looked lead. But for the new me, the only important aspect of the case was the resolution, finding out how the killer screwed up. So I tuned them out, finished my mediocre pie and coffee, and left.

Duty called.

I stood in the subway station, and waited for Dean Moretti.

Moretti was a Mafia wannabe, a small-time thug with ten-uous connections to the Tomassini crime family. Three months earlier, he had decided it was time to strike out on his own, so he'd made a deal with the nephew of a local drug lord. Together they'd set up business in a residential neigh-borhood that, oddly enough, no dealer had previously tapped—probably because it was under the protection of the Riccio family.

When the Riccios found out, they went to the Tomassinis, who went to the drug lord, and they decided, among the three of them, that this was not an acceptable entrepreneur-ial scheme. The drug lord's nephew had caught the first plane to South America and was probably hiding in the jun-gle, living on fish and berries. Moretti wasn't so easily spooked, which probably spoke more to a lack of intelli-gence than an excess of nerve.

While I waited for him, I wandered about the platform, taking note of every post, every garbage can, every doorway. Busywork, really. I already knew this station so well I could navigate it blindfolded.

I'd spent three days watching Moretti, long enough to know he was a man who liked routines. Right on schedule, he bounced down the steps, ready for his train home after a long day spent breaking kneecaps for a local bookie.

Partway down the stairs he stopped and surveyed the crowd below. His gaze paused on anyone of Italian ancestry, anyone wearing a trenchcoat, anyone carrying a bulky satchel, anyone who looked . . . dangerous. Too dumb to run, but not so dumb that he didn't know he was in deep shit with the Tomassinis. At work, he always had a partner with him. From here, he'd take the subway to a house where he was bunking down with friends, taking refuge in numbers. This short trip was the only time he could be found alone, obviously having decided public transit was safe enough.

As he scouted the crowd from the steps, people jostled him from behind, but he met their complaints with a snarl that sent them skittering around him. After a moment, he continued his descent into the subway pit. At the bottom, he cut through a group of young businessmen, then stopped amidst a gaggle of careworn older women chattering in Spanish. He kept watching the crowd, but his gaze swept past me. The invisible woman.

I made my way across the platform, eyes straining to see down the tunnel, pretending to look for my train, flexing my hands as I allowed myself one heart-tripping moment of anticipation. I closed my eyes and listened to the distant thumping of the oncoming train, felt the currents of air from the tunnel.

I felt as if I was standing in an airplane hatch, waiting to leap. Everything planned, checked, rechecked, every step of the next few minutes choreographed, the contingencies mapped out, should obstacles arise. Like skydiving, I control what I can, down to the most minute detail, creating the ordered perfection that sets my mind at ease. Yet I know that in a few seconds, when I make my move, I will still leave some small bit to fate. And that's what sets my pulse racing.

I don't think of what I'm about to do. It's too late. I have to clear my mind and concentrate on the end goal. Hesitate and I'll fail.

I inhale deeply, and concentrate on the moment, slowing my breathing, my pulse.

No fear. No time to second guess. No chance to turn back. No desire to turn back.

At the squeal of the approaching train, I opened my eyes, unclenched my hands and turned toward Moretti.

Free fall.

I quickened my pace until I was beside him. Tension blew off him in waves. His right hand was jammed into the pocket of his leather jacket, undoubtedly fondling a nice piece of hardware.

Finally, the train headlights broke through the darkness.

Moretti stepped forward. I stepped on the heel of the woman in front of me. She stumbled. The crowd, so tightly pressed together, wobbled as one body.

As I jostled against Moretti, my hand slid inside his jacket. A deft jab followed by a clumsy shove as I "recovered" my balance. Moretti only grunted and pushed back, then clamored onto the train with the crowd.

I stepped onto the subway car, took a seat at the back, then disembarked at the next stop, merging with the crowd once again.

Job done. Payment collected. Time to go home. Almost . . .

I sat in my rented car, outside the city. Just sat, drinking in my first unguarded moment in days, leaning back in my seat, feeling . . .

Feeling what? I suppose there are many things one should feel in the aftermath of taking a life. Dean Moretti may have earned his death, but it would affect someone who didn't deserve the pain of loss.

I knew that. I'd been there, knocking on the door of a parent, a wife, a lover, seeing them crumple as I gave them the news. Your father was knifed by a strung-out junkie client. Your daughter was shot by a rival gang member. Your husband was killed by a man he tried to rob. I'd seen their grief, the pangs made all the worse by knowing they'd seen that violent end coming . . . and been unable to stop it.

Yet in this case, it was the other victims I saw—the teens Moretti sold drugs to, the lives *he'd* touched.

Killing him didn't solve any problems, not on the scale they needed to be solved. It was like scooping water from the ocean. More would rush in to fill the empty place. Yet, the next time the Tomassinis called, if the job was right, I'd be back.

I started the car and headed for the highway. As the lights of New York faded behind me, the radio DJ paused his endless prattle with a "special bulletin," announcing that the Helter Skelter killer had struck again, this time in New York City.

"Good thing I'm leaving, then," I murmured.

The announcer continued, "Speculation is mounting that the Helter Skelter Killer is responsible for the rush-hour subway death of Dean Moretti . . ."

I nearly ran my car off the road.

Cool under pressure. If they posted employment ads for hit men, that'd be the number two requirement, right after detail-oriented. A good hit man must possess the perfect blend of personality type A and B traits, a control freak who obsesses over every clothing fiber yet who projects the demeanor of the most laid-back slacker. After pulling a hit, I can walk past police officers without so much as a twitch in my heart rate. I'd love to chalk it up to nerves of steel, but the truth is I just don't rattle that easily.

Driving up to the U.S./Canada border that morning, I was still so rattled I could hear my fillings clanking. How could Moretti's hit be mistaken for the work of some psycho? Any cop knows the difference between a professional hit and a serial killing.

Had I unintentionally copied part of the Helter Skelter killer's MO? The case had been plastered across the airwaves and newspapers for two weeks now, but I'd been good. If an update came on the radio, I changed the station. If the paper printed an article, I flipped past it. It hadn't been easy. Few aspects of American culture are as popular with the Canadian media as crime. We lap it up with equal parts fascination and condescension: "What an incredible case. Thank God things like that hardly ever happen up here." But I no longer allowed myself to be fascinated. In hindsight, a choice that warranted a special place on the overcrowded roster of "Nadia Stafford's Regrettable Life Decisions."

Now, as the queue inched forward, I rolled down my window, hoping the late-October air would freeze-dry my sweat before I reached the booth.

I eased my foot off the brake and moved forward another car length. Normally, crossing the border was no cause for alarm. Even post-9/11, it's easy enough, as long as you have photo ID. Mine was the best money could buy. Half the time, the guards never gave it more than the most cursory glance. I'm a thirty-three-year-old white middle-class woman. Run me through a racial profile and you get "cross-border shopper."

I pulled forward. Second in line now. I inhaled and plied myself with reassurances. Let's face it, how many terrorists enter Canada from the U.S.? Even illegal immigrants stream the other way.

As I told myself this, the agent manning my booth waved the vehicle in front of me over to the search area. It was a minivan driven by a white-haired woman who could barely see over the steering wheel. I was doomed. I assessed my chances of jumping into another line, where the agent might be in a better mood. Impossible. Nothing says smuggler like lane-jumping.

I removed my sunglasses and pulled up to the booth.

The agent peered down from his chair. "Destination?"

"Heading home," I said. "Hamilton."

I lifted my ID, but didn't hand it to him. Prepared, but not overeager.

"Where are you coming from?"

"Buffalo."

"Purpose?"

"Shopping trip."

"Length of stay?"

"Since Tuesday. Three days."

The agent waved away my receipts, but did accept the proffered driver's license. He looked at it, looked at me, looked back at it. It *was* my photo. A few years old but, hell, the last time I'd changed my hairstyle was in high school. I didn't exactly ride the cutting edge of fashion.

"Passport?" he asked.

"Never had any use for one, I'm afraid," I said. "This is about as far from home as I get." I dug into my purse and pulled out three other pieces of fake ID. "I have a library card, my health card, Social Insurance Number . . ."

I held them up. The agent lifted his hand to wave the cards away, then stopped. The wordless mumbling of a distant radio announcer turned to English.

"—fifth victim of the Helter Skelter killer," the DJ said.

"Sorry," I murmured, and reached for my radio volume, only to find it already off.

The agent didn't hear me. He'd turned his full attention to the radio, which seemed to be coming from the truck on the other side of the booth. As the announcer continued, in every booth, every car, the occupants seemed locked in a collective pause, listening.

"Police are searching for a suspect seen in the vicinity. The suspect is believed to be a white male . . ."

I exhaled so hard I missed the rest of the description.

"Although police are treating Dean Moretti's death as a homicide, they are dismissing rumors that he was the Helter

Skelter Killer's fifth victim. Yet speculation continues to mount after a witness at the scene claimed to have seen the killer's signature . . ."

The announcer's voice faded as the truck pulled away. As the world around us shifted into drive, the agent leaned out from his booth to check the back seat, gaze traveling over the crunched up drive-through bag. I'd had to grit my teeth every time I'd glanced in the rearview mirror and seen it, but a spotless car can seem as suspicious as one piled hip-high in trash.

I held my breath and waited for him to tell me to pull over.

"Have a nice day," he said, and handed me my fake license.

I nodded, drove to the garbage can by the currency exchange booth and threw out the fast-food bag.

The ten o'clock news on CBC brought word of the Moretti case.

"It is expected that police will provide a description of the man wanted in connection with yesterday's subway murder. Authorities stress that the man is wanted only for questioning. He is not considered a suspect, but police believe he may have witnessed . . ."

Uh-huh. Amazing how that "wanted for questioning" line actually works. I've known perps who've shown up at the station, thinking they're being smart, then been genuinely shocked when the interview turns out to be an interrogation.

Unless they really *were* looking for a witness . . . What if the "male suspect" being sought was really a witness, meaning someone had seen me shoot Moretti? No. It had been a good hit, a clean hit. No second-guessing allowed. Not now.

The newscaster continued, "Yesterday's subway killing is believed to be the fifth in a series of murders that began two weeks ago."

Okay, here it comes. The recap. I turned up the volume another notch.

"The last confirmed victim was sixty-eight-year-old Mary Lee, who was found strangled in her Atlanta convenience store yesterday morning. Again, we will bring you details from the press conference as they become available. Up next, a panel discussion on the problems with health care in this country . . ."

I whacked the volume button so hard it flew off and rolled under my feet.

So much for a decent recap.

Four killings in two weeks, in different states, seemed more like a cross-country spree killer than a serial killer. How were the police connecting the murders? Why would they think the hit on Moretti was part of the series? An elderly woman strangled in her shop and a Mafioso punk killed in a subway? How did you connect those?

I spun the radio dial, searching for more information, but, for once, the media was silent.

In Peterborough, I stopped at a storage shed I rented under another name and dropped off my subcompact workmobile. A few blocks away, I picked up my regular wheels, an ancient Ford pickup. Then I left the city and drove north until the fall foliage ceased being jaw-droppingly spectacular and became merely monotonous. Ontario cottage country. My year-round home.

I slowed near a roughhewn sign proclaiming *Red Oak Lodge: No Vacancy*. Well, that was a nice surprise. This time of year, the lodge was rarely at more than half-occupancy, even on weekends. Not that the lodge would make me rich anytime soon. It had yet to break even. In fact, my contract work with the Tomassinis was the only thing that kept it open, and there was only so far into the red a place could go before Revenue Canada would wonder why you hadn't declared bankruptcy.

Three years ago, I *had* almost declared bankruptcy, hanging on for months fueled by nearly irrational desperation. I'd destroyed my life once. To rebuild it only to lose it again . . . ? I didn't know if I was that strong. When that first job offer from the Tomassinis came, under circumstances I can only chalk up to fate, I took it, and the lodge and I survived.

I signaled my turn. No one was behind me, but I still signaled. It's the law.

Before I could steer into the lane, the roar of tires accelerating on dirt sounded behind me. I glanced in my rearview mirror to see a car pulling out to pass me. A small car, which around here meant tourists. I shook my head. Why come up for the autumn colors if you're not going to slow down enough to see them?

As the car zoomed up beside mine, gravel clinked against my fender. I raised my hand—my whole hand, not just my middle finger. Being semi-dependent on tourists for your livelihood means you can't afford to make obscene gestures, no matter how justifiable.

In mid-wave, I caught a glimpse of the driver. Dark-haired. Male. Features shaded into near-obscurity by the tinted glass, but the shape of his face familiar enough to warrant a double-take. The man leaned toward the window, so I could see him a little better.

"Jack?" I mouthed.

He nodded. I stopped the truck, but he'd already pulled away, message conveyed. He wanted to talk to me, but no such conversation would take place until the sun set.

Jack. In the world of professional killers, there are a million shades of mysterious. In my own zeal for secrecy, I'd be considered borderline paranoid. Compared to Jack, though, I might as well be advertising in the Yellow Pages with a photo. In the past two years, Jack had visited me over a dozen times and I'd never seen him in daylight. If he wanted to visit, he'd phone pretending to be my brother, Brad, which worked out well, since Brad himself last called me in 1999.

For Jack to just show up meant something was wrong, and I was sure that "something" had to do with the Moretti hit.